Kilbroney

KATHLEEN O'FARRELL

KILBRONEY

BRANDON

First published by
Brandon Book Publishers Ltd,
Dingle, Co. Kerry, Ireland

This book is published with the financial assistance of the Arts
Council/An Chomhairle Ealaíon, Ireland

British Library Cataloguing in Publication Data is available for this book

ISBN 0 86322 141 6

Typeset by Brandon
Cover illustration by Finbarr O'Connor
Cover design by The Graphiconies (Foreman)
Printed by Guernsey Press, Channel Islands

In memory of my parents, William John and Cathleen Rose Farrell,
who are both buried in Kilbroney

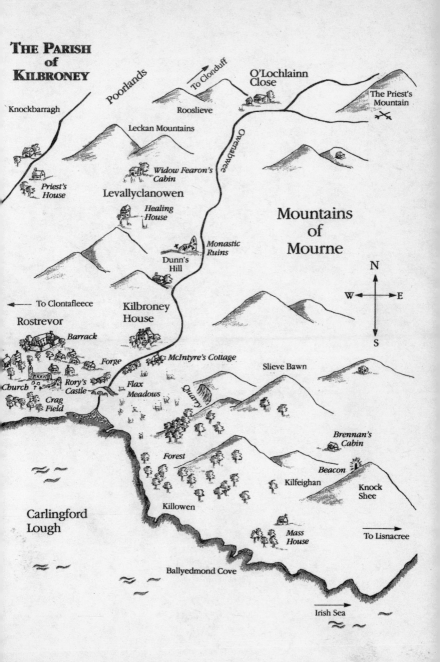

The Storm

April 4th 1780

'I AM GOING TO leave him,' Grace O'Lochlainn decided as she gazed on the image in the looking-glass. Within the oval frame she saw a cold waxen face, devoid of either beauty or character, lifeless eyes under a stark brow. The hair had been pulled back so severely that the scalp was stretched and numbed. Grace remained rapt by her own gaze for some moments before pulling out the hairpins. A pale cascade tumbled over the black housekeeper's gown as she rose to her feet.

Turning sadly away she plumped the pillows of her bed and smoothed the covers as she had always done. It was a vast bed, only a corner of which had been disturbed. She lay alone now, more often than not. The pristine sheets teased her, and she beat the pillows, sending a few downy feathers adrift to float indecisively before settling on her gown. Grace opened a window to clear the room, and heavy dank air invaded from outside. Dark storm clouds were gathering over the lough, its waters grey and turbulent. At such a time most ladies of quality would take to their beds to rest with kerchiefs doused in lavender water. But Grace felt a compulsion to go out, to escape, to face the elements. The house – his house – now felt claustrophobic, suffocating, with the mocking whispers and taunting sneers of those who, having predicted her fate, were now rejoicing in her downfall. Donning her great-cloak she walked slowly down the stairs, ignoring the sounds of scurrying feet and stifled laughter in the shadows. For years she had been protected from humiliation. Now she would protect herself.

Deciding against the shady secluded path that led to the woods, she walked stubbornly into the wind, crossing the lawns which led down to the banks of the Owenabwee river. She was aware of eyes on her back as she moved, but wondered only if the eyes were his.

❖ ❖ ❖

Thady O'Lochlainn pushed a cartful of blistered wrack up from the shore. There was a sizeable weed plot allocated for the folk of the Poorlands, although one had to wait for a low tide to get at it. The sweat was on his brow before he had reached the village of Rostrevor and he regretted not having waited for Seán to finish at the quarry. Anyone would have thought he had no sons to give him a hand. To make matters worse, Ned the Buller passed him on Dunn's Hill with his own ass-drawn cart, having left home a good hour after Thady.

'The skies'll open over you if you don't put a skip to your step,' the Buller advised Thady smugly as his cart trundled by. Thady could have danced with frustration as he saw the distance between himself and the Buller gradually increase.

'Where the hell's Seán when you need him!' he grumbled aloud, the wrack getting heavier by the minute. If it rained he would have to abandon half the slimy load, for the weight would be beyond him. To Thady's immense relief, a voice called out in welcome.

'Ahoy there, Thady O'Lochlainn!' Tom Dunn, leaving the flax meadows by the river, drew alongside Thady's cart. Within minutes Dunn's plough horse had been yoked and Thady was able to proceed, but not before leaving a complimentary load of seaweed with Annie, the woman of the house. Dunn had protested that the thin soil of upper Kilbroney was more in need of the sea's nourishing plant than the dark fields of Dunn's Hill, but he understood that the gift was a matter of pride to the impoverished Thady.

They reached the O'Lochlainn close only moments before the storm broke. 'God save you, Mistress O'Lochlainn,' said Dunn as his large frame filled the meagre cabin. 'I have brought your man home to you.'

Thunder sounded in the Cooley Mountains. The storm was sweeping nearer. Eily O'Lochlainn stoked the fire.

'Oh, Master Dunn! To think that he might have been caught

out in that! Him and his bones,' she cried gratefully.

'Look at that for a downpour,' said Thady, sitting down heavily on a stool. 'Only a fool would find himself caught out in such a squall!'

The storm blew up with an intensity which took all but the canny mountain dwellers by surprise. Great billowing grey mists had earlier ushered goats and sheep down from the rugged crags of the Mournes and sent gulls and snowy seabirds flying inland. These were timely warnings to the cautious to have a good supply of fuel and kindling to hand, and to board up gaps against the coming onslaught.

❖ ❖ ❖

Eamonn O'Lochlainn, the least weather-wise of men, was caught unawares. The hedge-school teacher was making his way home-ward when the heavens opened above him and the tempest broke. Pulling a shabby cloak around his thin shoulders, he bowed his head against the wind and forged onwards. Lashing rain whipped his face as he sought the protection of the hedgerows and ditches. A low rumble in the distance heralded the first shaft of lightning, and the young man lifted his pale face to the skies. He knew no fear, only excitement at this visual manifestation of the power of God, without limit, without restraint.

On impulse he veered from his homeward path and turned in-stead towards the Owenabwee, to the elevation above the river where stood the ruins of an early Christian monastic settlement and the church of Bronach. This ancient abode of saints and scholars suddenly stood framed by a second splendid bolt, the great carved cross of the virgin martyr stark against the beatific white light.

It was here on this hallowed ground that Eamonn first heard it, loud and clear above the ferocity of the storm, a sound so com-pelling, so beautiful, it touched his innermost soul and forced from his lips a cry of exaltation.

This was the sound men dreaded to hear: the voice of the Celtic storm god on his way to do battle with the Christian interloper.

Others heard only the Doom Bell with its awful cry prophesying a near and certain death for the listener. But Eamonn O'Lochlainn was none of these men. He heard only the Bell of Time, the Bell of Destiny.

From that moment onwards, he knew he was destined to leave the valley of Kilbroney.

Chapter One

April 29th 1780

OVER THE CREST of the hill they appeared, the prospect of a safe house beckoning from the valley below. It was their tenth day on the move, a harrowing journey through the remote mountain passes and lonely glens of the Mournes, living in fear of their pursuers, trusting no one. They had treated everyone with suspicion, even the most miserable inhabitants of the mountain booleys and poor cabins. Curious at their approach, ragged children scurried to call their parents, while cagey, inquisitive eyes peered from these dark hovels. Once in a while the woman of the house would appear with an offering of whey or potatoes, no doubt out of pity for the lame Dissenter. The younger traveller had been inclined to give friendly folk the benefit of the doubt, despite the dark warnings of his companion, until he had heard of the arrest of an innocent shepherd who had sheltered them some time previously. After that he was more reluctant to befriend strangers. The last safe house had belonged to a cooper on the outskirts of Ballynahinch. He was a dour, sullen man who had not as much as a word to throw to the dog. His talkative wife compensated for his silence, fed them and gave them a warm bed for a few nights. The cooper's parting advice had been characteristically brief.

'Keep along the high ground till ye arrive in Kilbroney. Ask for Dunn.'

They were undoubtedly an odd-looking trio, the young rapparee, his crippled elder companion, and the black and white terrier who always kept a few paces ahead of the field, peeping over his shoulder now and then to make sure he was being followed. On the steeper climbs the Dissenter was slow, spurning any assistance with a shrug. Then, as the little dog settled for a scratch, young Donal would leap ahead to the nearest vantage point and scan the surrounding countryside. From some elevations he could look across the Irish Sea as far as the Isle of Man, the haunt of pirates and privateers. To the west stretched the lowlands of Ulster, the youthful River Bann splashing over the rocks of its birthplace before diminishing to a silver thread on its way towards distant Lough Neagh. He took no notice of the muted hues of the Mournes, the many shades of brown, grey, green and purple. Even the vibrant gold of the whin blossoms and the blue and violet wildflowers of spring did not warrant his attention. His eyes were alert only for a certain shade of scarlet – the red of a military uniform.

He waited with barely disguised impatience for old Makepeace to catch up with him. It had been a clear, fresh day, and he felt the urge, not for the first time, to continue his journey alone. Master Makepeace was making slow progress, muttering various tracts to himself as his crutch poked the ground ahead.

The sudden swoop of a hawk caught Donal's attention and he gasped an exclamation.

'What is it? What did you see?' asked Makepeace in alarm.

'Nothing. Just a hawk,' replied Donal, trying to hide his own apprehension. He knew that they were no safer than the prey of the bird, whose freedom and life had come to an abrupt conclusion out here amidst the bog-cotton and the heather. At least the young coney's end was swift. No imprisonment, no flogging, no...

'No!' cried Donal. 'Not for us!'

'Not for us, you say?' The breathless Makepeace stumbled to a halt below Donal.

Donal did not answer. His thoughts were on his determination to avoid recapture. He had just witnessed Nature at her most cruel, and yet she did not compare with the evil to which his fellow man could stoop. He had seen flogged prisoners beg for death, and starving evicted women plead for food for their children. He wished he was immune to pity. That was the prize, they said, of the battle veteran, who could obey any order, no matter how cruel or unjust, and then sit down to a hearty meal. But as the grey-faced Makepeace eased himself to the ground to rest,

Donal felt thankful that he still had the capacity in his heart for compassion.

'I must find you something to eat,' he said.

They had covered more than ten miles that day, leaving behind the snow-capped crown of Slieve Donard, guarded by Binnion, Slieve na Muc, and the lesser peaks. Passing through the lonely Meadow of the Deer, they arrived in the Meadow of the Ox, the ancient parish of Clonduff. This was the Gaelic heartland of old Iveagh, where men had stood firm against their would-be conquerors long after the rest of Ireland had been subdued. They had fought for Iveagh, resisting attempted plantations through the reign of James I, until their townlands became embroiled in the insurrection of 1641. Then the great clans of southern Ulster, the O'Neill, the MacAongus, the MacArtain and their people, suffering the punishment of a vengeful crown, were scattered to the four winds. General Monroe laid waste the farmlands, putting mills, barns and homes to the torch, leaving only the mountain wilderness of Mourne to become a haven for the dispossessed and a refuge for the defeated. During the years that followed, legendary rapparees, tories, and outlaws of every description haunted the wild lands, swooping down on the new settlements of loyal subjects and ensuring that this part of the King's realm remained ungovernable. Military outposts manned by Welsh troopers and Irish mushroomed along the edges of the rich farmlands of Down, demarcating the boundaries of what came to be known as the Poorlands.

Makepeace had a little knowledge of the history of the area, patiently gleaned from the taciturn Ballynahinch cooper, and this he recounted to Donal as they passed through Clonduff.

'If you had listened to the man you might have learned something, instead of spending your time looking on his wife,' remarked Makepeace tersely.

'You would be surprised by what I learned in that house,' the younger man replied smugly. 'Did you know,' he went on, 'about the Brave Redmond O'Hanlon?'

'The rapparee! You would have to learn about rapparees!'

'He died here you know, betrayed by his own half-brother, a confounded bounty hunter!'

'What have I been telling you? There will always be men greedy for their thirty pieces of silver. Avaricious men... and women!' he added sourly. He looked ahead.

'I wonder would that be the boundary between Clonduff and Kilbroney?'

'You've been asking that question since noon, and one sheough looks the same as any other.'

'The cooper said we would know. Help me to my feet lad.' Makepeace winced with pain as he grappled with his crutch.

'Is it your leg that's hurting?'

'No! 'Tis my armpit. That part takes all my weight!' There was very little spare flesh on Makepeace, and Donal would have happily carried him for a few miles on his back, but the old man's stubborn nature was well known to him and he desisted from offering.

'I should find a shelter, Master Makepeace. We can bed down early.'

'You'll save yourself the bother. We'll keep going till we have the sea ahead of us. This man Dunn will have a dry bed waiting, if he's half as stout as they say,' was the obstinate reply.

'We'll not get there by nightfall!'

'Let thine eyes look forward, and thy gaze be straight! Take heed of the path of thy feet, then all thy ways shall be sure! Isaiah, chapter twenty-one, verse... four.'

Donal had perceived that the Dissenter's encyclopaedic biblical memory had been waning of late. 'Hand me your bundle,' he said.

'I carry my own burdens.'

'Your belt, then? I will take some of the weight of it, though God knows why you need all those odds and ends.'

'I'll die with it on!'

Master Makepeace Agnew was not in the mood for reason. His belt carried as much hardware as a tinker's donkey, with an assortment of blackened pots, a segment of iron chain and a rusted blade, the last picked up by a well some days earlier, the refuse, he declared, of some drunken vagabond. Safely stored in a stout leather purse was his King James bible, well bound but dog-eared, and the only remaining link with his Scottish childhood. He read it aloud on rising and retiring, in the tone of a preaching man, whether or not he had a listener. He did not count Donal MacArtain as such, for the godless youth turned a deaf ear to the precious words, be they the meticulous genealogies of Deuteronomy or the most edifying psalms.

The trio had barely covered another half-mile when Makepeace admitted defeat and stopped to rest. This evening he did not reach for his book, a sure sign, if any were needed, that the old traveller was well and truly exhausted. Donal fashioned his ragged cloak into a pillow and loosened his stock. It was grimy and threadbare, a condition which greatly offended Donal's sensibilities, for he liked to consider himself in the tradition of the white-throated gentleman tory. He did possess a decent set of leather boots, acquired from a diseased corpse which the prison warders had refused to touch. Makepeace, reared in Christian cleanliness, did not know about the origin of the boots, although in his heart he doubted the young knave's explanation concerning bountiful gifts from visiting Quakers. The Quakers, he surmised, were generous to a fault, but they were not fools.

His attention was caught by the alerted ears of the terrier. Two intense eyes were trained on a spot some way up the mountainside, now basking in the glow of the setting sun.

'Donal!' he hissed in alarm, 'what does he see?' The young man drew his sword and instinctively placed himself in front of Makepeace.

'Will you stand aside! How can I see from here?' Makepeace was notoriously short-sighted and even with the help of his spectacles was unlikely to see beyond the dog. Nevertheless, Donal stood back.

'There's nothing there,' he reassured Makepeace. He had endured many a sleepless night because of the Dissenter's misinterpretation of his dog's behaviour. 'He is in the mood for chasing a bitch, and come to that, so am...'

'Wheest!' The dog was growling threateningly. Donal sighed in exasperation. If he did not make some show of investigating the problem Master Makepeace would stay awake through the night. The stiff frame of the terrier was pointed accusingly in the direction of the mountain. He barked a few times before returning to his master's side. In the silence that followed the dull clank of a bell sounded in the evening air. Donal smiled in satisfaction.

'Redcoats be damned!' he called to Makepeace. ''Tis no less than a milking goat! Hand me your can – we'll sup well tonight.'

But Master Agnew was fast asleep, his spectacles askew on a careworn face. Donal looked quizzically at the old man and his expression softened. More than once he had been tempted to leave him, to continue his journey alone. He could have been in France by now were it not for that ailing leg, which not only added days to the journey but drew the attention of every vagabond and wayfarer along their path. He cut a distinctive figure, a small bespectacled cripple in the sober garb of a Non-conformist preacher. An unlikely outlaw – yet outlaw he was, by virtue of his choice of companion. As Donal watched, the thin face, with the grey stubble and quaint round spectacles, momentarily winced in pain. Donal tenderly removed the spectacles to a safer place and tucked the patched cloak around his friend. More than just a friend – he had been both father and mother from the age of five and, come what may, Donal would never desert Master Makepeace Theophilous Agnew.

It was fifteen years since he had first felt the reassuring hand of the Preacher Agnew on his shoulder, as the death sheet covered his mother's face, and the reek of ammonia stung his eyes. The resulting flood of tears was fed by bewilderment and desperation – not sorrow, for he did not realise how final was this parting. In the years that followed, try as he might, he could not conjure up a memory of her face, only of the sheet and the smell of the workhouse. The rough, dark shoulder of his rescuer he could clearly recall, and the quiet, comforting words of the man who was to become his adoptive father.

He had never known his real father. There were confused, disturbing visions of tall ships and swarthy mariners; how much was real, and how much imagined, he did not know. Once a fishwife in the port of Carrickfergus had taunted him about his whore of a mother. 'I suppose your father was the French sea captain! Or would he have been the king of Spain?' she had yelled from the crowd while Master Agnew delivered his personal testimony. Little Donal, not understanding the derision in her voice, was quite taken with the thought of a French sea captain father, and diligently inspected every large boat which docked in Carrickfergus. As he grew older he decided that his father might as well be someone grand, rather than a smooth-talking rascal or low-ranking sailor. High or low born, his mother had been abandoned, left to fend for herself and her son, so he bore her family's name, MacArtain. That was about all he knew of her, except that Master Makepeace had conscientiously tried to rear him in his mother's faith.

Donal turned to the terrier.

'Stay with your master!' he ordered, somewhat unnecessarily, for one hundred armed infantry would have been hard pushed to separate man and dog. Makepeace would sleep well guarded. In the meantime, the sound of the milking bell was making his mouth water, and he climbed towards it.

In the evening light the pale granite rocks jutted from the earth like the exposed bones of a dead animal. Donal did not believe in superstitious tales. He had no time for fireside yarns about ghosts and pookas. Now he wished he had never listened to them, for to deny the existence of such abominations was to invite their sudden appearance from behind a stone. He looked back for the comforting sight of man and dog, but both had disappeared from view, and even the bell had stopped sounding. He began to sweat. Should he go back? Tomorrow was, he realised, the eve of Bealtaine, one of the pagan festivals that provoked unwelcome denizens to appear from the depths of the earth. As if things were not bad enough, an eerie mist had begun to creep up the mountainside. The bell sounded again. He braced himself to go on, though his heart was pounding. The climb was deceptive. Every so often he seemed to be near the summit, but there was always further to go. He looked down again but the thin mist appeared even less friendly than the climb ahead so he went on, cursing every missed step or jagged rock underfoot. The goat must be trapped, he decided, or it would have run off before now.

Like the human inhabitants of the Mournes, the mountain goats were elusive creatures, sharing their craggy demesne with black-faced sheep and a few red deer. Their natural predators, apart from hungry men, were preying eagles which could lift young kids with their talons and spirit them away to their eyries on the rocky peaks.

The animal which had lured Donal was in no danger from birds of prey. A hardy creature, raised on the sweet herbs and shrubs of the higher pastures, it was prized for its milk rather than its flesh. Donal had been told the story of how a settler, some years back, had brought to Kilbroney a herd of pedigree milking goats which were carefully nurtured in a guarded enclosure. Gradually, for no apparent reason, the aristocratic animals began to take on the distinctive features of the native wild goats. No one had ever seen the determined wild billies scale the walls to service the newcomers, but there was no doubt that they were doing so. The allegorical nature of this tale had ensured that it would be widely repeated, but settlers and native alike agreed that the milk from these hybrids, most of which, in time, reverted to their wild state, was second to none. It was good, some said, for every ailment under the sun, from the pox to the scour.

Donal, having always enjoyed rude health, was unconcerned about such claims. Finally reaching his goal he saw that the bell rope of the animal had twisted around what appeared to be a small wooden crucifix, roughly fashioned but firmly implanted in the heather. Her udders were heavy and blue and Donal regretted not having brought a bigger can. He had never milked a goat before, but assumed that it was no more difficult than handling a cow. He had never milked a cow either, but as every woman in the country could, he did not anticipate any problems. He had already forgotten the uncomfortable climb, every other step of which had landed his good boots squelching in a boghole. He confidently advanced towards his quarry.

'Ho! That's my fine girl! I'm no wolf! I won't hurt thee!' The placid animal bucked at his touch and he staggered backwards with a cry, his rear end landing in the muck. Donal's anger exploded in a stream of curses. As he struggled to his feet his legs slid from beneath him, and this time he landed face down in the boggy quagmire, soaking wet from head to toe.

'Damn you and your breed,' the young man cried, 'I'll roast you for supper and feed your bones to the magpies! And then,' he finished darkly, 'I'll wipe my boots on your hide!'

The goat laughed. Donal looked up sharply at the sound. The goat stood alone, glaring at him defiantly. A fairy's goat? No wonder she would not milk.

'So that is what you are! A confounded fairy goat!' He dragged himself to his feet, recovering his sodden hat and all that remained of his dignity. The laughter grew clearer and it did not, he realised, come from the goat. He turned to see, silhouetted in the glow of the evening sun, the slight figure of a girl, beautiful but with a mocking laugh that made his young heart skip.

❖ ❖ ❖

Makepeace twisted and turned as the ache gnawed at each of his bones in turn. Tired as he was, his bed would not allow him to rest. The terrier nuzzled close, offering what comfort it could.

'Good dog! By tomorrow we will be under thatch, and you'll have a fine ram's bone for your supper.' Of the three travellers, the terrier had dined the most royally along the journey, usually while his master slept.

'I am too old. I should have let him set forth alone. He has sense enough by now.' The terrier scratched his ear. 'I think maybe you're right, boy. If it were not for me, he would be back in chains by now.' Makepeace did not voice his deeper fear, that his beloved foster son might suffer a more ignominious fate at the hands of the hangman – the brutal death of a condemned traitor. He shuddered, trusting in the mercy of providence to spare him from such a sentence. His boy was meant for better things, even though he was, at times, vain, stubborn and foolish. He needed the guiding hand of a level-headed mentor. That was why Make-peace refused to leave him. The old man seemed unaware that as far as impulsive natures were concerned, his was as fine an example as any.

It was this nature that made him agree to the request of a dying woman, an unspoken plea, made with sunken, pain-filled eyes which wandered between her little boy, playing unconcernedly at the foot of the pallet, and Master Agnew, the visiting preacher. The crusty bachelor, knowing little of the love of a woman and even less about children, suddenly found himself the foster father of little Donal MacArtain. Mistress Foster had tried to persuade him that he was under no obligation to take on such a burden, and that such a child would be much happier in the workhouse alongside his fellow waifs.

'Besides,' she had argued, 'the unfortunate woman was a Papist. She could not have intended that you should rear him. Perhaps he has living kin?'

'Tell me who she is then, and I will try to find them.'

'MacArtain. Rose MacArtain. She spun yarn for a living, or so she told me...'

Mistress Foster's expression suggested that she did not entirely believe this part of the story, as the woman had been found in a state of destitution, living among the crates and barrels on the dockside of Larne. She was in an advanced stage of illness; in all probability, Master Agnew was told, the consequence of a sinful life.

'And the lad? Who tended him?'

'The poor child! 'Twas he who led me to his mother.' Mistress Foster was so moved by the pathetic situation of mother and child that she had her moved to the infirmary at her own expense. She was equally concerned that the dying woman should have every opportunity to renounce sin and Romish superstition, and so save her soul from eternal damnation. To this end Mistress Foster had sent for Master Agnew, a bookbinder by profession and a preacher of scripture, by conviction; a man of high principle in whom she had considerable confidence. Armed with his bible and some suitable tracts, Makepeace had set off to the infirmary. He had shuddered in alarm at the sight of the dying woman and the prayer beads entwined in her emaciated fingers. He was reluctant to touch the beads and, judging by the wary expression on the face of the woman, so was she. He had seen a set before, in the possession of his mother, a former Highland Papist whose family, advocates of the Jacobite cause, had paid the price for being on the wrong side in war. She had been saved, in several senses of the word, by Theophilous Agnew, a strict adherent to the teachings of John Knox whose great ambition in life had been to purge his wife of the unhealthy superstition to which she continued to adhere. A pragmatic lady, she allowed herself to be spiritually wooed by her husband, thus giving him the pleasure of taking the credit for another soul saved from the Pope of Rome. She had hidden her rosary beads as if hedging her bets, and Makepeace had understood that they were to remain a secret.

So, as he gazed at the poor face of Rose MacArtain, he decided that if they could bring her any consolation at this dreadful hour, the beads should be left in her hands. He sat with her through the evening and into the night, through pain-wracked periods of wakefulness followed by merciful sleep. He read no tracts, preached no sermon. There was no point. He prayed silently, once or twice wetting her cracked lips from the water-bowl. The little boy slept through most of the night, and in the morning ate the porridge intended for Master Agnew. She died soon after dawn on a cold, stark morning, leaving her suffering behind her and her son to Makepeace.

❖ ❖ ❖

'All I wanted was a sup of milk,' Donal told the girl.

'Milk? 'Tis not yours either to want or to drink.'

Humbled before this slip of a girl, he rose with what dignity he could muster. She made no move to help him, and appeared to be highly amused by his appearance. He looked at her awkwardly and winced at the squelching of his boots in the mire. She had no such problems as, like the animals she tended, she went barefoot. The late sun had set a golden halo on her brown hair, and she had all the appearance of an unearthly sprite. Only her ragged skirt, gathered in folds around her waist, betrayed her mundane origins; her laughter, too, was very human.

'I will take my leave of you then!' the young man said stiffly.

'Pass me your can! You shall have your milk, and may it do you good!' She laughed again.

'Thank you,' Donal said. He was going to tell her not to bother, but his thoughts went quickly to his hungry companion. 'Thank you,' he repeated. 'You are a decent woman.'

The girl knelt by the goat and her nimble fingers performed the familiar routine. Donal stood back in admiration. She was a very comely girl indeed.

'You should not be wandering around so late in the evening; 'tis nearly dusk!' he admonished sternly.

'And so it is!'

'You might get attacked.'

'By who?'

'By a... a wild rapparee!'

'Like you?'

'Er... yes... like me!'

'Well I wish you a better way with women than you seem to have with goats. Here is your milk.'

'I thank you, Mistress...' he began, but as quickly as she had appeared she was gone.

❖ ❖ ❖

Makepeace relished the creamy milk. There was sufficient for them to breakfast on the following day.

'That will put an inch on your step!' declared Donal confidently. 'You'll not get as good a drop as that anywhere in Ireland.'

'You surprise me every day. I never thought you could catch a goat, let alone milk one.'

'Your wisdom is rubbing off on me,' was the smug reply.

24

'Tell me truly,' Makepeace was sceptical, 'what went on up that mountain while I was napping?'

'Aren't you a suspicious old gorsoon? I simply found my goat and milked her, that's all.'

'She must have been a docile animal. Are you sure it was a goat?'

'Did you not hear her bell? She was caught on a cross.'

'Cross? What was the cross for?'

'I didn't ask.'

'You didn't ask who?'

'Er... I didn't ask the girl.'

'Aha! So that's what has you mooning at your own face.'

'I'm only cleaning myself up.'

'You're shaving again. The last time you did was to impress the cooper's wife. You need not deny it, for I can see the back of your neck flaming red.'

Donal was lying flat on his belly, using a rock-pool as a looking-glass. His grubby shirt and stock lay draped over a thorn-bush. He twisted his head. 'Today we meet Thomas Dunn. I want him to know that I am a gentleman.'

Modesty, Makepeace had to admit, was a virtue he had patently failed to nurture in Donal. 'I wonder,' he asked the young man, 'who would set a cross up the mountain?'

'I wondered that myself. I did not like the place.'

Makepeace had dutifully had the boy raised in his mother's faith, but in spite of the efforts of his pious housekeeper to instill a sense of religious devotion in the lad, he had turned out to be a godless rapscallion. The old man gathered his oddments together for the next leg of their journey, keeping a careful tally of each item. The dog was lapping up the rest of the milk. Donal completed dressing by adding a newly acquired eagle tail feather to his tricorne.

'Are you sure you are not going to attract too much attention with that hat?'

'Not at all, Master Makepeace. We can keep within the trees from now on.' They headed off, the terrier skipping ahead.

It was a chilly but bright morning as the sun rose over lichen-encrusted ditches and ferny hollows. The stark moorland began to give way to a gentler terrain thick with the wildflowers of spring, clover and buttercups, coltsfoot and cranesbill. In the little wooded copses which pre-empted the oak forest blue hyacinths and violets thrived in the shade, while fragrant primroses lay scattered along the river-banks. The Owenabwee River, which rose in the peaks beyond the Priest's Mountain, splashed a determined path over the granite towards its destination in the lough below. The travellers caught their first glimpse of the sea which, bounded on one side by the steeply wooded southern slopes of the Mournes and on the other by the dark mountains of Cooley, had so much reminded Viking corsairs of their Norwegian homeland that they had named it Carlinn's Fjord. Carlingford Lough shimmered within its verdant setting, the varied foliage of oak, beech and chestnut spreading like a rich fabric over the slopes of Slieve Bawn and Slieve Dermot.

In the valley below, given away only by the rising wisps of smoke and the stone quay, lay the little village of Rostrevor. One or two small boats could be seen, making their way across the lough.

'You are sure that this is the place?' asked Makepeace warily.

"Tis what I was told,' Donal replied. 'Rostrevor, in the Parish of Kilbroney, and ask for Dunn.'

Chapter Two

'YOU SHOULD NOT be surprised at my situation. No one else seems to be.'

'And what is your situation, Grace?' asked Annie.

Mistress Dunn had known Grace O'Lochlainn since childhood, when, as a little girl of nine, she had arrived at Dunn's Hill requesting permission to join Master Tom Dunn's hedge-school. Her brothers had been on the roll of scholars for some time, but Grace had assured Mistress Dunn that she could already out-read them. There were no other girls in the school, and Tom Dunn would have turned down her request were it not for the persistence of his wife. Annie had ridiculed any suggestion that the girl would be a disruptive influence among the other pupils and vowed to tutor Grace herself, should she be denied the opportunity she sought. There was considerable rivalry between Grace and Seán, the two eldest children of Thady O'Lochlainn, and Annie Dunn took pleasure in the progress of her protégée. Then, all too soon, the O'Lochlainn family fell on hard times and, in spite of Master Dunn's attempts at persuasion, Thady had no choice but to hire out his children to labour. Seán was allowed to continue with his classes on the days during which work stopped at the quarry, but Grace had no such time to spare. In the years that followed, Eamonn, Thady's youngest son, fulfilled all the promise of his older siblings, and by the age of seventeen was teaching the younger hedge-scholars himself.

Now, more than twenty years after their first meeting, Annie Dunn was still Grace's champion, and as close a friend to her as anyone was likely to be. Yet, even to Annie, Grace rarely spoke of the controversy which had so scandalised the people of Kilbroney – her relationship with Henry Valentine.

'Don't be afraid to talk about your worries, Grace.' Annie was already concerned that she had said too much, as she noticed the familiar veil fall over unusually anxious grey eyes.

'You, at least, never uttered a word of censure,' Grace answered. Annie did not reply, and was rewarded with a further confidence.

'He would acquire a small townhouse for me in Dublin, south of Saint Stephen's Green. Where he can visit me.'

'Is that what you wish?' The women had met on the lough shore, where the Dunns, mother and daughter, were collecting shellfish. Grace had been wandering aimlessly along the water's edge and had seemed startled by Annie's warm greeting. Now, just as she was starting to speak, the sound of a splash distracted Mistress Dunn.

'Betsy!' she called. 'You will catch a chill if your feet get wet!' She picked her way over the wrack towards her daughter who was determined to procure the plumpest low-tide shellfish. As she turned back towards her friend, Grace was already walking away. She was well used to coping with loneliness. Not many stopped to speak with the landlord's mistress.

❖ ❖ ❖

It had turned out a fine evening, the last April had to offer. Further up the valley the slanted stones and walls of the ruins cast long shadows, shades of the past invoking the memory of the Druids who had worshipped here long before the advent of Christian Patrick. This evening would have had particular significance for the followers of the ancient cult of Bealtaine, Goddess of Spring, for it was May Eve. The oak grove had in medieval times become a centre of healing and learning, and a little monastery was built on the spot, under the patronage of Bronach, the virgin saint of the MacOwen clan. The sturdy granite walls had withstood the worst onslaughts of Carlinn and his Viking hordes and, more recently, a zealous Roundhead troop dispatched by Oliver Cromwell. This former scene of carnage had, through the passage of time, regained its original tranquil character. A haven of peace in a troubled world, it was no wonder that Eamonn O'Lochlainn chose to conduct his classes within the shelter of the ruins. Frothy white hawthorn blossom now filled the bower of the martyred saint, and thick fronds of ivy adorned the outer walls. In the immediate surrounds were the graves of the dead, the unmarked mounds of the poor, flanked by a few upright slabs bearing the names of planters' families and, on the southernmost sloping ground, a gnarled oak tree of great antiquity.

The oak tree was a constant source of distraction to the budding scholars of Eamonn's school, not least young Briony Fegan. Father Mackey, the Parish Priest, was forever chiding them to avoid temptation, and yet here was the most tantalising tree he had ever seen, and on the most sacred ground in Kilbroney. Even to think of climbing that tree was a sacrilege, therefore think of it Briony did. There were many taller and more impressive trees in the forest, but none so tempting, because it was forbidden.

It was the tree which occupied Briony's thoughts on this languorous evening as Owen MacOwen was tediously translating. 'If I climbed to the top,' he told himself, 'I could see to the end of nowhere.' Nothing stirred his imagination more than the prospect of what lay beyond the Cooley Mountains, his farthest horizon. Past the safe confines of the lough smugglers, corsairs and sea dragons roamed the oceans. There were the sunny isles of legend, where fierce knights fought heroic battles and the brave always won.

'Fegan!'

A censorious voice interrupted his reverie. Owen MacOwen, having laboriously completed his passage of text, was determined to see his classmate suffer in kind.

'Briony, the next verse if you please!' Eamonn O'Lochlainn carefully handed his precious tome to the boy. He began to read effortlessly, to the annoyance of the hapless Owen whose best endeavours were never good enough to earn the praise of Master Eamonn.

It was now Eamonn's turn to be distracted by the tree. As a potent symbol of paganism he felt its presence disturbing, not least because of its close proximity to the shrine. The See of Rome had no more ardent followers than the people of Iveagh, who had come through every test of faith and endurance in their recent history, paying the price of poverty, dispossession, imprisonment and death. Even now, the rallying cry of 'the Priest's Mountain' stirred the folk memory. Yet in spite of everything, the ancient pagan rituals still persisted. Father Mackey had laughed at Eamonn's anxiety, advising that Mother Church had to be pragmatic where such practices were concerned, and had wisely incorporated many of them into Christian worship. Eamonn, an intensely pious young man, was unconvinced, and Father Mackey was driven to issuing a warning lest Eamonn be tempted to cut down the tree himself. Now his eyes scanned the branches, bedecked with their customary outlandish collection of small rags and bits of clothing. They were pathetic invocations to the saint, or perhaps to a still potent pagan predecessor. He noticed a little shirt of white linen, a precious offering and the newest addition to the bizarre collection. He breathed a prayer for the tiny owner of the shirt, whose parents would not decry the aid of either saint or goddess.

'Superstition – the Devil's work.' Eamonn spoke suddenly, bringing Briony's translation to a sudden halt. The boys turned towards their mentor with questioning eyes.

'Carry on to the next page,' he instructed the puzzled reader, who shrugged his shoulder and continued.

Eamonn thought of the other customs of May Eve to which even the most devout households adhered. Tonight every lintel and threshold in Kilbroney would be adorned with wild flowers, a means of keeping the mischievous inhabitants of the netherworld where they belonged, away from the living. Eily O'Lochlainn, Eamonn's mother, told him that she would ignore the old custom at her peril, but, just to please him, would add an extra few prayers to her nightly litany to redress the balance. Eamonn she considered to be far too sober-minded for his own good.

'When I am a priest I will stamp out these heathen practices and profane indulgences,' he had declared, quoting old Priest Pullein, the warhorse of the mountain townlands. It was left to Eily to try to persuade her son that these harmless diversions did but introduce a little colour to otherwise drab, care-laden lives.

As Briony reached the end of his translation, he snapped the book closed and Eamonn realised with a start that he had not heard one word. Not that he need worry, for Briony was his brightest student and was unlikely to make any errors. Not so poor Owen, the last of the Clan MacOwen, hereditary Keepers of the Staff. On impulse Eamonn told Briony to return the book to Owen.

'I have had my turn, Master O'Lochlainn!' cried Owen in disappointment. To Eamonn's dismay, Briony tossed the precious book towards Owen, who fumbled and dropped it.

'Fegan!' Eamonn responded angrily, 'have some respect for these books. We are fortunate to have the use of them!'

Briony eyed him with a roguish expression. 'Tell me, Master,' he began, 'what do those signs of heraldry on the bindings mean?' Eamonn did not miss the sharp intake of breath from some of the boys. In anger he lashed out at the boy with open palm.

'You ask too many questions about matters which are not your concern!' Eamonn cried angrily. 'I will speak to your father when he comes.'

To hit a child was an uncharacteristic action for the young man, but he was over-sensitive where his sister Grace was concerned.

❖ ❖ ❖

Briony's father, Murtagh Fegan, jangled the coins in his pocket. Had he one hundred sovereigns he would still plead the poor mouth, for profit was transitory at the forge, and if business was good one year, it might not be so the next. Murtagh's dependable clientèle were the common people, who came back year after year with the same pots, shovels and scythes, to be moulded and mended until there was no life remaining in them. Murtagh also welcomed the custom of visiting gentlepeople who came to Rostrevor during the warm season to drink *meadhg*, the medicinal goat's whey. If the mountain air cured bodily ailments, the rocky mountain tracks did little for carriage wheels and suspensions, and Murtagh's skills were often in demand through the summer months.

The Fegan's forge, in a glade near the bridge, was home to Briony and his seven little sisters. The elder girls looked after the younger children, keeping them away from the brazier, the river's edge, prancing hooves and the hissing gander. The forge was a dangerous home, and yet the little Fegans appeared immune from serious injury. The youngest was a baby of six months who occupied whatever time her mother, Brigid, had left after tending to the men of the house, Murtagh and Briony. The baby, like Briony, sported the black curls and dimpled cheeks of her mother, a cowman's daughter from Lisnacree, although Murtagh liked to think that Briony had inherited the Fegan brains.

It was a happy, if noisy home, in which the only son enjoyed a privileged position among so many girls. While his sisters shared a straw mattress, curled together like a litter of pups for warmth, Briony slept on a comfortable pallet by the hearth; while the girls took it in turn to soothe the teething baby, Briony was left to rest undisturbed; and while Briony went off every day to Eamonn O' Lochlainn's hedge-school, his sisters cooked and cleaned and ran errands.

Strangers often called at the forge, consulting the blacksmith on the advisability of entering forests teeming with outlaws, brigands and cut-throats. He, in return for a few coppers, would soothe flustered ladies by pointing out the presence of the gallant garrison in the village, the troopers of the Welsh Horse.

To his own associates, and behind closed shutters, Murtagh would express a different opinion.

'Cut-throats? 'Tis the bastards in the red coats that would worry me more.' He did not like to see the Welsh Horse bringing their custom to the forge, and since there were military smiths and ostlers working within the walls of the Barrack, he suspected that his red-coated callers were intelligence gatherers, and duly instructed his family to say nothing if questioned.

'And what would I say to them?' his wife demanded as Murtagh got into bed one night. 'If they ask me about the Oakboys, am I to say that I won't tell them anything?'

'All you have to say is that you have no English.'

'If I say that so they understand me, they'll know I know English.'

'Ah, say nothing then, but don't come crying to me when they arrest you.'

Brigid looked at her husband in exasperation. 'Would it ever occur to you that they might be lonely, and missing their own wives and children?'

Murtagh sat up in shock. 'I knew they were up to no good. I'm going to see the Agent Coyle about this at first light.'

The suggestion that there might be any signs of familiarity towards his daughters struck a raw nerve within Murtagh. Brigid, having unintentionally stirred his anger, attempted to pacify her husband.

'If you wish, I'll tell the girls to keep away from the troopers,' she said. Murtagh had to agree that there was little else to be done. The Agent Coyle might only laugh at him or, worse, spread the rumour that his wife and daughters had already been tampered with.

'Look at what happened to Grace O'Lochlainn,' he began, but Brigid had heard enough.

'Go to sleep,' she yawned, and turned her back to him.

The following evening Murtagh removed his hide apron, which he did only when attending his lessons or the Mass House.

'I'm going to see Eamonn O'Lochlainn. He said he'd show me a few more letters,' he said.

'And what call is there for you to read or write?' asked Brigid, with doubt in her voice.

'Do you want to see me making a goat of myself in front of the customers?' he replied tetchily.

'I don't know how you managed before now.'

'I managed because I had to manage. If my father had had the chance of me learning and bettering myself, he would have taken it.'

''Twill be of no use to you,' persisted Brigid.

'I need to be able to write my name on bills of sale and the like. 'Tis the way business is done now.'

'What was wrong with a spit and a shake of the hand?'

'That was all right for some, but a man of quality will take neither my hand nor my spit.'

'I see. He's a man of quality when he pays you, and an accursed planter when he does not.'

'That's business. A woman wouldn't understand the difference.'

Feeling the better for having corrected his argumentative wife, he prepared to take his leave of the forge.

'That long spade is for Spendlove Bushel. He'll be preaching outside the alehouse this evening. And there's the Sparrow Magee's kettle. 'Tis the second time this month she's burned the arse out of it.'

Brigid Fegan pursed her lips in silent condemnation of the Sparrow's bad housekeeping and went to feed the geese.

'Good evening to you all!' Mistress Dunn, hurrying home from the shore with her daughter and a basket of mussels, called a friendly greeting to the Fegans on the opposite bank of the river. Betsy had sneezed twice already, so Annie did not stay to gossip. Further up the path they could ford the river to Dunn's Hill. To their right the encroaching forest had been cut well back to provide for more white-flowering flax fields and grazing meadows, although isolated copses of oak and beech still remained. Into view rode a hunting party of ladies and gentlemen, returning to Kilbroney House after a day's sport. The band of riders passed the Dunns without acknowledgement. Unlike the peasant tenantry, no obsequiousness was required, although Annie chastised Betsy for pointing.

'I have told you before, Betsy dear, that it is rude to... Oh, look!' She had to will herself not to point in the direction of two riders following in the rear of the hunt.

The taller of the two, a dark, broad-shouldered man, was undoubtedly Major Henry Valentine, the landlord of Kilbroney. As they approached, Annie pulled her baffled daughter behind a tree, from where she could indulge her curiosity at leisure. Not, she realised, that such a precaution was necessary, for Major Valentine seemed fully preoccupied with his companion, and would not have noticed had half the village been looking on. She was a doe-eyed beauty, fashionably clad in emerald velvet with a jaunty feathered bonnet. Her tinkling laughter rang across the meadows to the alert ears of Mistress Dunn.

'Why are we hiding, Mama?' Betsy began. The riders passed by, looking for all the world like two people in love.

'It had to happen like this,' Mistress Dunn murmured sadly. 'It was only a matter of time. Poor Grace.'

❖ ❖ ❖

On the opposite bank Murtagh Fegan took his leave of hissing geese and whingeing children and started up the river which, after the weekend rain, sported a good flood. He walked along the bank on the village side where the bleachers and scutchers lived. Most of these were skilled workers who had moved into the village, attracted by the prospects of good tenancy agreements and decent wages. They kept very much to themselves, as few even spoke the same language as the local peasants, and an air of mutual distrust reigned between them. Their cottages were built in neat rows along the lane to the back of the bleaching green. These were well-guarded lawns for such was the value of good linen that many a mountain rogue would take his chances and risk the hangman's curse. Murtagh's burly form was a familiar sight to the bleacher wives, and he was allowed to go his way unhindered.

If the blacksmith appeared to be in considerable haste it was because he wanted to get home before nightfall, as only the foolish would be caught in the river glen on May Eve. A particularly impish breed of fairy was known to inhabit the glen, and there had been many dependable eye-witness reports of their presence. Murtagh knew the mischief of which they were capable, and tried to concentrate his thoughts on matters of learning.

A sharp peal of laughter called his attention to a few ragged urchins jumping about from rock to rock above the salmon leap. As lithesome as the silver fish, the children appeared to dance on the foam in the evening light. They shrieked and sang as little white legs sprang from boulder to boulder until, inevitably, one of their number fell into the water. Murtagh rushed anxiously towards the spot, but the victim had already climbed on to the opposite bank and was shaking himself dry, ignoring Murtagh's shouted warnings about the power of the fairies.

The sharp report of a gunshot rang out, changing the children's laughter to cries of fear and alarm. The little fellow who had picked himself out of the water clasped his arm and stood rigid with fright while his companions ran off. Murtagh crossed the river to reach the panic-stricken child.

'Hush,' he comforted, 'you weren't shot. You'll be all right now.' The boy, not much more than five years old, was trembling violently, and Murtagh looked around to see a small girl timidly return to the scene.

'Here, girleen, is he from your house?' the blacksmith enquired. She nodded, accepting full responsibility.

'Away home with you now. Tell your ma he wasn't hurt,' Murtagh advised the girl, who shepherded her brother out of sight. Out of the trees appeared the tall figure of Samuel McIntyre, the Valentines' gamekeeper.

'You scurvy bastard!' roared Murtagh in fury. 'You might have killed the child!'

'Those children are not permitted here,' replied McIntyre dourly. The gamekeeper, whose concern was the welfare of the river stock, felt he had done no more than dispense a warning.

'The child has more right to be there than you and your pox-ridden master.'

'Would you care to repeat that opinion in the presence of Major Valentine, eh?' inquired the gamekeeper in his Lowland Scottish accent. Murtagh took a deep breath and suppressed his anger. He had no wish to meet Major Valentine.

The blacksmith continued on his way, but the spring had gone out of his step. He met Annie Dunn at the mill ford, noticing that she, too, was preoccupied. They exchanged a brief greeting before mother and daughter turned off towards Dunn's Hill.

Murtagh emerged from the woodlands and crossed the meadow. Further up the valley the land was marked by small lean patches of tillage and an abundance of yellow whins. Hawthorn and windswept trees marked the path towards the ruins of Bronach's monastery. Murtagh espoused great devotion to the saint, and attributed the well-being of his family to her benevolent patronage. Each new child had been blessed after baptism with the Staff of Bronach, the ancient symbol of the Abbess Bronach's authority. The MacOwens were hereditary Keepers of the Staff which was kept in their home, the Healing House, the reputed birthplace of the saint. The townland around the house, below Slieve Leckan, to the west of the ruined monastery, was Levallyclanowen, the homeland of the MacOwens. All that remained of this ancient and revered sect were the widow Dervla MacOwen and her son, Owen. A few thin spruce trees marked the landscape, now the only sentinels of the MacOwen inheritance.

Murtagh blinked. For a fleeting moment he thought he had seen two strange figures below Leckan, one of them clad in black and wielding a wand. He stared hard but the visions had disappeared. Murtagh blessed himself and invoked stronger powers than Saint Bronach for protection. A woman was all very well for healing and the like, but when the powers of Hell were ranged against a body... He commenced his litany by invoking the aid of Saint Michael the Archangel.

Murtagh was still mumbling his prayers when he interrupted Eamonn's class. His garbled warning about getting the children home before dusk was greeted frostily by Eamonn, who had been telling his young scholars that May Eve was no more or less dangerous than any other night of the year. He instructed Murtagh to wait, as he had no intention of wasting God-given daylight and dry weather. The scholars were working with varied degrees of enthusiasm, some writing with charcoal on the horizontal grave-slabs of old soldiers. Murtagh looked around for Briony, intending to take him home as soon as he decently could. He saw his son resting against a wall, cleaning his teeth with a straw. Murtagh beamed with pride. His boy was plainly too bright for the others.

Owen MacOwen started once more to read. His efforts were painfully slow.

'Agamemnon was the, er...'

'Try "the bravest",' suggested Eamonn after a long pause.

'And the thickest,' muttered Briony audibly. Owen brightened up.

'Agamemnon was the bravest and the thickest of the Greek warriors!'

The sniggers of his classmates brought a dull red flush to the neck of poor Owen as he realised that he was, yet again, the object of Briony's wit. He stammered an apology to his tutor, who inwardly resolved to give Briony a thorough lesson in the virtues of humility and charity.

'Master Eamonn,' the offender butted in, 'do we have to listen to MacOwen reading again? We would all be on the next book by now were it not for him.'

Suppressing some sympathy for this view, Eamonn bade the lanky youth continue, but Owen's pride had already suffered more than he could tolerate. To the despair of his mentor and the delight of his classmates, he threw a badly aimed punch at Briony, who was immediately on guard with raised fists. The two leaped at each other like spitting tomcats as an outburst of encouraging yells rang round the ancient ruins. The young scholars followed the action with enthusiasm, a welcome respite from a tedious lesson.

Briony Fegan was a good head smaller than Owen, and of lean build, like his grandfather in Lisnacree, but he had clearly inherited the Fegan strength of arm. Murtagh stood to one side and relished the spectacle, his thoughts diverted from fairies and pookas. He had no doubt as to the outcome of the quarrel for one well-aimed punch in Owen's direction followed another. Briony's nimble movements rendered the flailing arms of his opponent quite useless.

'Stop them, Murtagh,' pleaded Eamonn, 'for fighting is sinful, even if not on hallowed ground!'

Murtagh, engrossed in the progress of the battle, paid no heed. The combatants were, by now, hidden in the long grass, and the band of spectators had moved to a better vantage point. Eamonn buried his head in his hands and wished himself miles away. He picked up the books he had borrowed from Grace and prayed for a speedy end to the conflict.

'Rise up, ye hallions, and tremble before the righteous wrath of Zion!' The antagonists parted in haste as a fearful mace crashed onto the flat tombstone on which they had been wrestling. Briony blinked in amazement. Looking upwards he saw all the fury of the devil himself, a vision in black with bespectacled coal-fire eyes piercing him wrathfully. He scrambled to his feet in time to see his father scurry back down the valley.

'How dare ye pick a fight here! Have ye no respect for the dead? Woe betide ye who transgress the laws and violate the covenant! Now run away home with ye all!' commanded the vision. The boys did not wait for further instruction.

Donal MacArtain looked on in annoyance. Master Makepeace Theophilous Agnew would have it believed that he, Donal, was the flamboyant character, yet the old Dissenter had a theatrical style second to none.

'And now,' Makepeace inquired civilly of the bemused schoolmaster, 'I would be obliged if you would kindly direct me to the home of Master Thomas Dunn.'

Chapter Three

FURTHER UP THE Kilbroney valley, above the woodland and the sheltered meadows of Rostrevor, lay the Poorlands, mile upon mile of mountain wilderness and bog, marked by meagre cabins and crude turf dwellings wedged into the hillside. Unlike the sturdy stone cottages of the village, few of these homes possessed any sign of permanence, having neither chimneys nor windows.

As in other parts of the country, the native peasantry had been banished to the wilder land, to live as tenants of the great land-lords who, between them, had divided the spoils of Iveagh. Many did not officially exist at all, homeless vagrants condemned by poverty to a nomadic way of life. In summer they moved to the high pastures above the woods, taking shelter in the 'booley' huts, while a cold winter would force them on to the streets of Newry to beg. They were the dispossessed, to be at the one time despised and feared by those subjects of the king who chose to abide by the law.

The only group who prospered in the mountain wildernesses were those who ignored the law: tories, highwaymen and rappa-rees. They lived on the misfortunes of others, preying upon hap-less travellers and merchants who had strayed from the main roads. Even the arterial route between north and south was fre-quently ambushed with the Dublin-Belfast stage coach, the 'Cock o' the North', a popular victim of the outlaws of South Down and Armagh. Robberies were usually executed with such speed that even the outriders, following at a short distance, often came upon a looted coach and a driver without a whip. Only the mail coaches were sufficiently well guarded, with armed dragoons and loaded pistols. These outlaws and robbers were folk heroes to many poor people, not because they were in any way benevolent, but because they were the only people who seemed able to outwit the law and flout the authority of the planters.

From his vantage point by the Swallow's Rock above Rooslieve, Thady O'Lochlainn surveyed the scene below. A wizened man in his late sixties, Thady feared neither tories nor wild rapparees, for he owned nothing worth stealing. 'Good luck and long life to them!' he declared, aiming a spit at a working beetle. He had dug a drill of good black turf which, given some summer sun, would fill many a good hearth the following winter.

A spasm of pain shot through his back as he eased himself into a sitting position. He cursed and fumbled in his waistcoat pocket, producing from it the latest gift of the merchant Dwyer, a small clay pipe. He did not light it for it was too good to use, but he liked the feel of it between his teeth. He would wait for his son Seán to arrive with the turf car.

Far below, on the dark waters of the lough, shimmered a single streak of molten evening sun. A tiny fishing boat was bound for the shore with its catch. At the quayside women and children would be standing by with sharpened knives, ready to gut the fish for the Barrack and the inn to eat the following day. The brown sails were furled as the boat disappeared behind the tops of the trees. Thady himself was not averse to a nice bit of salted herring, should the occasion arise, and that was usually when the merchant William Dwyer came calling with his wares.

William Dwyer delighted in bringing small gifts and surprises to the O'Lochlainn close. It could be some herring, a piece of fat bacon, or a pretty ribbon for Sosanna's hair. Lately the generosity of their benefactor had shown a significant increase, and the end of the Lenten fast had been marked by a bottle of Spanish wine for Eily and a pipe for Thady. Thady's wife had never tasted wine before, and the gift had caused considerable glee in the close. Thady found the brown liquid sweet and sickly and earned Eily's wrath when he suggested to William that he might use it to empty his bowels. Eily was of the opinion that William Dwyer, a man of good Clonduff stock, could do no wrong.

The ruddy-faced merchant was a popular and much respected

caller around Kilbroney. Although past fifty, he was considered to be well preserved and comfortable-looking with a quiet, sanguine disposition. As his business was with planter and native alike he was always first with the news, be it the price of hoggets at Hill Town fair, the state of King George's health, or the latest manœuvres of the sparring couple of Upper Knockbarragh. His principal source of information, though, was undoubtedly his elderly mother who kept a small shop in Hill Town; a formidable dame, whose hearing was as good as her corns were bad.

Every Tuesday and Friday he journeyed across the Poorlands, down by Knockbarragh, through the townland of Drumreagh and into Rostrevor. There he conducted his business with the waspish mistress of the inn, before moving on to the Barrack and the two lodging houses. The vicar's wife was a favourite client, with whom he had a private arrangement to supply contraband brandy under the guise of a linament for her joints.

Bella Morgan, the seamstress, who had a flourishing trade in ladies' fashions, was interested not only in William's supply of laces, buttons and trimmings, but also in his person. The merchant was surprisingly coy in the company of women and had always managed to avoid Bella's lures, without losing her valued custom. Her ingenious tricks included a rat in the rain-barrell, an alluring display of corsetry, and the latest, most alarming, a cockroach in her boudoir. After that incident William went to great lengths to avoid being left alone with the amorous seamstress.

Mistress O'Lochlainn had remarked on his shyness. 'I would say 'tis that old mother of his. 'Tis she who has done the harm,' Eily confided in the Widow Fearon. The Widow, no mean expert on the subject, reassured Eily that not all of the breed were cut out for pairing with a woman, and that it was not necessarily the fault of his mother. Mistress O'Lochlainn considered this information for some moments.

'You think that he has no...'

'Oh, I have no doubt that he has all his bits and pieces It's what he does with them I'm not sure.'

'You think he might have been cut out for the clergy then?'

William Dwyer had been calling at the close for ten years or more, but lately his visits were becoming more frequent. Eily, concerned with the doubts implanted by the Widow, found the quiet man even harder to talk to, although he always seemed quite at ease in the presence of Thady, Seán and Eamonn. There was no doubt that William enjoyed the company of the O'Lochlainns, and there was always a good hearth by which to warm his feet on a cold night. He never stayed over, for his mother would wait to hear his footstep before starting her night prayers. Thady himself had no doubt that William was lost for a bit of companionship, for his mother was too odd to encourage any company by her own fireside. He also knew that William had once had eyes for Grace, but that was before she went away.

Mistress Dwyer also knew about Grace, and daily thanked God that her son had been delivered from the snares of the 'Planter's Whore'. William had tried to placate his mother.

'If I was taken with her, so was every other man for miles around. She was a very comely girl.' He further cautioned Mistress Dwyer that as he did business with all sorts, her comments might do untold harm to trade should Major Valentine ever get to hear them.

Thady sometimes expressed his concern for the merchant's safety, as the route back to Clonduff was bleak and lonely.

'Be careful, lad,' he would whisper, 'for those raw dogs from the Bolie would take your ass for soup.'

William would confidently reassure Thady that his ass could outrun any rascal with a cudgel. He showed him the loaded pistol which he kept hidden on the cart.

'Take care,' Thady warned, 'for if the troopers knew you kept such a weapon you might have more to worry about than a blackguard wielding a shillelagh.' William made no further comment, discretion being his greatest virtue.

❖ ❖ ❖

The O'Lochlainn close was set within a hollow scooped from the mountainside by a stream which had long since taken an underground route. Old Felim O'Lochlainn had begun to clear a couple of fields down to the river, a tedious labour, for there was more bare rock than fertile soil. Over the years Thady had tried to feed nutrients into the earth, pulling his cart down to the shore and loading it with sea-wrack. Such a practice had been forbidden by George Valentine but his son, the Major, had relaxed the rules because the weed was too unsightly on the shore. There was a poor return of small, misshapen potatoes, but it fed Thady's family. Apart from the cabin, a single room with a chimney and rickety roof-loft constructed by Seán, there was a crude three-walled shelter for turf and livestock, and a small byre, which had housed Thady's widowed mother until her death. The neighbouring cottiers, Paddy O'Linden, Ned 'the Buller', the Kieltys and the Murphys had similiar dwellings, but only Thady paid the Hearth Tax.

Murtagh Fegan was a regular visitor to his great aunt in Upper Kilbroney, where generations of Fegans once lived. The black-smith had a close affinity with his native townland, and although he had no intention of leaving his comfortable village home and profitable business he liked to visit the mountain land, if only to remind folk of his success. He made sure that Briony dutifully visited the old woman as well, for there were strong rumours that she kept more than the chamber-pot hidden under the bed, and Briony's charms might encourage a financial windfall in the event of her demise, much regretted though this might be.

Murtagh enjoyed the occasional night's *céilí* in the O'Lochlainn close, proclaiming that Thady was a born innkeeper. The Buller and Paddy O'Linden liked to gather around the same hearthside on a winter's evening when the work was done, and the bold Widow Fearon often called on her way from a confinement or a wake, to hear and give the latest news. Sometimes a song or two would be requested, or the Buller might entertain with a ghostly tale, but most of the time was spent in conversation.

They debated the merits of the man Grattan in Dublin. They revelled in the latest news from the American rebels. They cursed the mean rascal who called himself the Poundwarden, and anticipated the latest evictions. They predicted the following week's weather, but more than ever they wondered if this was the year in which the French would finally come.

One man whom the Buller never liked to see in the townland was Father Mackey, the Parish Priest. When his companions berated him for voicing such a sacrilegious opinion, he replied, 'What do you think takes him up here at this hour of night? 'Tis not for the sake of a wedding, nor a christening.' And it was indeed one of life's unexplained mysteries that people required the sacrament of Extreme Unction more often at night than during the day, and rarely when the weather was dry. Father Mackey, one of the old school, stoically brushed aside any inclination to grumble, as he saw the care of the sick and the dying as the most important feature of his ministry.

Eamonn O'Lochlainn, his unofficial acolyte, always accompanied him on calls to the Upper Kilbroney area. Eily clucked and fussed every wild night which brought him out on his mission, for Eamonn had a weak chest. It would not, she commented, be the priest who would have to endure the subsequent wheezing and coughing. She received a terse refusal from the irreligious Seán when it was suggested that he might, occasionally, take his younger brother's place. Seán had a suspicion that the wily old priest had a motive of his own for exposing Eamonn to the most rigorous functions of priestly life.

Eily always made a point of watching from the head of the track as the priest and his acolyte set off on their rounds.

'And don't forget to mind yon boghole.'

'Which boghole?'

'The one you always end up in!'

She stood until the dim lantern glow faded into the blackness. Eamonn, in spite of the impression he would give, did not relish these morbid journeys to the dying. He dreaded most of all the crossing of a stream, for the old Celtic superstitions which he scorned in daylight took on a new potency during the dead of night. The same inner eye which allowed him to see angels while at prayer was also capable of conjuring up the most dreadful demons to haunt these lonely, God-forsaken places.

Once, he recalled to the Buller, he was leading the priest across a stream just below the Priest's Mountain. On reaching the opposite bank he turned to guide Father Mackey over the last of the stepping stones. There in the pale glow of the lamp was the shocked white face of the priest, who seemed to be confronting some invisible power, his trembling hands grasping the purse which held the sacred wafer and his lips incanting silently. When they reached the home of the dying man he prayed by the bedside until daybreak before venturing home. Eamonn's tentative enquiries were met by the priest's customary brusqueness.

'Away home and say your prayers. And don't be tempted to dabble in what does not concern you!'

Seán smiled when he heard Eamonn's tale.

'That is how all priests reply to questions when they do not know the answer,' he scoffed, having little time for the clergy. Eamonn, aware of his brother's scepticism, did not indulge in argument. The Buller had no such scruples. Before an attentive audience in O'Lochlainn's, he volunteered his own explanation.

'A stream is a refuge for lost souls,' he began mysteriously, 'those who died unshriven and unmourned, doomed to wander between earth and purgatory for want of a few prayers. In dark and lonely places, you will hear their despairing wails...' His silent audience listened to the wind moaning in the eaves.

'A lost soul? So that's all it was,' remarked Seán irreverently. 'I'd be more scared of the Agent Coyle coming looking for the quarter's rent.'

'A lost soul! No doubt one who scorned the old customs when he was alive!' declared the Buller with authority, glancing meaningfully at Seán. 'Any priest,' he continued, 'properly ordained to Holy Orders has strange and unusual powers. When he carries the Blessed Sacrament over water, he can look into the realms of evil and see the torment, and hear the wailing cries of the damned!'

The silence that followed was broken only by a smothered chortle from Seán. But Sosanna, his young sister, was visibly shaken, and she rose and left the smoke-filled cabin.

'You had no call to frighten the child with your nonsense,' Seán barked crossly at Eamonn.

'But it did happen. I was there!' he protested.

'Nothing at all happened, brother, save that the priest had a dose of indigestion from being too well fed! Why can you not carry home some cheerful tale for a change.'

Few seemed to accept Seán's interpretation of the incident, and the righteous Buller stood vindicated by popular acclaim.

If the proximity of Father Mackey concentrated minds on spiritual matters, a call from Tom Dunn had the opposite effect. Dunn's grandfather, in a desperate effort to hold on to his small farm against the punitive excesses of the Penal Laws, had declared himself a convert to Protestantism. Dunn's Hill was saved from confiscation and he was allowed to pass on the land to his son. For the next generation, the family had to endure the taunts of 'Turncoat!' from their former neighbours and co-religionists, but as each in turn was impoverished and banished to the Poorlands, young Tom began to despise the system which turned Irishman against fellow Irishman. Having gained the benefit of a Protestant education at Trinity College, Dublin, and a degree in law, he reverted to the religion of the peasants, making an occasional but conspicuous Sunday appearance at the Mass House by the mill. Some said it was a hollow gesture of political defiance, as Tom was not the most pious of believers.

To the further confusion of friend and foe, his wife Annie was a staunch Presbyterian, and through this relationship he moved at liberty around the Meeting Houses of Ulster. Yet he was much loved among the deprived people of the Poorlands and became their stoutest champion. As Thady O'Lochlainn often said, 'Does it matter a damn who owns his soul, when we know where his heart is?' Thady's family were not the only beneficiaries of Dunn's hedge-school, but were among the most appreciative, and Tom Dunn was always welcomed at the close.

Thady marvelled at the way news could travel in Kilbroney, for no sooner would he hear that Master Dunn was on his way than a host of other callers would appear, some seeking advice on legal matters, others just to listen. Thady liked to watch from the head of the track for the familiar figure leading his dappled mare in the company, usually, of the neighbours' children. He was a very tall, well-built man who wore his greying hair swept back from his face. Stern, aquiline features were relieved by kindly eyes and a mouth quick to smile. Because of his height he had to stoop to enter Thady's cabin, where a seat by the hearthside invariably awaited him.

Dunn spoke as fluently in the native tongue as in the English, a language which was no more than gibberish to many mountainy men. The conversation usually commenced with local issues, such as the recent impounding of Barney Cole's cow and the Agent Coyle's latest devious plan to further limit grazing rights. Evictions were always a cause for concern.

'I hear the Widow MacOwen got her final notice,' remarked Thady one evening. Dunn would often agree to intervene on behalf of a tenant, not that he was well thought of by the Agent, but because he had a superior understanding of the law.

'There is nothing I can do for the Widow MacOwen. She refuses to plead her circumstances.' Even Dunn could not prevent the inevitable. The younger men like Seán still had enough anger and defiance to challenge the injustice of such a case, while most of Thady's generation could only despair. Dunn admired the fighting spirit in the young men, but had seen too many end up on a prison ship or the gallows for giving vent to their anger. He warned them against becoming involved in some of the fast-growing bands of secret societies. The Oakboys were, he declared, mindless scoundrels who only managed to make a bad situation worse.

'I hear,' declared the merchant Dwyer, 'that they're drilling and training around Rathfriland for all they're worth. Dissenters alongside Protestants. I wonder who their intended victims could be.' A murmur of concern followed this revelation for there was deep mistrust of the men of Rathfriland.

'Who else but ourselves?' Thady responded angrily. 'And we're

48

sitting here like beasts for the slaughter.'

'No,' Dunn reassured him, 'they don't have the O'Lochlainn family in mind just yet. They are volunteers. They march in Newry and Downpatrick and Belfast.'

'Aye, and march on Kilbroney for practice,' Thady persisted.

'They are armed against the threat of a French invasion, or so they say,' continued Dunn; 'with many of the King's men fighting the American colonists, some fear the French might take advantage of the situation.'

'The French!' cried Thady. 'So they're coming at last, God bless them! But what the hell would take them to Rathfriland?'

Dunn sometimes felt that the wider issues escaped the Kilbroney man, much as he admired his fighting spirit.

Like the men of previous generations, Thady's nightly prayer was that the French might come and deliver them from their misery. Tom Dunn was not so sure, and was more inclined to take inspiration from the Americans. The French monarchy could be just as corrupt as that of King George, but if the people held power in their own hands... He looked towards Seán and the young men present. Then, eyes aglow, he sat forward in his chair. What, he suggested, if a man like George Washington was to step forth in Ireland? What if people were to follow him, to take responsibility for their own government? Puzzled faces regarded him with curiosity, and he sat back. No, he thought, the time was not yet right. The new idea needed time to settle on the mind. The idea that a land did not need a King. He was doubtful of King Louis' support for an uprising against a brother monarch. In the Americas perhaps, but that was far away. Ireland would be a different matter.

The activities of Tom Dunn were closely monitored by the local garrison. To be sympathetic towards the native peasants, often lawless and belligerent folk, was grounds enough for suspicion. To be educated and liberal compounded the crime.

Towards the end of March Dunn was involved in an incident at the O'Lochlainn close. It began when Thady noticed the alerted ears of Bran, the Buller's dog, while on a personal mission behind the byre. Fastening his breeches and walking to the head of the track, he looked down the valley. It was bathed in moonlight and all looked peaceful, yet something seemed to bother the dog.

'You cur,' spat Thady in annoyance. 'Could you not have the manners to wait till I finished my business?'

He stopped to listen. From some distance came the barely perceptible sound of several sets of well-shod hooves. He hastened back to the cabin and flung open the door.

'Away home with you lads, 'tis the Welsh Horsemen.'

The Welsh Horse, as they were commonly known, were stationed in the town of Newry, a citadel of growing commercial prosperity, from which the wild and troubled lands of the Mournes, South Armagh and North Louth were governed. The small garrison based in the village of Rostrevor had a particular responsibility to protect the life and property of the landlords and lesser gentry, but particularly that of the influential Major Valentine, whose lands extended over most of Kilbroney parish. Sergeant Pollard had orders to keep an eye out for potential trouble-makers, especially those identified by the Valentines' perspicacious agent, Coyle, and now and then patrols were sent into the farther regions in search of unauthorised assemblies of any kind. The presence of one Thomas Dunn at such a meeting would suggest an attempt to involve simple people in dubious political activity.

Thady, keeping one eye on the approaching horsemen, watched his callers scatter and scramble across the fields to the safety of their own homes. Tom Dunn, as he prepared to depart, suddenly inveigled the daughter of the house into a mischievous scheme to mislead the Welshmen.

'Sosanna! Walk out with me for a while! They'll think I've come here on other business,' he said.

So the night patrol observed Dunn appearing from behind a hawthorn clump with his arm entwined around the waist of a woman who was clearly not Mistress Dunn. There was some chortling and unholy delight as the troopers found that the righteous Dunn had a chink in his armour, after all, and his preference was for very young maids.

'He's some woodcock!'

'Woodcock? Where I come from, we'd call him a roving rooster. Scratching in somebody else's barnyard!'

Still laughing, they turned their horses down the glen with the information for Sergeant Pollard. Annie Dunn would also get to hear of it soon, for such news spread rapidly in Rostrevor.

Dunn kissed the bemused Sosanna with a resounding smack. Annie would understand the diversion had been necessary. There was nothing to be gained by drawing the attention of the troopers to the men in his company. He was well able to stand up to their threats, but his companions would be subjected to unwelcome scrutiny.

No one had asked Sosanna how she felt about the conspiracy. And William Dwyer, for his part, failed to see any humour in the situation. As Dunn took his leave of the close leaving the merchant alone with Thady and his wife, William decided to speak his mind.

❖ ❖ ❖

Sosanna was always uneasy with Tom Dunn. Unlike the other O'Lochlainns, she had no learning and could neither read nor write. In this she was no different from other country girls, for Grace was the exception. It was no wonder that the younger girl felt stupid and ignorant in the company of the learned Master Dunn, for she had often heard that she was not in the least like Grace. She had neither her beauty nor her intellect, but one thing she knew they shared was a burning ambition to escape from the poverty of the close in Kilbroney.

Clasping her shawl tightly, Sosanna left William Dwyer with her parents and forded the river to Murphy's field, where her friend Cáit, a recently widowed young mother, lived in a tiny cabin. It was bedtime when she arrived and the two youngest, still in kilts, were being ordered to bed when Sosanna entered.

'Sosaí!' they cried, welcoming the diversion. Cáit was also pleased to see her friend. Her tired, drawn looks drew a wave of sympathy from Sosanna. Cáit was not as old as Grace, and yet she could pass for a woman of fifty, for her hair had greyed and her face was lined with care. She never rested; if she was not toiling in her stony plot or tending to her children, she was spinning yarn for the village weavers.

'I'll bed them down for you, Cáit,' offered Sosanna, lifting the smallest child into the cot with the promise of a story or two. Within twenty minutes all the children were asleep and so was Cáit, drooped over the spinning wheel where she worked. Sosanna prised her fingers from the spindle and gently eased her down on the heap of rags and reeds she called a bed.

'This,' whispered Sosanna, 'will not do for me.'

The escapade with Thomas Dunn still rankled. They had laughed at her! Even the troopers had found the idea of an educated man with a peasant girl amusing. She wondered what Thady and Eily planned for her future. She suspected that her father was quite happy to keep her at home to look after them in their old age. Eily probably had one of the O'Lindens or Murphys in mind as a husband. Hard-working lads they were, but dull as wretting flax.

The more she thought about the options which awaited her the more miserable she became, envying Mistress Dunn with her rooms and glass windows and clean clothes. As she walked towards the close, the sound of laughter spilled out from the cabin. Tom Dunn was probably making fun of her at his house, too, telling his wife about her embarrassment. Sosanna lifted the tail of her skirt to wipe away the tears. She found her favourite spot above the well, a little hollow in the hillside from where she could watch the moonlit lough. There she shivered and hugged herself in confusion. A man had kissed her – dare any of them call her a child now. The sound of muffled laughter had died away. She sat up in anger. Let them talk: she would show them how much she cared for their opinion. Lifting her chin, she walked purposefully towards the cabin.

❖ ❖ ❖

'I would take your daughter for my wife,' stammered William Dwyer before Sosanna's astonished parents. 'Wait,' he lifted his hand as Thady tried to speak. 'I know that she's young...'

'Barely seventeen,' interjected Eily.

'Yes, she is young, and I am a good lock of years older, but consider: I can give her everything a girl could wish for. No country youth of her age could hope to provide a fine stone house, newly thatched with yellow straw, and a feather bed; five acres of green meadow and her very own milch cow.'

Eily was most impressed, so William felt emboldened to continue with his much-rehearsed words.

'Everything she ever wants will be hers, be it in my power to provide.' Eily was now smiling and William digressed from the speech he had prepared. 'I have watched her grow from childhood, a charming little maid she was, with a smile and a pretty curtsy for me every time I called.'

Thady was tempted to remind him that Sosanna, like any artful child, was merely exchanging a few pleasantries in return for an apple or a piece of ribbon. 'When she's a year or so older, Master Dwyer,' he suggested, but William, having grasped the nettle, would not be deterred.

'I love her so much that I cannot wait until she is older!' It was his first declaration of love, and one of the few times that the merchant, shrewd in matters of dealing and selling, had ever bared his soul. He looked at Thady, seeking a response.

'Thady,' enthused Eily, 'a milch cow of her own – and a feather bed,' she added ecstatically. Thady harboured considerable doubts about the comfort of a feather bed if it had to be shared with a Clonduff dealer, however prosperous, but he was impressed by the cow.

'She has a good yield, this cow of yours?' he enquired civilly. William, who felt that he was being diverted from the vital subject, nevertheless answered courteously.

'The best in Clonduff! I could have sold her a dozen times had I the mind to. But,' he continued with determination, 'I want Sosanna to have her.' As Thady appeared to deliberate, the suitor played his trump card. 'Why,' he declared magnanimously, 'she can have the cow even if she chooses not to marry me.'

Eily, whose sense of justice preceded that of reason, chimed in. 'Why, that wouldn't be fair. She'll have to marry you!'

'Poor and all as I am, I have no notion of selling the girl off for a cow, whatever the yield,' Thady rebuked his wife. He turned to the merchant.

'You're a good man, William Dwyer,' he consoled him, 'and I would look no further for a husband for Sosanna. But she's not much more than a child, for all her winning ways, and happy with us for the moment. Having said that, I will put the question to her, and if she agrees, well then, I'll gladly give my blessing.'

Thady chided himself for having paid no attention to the warning signs. He should have known that William was after more than just the warmth of the fire on his backside all these years, with his gifts and offerings. The plug in his pipe was an example of such. He lifted a spark from the embers and watched the merchant as he and Eily discussed the present state of his mother's bad feet and the pitfalls of trading with men from Attical. Eily had clearly aligned herself with William who was now laughing politely at the story of Madam Patterson's flatulence. Thady, like William, had heard the same yarn often before.

He sat back and observed the merchant through the haze of smoke. He saw a well-preserved man all right, with a carefully trussed belly and bottle-green waistcoat; he wore no fripperies, although his neck cloth was spotless, and his demeanour betrayed no sign of the desperate longing Thady had seen just a few moments earlier.

''Tis well seeing his mother is still alive, to turn him out looking so neat,' thought the Kilbroney man. William's laughter had subsided and Eily was prattling on, her words wafting around with the smoke. The merchant's bushy grey eyebrows hooded an expression which Thady could not interpret. A man like that, he decided, could have married years ago, had he so wished.

The latch rattled and Sosanna entered, tossing her great-shawl aside. William stood up to gaze at her. Thady could now see why

William was so taken with his daughter, with her flushed cheeks and eyes sparkling with emotion. Perhaps she was not ready to discuss such a subject, and he regretted having made any promises. With a nod of the head towards William and her parents, she turned towards the loft ladder, to be halted at the first step by Thady's hand. Her shoulder felt rigid, and he wondered what ailed her.

'A chroí,'* he said gently, 'we were talking about you here.'

The girl turned to face them.

'This man,' hurried Thady, confident that William would be refused, 'would marry you, should your wish be his.'

Sosanna's eyes turned in wide surprise to meet William's anxious gaze, and a few tense seconds followed. She relaxed her shoulders and smiled. 'Marry old Master Dwyer? And why should I not?'

'You... you'll be my wife?'

'Some will tell me I could do a lot worse. Aye! I'll be your wife,' and she scrambled up the ladder to the privacy of her own bed, leaving an astonished Thady to shake the hand of his future son-in-law.

❖ ❖ ❖

Some months had passed since that night, and Thady was beginning to enjoy the prospect of a son-in-law with more to his name than the breeches in which he stood. He looked forward to the comfort of the newly thatched roof promised by William Dwyer, and lauded himself on having reared at least one lass with some sense in her head.

It was not the custom to marry during Lent; then, after Easter, old Mistress Dwyer came out in a fiery rash, ordering the postponement of the nuptials. Her dutiful son, following the habit of a lifetime, obeyed without question, although there were neighbours in Clonduff who saw the old dame's illness as being self-inflicted. She would not surrender her position to a young rival without a

---

*A chroí: used to refer to someone as 'love' is in English.

fight. 'Too much spring cabbage,' was the preferred explanation for the ailment.

Now a new date had been fixed in mid-May, and shrewd William had devised a solution, should a similiar situation again arise. Sosanna O'Lochlainn, he told Mistress Dwyer, would be only too happy to nurse an ailing mother-in-law, and to relieve her of most of her burdensome duties. This had the desired effect, and within hours the widow was back in her shop, stoically bearing her cross 'for the sake of William'.

It was now no more than a fortnight before Sosanna would be leaving home and Thady, on his mountain perch, examined his clay pipe and wondered, not for the first time, about the wisdom of it all. He had not expected his daughter to be so content with the situation, but then, he thought as he pocketed the pipe, you could never tell what a young lass might be thinking.

'Are you not away home yet?' Seán's voice called out, rousing Thady from his day-dreams. It was late in the evening, and Seán had only just arrived with the mountain car.

'And what kept you?' Thady enquired crossly. 'I'm sitting here so long my arse is stuck fast and I couldn't move if I tried.'

'Now here's the man to shift you,' replied Seán, indicating his companion. The tall figure following Seán was unmistakable.

'God save you, Master Dunn,' Thady cried, 'and what takes you up this way?' He had not seen Dunn since the night the troopers called.

'I need a favour of you and your house.'

'For yourself?'

Dunn did not answer immediately, choosing instead to assist Seán in loading the spades and a few sods on the broad-wheeled car. He turned, wiping his hands.

'I need a safe house for a night or so.'

'In Kilbroney?'

'Just until one of the fugitives is fit to be moved elsewhere.'

'How many are there?'

'Two good men, in sore need,' explained Dunn. 'I dare not keep them myself, for only yesterday I had a call from Pollard. So, you see my predicament: they have been living wild for weeks, and are weak and ill. They think they have shaken off any pursuers, but it would be wise for them to lie low. It occurred to me that if you could give them a space in your byre, you might pass them off as kinsfolk. Just in case anyone asks.'

'Relations... calling to see the young one wed, you mean?' pondered Thady.

'I'll get word to you, should there be any sign of house raids. Murtagh Fegan keeps a sharp eye on the Barrack and he'll let us know of any activity.'

'It should be safe enough then,' Thady quelled his doubts.

'I knew the O'Lochlainns wouldn't turn me down,' Dunn declared as they made their way back to the close.

'Who are they, or can you say as much?' asked Seán.

'Two men destined for France. For the Irish Brigade of King Louis.'

'The Irish Brigade!' Thady's tone was hushed with reverence. 'God bless them all.'

'The younger man is the son of a MacArtain of Down, I believe.'

'A connection of old Briony MacArtain? Of Tullylish?' Thady, like many mountainy men, had a keen interest in genealogy.

'The elder of the two,' Dunn informed them, 'MacArtain's foster father, is a brave Dissenter. Makepeace Theophilous Agnew is how he describes himself, and his character is as stout as his name.'

This outlandish collection of names was beyond Thady, and he abandoned any hope of tracing the clan to which the young man belonged.

As they neared the close, Tom Dunn was offered the usual hospitality, which he regretfully declined.

'My compliments to Mistress O'Lochlainn,' he called as he mounted his mare, 'and tell her she may expect her guests shortly.' He rode off in haste down the glen, hoping that the O'Lochlainn family would not have reason to regret their generosity to strangers.

Chapter Four

May 1st 1780

THE SUN WAS some hours from rising on the first day of May when the Buller called to rouse Seán. After washing the sleep out of his eyes at O'Lochlainn's well, he went over to rattle the latch. To his surprise, this customary greeting was interrupted by a cudgel-waving Thady.

'What the devil are you doing snooping round here at such an hour,' shouted the angry master of the house. 'You scared the breeches off me, pounding the door like that.'

The Buller, having recovered from his initial bewilderment, respondered with vigour. 'You big-mouthed braggart! Threatening decent men going about their business. 'Tis only a wastrel would be still lying abed this hour of the morning, with the sun splitting the stones!'

'Are you blind or are you drunk? 'Tis pitch black. Only a fly-by-night or a grave robber would be abroad at such an hour.'

Seán emerged from the byre, blinking at the sight of the two old neighbours sparring with each other. This was not an unusual occurrance, though earlier in the morning than was customary. Without doubt the Buller would be around that evening as usual, as though no words had ever been spoken.

'I don't know what has come over your father,' remarked the Buller tersely. 'Is he gone soft in his old age?'

'How was I to know it was yourself? You should have declared your name,' answered Thady sheepishly.

'And who else could it have been?' the Buller asked. 'The excise men aren't on your trail again, don't tell me.'

'God knows, it must be twenty years since we buried that still,' Thady began. 'Do you mind the time...'

'What was it you wanted,' Seán interrupted. 'Is it the year-old we took down yesterday?'

'Thady!' a voice called from within, 'you needn't think of going anywhere at this hour without your stirabout!'

'Now look!' charged Thady, recovering the high moral ground. 'You went and roused half Kilbroney with your roaring. Are you happy now?'

The Buller, leaving Thady to continue arguing with Eily, shook his head and followed Seán up the track.

'Every rooster's brave in his own barnyard,' he grumbled.

'He has good reason to be suspicious,' confided Seán as they searched for the ewe. There were a few men who could be trusted with the news, although he suspected his inquisitive neighbours would not be long finding out.

'They are cousins of my mother's, that's what you have to say, Buller.'

'Seán O'Lochlainn, you should not be trusting people with such a story. It might be worth a shilling at the Barrack.'

'Come on now! 'Tis not every man I would trust! Master Dunn, Murtagh Fegan and yourself, of course.'

'I suppose Tom Dunn knows his business...' the Buller seemed uneasy. 'Just watch yourself, that's all I'm saying.'

'I'll take care!'

'So explain to me why this Master Agnew is in your bed, and you are lying in the byre?'

'My mother thought he had a bit of an ague and needed the heat. I don't know how any of them slept last night, for the snores of him could be heard from the top of Rooslieve. The other one slept like a young pup.'

They walked on in silence. As the first light of dawn was slowly breaking over the glen, the sheep began making their way down from the mountainside towards the sheltered ditches and hollows at the head of the valley, a forewarning of bad weather. Much of the lambing had already taken place, but there were many still to be accounted for, mostly from the young ewes which were only born the previous year. The Buller had responsibility for the husbandry of Major Valentine's flocks on the mountain pasture between Kilbroney and the glen of Knockbarragh, and this involved watching closely over the lambing. In return he was permitted a limited number of ewes of his own, which, like those of the other peasants, were marked with his own symbol. All unmarked sheep automatically belonged to Major Valentine. The Warden knew the number of expectant ewes and called the local men to account for any missing lambs.

The young ewe which the Buller sought to save was unbranded and therefore belonged to the landlord. She cried in pain and fear as the two shepherds regarded her in the hollow where she lay.

'Do your best with her, Seán. You have great healer's hands.' The Buller struggled to pacify the panic-stricken animal as his companion tried to extricate the spindly legs of the half-born lamb.

'Look at the cut of her. This is what comes of sending cross-breeds up here. She's not hardy enough for the mountain and 'tis tough enough on any poor hogget to be lambing, without a pick of meat on her back,' Seán said angrily. It began to rain, creating rivulets of blood as the lamb was brought struggling into the world. The ewe was beyond help, and her frantic struggling gradually ebbed away.

'Do you think it was worth the bother, for the sake of an animal he did not know he had?' Seán was disappointed.

'We've saved the lamb!' replied the Buller. ''Tis a good morning's work! Ask your mother to keep her warm for me till I get her fostered.'

'And what good will it do you? All they'll take into account is that you lost the ewe. You'll be lucky if they don't say you killed it.'

'They'll see the carcass. 'Tis beyond salvage.' The Buller tipped the dead animal with his boot. There was no eating on her.

It took very little to raise the ire in Seán, the Buller knew, as he watched the younger man place the lamb under his coat for warmth. Yes, and little to soften his stout heart.

'Damn Valentine and his half-breeds. 'Tis against nature.'

'What is?'

'Mixing the races – and I'm not just talking about sheep.'

The Buller knew well what was in Seán's mind, but did not

choose to comment. Instead he issued Seán a warning. 'Mind you do your best for the lamb. You don't want to lose your grazing rights, as others before you lost theirs.'

'Rights? On land that's barely fit for burying the dead? Have you ever noticed, Buller? The only place where the grass grows here is over the graves.'

❖   ❖   ❖

As Eily O'Lochlainn had often remarked, a stranger to Kilbroney would never take Seán and Eamonn for brothers, so different were they in character. Seán was over ten years the senior of the two, thick-set, dark, whiskered and fierce, while Eamonn was taller, of slight build and pale, fair complexion. Eamonn was one of those children who should never have survived childbirth but in spite of all the odds was still alive and fighting. Eily was the first to admit that she had done much of the fighting for him, nursing him through a childhood marred by rheumatic fever and epilepsy. He had been cosseted by the older children, Seán and Grace, and although Thady had often accused them of spoiling the little boy, it was he who had insisted on Eamonn going to Master Dunn's school. 'So that he could earn his living without breaking his back,' he told Eily. Eamonn, being spared the usual household duties, had plenty of time to devote himself to his studies, while Seán, hired out from an early age, continued to labour at the quarry.

Seán's first few years at the quarry involved carrying endless buckets of water to and fro and gathering splinters and gravel. The hard green granite known as syenite was used in the construction of Kilbroney House, the Barrack and other buildings on the Valentine estate. Its enduring qualities gave the occupiers a sense of security and permanence, both real and symbolic, in an otherwise alien environment. When Seán grew strong enough to wield a pick he was sentenced to the back-breaking task of splitting the rock, a challenge which he at first welcomed as an advancement from the more childish chores. When the building programme was at its most intense, he rose each morning well before dawn,

Eily feeding him up as best she could with potatoes, or oatmeal stirabout when she could get it. He would leave, armed with pick and shovel, returning only after dark, his face worn and grimy, and his hair matted with dust. During the worst of the winter months he would sleep overnight in the woodman's hut, sometimes in the company of the Buller, an occasional worker. There were many accidents at the quarry, mostly broken bones and crushed limbs. Seán himself retained only partial sight in his left eye after a splinter had embedded itself there. He was lucky, Eily told him, that he was still able to work, for other men had injuries that made them fit only for the begging bowl. Yet the pain had been excruciating, and added fuel to Seán's smouldering anger.

Seán's strong personal dislike of the Valentines was equalled only by his sense of frustration at being completely at their mercy. He hated to work for them, but needed the money to pay rent and taxes. Eily was forever at pains to warn him against speaking ill of his master, lest some turncoat would carry the tale back to the Agent Coyle. He was the only remaining son who was fit to earn a day's wages, circumstances which also caused him grief. There had been two other boys in the O'Lochlainn family, both close in age to Seán, strapping healthy lads with curling hair and freckled faces. Donogh and Tadhg had both fallen victim to smallpox in one night. Thady had said little, leaving Eily and the Widow Fearon to bind up the bodies while he went in search of the Buller to dig the graves.

Seán had been old enough for sorrow, too young for understanding. He heard his grandmother moaning to Father Pullein about his brothers dying unshriven, while the tired old priest, heartsore from like tragedies all over his mountain parish, rambled on about angels and heaven. The priest told him how privileged he was to be so close to Our Lord, that he should be asked to share in such suffering. The 'Planter' as Father Pullein called him, was so far from God that he was not fit to shoulder the cross. Seán had watched with incredulity his parents' docile acceptance of this explanation of their tragedy, while his own heart raged and bled within.

'God is saving Eamonn for some special task!' Eily had whispered through her tears. Seán was not impressed by God's generosity, a bountiful deity who took much more than he ever gave.

Other, deeper scars were etched on his consciousness: memories of his grandfather Felim's senile ravings, his tales of clashing steel, spurting blood and screaming children; of a priest, Father MacOwen, who had bade his flock to stay at prayer while the priest-hunter Whitechurch attacked the little congregation of fugitive worshippers out on the grey slopes of the Priest's Mountain. Felim had died with the words he had been unable to utter on that terrible Sunday, which he alone had survived. Seán had often visited that dark place, not to pray for the dead, but to ask the question, why? 'Father MacOwen, why did you incite such fine people to martyrdom? Could they not have prayed while they ran? It was your choice to be a martyr, not theirs!' His mother and father had disapproved of his unholy curiosity. Had they not heard, Seán asked himself, Felim's last tortured recollection and his dying words: 'Run for your lives!'

❖ ❖ ❖

Eily was throwing skins to the fowl when Seán arrived home with his charge.

'I have a lamb for Sosanna to tend!' he called. 'Is she away with the goats?'

'She slept down at Murphy's. I think the two strange men upset her.'

'They did what?' exclaimed Seán. 'They annoyed a wee girl?'

'No, no!' his mother replied. 'She just did not like the thought of strangers in the house, what with her getting wed. Away now and take your stirabout before you go to the quarry.'

'I'm not wanted this day.'

'Oh?'

'Not until Tuesday. It seems that Madam Ward doesn't like the sound and sight of us when there's a hunting party on. Some important folk, I hear.'

'Oh?'

'That is all I can tell you,' he replied, seeing a look of curiosity on his mother's face. 'I can help my father with the turf.'

Seán pushed open the half-door to find Donal MacArtain stripped to his breeches and shaving himself over a basin. Draped by the hearthside was his linen shirt and stock, less some of the last month's grime.

'Good morning, O'Lochlainn, 'tis a poor enough Mayday!' he exclaimed courteously.

'No worse than any other, and better for them that has the time to look after themselves,' Seán replied while looking to see if his guest had left anything in the pot. 'I see you were hungry.'

'Thank you! The stirabout was most tasty. When you've been living in the wilds for as long as we have, a good pot of hot oats is well appreciated.'

'You can thank William Dwyer for the oats. Praties is the usual fare in this house.' Seán settled the lamb in a haybox, where it would remain until the Buller found it a foster mother. He dipped his fingers in goat's milk, and after some coaxing the lamb allowed herself a taste.

'Bully girl! You have a good strong suck,' said Seán with satisfaction. 'All you need now is a new mother!' A sudden snort from the corner startled him.

'In the name of the Devil!' he roared as vengeful eyes peered from under the pile of rugs where he usually slept. One angry looking terrier emerged, growling. 'You're all right lad,' Seán soothed the dog, 'we'll not disturb your master.' The terrier sunk his head, but kept his beady eyes in the direction of the lamb. His tail beat slowly. 'Thon companion of yours,' Seán looked at Donal, 'is no early riser.'

'Ah now, don't begrudge him his rest, for 'tis the first sleep he has enjoyed under a dry roof for nigh on a week.'

'And what did he do to his leg?'

'Nothing. He wounded himself leaping over a ditch. You know how it is with old warriors. He would take no help. Yet he would not get it seen to.'

'Aye. I know how it is.'

'Well he's not the type to complain... about himself that is, and I did not know how bad it was until it collapsed under him.'

'Collapsed! I hope it's not bloodrot!'

'We were hoping Master Dunn would help.'

'He will,' Seán reassured him, 'but the best healer around this country is the Widow Fearon of Levallyclanowen.'

❖ ❖ ❖

In darker times, and in other lands, the Widow Fearon might have ended up in the ducking-stool for crimes of witchcraft, but the people of Kilbroney recognised her for what she was, a competent midwife and healer. She also laid out the dead, a more sombre but frequently requested skill. Her remote cot in the townland of Levallyclanowen allowed her the opportunity to indulge in practices which bordered on the occult, but though this troubled Eamonn O'Lochlainn, most people were unconcerned. If her curses were as effective as her love charms, the Buller often said, then there was damn all to worry about.

The Widow was of uncertain age, with thick hair which had been dyed with a syrup of whin blossom and sea-wrack. The hair was an orangey colour most of the time, but when it rained it turned to purple. She had retained most of her teeth, and they were stained greeny yellow from chewing stems, so, together with her rosy cheeks and blue eyes, the Widow made a colourful character. Her little cabin was hung with plants, weeds and herbs of all descriptions from mountain, forest, meadow and shore, all of which were within a few hours of her home. A formidable array of balms, ointments, potions and lotions were hidden under ditches and within hedgerows known only to herself and to young Owen MacOwen, her nearest neighbour and acolyte, although some secrets were kept hidden even from him. She knew which fungi and seed-heads had hallucinogenic qualities, and although they were mainly for personal use she was not beyond using them to intoxicate a woman in labour. She was an authority on childbirth, having had nine of her own, none of which survived past infancy. Not known for her high standards of personal hygiene, she was nevertheless a good midwife.

Early on the morning of the first day of May, Owen MacOwen arrived breathless at Widow Fearon's door with the rain dripping from the end of his nose.

'Master Dunn wants you!' he called out, rapping at the old timber. It was some months since the Widow had received such an important summons and she wasted no time about rising from her bed.

'What harm's come by Master Dunn?' she asked.

'No harm! 'Tis a stranger, up at Thady O'Lochlainn's close. I think he's an uncle or something.'

'Have I to lay him out or what?'

'I don't know. He didn't say,' said Owen helpfully.

'For Holy Mary's sake, is he alive or dead?' asked the exasperated woman.

'Sure I saw him myself yesterday.'

'Where?'

'In the graveyard.'

'Was he dead then?' Widow Fearon was losing her patience.

'Dead? He near hit me a thump with his crutch!'

'And that's what I'd like to do to you now!' She left a rather hurt Owen standing and, armed with a balm she had prepared for Thady's bad back, she set out to cross Leckan Mountain into upper Kilbroney.

❖ ❖ ❖

Seán had sympathy for the old Dissenter and did not begrudge him his bed, but he had to admit to himself that the King of France must be in a state of sore need if he was depending on the arrival of this Master Agnew. Tom Dunn, he thought, could not have told them the full story. He watched Donal MacArtain, the young popinjay, who had eaten a full breakfast and was now cleaning his boots with Eily's best fleece. Seán settled his lamb before casting a cautious look towards the mound which concealed the terrier.

'He'll not touch the lamb,' said Donal, combing his hair. Seán, being not altogether reassured, attempted to remove the dog from his snug refuge. The animal's growl of protest disturbed Master Agnew.

'Come on! I'm ready for ye!' he cried in confusion, flailing out blindly, hands fumbling in search of his blade and spectacles.

'Hush, Makepeace! Go back to sleep!' soothed Donal. 'We're safe now.' The old man stared wildly at him before he realised where he was; his arm relaxed and he returned the knife to its resting place by his side.

'He has the makings of a fever,' began Seán warily. It would be just their luck to have given shelter to the harbinger of some pestilential epidemic.

'He's exhausted! He was so determined not to hold me back. I would never have left him behind.'

Donal tenderly fixed the rug over the old man, and Seán could see his affection for Makepeace. A popinjay no more, Seán saw a young man with a dark past, and an even darker future.

'The Widow Fearon is surely the woman he needs,' the Kilbroney man suggested.

'A healer?' asked Donal.

'You could say that. If she can't cure him he'd be better off dead, and she'll come in handy, even then.'

❖ ❖ ❖

Donal had been relieved to reach the end of the journey on the previous evening, but Tom Dunn had obviously been worried by the condition of Makepeace.

'He is in no state to travel further,' Dunn had said. He was anxious that Donal should waste no time about his own departure. 'Ned Maguire of Clonduff – he'll want you gone as soon as possible.'

'I can't go without Master Makepeace!'

'You may have no choice. 'Tis a matter of sailing when the tides are right and the risk is lowest,' Dunn warned. 'There are good people around here. They will do their best to help you. But if you put their lives or liberty at risk for the sake of your own plans –

I'll turn you in myself.' Donal was quick to reassure Master Dunn that he was the soul of discretion, but his natural concern for his foster father made him anxious.

The safe house, he discovered, was the home of Eamonn O'Lochlainn, the hedge-school teacher they had already encountered. It was nearly dark when they arrived at the close in Kilbroney, and Makepeace had to be assisted from Tom Dunn's mare. The woman of the house was clucking and fussing around the sick man as Donal unsaddled the horse. It was a poor cabin, and he hoped that their sojourn there would be brief.

Then his attention was caught by a most welcome vision, the girl he had encountered on the previous evening, looking even more elfin than before. She carried a basket of spring primroses, the traditional protection against the mischievous fairies who could cause domestic havoc on May Eve. His appearance startled her for she dropped all her flowers, enough for five houses, in a heap by the door.

'Sosanna!' the father of the house appeared from behind the byre. 'What hour is this to be coming home at? Your mother was worrying about you being abroad so late, and on such a night!' The girl did not appear to hear his words.

'God save you, young Mistress Sosanna!' Donal removed his hat. 'For whatever else passes your threshold this night, it will not be the fairies,' he continued under his breath.

Now he stood at one end of the cabin as the women tended to his foster father.

'This man's burning up!' whispered the Widow to Eily. 'We'll have to sweat it out of him.'

'Fever?' asked Eily in alarm. 'What about the rest of us?' She pushed the Widow to the door.

'You can't turn your uncle out like that!'

'Uncle? He's no uncle! Thady took him in as a favour to Tom Dunn. Only I'm not supposed to say who he is.'

'If it's any comfort to you, he has neither cough nor rash. It could be nothing more than a passing ailment due to his years. Make up as good a blaze as you can,' advised the Widow, 'and I'll mix up a dose for him.'

'Do you think this will work?' asked Eily as she watched the healer infuse a mixture of wild barley, clover, and some root of her own.

'This is what the old boy in Clonduff uses when all else fails. "Kill or cure" he calls it, and in truth nobody's ever complained yet.'

As the fever persisted through the following days, Eily prayed and Thady cursed. Donal alone showed little sign of anxiety.

'He's pulled out of worse than this before. He's as strong as a plough horse, in spite of his looks.'

'We may be grateful about one thing,' said Seán wryly. 'Not even the troopers will want a man with the pox.'

'Jesus! The pox?' cried the Buller, taking a step away from his companion.

'It could turn out to be that. You would never know with these Dissenters.'

❖ ❖ ❖

The most concerned person appeared to be William Dwyer, who arrived at the close only to be shooed away by Eily. Sosanna, she assured him, was sleeping in the Murphy cabin across the river, and would be safe enough. It was a pity this had to happen just before her wedding, but it could not be helped. William foresaw another excuse for his mother to plead for a postponement and left despondently.

But three days after his arrival Makepeace was sitting up drinking good barley broth sent up from Dunn's Hill. Owen MacOwen, Tom Dunn's courier, brought a written billet to Donal urging him to contact Ned Maguire as soon as he was able.

'Tomorrow is fair day in Hill Town,' remarked Thady. 'You'll find Maguire in the alehouse, if I'm any judge.'

'I have no work so I'll go with you!' suggested Seán eagerly.

At the mention of 'alehouse' Makepeace stirred in his bed and declared his intention to accompany his foster son.

'You will not enter a house of sin while you're in my care,' he cried sternly. It took some time for Thady to persuade him that he was not fit to walk as far as the door, let alone to Hill Town.

'My only reason for visiting the alehouse is to make my arrangements with Ned Maguire,' Donal placated him. It was agreed that Seán would keep the young man company and away, he promised, from 'sinful influences'.

That night the Buller arrived, at last safe from contracting a variety of pox, and keen to exchange news with these strangers from the north. Thady presided as usual by the fireside while Eily darned his hose on her corner stool. The Dissenter was still too weak to rise out of his bed, but able to contribute his fair share, and more, to the conversation.

Donal asked them about the landlord.

'What kind of a man is he? Is he like most of them, living in London, on the backs of poor people like yourselves?' he enquired.

'Ach, you would see worse...' the Buller trailed off, looking to Thady for a lead, but their host just pulled on his pipe and shook his head. Then Eamonn spoke.

'I believe him to be a good man. If there is injustice, it is because he lives the only way he knows how. He has not been blessed with the True Faith as we have! Begging your pardon Master Agnew!' he added hastily.

'Pardon granted!' Makepeace replied civilly.

Seán burst out in anger. 'Good? There is not a decent bone in his body. I would say he's the greatest bastard that ever wore a coat. The spawn of the devil!'

'Watch that tongue of yours,' Thady roared at the glowering Seán. 'You're not that old that I'm past hitting you a thump to put some manners on you.' Makepeace hastily thought of a diversion to end this domestic dispute.

'Master Thady! You know that I am no disciple of the Popish faith. That is why I respectfully refused your kind offer to send for the priest when you thought I was near death.' Makepeace referred to a whispered conversation he had overheard the night before last.

'Ah now, 'twas well intentioned,' said Thady sheepishly, 'they talk about deathbed confessions...'

'As I say, I know little of Popish customs. Yet my young friend and I were curious about the presence, high upon the mountainside, of a lone cross. You saw it, did you not Donal?'

'Yes,' Donal nodded, excusing himself as he got to his feet.

'The Mass Rock,' said Thady in a respectful tone. 'On the Priest's Mountain – *Alt na Sagart*. To us it's as sacred as Mount Sinai was to the Jews.'

'I see. 'Tis a place of pilgrimage?'

''Tis that and more. I'll let the Buller tell you the story. It might explain Seán's anger.'

The Buller, not needing to be asked twice, began his tale. It was one told often, in case, as he said, people might forget. Makepeace listened as he spoke, but every so often his eyes were drawn to the door, where Donal had gone.

'It was in my grandfather's time,' began the Buller, 'that the only way to hear the Mass was in the wild forlorn places of the world, where the sole witnesses were them that had no spoken word in their mouths, the wild goats and mountain eagles. *Alt na Coillte* was such a place, a lonely barren mountain pass between Kilbroney and Clonduff. It was here that a pitiful, bedraggled group gathered, folk from all parts of Iveagh, footsore and weary, but full of hope and courage. There they met Father MacOwen, "the Shepherd of the Mountains" they called him. He was visiting them for the last time, for the priest-hunters and their bloodhounds were on his trail, and, like yourselves, he was preparing to flee to the sanctuary of France. The people welcomed him eagerly and they followed him uphill, a long climb through the bracken, above Owenabwee, to the Mass Rock. Now I'm telling you to close your eyes, and see as I do no great cathedral built by man, but God's own creation with its high altar of white granite, and vaulted blue roof. There they stood, young and old, mothers with babes in arms, little boys by their grandsire's sides...'

The Buller had closed his eyes as he always did, and the others listened intently. They knew this story, and would hear it again –

it never changed. If most of the faces were sad, Seán's wore an expression of anger. He did not need to imagine that little boy the Buller spoke of, for it was his own grandfather, Felim, no more than six years old.

'A few sharp-eyed lads were delegated to be lookouts, for that was the way it was done,' continued the storyteller, 'and they stood where they could see across the countryside in all directions, God help them. As the Holy Mass commenced, there were between forty and fifty folk gathered, and the sky was cloudless. But the Enemy of God is powerful too, and midway into the prayers a grey mist stole out of the earth, as sinister as the breath of hell. Slowly it slithered down the mountainside, until it had enfolded the praying company. 'Tis no wonder that no man paid heed, for all eyes were on the Mass Rock, where the priest, framed by the glow of two torches, had reached the most sacred part of the Mass. "Hoc est enim corpus meam," he chanted, and all heads bowed before the sacred host.' Thady blessed himself, as though reliving the experience. The Buller's voice quivered.

'The Mass was drawing to a close when Father MacOwen turned and spoke, not in Latin but in Irish.

'"Have faith in God's guiding hand," he said quietly, "not only in the sunshine of harvest, but in the tempest of winter, not only in the light of power, but in the darkness of oppression!"

'Then he moved among his people, blessing them and embracing the little children.

'"Now farewell," he cried, "and should we never meet again upon earth, God grant we may meet where the true Shepherd of the Mountain gathers his flock in the sunshine of bliss."

'Then a shot rang out...'

Seán clenched his teeth. He remembered this bit as though he himself were Felim clinging to his grandfather's side.

The storyteller continued. 'It is believed that the first man to fall was old Eamonn O'Lochlainn – Thady's great-grandfather,' he added for the benefit of Makepeace.

'No one ran; they stayed put, the men closing around the altar to protect the priest. He swallowed the sacred bread and wine to avoid the desecration that would surely follow. No mercy was shown. First with musket and then with sword every man, woman and child was massacred, save for one young boy, left for dead, who lived to tell the tale. That boy lived to hear the screams of the tortured priest and the mockery of his tormentors. He lived to see them set off with the head of Father MacOwen impaled on a stake. He lived, and yet he wished he had died with the rest, such was the horror that followed him through life.'

Makepeace had heard many such tales from the Penal times. His own mother carried accounts of similiar happenings at Glencoe. But here the grievance was still very immediate, very real, for no one could be certain that it would not be repeated.

'And was the wrongdoer ever punished?' he asked quietly.

'Punished?' cried Seán. 'He profited. His reward was the lands and property of his victims, and the King's commendation. His name was Colonel Whitechurch. They say he lived to a ripe old age and died in his bed with his grandson by his side.'

'His grandson,' explained the Buller, 'was George Valentine, Henry Valentine's father.'

❖   ❖   ❖

Donal stood outside, savouring the sweet mountain air. He would see Ned Maguire and leave as soon as possible. If Makepeace was unable to travel, the old man would just have to stay put until he was well. After all, he himself was the wanted man, and it might be safer to split up; they would be less easily recognised. He helped himself to a cooling draught from the well. Then, from out of the darkness, he heard the faint sound of singing.

It came from the direction of the cabin across the stream, and he moved closer to the source. It was the young maid of the house who sang; it was a sad song, one of hopes unfulfilled. She sang 'The Killing of the Swan' until the sound was lost in the wind.

Chapter Five

September 1762

I T WAS A late harvest, September of 1762 having settled to a sleepy golden calm after an indifferent summer which gave headaches to farmers, bleachers and washerwomen with its unpredictability.

It was as though Nature wished to compensate for her earlier churlishness, and the people of Kilbroney, gracious to the last, were quite prepared to take advantage of her generosity. On mountain and meadow mighty oaks and beeches blazed in tawny glory, while beneath them the hedgerows and ditches melted under the weight of mouldering berries and rosy haws. Even the Poorlands were bountiful, with woody copses giving forth brambleberries, hazelnuts, crab-apples and the fruit of the elder. The Widow Fearon, declaring that she had never seen a finer harvest, was on the go from first light to dusk, stocking up her little home. She prayed as she picked that no unexpected confinements or sudden deaths would interrupt her few precious weeks.

The orchards of the Valentines promised a record crop of apples and pears, but the purple black plums, swollen by the summer rain, had to be harvested promptly. The kitchens at Kilbroney House were busy with bottling and preserving, boiling and baking, while saving the most luscious samples for the family's immediate enjoyment. These were carefully polished and placed in parian china dishes, in the hope of tempting Madam Valentine, who was in residence with her two children, Miss Fanny and Master Henry. Rotting or under-ripe fruit was generously tipped into rush baskets to be distributed among the poor, the elderly and the infirm. Madam Valentine, adorned by the smile of Lady Bountiful, basked in their gratitude, although it was not unknown for some ungrateful recipients to remove their allotted portion to the nearest dung-heap. Such little acts of defiance, if unnoticed by their benefactress, were carefully stored in the record book of the vigilant Agent Coyle for future reference.

With the harvest came the usual bands of migrant labourers, poor starving spalpeens from as far away as Connaught, in desperate need of food. Temporary dwellings mushroomed by the roadsides, wretched little hovels held together with dirt and a few sticks, causing the decent residents of Rostrevor to complain about the smell and the unsightliness. When reports of stolen washing and food reached the ears of the Agent Coyle he took steps against the newcomers, terminating any employment in the fields and setting the troopers from the Barrack on them. To compensate for the shortfall in labour, the local men and women of the Poorlands, tenants, subtenants and cottiers, were called upon to pull their weight before the weather turned. With wages of fourpence a day quoted for the fittest men, this opportunity was not to be ignored, for it could add up to the price of a pig. Children, depending on their productivity, received less than a penny a day, but good nourishing food was promised as an encouragement. Those too young to leave their mothers stayed at home to pick potatoes, while their elder siblings joined Squire Valentine's harvesters.

Thady, armed with sharpened scythe, with Grace and the boys, Seán, Donogh and Tadhg, joined the little army marching down the valley. It was a long time since there had been such a spirit of truce and bonhomie; since it seemed likely to last only as long as the rain kept off, Thady and his boys were prepared to make the most of it. What Grace thought of it all no one could tell, for she was a quiet girl. The Buller was in rare form, calculating that if he managed to meet this and the next quarter's rent, he would buy an old ass for himself at the fair, come the spring. Thady harboured more ambitious plans. He would build himself a stone hearth and chimney.

'But that will raise your rent, man, and you'll be caught for the Hearth Tax. Besides,' the Buller went on in a disgruntled tone, 'there are no chimneys in Kilbroney.'

'None except on the O'Lochlainn house!' said Thady to himself with satisfaction. 'That will give them all something to talk about.'

The workers were divided mainly between the barley and the flax. High prices in the linen market had prompted George Valentine to put more acreage over to flax production, and he had even sanctioned the building of another mill along the river. It was to the barley that Thady and the boys were allocated, fields bleached ashen white by the weather and crying out for the cut of the scythe.

The young boys enjoyed the diversion, ducking and hiding under the haycarts. As long as Coyle wasn't around nobody passed any remarks or begrudged them their play.

In the mornings the harvested grain was removed for threshing, and a blizzard of white chaff rose over the scene. The pails and baskets of barley were emptied into the panniers of the farm donkeys and taken to the grain barns. The barns, large shells of stone and wood, were built close to the big house, where they were guarded by a pack of fierce hounds and a few ratting terriers. Held as securely as any city's merchant bank, the barns were, like the pedigree grazing herds, symbols of the landlord's – and the nation's – growing prosperity. They stood for a land of plenty, a land at peace. They rebuffed any suggestion that the people were anything other than content with their lot.

Thady too had his bit of sport in the late evenings when he could sit down with men from Killowen and Knockbarragh and enjoy a generous draught of ale and baked oaten bread from the farmhouse kitchen. The belligerent men of Killowen liked to challenge all comers to a tug o' war match, or even a hurling free-for-all across the stubble. In such games, it was acknowledged that the advantage lay with the better shod, and Killowen boasted a cobbler who could make a pair of decent boots from a catskin. Not that a final score was ever reached, for when the lookout heralded the approach of the Agent, sticks and cudgels were dropped on the spot and all contestants returned to their duties.

The uncanny gift of Adam Coyle was his ability to see behind his own back. He had been the land agent since before Grace was born, a short stout man with the appearance of a good-natured uncle but the reputation of an Oliver Cromwell. He kept meticulous records on every resident of the Parish of Kilbroney, down to the last newborn infant. He could, at any given time, recite the breed, the age and the milking capacity of any cow in the meadow, and was totally dedicated to the rule of the laws of the country and, especially, the rule of the Valentines. Coyle worked hard and to order, whether his masters were in residence or not, his obedience and loyalty beyond question. While not the villainous middleman of legend, cheating both tenant and master, he was, without question, unpopular. He lacked imagination, humour and foresight, and would go to any lengths to ensure that the letter of the law was complied with. His wife, Bess, had found this inability to compromise and obsession with order beyond what any reasonable woman could bear, so she had lifted her copper pots and pewter candlesticks and returned to her own people in Clontafleece. When her mother tried to intervene in the marital dispute she received a frosty rebuff from her erring son-in-law. When the meticulous Coyle returned a set of dowry forks which his wife had overlooked, his mother-in-law lashed out in fury, almost blinding him and leaving him with a distinctive scar.

Coyle was irritated only because the law of the land forbade him to take another wife while the Clontafleece vixen still lived, so he fulfilled his carnal needs with a whore who frequented the Barrack area on a basis so regular that Sergeant Pollard swore he could set his watch by the lamplight from the Agent's bedroom window. That, he would say, was the best time to get drunk or to fornicate, for it was the only time that Coyle would not notice and record it in his little book.

❖ ❖ ❖

The Agent had clean and comfortable lodgings in the village, from where he had an excellent view of the inn, the church, the Barrack and the pump. He was interested in the clientèle of the alehouse behind the inn and kept a written record of their names, putting a tick beside those who left in an obvious state of inebriation and a circle around the legless who had to be carried out. If the names of Napper Donnan and Mick the Fox appeared more frequently than most, they were in good company, for Coyle also kept a tally of those who attended church. The gates of the Barrack he watched with equal interest, for in his opinion the garrison was there only to protect his master and the Valentine interests, a matter with which Sergeant Pollard took issue. There was only a handful of troopers there at any one time, and they were responsible to their superiors in Newry, who in turn saw their duty in relation to the law of Ireland, and not, as the Sergeant often said, to some nosy interfering snipe of an agent.

Another source of conflict in Coyle's life was the presence of freeholders, men who owned their land and owed no loyalty to the Valentines. Tom Dunn was a constant thorn in his side, not least because he had the affrontery to teach the children of the peasantry to read and write. Squire Valentine thought this highly amusing, even more so when he was told that the 'bog-Latin' tutor was attempting to educate the brats from the Poorlands who had not a word of the King's English. Such things, Coyle protested, were not natural.

❖ ❖ ❖

Grace O'Lochlainn always had a hunger for learning. Even when she could no longer attend lessons she coaxed Seán to tell her every word of every lesson. It was the only time Eily ever saw her get anxious, for she was normally a shy, reserved child with not much warmth about her. She had been christened with the name of Bronach, but had never been called anything but Grace since Tom Dunn had told Thady that she would suit no other name. Thady, a proud father, agreed and thus Grace she became. Although endowed with the cool appearance of a marble goddess, she showed great affection towards her grandmother who shared the little byre with her. Eily suspected that it was she who was putting notions in the girl's head about learning, although the old woman herself had never been further than Hill Town.

'If I did not go to school, child, I at least met the scholars,' the old woman would say to Grace.

Their tiny house was not much better than the booley cabins or cottiers' dwellings, consisting of a single room with a rush-clad floor, and lacking windows and chimney. When a fire was lit the smoke filled the cabin, making her grey eyes sting and her throat raw. Her grandmother maintained that it was good for her and that the smoke purified the lungs.

'Look how it makes me cough!' she would explain. 'It brings the phlegm up.'

On stormy nights the wind came whistling through the gaps in the turf walls making the smoke billow in all directions and the normally somnolent fire spit and hiss as though there was some spirit in the house which, like Grace, wanted desperately to escape. Eily was always pregnant. Sometimes there was a child at the end, but more often there was none, and many little half-formed bodies were destined for limbo. When her mother was laid up with the sickness, the responsibility of caring for the other children fell on Grace. She was good with them and with the neighbouring children, and sometimes Eily, watching from her bed, dreamed of a great future for her daughter, as a nursemaid to some grand lady's offspring. Maybe, she thought, her learning would not be wasted after all.

❖ ❖ ❖

Learning and books were far from Grace's mind as she joined other girls of her age in the flaxfields. The work was thought to be more suitable for women as no tool or weapon was needed. Besides, Coyle thought it prudent to separate the sexes and thus avoid any disruptive behaviour.

The harvesting was a laborious process. The whole plant had to be pulled from the roots by hand so that the long fibres remained undamaged and intact. The plants were removed to the various flax dams and ponds to wret before being spread in the sun to dry, waiting to be lifted and baled by the workers.

The older women were uncomplaining, but tender young hands soon grew red and blistered with the stinging fibres. The two girls who shared Grace's toil engaged in a continuous stream of banter about young men, and who they should meet at the next year's

Greencastle fair. As the day wore on they began to complain about the soreness of their hands and were advised by the more experienced women to bind their palms with rags. This worked for a while, but eventually the rags became knotted and useless. Her two companions abandoned their task in tears, but Grace determined to continue for as long as she could, bearing in mind her father's dream of a stone chimney. Her eyes were cool, but her cheeks were flushed and her hands stung painfully. Laying down her bundle of flax, she knelt to remove the rags which were now tattered beyond use. Then, pulling off the kerchief which bound her hair, she began to make new mittens. Suddenly a shadow masked the light of the evening sun from her eyes.

Before her, mounted on a prancing roan was a boy, nearly a man. His hair, ebony black against the sun, inclined to a vigorous curl beneath his hat. His features were perfect: flashing eyes of vivid green beneath stark black brows, a soft gentle mouth and skin free from blemish. He wore a startled expression. Grace was not used to beauty in her menfolk, with their grimy skin, tattered beards and ill-fitting garments. Even the horse, immaculately groomed, was perfect in every detail.

The lively colt danced with impatience as they eyed each other. He parted his lips to speak but the words caught tightly in his throat. He saw no rags, no shabby grey homespun, no dirt-stained feet, but rather a girl with golden hair and proud grey eyes. His eyes were drawn to her poor hands and he felt a stab of shame as he involuntarily compared them with his own well-manicured fingers. She did not move, let alone curtsy as any peasant girl would: *he* found himself removing his hat and bowing in deep reverence. At that moment she was his queen, he her humble subject. But in an instant the spell was broken. A swift expression fleetingly passed her eyes before she bowed her head. Then she lifted her bundle of flax and ran from his sight.

Observing this encounter was the Agent Coyle. He was annoyed at the apparent humiliation of Henry Valentine by a peasant's brat. If the young gentleman wished, he could select several prettier, more beguiling girls than this impudent wench who would give Master Henry the respect due to his ancestry.

His great-grandfather, the priest-hunter, had been a firebrand frontiersman with a mission to tame the wild natives of Ireland and to rid the land of Romish Popery, or so Coyle's grandmother, a fervent admirer of Colonel Whitechurch, had informed him. He had lived in the grand style, like a king out of the dark ages, building up his estate, acre upon acre of sequestrated land, with his own private militia to enforce his will. What the country needed, Grandmother would say, was a few more righteous men like Whitechurch. She had not told him if he was a womaniser – he suspected not. These God-fearing types might hang women, but they would not blemish their souls by lusting after them. Squire George: now that was a different matter entirely. Whitechurch would twist in his grave if he knew about the lifestyle of his grandson George.

George, the present Squire, hated country life, never drew breath in a church and spent most of his days drinking and gambling in the clubs of Dublin. During the few months of the year when funds were low, George would return to Kilbroney House to rusticate on a low budget and to amuse himself with the servant girls. Coyle was instructed to keep a sharp eye out for any 'by-blows' which might be born between visits. With Whitechurch blood in their veins they could not be reared by Papist mothers so they had to be taken to a charitable institution, endowed by the Valentines, to be brought up within the established church.

Madam Valentine, Henry's mother, was quite happy to spend long periods in the country, where one could live in splendid style at a fraction of the cost it would take to live in England in a similar manner. The daughter of an impoverished aristocrat, Daphne Valentine spent all her time trying to prevent her husband from getting his greedy hands on her Gloucestershire estate. George, forever up to his neck in gambling debts, simply had to rely on Coyle to whip up the money from somewhere.

The Agent began to walk homewards when Madam Valentine, elegant in slate-blue velvet hunting attire, reined in her horse by his side.

'Where is my son, Coyle?' she called. The old women still toiling in the fields turned at her voice. In their threadbare rags they stopped to watch the vision mounted on the white mare canter down the river-bank, but Coyle curtly instructed them to get on with their work.

'I have no wish to see idlers here!' he barked. He thought about the situation with Thady O'Lochlainn's lass. She needed a lesson, he decided, in humility and respect for her betters. He would see Mistress Cunningham, the housekeeper at the big house.

❖ ❖ ❖

Thady O'Lochlainn's daughter commenced service with the Valentines at the age of fourteen. No questions were asked. They never were. A lad from the village, much more smartly clad than anyone from Kilbroney, walked gingerly into the close with a message from Agent Coyle. Grace, he informed her mother, was to present herself at the big house at daybreak the following morning. Eily did not understand a word he was saying, even though he repeated himself slowly and loudly. She called shrilly for her daughter. The lad, who had had to skirt several inches of muck to reach the O'Lochlainn cabin, was obviously puzzled as to the nature of this command until Grace herself, flushed and breathless, came running down the mountainside in answer to her mother's call.

The lad made sure that Grace understood the message and was rewarded with a shy smile. Then she explained to her mother that she would have to go to work in the big house and she needed to have a skirt that decently covered her.

❖ ❖ ❖

The Valentine family were rarely in residence, choosing instead to divide their time between Dublin, London and Madam Valentine's Gloucestershire estate. Grace knew little of them. They belonged to another world, as remote, all powerful and dazzling as heaven itself. More so even, for one always had a chance of reaching heaven.

Grace rose well before dawn the next day. In truth, she had hardly slept since the summons to Kilbroney House.

'Why do you think they want me?' she asked her mother. Eily was afraid to answer, lest she frighten the girl. One thing was certain, they could not afford to ignore such a command. Grace looked a frail young figure in her ill-fitting dark gown and hard wooden clogs. At least, her mother thought, she would be warm and well fed during the winter months.

'I saved that gown since I went into service myself, before I wed your father. 'Twas with a moneylender's mother in Tamnaharry. They called me Eliza, after a queen that died. Old Madam couldn't get her tongue round my right name, Eilís.' Grace knelt to allow her mother to braid her hair.

'I was younger than you, half the height and twice the width. Look at your legs! You're like a sick sparrow! You'll have to eat up when you go to the big house or no man will look twice at you.'

'I'm not concerned,' replied Grace, 'if I should never have a man.'

'I know you're not, daughter, and I would wish for better things for you than this.' Eily, cursed yet again with the morning sickness, regretted that she was not fit to accompany the girl down the glen. Grace kissed her mother, leaving the house as the moon waned behind the mountains of Cooley. Her step was light as she made her way to the head of the track, but once on the mountain a deep loneliness overcame her.

'Grace!' a voice rang out. To her great delight Seán was racing after her, pulling on his coat as he went. He was younger than her, but sturdier, with a head of wiry black hair.

'And where are you going?' she asked.

'I'll keep you company down the hill!' he said.

'You might as well,' she answered. 'I'll be glad of somebody to talk to.'

'Master Dunn has a new book for me,' Seán began as they walked.

'A new book? Read it and tell me what it's about, won't you?'

'When I said a new book, I meant an old book. *The Elements of*

Euclid,' he explained. 'They say 'tis worth reading.'

'Ah, Euclid! Master Dunn speaks of him.'

''Tis his own book. So, I thought that if I have to call at Dunn's Hill, I might as well accompany you along your way.'

Grace smiled to herself. Seán would die before admitting to her that she was the main reason for his journey, and not Tom Dunn's book. 'Yes,' she answered, 'you might as well.'

They walked on some distance in companionable silence, speeding up a little as they passed the burial ground at the old monastery.

'Do you ever get frightened walking here in the dark?' she asked him.

'Me? Not at all!' They crossed by the copse below Dunn's Hill and continued down towards the gates of the big house. In the distance they could see many bright lights.

'So many windows!' exclaimed Grace breathlessly. 'With glass for seeing in.'

'I'd say the glass was for seeing out,' Seán suggested. The twinkling windows that so captivated the young O'Lochlainns were the first indication that Grace was about to enter a world very different from her own.

'Are you scared?' Seán asked.

'Why should I be? Think of all that I'll learn!'

'I'll leave you here, unless you want me to see you to the front door.'

'No, I will be safe enough.' Grace swallowed a lump in her throat. 'Good morning then,' she said, 'and don't forget Euclid.'

Seán stood at the gates and watched her go. 'If they're bad to you, just you up and run off!' he called anxiously as she disappeared from his sight.

She had never been so close to such a large building before, crowned by so many chimney-pots, billowing smoke of coal and wood. It surpassed the inn in size, and yet only one family dwelled here. She surveyed the house for some time, calculating the number of windows and trying to decide how many people must be inside.

She walked to the front door and looked around for the latch. There was none. A rope dangled alongside the door and out of curiosity she gave it a yank. Somewhere in the distance a bell tinkled. Immediately one of the sash windows at the top of the house flew open. A head crowned with a white mob cap appeared and a shrill voice screamed:

'Here you! Away round the back! Are you daft?'

The girl gazed at the head, and wondered how it could find its way around such a labyrinth. She took a few steps backwards to recover her bearings.

'It must have two doors,' she decided, 'like Dunn's barn.' She pulled her shawl tightly around her shoulders and set out to look for the back entrance. A confusion of walls and hedges confronted her but she finally found herself in a busy yard where a tethered guard dog bared his teeth.

'What are you looking for, girl?' asked a woman bent under a milk yoke.

'I was sent for,' Grace replied. Her eyes followed the bustle of aproned laundry maids carrying great baskets back and forth under the supervision of a big red-faced woman.

'You'll have to ask her,' whispered the milkwoman. 'That's Mistress Cunningham, the housekeeper. Watch yourself. She's one quare bitch.' With this encouragement, Grace approached the gorgon.

'Here you!' barked the housekeeper. 'What sort of behaviour was that? Going to the front door indeed. Are you mad? I heard you were an impudent pup, but that beats all.'

'I thought...'

'You're not here to think. What if you'd woken up a lady or gentleman?'

Grace hung her head in a gesture of submission.

'Leave your boots there. Were you wading in cowclap?' Mistress Cunningham grumbled. She was annoyed at Coyle's insistence that she take on the girl. When the family was in residence they brought their personal staff from the townhouse in Dublin. There were very few from the Parish of Kilbroney employed domestically.

The extra maids required from time to time were orphans from Newry who knew how to show gratitude, 'by-blows of the Squire,' it was rumoured. Country lasses like Grace O'Lochlainn lacked both demeanour and industry.

'Now my girl!' she declared. 'This here is the scullery, and it's as high up as you'll ever get in this house.'

❖ ❖ ❖

Henry Valentine could not forget the girl – nor did he want to. They had not spoken; he didn't even know if they would understand each other: she was a girl from the Poorlands. One only saw these people from a distance, toiling in the fields. Mother had said that it was better that way, for the peasants carried infections and lice and smelled to high heaven. Henry cherished a secret belief that she was really a well-born maid cast by fate into humble circumstances. It was his duty therefore to rescue her from her drudgery. What he could not entertain was the possibility that he had truly fallen in love with a simple native.

The love-lorn youth submitted himself to the appropriate pastimes of writing poems and going off his food. He was confused by his infatuation, for on the one hand he wanted to shout her name from the rooftop, and on the other he feared to mention it to his mother or his sister. What was her name? He could not guess. His sister Fanny would be too busy to listen to him, preparing as she was for her forthcoming nuptials to Frederick Ward. Oh Fanny might listen all right, but she would not take him seriously and would probably moralise about waiting for a suitable match with one of one's own class – a rarity in this part of the world. He was even less inclined to talk to his mother who was presently indulging in a mild flirtation with Squire Nedham, a county friend. She would not moralise, he was sure, but neither would she sympathise. A young man of seventeen, she would say, should have more sense. And as for his father: he would surely want the girl for himself. Fortunately the reprobate was in Dublin and likely to stay there until his money ran out.

Those who knew Henry Valentine saw him as a serious young

man with a strong sense of duty. 'More of a Whitechurch than his father' was the common belief, mainly because the youth was a frequent church attender, and the complete antithesis of his father. Squire Hall of Narrow Water thought that Henry would have the makings of a fine officer once he had completed his cadetship. Henry had always made known his intention to serve the Crown and to bring peace and prosperity to this part of the king's realm.

'Most definitely a Whitechurch,' Squire Hall had insisted, noting that the boy was straightlaced and humourless, like his famous ancestor. Henry's nurses and tutors – there were many of them – would not agree that he lacked humour, simply parental love and affection.

The youth had all but resigned himself to never again seeing the subject of his infatuation, when he encountered her once more, and this time it was he who had the upper hand.

He was returning home with a hunting party comprising his own family and their friends, the Nedhams and Halls. They would dine in Kilbroney House, after which there would be a merry party. Henry dreaded such occasions. Squire Hall might be persuaded to sing one of Mr Handel's airs, and John Nedham always had a ready repertoire of humorous songs. Fanny would accompany her mother on the new harpsichord and she would sing tunelessly, as usual. Then she would complain of the difficulty of keeping a harpsichord well tempered in this part of the world where the nearest thing to a music maestro was Giddyhead Magee the piper. Henry himself was a competent viola player and a useful component of any household ensemble, but he hated having to perform alone, and his mother was prepared to make no concessions to his wishes. In such petulant frame of mind he led his roan to the stables. It appeared to have an injured fetlock and he intended to see that the groom took no short cuts with the treatment. It was then, just as he passed the kitchen yard, that he saw her. It was the sheerest chance, he told himself, which led him to her for a second time. Fate was undoubtedly playing a hand, for there she was, sitting amidst a mountain of apples, paring and coring. He watched her for as long as he dared, noticing that she wore the simple livery of a lesser house servant.

◇   ◇   ◇

Mistress Cunningham inspected the drawing-room. Her eye for detail was meticulous, and she distrusted the housemaid's efforts. She checked under the rugs, straightened the porcelain figurines and rearranged the cushions to her satisfaction. Pink brocade – they would be going soon, as Madam wanted the place completely redecorated. Mistress Cunningham regretted the upheaval of having painters and craftsmen from Dublin about the place, but looked forward to a new location for the cushions. What better place than in her own room. She had quite a little nest egg of knick-knacks that the gentry had discarded, and had, unknown to herself, been christened 'The Magpie'. Yes, she would have to keep a sharp eye on the Dublin rogues lest they have the same idea. She lifted one of the plums from a side table and, with her apron, carefully removed the last remnants of bloom. She stood back to admire her handiwork.

'Cunningham!' She jumped at the unexpected voice behind her. 'I would like a word with you.' She sighed in relief as she recognised the young man who had entered the room.

'Oh, Master Henry! And there was I thinking about thieves in the drawing-room.'

'Thieves? My mother will have them hanged.'

'No. I did not mean that...' The embarrassed housekeeper was obliged to explain that the theft in question was hypothetical.

'I'm not so sure of that!' he replied darkly. To her surprise, he engaged her for some minutes on the subject of dishonesty and moral weaknesses among the simple people. She was feeling decidedly uneasy when he broached the subject.

'My gold studs. Have you seen them?' Mistress Cunningham held on weakly to the back of a chair.

'Master Henry! In all the years I have been in this family's service, I have never been anything but scrupulously honest!'

'I know, I know. That is not what I meant. Of course, dear Cunningham, you must be above suspicion. Now, are all the members of this household as upright as you?'

The moral elasticity of the lesser servants was a subject close to the woman's heart, and she lost no time in unburdening herself to Master Henry. He listened gravely to an exhaustive pedigree of every servant in the house, but still the name of the scullery maid eluded him.

'Oh, Master Henry! Your gold studs! I'm sure they'll turn up! The Master was always losing his.' She did not add that they had a habit of turning up in the many strange venues in which old George chose to undress. 'And 'tis not,' she simpered, 'the first time you have mislaid something, now is it?'

He pressed on regardless. 'Tell me about the kitchen staff.'

'Dare they put one foot past the kitchen door. Cook would roast them.'

'Would she know?'

'Would she what? She'd miss a raisin from a spotted pudding.' His mind's eye went to the vicious gargoyle who patrolled the nether regions of the house.

'There's Minnie the Fox, and Bendy Biddy.'

No, his love could not possibly be described as a 'Bendy Biddy'.

'That is all I can think of. Just two in the kitchen.' Henry was about to give up in despair when it dropped like a gift from heaven.

'And that only leaves the scullery maid, but Grace O'Lochlainn would not know a gold stud from a boot button.'

Mistress Cunningham continued on the subject of unsuitable servants, but Henry's young heart was soaring above the clouds. He felt he had always known that her name would be 'Grace'.

❖ ❖ ❖

'Go straight home now, O'Lochlainn, and do not linger along the way.' The housekeeper was pleased with Grace. Not that she had many occasions to visit the scullery where Grace spent most of her working hours scouring greasy pots. Minnie the Fox had been delighted to hear that she no longer had to do that tedious task and was now allowed to sleep by the kitchen spit at night. If

Grace hated the cold pallet by the kitchen door which Minnie had vacated, she did not voice any complaints to either the cook or to Mistress Cunningham. Had she done so, Minnie had warned, she would have earned a crack on the ear. Grace was a quiet girl, and even by the housekeeper's standards a hard worker. She had a pleasant submissive manner which was very promising, for Cunningham was alert for the insolent flash she had previously detected in Kilbroney girls. Many a cheeky wench had been locked in the coal hole for a penitential period in the past, but there seemed to be no such impudence about Grace. She would take pleasure in informing the Agent that he had been wrong about her. So wrong in fact, that she had decided to keep Grace. The housekeeper's tone was not unkind when she gave the young girl a bag of fowl carcasses and told her to take them home for soup.

'Thank you, ma'am. My mother will be glad of them.'

Grace was pleased to be allowed home for the night. She knew that they would all be happy to see her, and she wondered if Seán had got hold of that book. Minnie the Fox had told her that she would be let home every other Sunday, if she kept her nose clean and annoyed nobody. Minnie, a Newry orphan who had wed a McCann of Knockbarragh, claimed relationship with Grace through her late husband on her mother's side, and told her that she could make her a good match with her son Mick. Eily would enjoy that story almost as much as she would like the chicken bones.

It was getting dark and the burial ground had to be passed. She wished Seán had come to meet her. Maybe he would walk back with her in the morning. Rustling noises in the trees and scudding clouds casting eerie shadows against the ruins did nothing to calm her fears. Legends of the phantom Bell of Bronach and ghosts long dead came to mind. She shivered and tried to breathe the cold from her hands.

'Grace!' She caught her breath. It was not the voice of a mountainy man. Her panic intensified as she realised that she was being followed by someone on horseback. She heard her name called again and she shouted.

'Go away! I have nothing!'

'Please, Grace. I would escort you home.' She looked up to see the hopeful face of Henry Valentine. He was immaculately attired in pale beige breeches and well-tailored coat, and cut a fine figure on horseback. His eyes were shining with admiration, and she wondered what he could find to admire about her, in her ill-fitting rags.

'Go home, sir. 'Tis dangerous for the like of you to be about at this time.'

He noticed her flushed cheeks and parted lips, and felt encouraged in spite of her verbal rebuff. 'I would risk any danger, if only to be by your side,' he declared. He dismounted and walked alongside her.

'Since we met,' he continued, 'I have thought of nothing but you. I have neither eaten nor slept since!'

'You look well enough fed to me, Master Valentine.'

'So you do know me!'

'Who else could you be?'

'Then, since you know me, may I walk with you?'

'Why, 'tis your land. I cannot stop you.' She smiled shyly. 'Even if I had a mind to do so.'

He looked at her threadbare clothing and wondered how she could bear the cold. Such a thought had never occurred to him before and he removed his coat to place it over her shoulders. She looked astonished.

'No! You will be foundered. I'll take no hurt!' she told him. Their hands accidentally brushed and he shivered at the touch. 'See! You are cold!' Grace said, and there was an uncertain tremor in her voice. He lifted her hands in his.

'Grace,' he whispered, 'I cannot feel any cold.'

He raised her fingers to his lips. The nails were grey and broken, but he did not see anything but their slenderness. Her face was grimy, but he saw only its beauty. She allowed herself to be kissed.

And so their courtship began. They met furtively, whenever Grace saw an opportunity to escape from her duties, inveigling a reluctant Minnie the Fox into covering for her.

No one ever paid much attention to a scullion, but the behaviour of Henry Valentine certainly gave cause for concern. He cried off from visits to Narrow Water and offended Madam Hall by playing truant from her picnic. It was only a matter of time before youthful enthusiasm and indiscretion betrayed them both, and the liaison between the Valentine heir and Thady O'Lochlainn's daughter became the talk of the house. Minnie the Fox did her best to warn her friend.

'Take care,' she warned, 'for the cook has a face like she has one foot in the piss pot...'

❖ ❖ ❖

'You were right to bring this matter to my attention!' Mistress Cunningham praised the vigilance of the cook. 'Something will have to be done!'

'In my opinion, for such as it's worth, that hussy needs to be made an example of,' replied the cook.

Cunningham had to admit to a feeling of having been let down by Grace. Inasmuch as it was possible for her to feel motherly towards anyone, she had taken a personal interest in the girl's welfare. The matter must now be placed in the hands of Madam Valentine.

Madam was in her boudoir when the housekeeper went to broach the delicate matter. She sat at her dressing-table scrutinising herself in the looking-glass when the housekeeper's fat red face suddenly appeared in the mirror.

'So! Henry is taking after his father. What a surprise.' A languid hand reached for a pot of lip-salve. The red lip-salve was almost the last touch to a fifteen minute face toilet, and the first thing on Daphne Valentine's mind. She considered a face patch for the mole on her chin, choosing one in the shape of a tall ship.

'Damn the pair of them!' she exploded as the patch sank into the salve. 'Cunningham! That kerchief!' Her mouse-like maid was dressing her mistress's wig on a stand by the window, while feigning a complete lack of interest in the amorous affairs of the youth. But with her attention distracted she added too much powder to the wig and began to cough.

'Stop that!' snapped the lady, 'I am trying to think!'

Cunningham pressed on, regardless of the interruption.

'The girl is very young. Barely fourteen and just into service.'

'The little slut.'

'And they say...'

'Who says?'

'Oh, folk around the village...'

'And what do these "folk" presume to say?'

'Ah... that she has him smitten.'

Madam Valentine had had enough. 'My boots! Get my boots!'

The maid scrambled to produce an elegant pair of beige button-boots to match her mistress's gown.

'And where is my son at this minute?'

'I saw them, I, er, happened to be looking out...'

'You were spying, as usual. Go on.'

Cunningham looked offended, then glanced over at the maid. 'In the stables,' she whispered discreetly.

'In the stables?' barked Madam Valentine. 'Hurry up with that boot! And have my wig dressed by the time I return.' She flounced out of the room followed by a satisfied housekeeper.

They were not in the stables. There was no one there, although Cunningham thought she heard the sound of distant laughter.

'Well then,' demanded Madam Valentine, 'where are they?'

'I saw them head in this direction. I was sure...'

'Damn you, woman! Just look at my boot!' One of the delicate little boots was now submerged in smelly brown muck. Mistress Cunningham's hand moved to her mouth in nervous panic, but too late. Madam noticed the smirk. 'You impudent hag!' She slapped the housekeeper across the face.

❖ ❖ ❖

As if knowing that their time was running out, the lovers had met as far from the house as they could manage. They cantered through fiery autumn glades and across the heather moors, not

93

caring who was watching. He held her close to him, for she was unused to riding horses. The wood rang with the sound of their chatter as they approached the sun-drenched mountain-top from where the lowlands of Iveagh stretched out before them. Henry left his horse at the wood's end and together they walked to the summit of Slieve Bawn. The wind pulled and tugged at her un-braided hair, and his hat was blown away. They laughed and squealed as he made a futile attempt to recover it before collapsing breathless on the grass. Grace knew this spot well. She had climbed there before in search of missing goats, but he, whose father owned the mountain, was there for the first time. She knelt beside him. They both knew that for them there was no future, but the present was there for the taking.

'I love you, Grace. I have never loved anyone else, and I never will.' His green eyes blazed with emotion as he traced his finger down her forehead and nose, and then over her lips.

'That day, in the flaxfield,' she whispered, 'I thought I had imagined it. I thought that the sun had got to me.'

'You were so lovely then, I felt that if I were to touch you, you would melt away.' They kissed, and then for the first time, in an act of great tenderness, they made love. She had heard the priest and her mother talking about vile carnal acts and unholy lust, but this she knew was different, for her love for Henry Valentine transcended all sin.

Afterwards he wiped away her tears. She shivered and he held her close, for the mountain sun, although bright, gave little warmth.

'I could hold you thus forever!' he cried. 'We will build ourselves a home here, where no one will notice us! No one will bother us!' Everything around him seemed different. The lough looked deeper, the air clearer and the sky more blue.

'Come with me, Grace!' he urged. 'Come and we'll sail away on a privateer to a land where there are no servants, or no masters.'

'On a privateer? They would hold you to ransom.'

'Why, I would don the garb of a peasant! No one would notice me!'

She was three years his junior, but Grace wondered if he had spent most of his life with a langle around his neck. With his strange English voice and lily-white hands, any half-wise tinker would take him like a new loaf from the griddle. He was already planning an impossible escapade as together they surveyed the miniature world below the mountain. He was full of hope and expectation but she, the peasant's daughter, knew the value of hope in a darkened world.

❖ ❖ ❖

'I have arranged for you to leave in the morning.'

'I could not leave her. I will never leave her. I love her!'

'No, my dear. It just seems that way.'

'I know the way I feel!'

Madam Valentine jumped to her feet in exasperation. 'For heavens sake, child! Remember who you are. Amuse yourself if you must. But do not let me hear you talk of love. There is no more harmful or destructive emotion.'

'You cannot keep us apart.' The boy was adamant.

'Oh can't I? I could have her horsewhipped until the skin fell off her back.'

Henry glared at his mother. At that moment he could only hate her. He felt trapped and helpless. He would fight a duel on her behalf, he would go to prison for her, he would even suffer disinheritance for her, but the thought that any harm might befall her came like an icy shock. In that moment Henry Valentine's youth and innocence took wings and fled forever. He closed his eyes for one long moment. When he opened them, his voice was cold and resigned.

'If I go with you, will you promise not to harm her?'

'Good! That is that.'

Madam Valentine vowed to do her best to take Henry's mind off the girl. 'Once Fanny's wedding is off my hands, I must see that you have the opportunity to meet some suitable girls. Of course, you are very young.' She looked at the bowed head of the unhappy boy. 'We all fall in love at your age, but it is meaningless.

It does not last. And in this case it could not last.'

'When I am my own master, I will marry her.'

'Yes, dear,' she purred, 'and when we get to Dublin you can talk to your father about Sandhurst.'

In accordance with her instructions immediate frenzied arrangements were made for the journey to Dublin. Madam, it seemed, was bored with rustic life, and would return early to the townhouse to prepare for Parliament winter.

Next morning, soon after a warming breakfast, the family prepared to depart for Dublin. As it was unlikely that they would be returning until the following year, all but the most senior retainers were to be dismissed and the maids returned to the orphan asylum in Newry. The cook, grooms and personal servants prepared to accompany Madam Valentine to the Dublin townhouse. Grace, aware that something had changed, did not see Henry leave, and there was no time for goodbyes or explanations. The departing coaches left a haze of dust in their wake.

Grace, on Madam's instruction, was dismissed immediately, but not before receiving a severe beating. The groom who wielded the whip did so with the detachment of one who regularly castrated foals and cut the tails of pups, disregardful of the pain that he inflicted. Mistress Cunningham had decided that it would do the rest of the household good to witness the edifying spectacle. The order and precedence which governed their lives must be maintained and upheld, otherwise there would be chaos. And that order did not allow for the type of relationship which Madam had so wisely nipped in the bud. She felt a certain sense of moral gratification when two of the girls, trembling and holding hands, rushed from the scene to vomit in the corner. When Grace's screams had died down, she took them aside to lecture them on decency and modesty. Should either of them ever attempt to beguile a member of the family, she would receive exactly the same treatment. They both assured her that under no circumstances would they ever attempt such a seduction.

❖　❖　❖

Like a wounded animal, Grace wanted to take her pain and hide. She wished that the whip had killed her, for her heart was as sore as her back, and that was almost unbearable. With great effort, she began to retrace the steps which had first brought her to the house. The Indian summer had come to an end and it was bitterly cold. She could not wear her great-shawl and dragged it behind her as she took each aching step home.

'Young O'Lochlainn!' The Agent's voice almost had a jocular ring to it. 'Your duty is at the house, girl. Mistress Cunningham will have you beaten.' She looked at him, forgetting to be submissive, her grey eyes burning with anger. Then she dropped her head as if there was no fight left in her. Coyle noticed her bloodied clothes.

'Did Madam order this, or did the housekeeper?' Coyle, jealous of the autonomy of the household, was considering the question of jurisdiction. 'Well, girl!' he commented. 'You'll have to learn your place, for your own good. And yours is back in the Poorlands.'

Grace painfully struggled up Dunn's Hill and all but collapsed on Mistress Dunn's doorstep. Annie had just settled her infant in the cradle when the sound of sobbing caught her attention. She was appalled at the sight of her visitor and helped her into the kitchen.

'You cannot walk home in such a state!' she exclaimed, her eyes wide with revulsion. 'Who could do such a thing?'

'They did it. Down there...' sobbed Grace.

'Take off your shift. I must bathe those wounds.'

The kitchen was warm and comforting, with smells of baking bread and baby's rosewater. It was a real stone house with two good-sized rooms and little windows, and everything about it was welcoming.

'Drink this down! You are cold as stone.' Annie handed her a hot posset, watching as some colour seeped back into the girl's cheeks. Her fingers seemed transparent as she clutched the bowl, slowly sipping, as if each mouthful was painful.

Annie considered what action she needed to take. If Tom were here she would send him for the Widow Fearon. She chatted on, trying to put Grace at her ease.

'Lie down, I'll bathe the cuts with rosewater. It was purchased from a Newry apothecary; it should halt any infection.' Annie tried to hide her distress at the sight of the wounds.

'Is it bad?' Grace's voice trembled.

'No! You will not scar... and it is not very noticeable.' Annie, a strict Presbyterian, did not choose to lie lightly. The girl's pale skin bore a pattern of ugly stripes and weals, and there was much heavy bruising and abrased, ragged skin. Annie dabbed the sores and rubbed ointment on the bruising. Grace began to shiver.

'I will make a bed for you here; you must not lie on your back.' She rummaged for a clean linen shift of her own and gingerly helped the girl dress.

By the warmth of the fire Grace began to talk, at first tentatively and then in a flood of grief. Annie could say nothing to help, so she just listened, but she was appalled by the ferocity of the assault on one so young and fragile.

'It was not my fault, Mistress Dunn, really it was not!' She straightened herself up and looked straight at Annie. 'But neither was it his!' she added loyally.

'No. It was no one's fault. These things happen. The Lord ordained that it should be so, and no one can censure you for that. No decent folk would.'

'Mistress Dunn,' luminous tear-filled eyes revealed a new concern. 'I dare not go home. You know what my father is like. He is a mild man, but with a wild temper when roused.' Annie knew her fears were well founded. The men from the Poorlands had very little, but what they had they would protect to the death, and most precious of all in their eyes were their children. Thady O'Lochlainn was notoriously hot-headed. If he were to see his lovely young daughter sent home in this condition, there was no telling how he would react.

'Do not concern yourself! Bide here awhile and keep me company for 'twill be a day or two before Master Dunn returns from Belfast.' Grace began to sob again.

'You can help mind the baby! And I'll send for the Widow Fearon. Oh, she holds more secrets than Priest Pullein.'

Annie sat by the girl until she had cried herself to sleep, a child no more.

✧ ✧ ✧

The itinerant Priest Pullein strode down the track to the O'Lochlainn close. 'Another wild goose chase, I'll be bound!' he told himself. His errand was to administer the Last Rites to Thady's mother who was dying 'again'. She had dreamed of old Felim the previous night, and felt sure that he was coming for her. Father Pullein wore a somewhat sceptical expression as he produced the oils of Extreme Unction. He wished that old Felim was less venturesome instead of continually raising false alarms.

'How long do you think she'll last, Father?' whispered Thady, out of her hearing.

'Another ten years – which is more than I will if you continue calling me out of my bed,' whispered the priest in return. He then confessed to having a more serious matter to discuss with Thady. This he tackled in his usual roundabout way, littered with coded references.

'You must know, O'Lochlainn, that the Planter [George Valentine] voted with the Devil's Cub [Lord Clanbrassil] in his latest perfidious attempt to do his father's work.' The wily old cleric had a nickname for everyone in authority, as a protection against accusations of sedition. If anyone were to censure him for stirring up the feelings of the simple natives, he could look them in the eye and deny that he had ever mentioned Lord Clanbrassil's name.

'Oh, Clanbrassil!' Thady understood. 'They say he plans to hunt every priest from Ireland.'

'As they did many times in the past. Now that Heretic Council [the Irish Parliament] in Dublin has done it: they would ban all religious orders, friars, nuns and the like from our shore. Now what do you think of that?' Thady was not given the chance to answer for the priest continued, 'As for the rest of us, we would be bound by so many restrictions that our ministry would be impossible.

God knows, 'tis hard enough now. Why, were it not for his good Majesty and the Privy Council, the Devil's Cub would have had his way.'

Thady had good reason to scratch his head. On this occasion, it seemed, George of Hanover, the very symbol of Protestantism, was protecting his Irish Catholic subjects from the over-zealous reforming Parliament in Dublin.

'And you say Val... 'The Planter' is behind this?'

'Undoubtedly. So you must know where your duty lies now.' Thady hated to hear a priest talk in such terms for it usually led to a demand for money. That, on this occasion, was not Father Pullein's intent.

'It has come to my notice,' he began, 'that your daughter, baptised into the true church has gone into the service of the Planter!'

'Only to scrub a few old pots, from what I hear,' shrugged Thady.

'You should have refused to let her go!'

'And be turned out of my house and home?'

'A small price for the salvation of a soul.'

Thady was in a quandary. The care of souls was the priest's concern, but the care of bodies was his. With an ailing mother, an expectant wife and a hungry family he was hard pressed to keep a dry roof. He paid rent, tithes, taxes, dues, Peter's Pence. He bowed his head under the weight of the worry. And to think that only a few weeks ago he had been planning a chimney.

'Your daughter, Bronach – I will call her so for thus she was baptised – she is a handsome child, without doubt. First of all they will commence proselytising. Then they will forbid her any contact with the true church, including her family. Finally, they will rob her of her virtue and leave her destitute, provided she does not first die of shame and without repentance. Any unblessed issue of her body will be dragged from her side to be brought up in darkness.' The priest was pleased to notice Eily's gaunt eyes as they drank in these auguries of ill-fortune.

'Holy Mary!' shrieked Eily. 'What are we going to do?'

'We'll do what we're doing now. Nothing,' barked Thady in annoyance. 'That girl of ours has a head on her like a woman of forty. There is nothing soft about her.' Eily bristled at this.

'His Reverence knows what he is talking about,' she cried.

'And I know Grace. She'll have more sense in that head of hers than all the planters put together.' Thady stuck to his guns. The priest made as if to go, while murmuring something about praying for the sinner, although no one was sure to whom he was referring.

'Will you partake of a cup of buttermilk, your Reverence?' enquired Eily politely, delving into the churn.

'Thank you, no, Mistress O'Lochlainn, I have many more such visits to make this night.'

The hurdle in the doorway was pushed aside and there stood Grace who dropped a curtsy in the direction of Father Pullein.

'They sent me home,' she said, quietly. 'They have gone away to Dublin and will not be back for the present.' If Grace expected her family to register disappointment, she was taken by surprise.

'We must give thanks to Almighty God that he has seen fit to deliver his unworthy handmaiden!'

Grace raised an enquiring eyebrow towards her father, but he just blessed himself with the others and welcomed her home.

Chapter Six

May 5th 1780

THE HUSTLE AT the monthly fair day in Hill Town was more intense than usual due to the fine weather and a surfeit of spring lambs. The cautious old women of Clonduff who had hibernated through the winter appeared at their doorposts, still well wrapped up but eager not to miss out on anything of interest.

The men of the Kilbroney townlands took the usual routes over the Poorlands or down by the Bolie, by ass-cart or on foot, some driving livestock before them. Seán took the low road, conscious of his promise to the Dissenter to keep a careful eye on his foster son.

'I'll walk alongside your sister!' Donal smiled. 'The troopers will take us for man and wife.'

'Dare you come within a yard of me and I'll cut the legs from under you!' Sosanna replied with such venom that even Seán was taken by surprise.

He chuckled at Donal's discomfiture. 'Sosaí will be a wife soon enough. Maybe she is not as pleased as she should be!'

Sosanna joined the Buller with his ass and cart some distance ahead, while Donal had to be content with the opportunity to appreciate her shapely form from behind. A few beggars from the Bolie were trying their luck along the fair route and Donal expressed sympathy for their apparent misfortune. Seán stopped him from digging into his pocket.

'Hold on to your money,' he hissed, 'for thon boy has two pigs and a milk cow, and only one child.'

'Two childer and only one sow!' returned the beggar angrily.

'You see?' concluded Seán.

The village of Hill Town lay where the mountain gave way to green meadow land.

'Hill Town? 'Tis on the flat.,' remarked Donal.

'The Planter Hill called it for himself.'

'Hill? Ach, I know that name. The Marquess of Downshire, no less. Master Makepeace once bound some books for him. Ledgers and the like.'

'Whoever he is, he likes the sound of his own name. "Cluan Dabh" was the old name for the place – the Ox Meadow. They held the fair on that spot even before Saint Patrick came. Twenty years ago there was nothing here but the inn and a few cots at the Eight Mile Bridge. Now there's a town.'

'Is it just a sheep mart then?'

'Never you mind the sheep. You'll meet a great set of women here, if you've a mind in that direction, with arms that could pull a quarry cart and a kiss to send the teeth through the back of your head.'

'Thank you. I will keep my teeth and wait for the French women.' But Donal was not truly concerned about French women either. His thoughts were on the girl walking the road ahead.

Sosanna was looking forward to her first visit to her new home. Her toes pinched in her mother's old clogs but, aware that she was being scrutinised from behind, she refused to hobble, or to give any indication that she was unused to footwear.

'Are your feet hurting you?' enquired the Buller. 'Leap up there on the cart and save your soles.' Sosanna cast an eye on the bony ass which badly needed its own hooves pared and declined her neighbour's offer. In a few weeks time she would be able to have her own shoes, if she wanted them.

❖   ❖   ❖

Sergeant Pollard of the Rostrevor Barrack had arrived in Hill Town some hours before the dealing started. Fairs were always a potential source of unrest among the drunks and gamblers, and, although the local garrison could deal with the usual influx of ne'er-do-wells, help was requested for this particularly busy time of the year. Pollard was suspicious of crowds and wary of the ease with which anything from illicit liquor to seditious broadsheets could be circulated. He surveyed the arrival of scores of people from the neighbouring parishes and townlands. There were farmers from the Bridge of Mayo and the Burren, dealing men from Rathfriland, and an old man selling hand-carved crucifixes from Barnmeen. There were folk of all shapes and ages enjoying the fine weather and the chance to exchange news and gossip.

From his station outside the parish church Pollard regarded the scene. Beside the horse trough Spendlove Bushel, the roving preacher, called on all men to repent, reminding his somnolent listeners that the wages of their sinning ways were eternal hell-fire and suffering. Pollard wondered wryly if the wrinkled old women bent double under their heavy bundles, who formed the majority of Bushel's audience, had ever had the chance to enjoy a decent sin in their miserable lives.

Grouped at one corner of the square, distinct from the peasant horde, were several sober citizens, members of the Rathfriland Volunteers. Permitted by law to carry arms, to drill and to train, on the off-chance that Rathfriland might be the target of a French invasion, the men were engaged in serious discussion with the local Presbyterian minister. The debate on this occasion was not about the French, but on the issue of whether or not to parade on a Sunday. The subject of the Sabbath observance, Pollard knew, could not be treated lightly as it was one of the major causes of dissension in the country. Various viewpoints were being forcefully aired, although the Sergeant had to admit to some confusion over the purpose of the parade in the first place. The loudest voice was that of the saddler, Wylie. As long as arms were presented before the Parish Church and the Meeting House, and the marching Volunteers sang the Doxology, he argued, an act of worship had taken place which was not only permissible, but essential, to carry out God's work in this barbarous land of heathens.

The peace had lain uneasy in this part of Iveagh since Clan Aongus had been routed from their hilltop fortress. Those left were a bedraggled and leaderless flock, prey to any rabble-rousing rapparee who could stir up discontent and inflame passions. The loyal Scots planters who had replaced the Gaelic hill-dwellers harboured a deep fear of their native adversaries with their Popish loyalties and did not rest easy in their new homes. Pollard himself had often stood on the hill at Rathfriland, scanning the surrounding countryside and imagining that the dispossessed mountain dwellers were plotting their revenge. From there it was easy to envisage the glint of unsheathed steel, and to imagine the grey crags sheltering hordes of vengeful natives. Such a thing was not impossible, he had heard argued, with the Devil's power ranged against the Citadel of God.

If Sergeant Pollard understood their fears, he did not share them. His duty was to keep the peace and uphold the law, goals not always compatible. In the prospering port of Newry, not many miles away, Papists and Dissenters marched alongside each other and banded together to protest against common grievances such as the payment of tithes. The authorities, the Sergeant liked to admit, mistrusted that situation much more than if they were at each others throats.

'A few more months!' he whispered to himself. 'Just a few more months and I'll be back home, away from this bloody quagmire of a country.' He tried not to think of the fate of his predecessor, found with a knife in his back behind the inn, but such considerations were never far from a soldier's mind. The Rathfriland men were departing. Saddler Wylie's case had won the day.

Pollard strode across the cobbled square, shaking his fist in anger at two hard-riding young bucks who had come thundering down the street, leaving a cloud of dust in their wake.

'Watch those damned horses!' he roared after them, just as one of the riders lost his hat. He returned to retrieve it, but a nimble-footed urchin had got there before him and would, no doubt, sport the hat when the coast had cleared.

'Serve you bloody right!' called the Sergeant with some satisfaction. He passed the Preacher Bushel whose enthusiasm seemed undiminished by the sudden dispersal of his audience. Pollard noted wryly that his presence had that effect on people. They feared that someone would take a shot at him and miss. The black-shawled crones remained in their doorways, puffing away at clay pipes, eyes wary. Their weather-beaten faces followed his footsteps across to the sheep pens before resuming their animated conversation in the Gaelic tongue.

At the heart of the fair were the animal enclosures, where the liveliest exchanges took place. Hoggets, old ewes and bleating lambs stood alongside a few milch cows. This was the day, Pollard had been told, to buy a young pig for Christmas fattening. Behind were wooden cages bound with straw, confining a variety of poultry, laying hens, young chicks, geese and ducks, all piled on top of one another in an uneasy fashion. Pollard's military rank was sufficient to encourage a few young lads to throw rushes over fresh dung, although he doubted that the shine on his boots would survive the running sewer he had to ford in order to reach the fighting cocks. Two women with spades squabbled over the dung, both claiming priority for their rhubarb, but he was not inclined to interfere in such a dispute. He ran an experienced eye over the roosters. They took pride of place among the fowl as they strutted and preened in individual pens. He compared two specimens, already scratching the dirt and eyeing each other wickedly. He admired the small brown cock with the clean plumage and long leggings as an unlicensed bookmaker operated discreetly in the crowd. The white bird was twice as big, but its opponent had the mean, hungry look and vicious spurs of a champion. As if to prove his point, it nearly took the nose off a boy who was goading it with a stick.

'Stick to pitch and toss, boy!' advised Sergeant Pollard.

His stomach rumbled as the smell of bread fresh from the griddle reached his nose. A few enterprising country wives from the Burren, dressed neatly in starched kerchieves and caps, were offering any hungry man with a halfpenny to spare a draught of sweet milk and a baked oatcake. A lazy townswoman could avail of somebody else's butter, eggs or sweet preserves. At the bottom of the street a variety of tradesmen conducted their transactions as usual. Cobbler McChesney tapped away in a corner while his neighbour, a quack doctor selling a potion guaranteed to cure all ills, packed up in disgust. There were few gullible people in town.

Then there was the hiring, where people put themselves and their families on the market, poor homeless people with no futures together. It was not called slavery, but any man forced to hire out his children was condemning them to a life of just as much drudgery. The people of Hill Town had a great reputation for hard work. There were also destitute families from the west, pathetically hoping for a temporary respite from their misery. Pollard was a battle-hardened soldier, but his heart went out to some of the little girls, barely old enough to leave their mothers, who would end up in the household of some conniving ogre. He saw himself in some of the lads, gangly youths with both hope and apprehension in their eyes.

'In a few years,' he decided, recalling the time he first enlisted, 'they'll be taking the shilling just as I did.'

'Was this one ever deloused?' someone was shouting, when Pollard noticed a familiar face in the crowd.

He knew Seán O'Lochlainn. He knew all the Kilbroney O'Lochlainns. This O'Lochlainn wore a furtive expression as he dodged in and out among the crowd. He was either looking for or avoiding someone, and seemed startled when he noticed the Sergeant's scrutiny.

'Most likely sold some man a lame sow,' Pollard surmised. He stopped and sniffed. Aha! So that was what had O'Lochlainn looking sheepish. He was trading moonshine. There were plenty of poteen stills around the mountains and just as many sharp boys who were the scourge of His Majesty's Excise men. He had not thought that any of the O'Lochlainn's... Still, there seemed to be something amiss; he would apprehend Seán. Into the foray he strode. A few shifty lads from Kilcoo removed themselves from his gaze, but he paid them no attention.

'O'Lochlainn!'

'Sergeant!'

'What have you got under your coat?'

'An empty belly. But don't be concerning yourself about me.'

The Sergeant admitted to himself that he had been wrong. There was no sign of any liquor on the person of the Kilbroney man. For once he had misread the signs. As Pollard went towards the inn, unlabelled green bottles and crude flagons exchanged hands safely behind his back. Seán had reminded him that he could do with a bite to eat.

❖ ❖ ❖

Donal MacArtain was enjoying his freedom. There were plenty of redcoats around, but he felt smart enough to avoid them. Seán was a good companion but overly protective, and Donal had some trouble giving the Kilbroney man the slip. He was not interested in the livestock or the wares of the pedlars, but his ear was drawn towards the sound of a fiddle. The nimble bow-arm of the itinerant fiddler of Carryduff had attracted an appreciative gathering of those who liked a good tune well played. Donal was more interested in the flashing white shins of the women dancing on the sward. Hill Town fair was full of diversions, and yet there was no sign of Sosanna.

From the Cabra direction came a coach of some style. Barking dogs heralded the approach of the vehicle, and small children were snatched from its path. A sizeable crowd gathered to view the spectacle as the steps were let down. Two elderly fops descended from the coach, their appearance drawing gasps of admiration from the fashion-conscious and gasps of astonishment from all others. Primrose and violet satin vied with flamingo pink and azure damask, a bizarre splash of the exotic amidst the drab greys and browns of the local homespun garb. The sense of the ridiculous was not wasted on the onlookers who threw a few ribald comments in the direction of the gentlemen.

Turning a deaf ear to the rabble, the taller of the two requested his mincing companion to step ahead of him, which he did somewhat tentatively. Country inns, he protested, could be damned un civilised places. The road had been terribly bumpy, and the springs of the coach far from London standards, so with the welfare of their own seats in mind they decided to sojourn at Hill Town. A mountain of baggage was lifted from the coach, under the supervision of the landlord, to facilitate a change of costume.

One of the fops stood back to admire the rustic charm of a briar rose, already sporting tiny buds. The other walked past him only to have his powdered wig caught by an overhanging bramble. Expressions of horror crossed the painted faces as a coachman attempted to retrieve the wig. An explosion of mirth and taunts from the vulgar onlookers had to be endured by one very bald and cross gentleman who could not be mollified by the obsequious apologies of the landlord. During this diversion, Donal MacArtain entered the inn by the kitchen door.

He left some time later wearing an expression akin to worry. His eyes scanned the crowd for Seán without success. He spied a familiar hat and called out, but it was not his companion. Then, as he considered his next move, a voice spoke from behind.

'You will find him with Murtagh Fegan. They're eyeing up a young pony. Or do you want me to call him for you, seeing as you're supposed to be in hiding?' Sosanna jumped down from the bale of hay on which she was perched. Donal's immediate objectives changed.

'Stay, there is no great urgency. If he is busy, I can wait. 'Tis not good to disturb a man making a purchase.'

'Seán? Making a purchase? What would we be doing with a pony?'

'Well, at any rate, I have all the time in the world. He is sure to find me later.' He went as if to detain her but she deftly sidestepped him and continued on her way down the street.

'You know, 'tis good to have company when you're a stranger,' he said hopefully.

'I suppose you were arranging your passage out of Ireland?' she enquired.

'I am to leave on the morning tide.'

'That's good news for you!'

'I leave in the morning without Master Agnew, or wait two weeks for the next opportunity.'

'A fortnight? What would you do with yourself?'

'I would find some form of diversion.' He wondered what she was thinking. There was no indication that she returned his interest. Still, Donal was an optimist, and there was no indication that she disliked him either.

'Yes,' he continued, 'a fortnight is a long time to be in hiding. I'd be as well to take my chances and go now.'

'You would be as well,' she replied.

'Sosanna!' William's voice sounded from across the square. He hurried over towards the pair, dressed in a billowing working smock.

'This,' sighed the girl, 'is my diversion. My intended husband.'

◇ ◇ ◇

At the other end of the fair, Seán stood examining a small piebald pony. The vendor eyed the Kilbroney man just as thoroughly. Murtagh Fegan stood by, awaiting his opinion.

'There's no doubt she's a healthy beast,' agreed Seán.

''Twould be useful to have her 'round the forge. I could do with a beast for delivering items.' Murtagh rattled his pockets but the vendor seemed unimpressed. He knew threadbare breeches when he saw them. He spat within an inch of the blacksmith's boot.

'Would you not be better fixed with a good strong ass?' suggested Seán in a dubious tone.

'I thought our Briony might like a young pony to call his own.' Seán rolled his eyes to heaven while those of the vendor brightened. Fools and their money were easily parted, and there was no fool like a doting parent. Seán felt that the last thing Briony Fegan needed was any more pampering and suggested that his friend give the purchase some more thought. Fortunately common sense prevailed, for Murtagh remembered that he had eight other mouths to feed, and a pony would eat as much as the rest put together. He declined the vendor's offer of a reduction in price, 'on account of it being for a child', and moved off. Donal MacArtain approached them.

'Where did you go? I lost track of you,' hissed Seán. 'Look at the troopers! Do you want to get us all shot?'

'You'll be all right. They would not know me without Master Agnew and his dog.'

'Look here!' Seán warned him. 'You can take whatever risk you like with your own life, but I'll go to hell before I'll let you bring the troopers down on our house!'

'There was business to be done, and Ned Maguire did not want any witnesses, or so he told me.'

'If your business is done, we can go for a sup of ale before we go home,' invited Murtagh Fegan.

'The alehouse?' Seán sounded doubtful. 'I promised I'd stay clear of it.' Donal and the blacksmith coaxed him into changing his mind. 'All right, but remember I did my best to talk you out of it. Mind you, watch who might be listening to you!'

Donal was in a quandary. Common sense told him that he should take the opportunity presented and leave in the morning, although it would be hard to leave his old friend. He certainly knew that Makepeace would advise him to do so, for it was only a matter of time before the Welsh Horse and its bloodhounds picked up the scent of their trail. The older man could follow him in two weeks time, for there would be less notice taken of them travelling separately. If Makepeace could stay with the O'Lochlainns, or some other safe house in Kilbroney, Tom Dunn would keep an eye on him. Having come to a decision, Donal followed his companions into the alehouse.

'You, er, will not tell Master Agnew that I have been here?' he whispered to Seán.

'As long as you don't.'

'Get that into you son!' Murtagh handed him a brimming tankard. 'You'll not get as fine a brew in France.'

Some hours later, having met the Buller in the inn, Murtagh was still drinking and Seán was growing worried. Donal had had little to drink, but there was an ominous red flush at the back of his neck. Seán rued having agreed to come in. The haze of smoke was so dense in the alehouse that one would not see a redcoat be he sitting a foot away. He was confident that none would be drinking in Clonduff, but there were plenty of sharp ears and loose tongues around. Murtagh, to the horror of his companions suddenly stood up.

'God bless the men of the Irish Brigade!' he proclaimed to the assembly and received a few muffled cries of 'Huzza!' in return.

Donal stiffened. He had not realised how much Murtagh was drinking. He glanced around, but no one in the alehouse appeared to have taken much notice. All the same, he was amply warned: drink and Murtagh Fegan made a dangerous combination. Seán tried to divert the blacksmith.

'The Irish Brigade? 'Tis the Irish College you are thinking of.'

'The Irish College?'

'Our Eamonn has a yearning to be a priest. He wants to go to Paris, to the Irish College. I don't know why.'

'The holy priesthood?' declared Murtagh, 'I always knew that there was something different about Eamonn O'Lochlainn! You should be a proud man, Seán, to have a Holy Father from the close!'

'Jesus! The last thing we need around Kilbroney is another priest! You are talking about people who can barely keep body and soul together! They pay rents, taxes, tithes – and you're suggesting that they should finance Eamonn's flight of fancy.'

'They sent Matthew Lennon to the Irish College,' Murtagh reminisced. 'I mind that time well. Even widows and cripples gave up their pennies to raise the fare.'

'Who is this Matthew Lennon?' enquired Donal, glad that the topic had changed.

'Matthew Lennon? Why, he's the Bishop of Dromore. A lad from Kilbroney Parish, just like ourselves.' Murtagh looked around him. 'Bishop of Dromore, that's what he is,' he yelled, 'and the Clonduff gorsoons don't like it!'

'Holy God! Get him out of here MacArtain!' Seán knew that of all the causes of strife in Ireland, an inter-parish dispute was by far the worst. Between them they ushered Murtagh into the sunshine, while making conciliatory noises to the assembly.

The Buller set off home with Murtagh Fegan in his charge, dozing off the effects of his indulgence in the back of the cart.

'I must see Maguire before we go!' Donal informed Seán. 'It would be best if I sailed in the morning.'

'Well you had best make haste with your business, for once I find Sosanna, we're leaving,' Seán replied with determination.

As Donal walked back to the inn he wondered once more if Makepeace would ever be able to follow him to France on his own. It might be better for both of them if the old man were to choose to stay behind in Ireland. Keeping a sharp eye open for any sign of a red uniform, he almost missed meeting Sosanna.

'Master MacArtain!' she called. 'Are we ready for home, or are you going back to the inn?' She wore a smile and a new hair ribbon.

In an instant Donal had decided that he could not, after all, leave Master Agnew. The old man had come with him this far, and it would be cruel to desert him at the last stage of their journey. He would wait another fortnight.

'No,' he replied. 'I'm ready for home.' With a lighter step he left for the Parish of Clonduff.

Chapter Seven

'THE PRIEST'S MOUNTAIN! Your folk still hold bitter memories of it,' commented Makepeace Agnew. He was watching Eamonn O'Lochlainn languidly picking over his dinner. The lad had the appetite of a sparrow.

'I suppose that it will never be forgotten, on account of how they died. You see, they died as martyrs, in a state of grace.'

'And you have had to watch the perpetrator of the deed prosper. That must be hard to take.'

'There is no doubt,' agreed Eamonn, 'that the name Whitechurch is reviled. Evil men can cause untold suffering.'

'I'm not so sure that strife is caused by evil men. Perhaps by good men who are so sure of their cause that they are blind to any other argument.' Makepeace spoke of his mother's recollections of Glencoe. Eamonn seemed surprised.

'That my own folk wore the White Cockade? Oh, yes! There are none of them left now. I'm the last of my kin for there's nobody coming after me. I had no sons of my own, but my brave Donal is as good as any son could be. My father was a preacher too, a Lowlander with different loyalties. I've often wondered how things would have been if the clans that fought for Charlie had left the Kings to do their own fighting. But maybe 'tis best not to dwell on such things, for it does no good.'

'You can see why it is difficult for us to forget? You have left Scotland behind you, and you don't have to walk on the ground where your own people's blood was spilled, day after day, and to see the same uniforms on the backs of the troopers. I can forgive them in the spirit of Christ, but I could not forget. Folk still whisper about hearing ghostly cries on the mountain, and of finding blood-stained rocks where the perpetrator died. 'Tis indeed hard for folk to forget...'

'Whitechurch? He died in his bed, I heard.'

'No, I meant the informer. He was one of ourselves. That was the worst of it all.'

Makepeace was recovering. The grey look had gone from his face and, apart from his leg, he was in robust health. That leg, he assured everyone, would heal in its own good time. From his pallet in the corner he had marked the change in Donal over the past few days. The lad had a constant, wistful look in his eyes, especially when the daughter of the house was around. When Sosanna's marriage was mentioned, he would make pointed remarks which only revealed his youthful vulnerability.

'I'll move down to the byre!' Makepeace suggested to Eily. 'I should keep an eye on the young rapscallion.'

'Indeed you'll do no such thing, Master Agnew. Do you want to go and get another dose in your kidneys? You're nice and warm where you are. And,' she interrupted his protests, 'you bother not a one.'

'I don't want him to cause any rows in this house. 'Twould be a dreadful abuse of your good hospitality.' Eily was aware of Donal's interest in her daughter, and she and Thady had been amused at his antics.

'Seán will keep an eye on him. He must find the time dragging waiting for word to come. Anyway, I blame my daughter for it all. She should have enough sense to keep out of his way.'

❖ ❖ ❖

Tom Dunn tactfully avoided the O'Lochlainn house, but occasionally sent messages with Owen MacOwen or Murtagh Fegan. Owen and Briony Fegan were good friends, in spite of the odd squabble.

'You are lucky,' Owen told Briony. 'There I am stuck with an ailing mother and the rent in arrears. You have the forge and a da who will give you anything you want.' Briony was not so sure of Murtagh's beneficence.

'I want to be a sea captain. Or a pirate. I want to see what's past those mountains. I want to find treasure!'

115

Briony was fascinated by the strangers in the O'Lochlainn house, especially as he had been well warned not to breathe a word of their presence to anyone. On a few occasions Makepeace had noticed him peeping over the half-door with an inquisitive look on his face, but he had run away when the old man spoke. Eventually, curiosity got the better of Briony and he tentatively crept into the cabin, where the veteran was resting his leg by the fire.

'Come in!' invited Makepeace, 'I'll not eat you!'

It was a perfect combination. A lad who was hungry to learn, and a man who had as much to teach. Makepeace was in his element with a willing and enthusiastic listener, telling tales from scripture, reciting psalms and inventing moral fables. Briony was not particularly partial to sacred scripture, although he listened politely, but he did like to hear of the military campaigns of the children of Israel.

'How was it that Joshua was able to bring down the walls with a ram's horn?'

'Why, 'twas the work of the Lord.'

'Can the Lord not work the same thing for us, here?'

'It could be that no one here would put their faith in a ram's horn.' Briony had faith. He could at least try the same trick on the Barrack walls. He set out to look for a good curling specimen around Rooslieve, and next day presented it to Master Agnew.

'Would this one do?' he enquired eagerly. Makepeace took the grubby object and worked on it with his blade.

'Watch this. You insert the mouthpiece thus, and you blow thus.' From near and far the neighbours jumped in fright at the demonic sound. The Buller left a good bowl of champ and onions to investigate the source of the noise.

'Look!' Briony told him, 'Master Agnew made this himself. It has a magical noise.' Before he blew it again, the Buller cupped a hand over the trumpet.

'Are you trying to bring the military down on us? God knows, haven't we enough ghostly noises around Kilbroney with this phantom bell of Eamonn's?' he barked at the embarrassed Dissenter. The disgruntled Buller returned to his champ convinced that Thady O'Lochlainn was taking a great risk in letting Makepeace Agnew through his door.

'Give me that, Briony. It could be that the Lord was thinking not of mountainy rams. They have a different breed of sheep over there.' Seeing Briony's disappointment, he sought to divert him. 'Now did I tell you about David? Yes, he was a small lad like yourself, only he played a harp, a soft gentle instrument with a sound to soothe you to sleep...'

'Makepeace,' Briony asked suddenly, 'tell me about your travels.'

'Briony, my lad!' Makepeace brightened. 'You look at a well-travelled man.'

'I don't suppose you were ever captured by bloodthirsty buccaneers?'

'Buccaneers? We'll say nothing about that!'

'So you were?'

'Some things are best not spoken of.' The Dissenter's tone was hushed and mysterious.

'I knew you had adventures with pirates!' Briony could not contain his excitement.

It was the first time in his life that the old man had been regarded as a hero by anyone and Makepeace quickly convinced himself that it was all harmless fun. As Briony's imagination caught fire in front of him, the Dissenter absently picked up his travel knife.

'Master Agnew! Did you ever kill anybody with that?'

'No, not with this particular knife.' Makepeace was incapable of setting a trap for a mouse.

''Tis a fine blade,' Briony encouraged.

'Can you keep a secret, lad?' Makepeace whispered. The little boy's eyes lit up.

'I swear I will never tell a living soul.'

'Why, 'tis blasphemous to swear. Your word will do.' Briony licked his lips in anticipation as Makepeace raised the blade aloft. 'Behold, the sword of Achilles!'

After a few moments silence a disappointed voice spoke. 'A

sword? 'Tis a mite small for a sword.'

'Ah! Many have been fooled thus! But even Achilles was once a lad like thee! 'Tis a boy's sword.' Makepeace started at the sound of an outburst of laughter. Seán was standing in the doorway, enjoying the story.

'Your ma will skelp you if you bring that home with you!' he advised, sizing up Briony's small frame. Achilles had been the hero of the hedge-school, even in Seán's youth.

'I give this sword to Briony Fegan, chevalier of Kilbroney!' Makepeace grandly presented the knife. 'Now keep it sheathed, for the Sword of Achilles was always wielded with honour.'

'The Sword of Achilles. I will treasure it all my life!'

'Did you see Maguire?' Makepeace enquired when Briony had left.

'I did,' replied Donal. 'I told him you would soon be ready for the road. He says he has to fix things up with a sea captain bound for the Isle of Man.'

'The Isle of Man? What good is that to us?'

'That is where all the pirates and privateers go to harbour. He'll get word through to the French ship. It has already sailed from La Rochelle. He says they take an oceanward route to avoid the King's patrols.' Makepeace closed his eyes at the thought: he had once been sea-sick on the short trip to Rathlin Island.

'I'll be back on my feet in no time,' he reassured Donal stoically. 'At least there will be little walking to do on board ship.'

'If you can make it as far as the ship, that's our worst problem.'

'Don't concern yourself, Master Agnew! We'll see you're not short of a mount,' Seán reassured the old man.

The thought of their departure did little to cheer up Donal; he had grown to like the valley folk.

'Jesus! Where the hell's my boot gone?' Seán exploded all of a sudden, and Makepeace winced at the blasphemy. He felt his dog nuzzling something under the blanket which could possibly be a boot. 'Are you sure you had two?' he began lamely.

Donal, standing in the doorway, could see a small distinctive figure on the mountainside with her flock.

'Your pardon, Makepeace,' he called, taking advantage of the temporary diversion, 'I'll be gone awhile.'

'Away off and see where he's going!' Makepeace urged Seán.

'With one boot? How can I go anywhere?'

❖ ❖ ❖

Eily, washing duck eggs in the close, spotted the Widow Fearon making her way down the track. Her orange hair flew unbraided, and her lips were stained with one of her homemade mouth dyes.

'Musha!' exclaimed Eily. 'She's out after a man.' The Widow knelt and helped herself to some plants growing under the hedgerow.

'A fine day, Mistress O'Lochlainn. You could get out two washes, had you the mind to.'

'I'll not be washing any more. Madam Patterson dropped dead yesterday.'

'So the veins got her at last!'

'A woman said she ate a dose of mushrooms, or so she thought; but they weren't mushrooms at all, so she died.'

'Now wasn't she foolish.'

'She'll never know how foolish.'

Madam Patterson was an eccentric old soldier's widow who had had a stone cottage near the mill. Like many others, she was too nervous to let a local servant into the house, so left her washing in a basket by the door for Eily to collect.

'I wonder should I leave this load back? When she's buried, they'll never know she had it.'

'I wouldn't be tempted. They'd hang you for her drawers alone. Do you mind the time she got Sammy Shields put away for stealing her rhubarb?'

From the darkness of the cabin, Makepeace heard them chatter. 'That nosy Widow!' he muttered to himself, before turning over and feigning sleep. He listened to her approaching footsteps.

'How is the sick man? Asleep, are you?' The Widow was hovering over the pallet. 'Listen to that, Eily, don't you like to hear a man that snores? It shows he has good strong lungs.'

'I doubt he wants to be disturbed,' replied Eily. 'Now, if you'll pardon me, I'll go and polish my duck eggs.'

'Don't concern yourself Eily. Just leave him to me. I'll sit here till he wakens, and faith, if I get dozy myself I won't be long squeezing in beside him.' Makepeace 'woke up' in horror.

'Er... good day to you, Widow Fearon, I did not hear you enter.'

'I have nothing if not a light step. I heard from MacOwen that your leg was paining you.'

'My leg? 'Tis as good as ever 'tis going to be.'

'I'm glad to hear that. But maybe then you'll let me see you walking on it.'

'Maybe then I won't.' He stubbornly folded his arms.

'Well far be it from me to force you.'

From behind the house a voice cried in panic: 'Away and hide! The redcoats are coming!'

Makepeace leapt to his feet in blind panic. 'Get out of my way, woman!' He stumbled on the rush-strewn floor and winced in pain. The Widow cackled a coarse laugh that threatened to split her corset.

'Away you go, Eily!' she cried. 'I told you that would shift him!'

'Oh, you're the crafty one, aren't you?' he barked angrily as he hobbled back to bed.

'Take off your breeches now,' she coaxed, 'I want to see your leg.' Two steely eyes pierced her from behind the spectacles.

'Now you look hard and long! For this is as much of me as you are ever going to see!'

'Think again! When you die of the blood poisoning, and I come along to lay you out, faith, I can look at you at my leisure. Every last inch of you.'

'Well, all right, but turn yourself around woman and don't be looking at me.'

'Will I give you a hand to loosen your...'

'No! I can take my breeches off myself.' As Makepeace fumbled around under the blankets, the Widow began to make up a poultice. She carried her own little pestle and mortar, and began grinding barley meal with ragwort and dalkin. A splurge of freshly squeezed milk of dandelions was added to bind the mixture. Makepeace did not like the sound of the accompanying incantation.

'What are you moaning about?' he enquired suspiciously.

'I was wondering if you had warts on any part of you, for I have some wartweed and elder flower with me.'

'I have no warts anywhere on my person,' declared the old man stoutly.

'And when did you last look?'

She put the poultice to steam over a hot stone. Makepeace felt his eyes water with the pungent smell as the healer with some difficulty extracted his leg from under the blankets.

'Does it look bad?' he asked nervously, suspicious of her silence. 'You may tell me the worst, for I want to know.'

'I can't tell you whether it's bad or not till you get them under-breeches off you first.'

'They will stay put,' he answered firmly. 'Those under-breeches and I never part company. They've been on since last November, and there they're going to stay!'

'By God, I've had enough of your complaining!' she burst out suddenly, throwing aside the blankets and catching the strings of the petrified Dissenter's drawers. With one practised move she had whipped them around his ankles.

'There. That didn't hurt you now, did it?' She deftly tossed both garments out to the waiting Eily. Her affronted patient tried to protect his modesty with his shirt-tail.

'Well now, I don't see that you have anything there to be ashamed about, for that's as fine a set as ever I've seen. Mind you, most of them were dead. At least yours have a bit of life in them.'

'Watch where you're putting your hands!' Makepeace almost screamed.

'Of all the men I've ever tended,' she scolded, 'you're the worst. You would try the patience of the Pope in Rome.'

'If you were to tell me now that you had the breeches off the Pope, why, I would believe you.' The poultice stung where she had slapped it on his leg.

'The Pope never wears breeches, just a long thing that takes him in all over. But I would not expect a Protestant like yourself to know such things.'

'I am not a Protestant. I am a Presbyterian. Non-subscribing, if you want to know.'

'You're Scottish.'

'I'm Irish. My mother and father were from Scotland. As different as brandy from barley. They were of two different faiths, but they never ever argued about religion.'

'And why was that?'

'Because my father would give my mother a good hiding if they did.' Makepeace relaxed. The poultice was beginning to take effect, and a warm tingling feeling came over his leg.

'How did you learn your art?' he enquired.

'From an oul' boy in Clonduff. He was a seventh son of a seventh son.'

'And had he any sons?'

'No. But it wasn't for the want of trying. I suppose they were just bred out. I am going to bind that up for you, so keep it very still. Now tell me if that's too tight, for there's no sense in healing the sore only to have the rest of your leg dropping off.'

Makepeace heaved a sigh of relief as the Widow gathered her bits and pieces together.

'Keep that still there awhile, and then you can get up and step around outside for a bit. 'Twill do you no harm at all, and a bit of clean air will do you good.'

'Thank you, ma'am. I'm in your debt. Now before you go, will you fetch me my under-breeches and things.'

The Widow scoffed. 'You daren't put on them wet drawers, or you'll catch a dose of the scour,' she declared, pulling the half-door closed behind her. 'Mistress O'Lochlainn is scrubbing them out for you. A bit of clean air won't do them any harm either. Now, good day to you, Master Makepeace.'

❖ ❖ ❖

Briony was delighted with the gift from Makepeace, and wasted no

122

time in showing it off to the other boys in Eamonn's school. This time it was he and not Owen who was subjected to their taunts. He refused to see what they saw – a rusty old knife, discarded and useless.

Brigid Fegan let her displeasure be known. 'Where did you come by that knife?' she asked her son.

''Twas a gift from the Dissenter. It looks like a knife but, in truth, 'tis the Sword of Achilles.'

'Well tell Achilles, whoever he is, that he can keep his knife. I do not want to see it about the place again. What would happen if the baby got hold of it?'

It was a commonly held belief around Rostrevor that the Fegan's were immune to injury, the forge being fraught with dangers for the very young. What with the scorching brazier, the close proximity of the river-bank, the unannounced arrival of galloping hooves and the cross old gander, the young boy's blade seemed to pose an insignificant threat to the charmed children of Murtagh Fegan.

''Tis all your fault!' Brigid barged, 'for letting him talk with that foreigner.' Like many other women of Kilbroney, a foreigner to Brigid was one who lived more than half a mile from her home. Murtagh laughed indulgently.

'What harm will it do him?' he asked. 'All lads enjoy tall tales.' Brigid was not reassured.

'As soon as he's asleep I'll take it from him.' Then she noticed that her husband was fashioning a small sheath to hold the knife. He was, she decided, going altogether soft in the head.

❖ ❖ ❖

Thady, satisfied that his recently sown potato crop was progressing according to schedule, asked the Buller's advice regarding a few onions. The Buller was quick to suggest that he would be better equipped to discuss the subject with a drop of William Dwyer's Indian tea to quench his thirst. On arriving at the cabin door they were greeted by an apoplectic Makepeace Agnew, hobbling around like a rabid dog and clutching his great-cloak about his person.

''Tis a good job he's not a cursing man,' whispered the Buller.

'What happened to your breeches, man?' quizzed Thady.

'She took them off me, the cunning old witch!'

'Who did?'

'That conniving hag you turned on me, the Widow Fearon!'

'So that's what the two of you get up to when my back is turned. My, you're a fast-working boy, and her crossed this threshold less than an hour ago!' chortled Thady. The Buller, choking with the laughter, could not get a word out.

'Vermin! That's what the lot of you are!' Makepeace exploded.

'Was she as good as they say?' continued Thady.

'She's a first-class healing woman, if that's what you mean!'

'That's what I meant! Now calm yourself down, sure we're only jesting.'

The Buller, recovering from his choking fit, spoke: 'If you don't take things easy, you'll die of the rage.'

'I'll die of the cold if you don't get me a pair of breeches.'

'I know a man who wouldn't raise an objection if I were to give you a pair of his!' suggested the Buller.

'You're a sound man! Who is he?'

'Who was he? Mickeen McGurk was buried yesterday, may he rest in peace; and not a one would think of wearing his breeches, for fear of bringing bad luck on himself.' The Buller settled himself by the hearth. 'But then, you don't pay heed to such things.' Makepeace had no comment to offer.

'Well?' asked Thady. 'Will they do you for now?'

'Er... is he long dead this..?'

'Mickeen McGurk? Nobody knows. They found him a few days back. I'm glad I wasn't there, for they say that the stench was damnable.' Makepeace paled visibly.

'They say,' added the Buller ominously, 'that he'll be warm enough where he's heading without any breeches.' The Dissenter hobbled back to his pallet.

'Thank you! I'll wait for my own to dry.'

'Now wouldn't it be the poor house that couldn't lend a man a spare pair of breeches.' Thady began to rummage among a bundle of clothing.

'How is it, Thady O'Lochlainn,' commented Makepeace wryly, that you're all such smart men around Kilbroney?'

'I don't know, sir, but I can tell you that the smartest boys of all are them that get out of Kilbroney.'

❖ ❖ ❖

Donal followed the girl from a distance as she weaved a path in and out through copses and rocky crags, finally disappearing behind the shoulder of the mountain. Her destination, he supposed, was the upper meadow where even cattle were grazed during the summer months. Climbing upwards, he made towards the occasional sound of the milking bells, confident that he could not lose her trail. He covered several miles, for Sosanna was intent on leading her charges to the sweetest pasture. So intent was he on stalking his quarry that he failed to notice the ominous signs of changing weather, the downhill movement of the sheep and the threatening light casting grey and brown shadows on the lough below. Almost without warning, a heavy grey mist enveloped him like a billowing blanket, cutting him off from his surroundings.

'Now where the hell do I go from here?' he asked himself angrily. The lough had disappeared, along with the minute village in the distance. So had the forest and surrounding peaks, and so had the girl.

'Sosanna!' he cried in panic. 'Where did you go to?' He listened, but there was no sound of the bells. 'Sosanna!' he cried again. Within moments she was by his side. The heavens opened before he could speak, and she pulled her shawl tightly around her head. Then, grabbing his hand, she ran lightly over the turf, pulling him with her, until they reached the overhanging bank of a deep cleft carved out by a vigorous mountain stream.

They huddled side by side in their rude shelter, watching the rain swell the tumbling torrent below them. He knew she was angry with him.

'If I did not have to turn back for you, I could have taken shelter in the shepherds' booley. 'Tis much drier there.'

'Forgive me! I would not have put you to any bother.' She did not reply so he continued. 'Did you know I had followed you?'

'Did I know? You may be sure that the half of Kilbroney saw you. Do you want to have me talked about or what?' she answered crossly.

'I am sorry,' he said, trying to sound as though he meant what he was saying. 'I would not like to have been caught in that deluge.'

'If you're quick enough you will never let yourself be caught. 'Tis easy to see the rain moving across. The birds are the best guide, for they feel the damp in the air long before we do.' The weather topic exhausted, they moved on to talk about animal husbandry. He, having spent most of his life living over a printer's shop, could contribute little.

'You'll be gone any day now!' she said suddenly.

'Yes!' He was going to add the words, 'Will you miss me?' but the courage failed him.

'Will you miss me?' she asked. He caught his breath, afraid to look at her lest he see the twinkle of a jest. Staring ahead he whispered.

'I will miss you sorely.' Daring to face her, his heart leapt when he saw the tenderness in her green eyes. They kissed – a sweet gentle kiss with the rain cascading like a silver cage around them. Both savoured the moment, for they were young and in love for the first time in their lives. Then she pushed him away.

'You'll never make a whore out of me!' He looked in astonishment at the flushed face, the eyes clouded with shame and hurt. He winced, as though he had received a physical blow.

'Would you debase me so?' he cried, 'and make so little of my love? I would rather die here and now than have you cast me off in such a way!' He rose to his feet and walked into the rain, oblivious of the downpour.

'Forgive me!' she wept, 'I have belittled myself, not you!' She stood behind him, tears pouring down her cheeks. He turned and took her hands in his.

'Were I the greatest prince in Christendom with all the power of

126

heaven and earth, I would throw everything away, if only I were the one to stand by your side when you marry.' Her doubts were washed away with the rain and once again she was held in his arms. There they remained until a brave evening sun burst forth a short brilliant ray of light, before settling to rest behind the mountains for the night.

Chapter Eight

EAMONN O'LOCHLAINN left the hedge-school to walk to the priest's house in Knockbarragh, taking the route past the MacOwen house in Levallyclanowen. The MacOwens were old nobility, like the O'Neills of Clonduff. Dervla MacOwen, Owen's mother, was a daughter of Clan Aongus, but the family into which she married was of much older lineage, albeit much poorer. Dervla was a proud woman who had become trapped in her own lonely world. She had turned down Tom Dunn's offer to speak with the Agent Coyle on her behalf, and looked on any kindness shown to her by her neighbours as interference. She had insisted on her son Owen attending the hedge-school, while all the time regretting that she could not send him to Salamanca where his father had gone in his youth. Owen was a reluctant scholar at the best of times, but of late he had missed several lessons, a matter which Eamonn thought that he should take up with his mother. Tom Dunn had warned him that payment was a sensitive subject, and that the widow might see his offer to waive the usual penny a week as an insulting gesture.

The MacOwens lived in a two-storey stone house, the remains of a medieval 'Healing House', the home of a leper colony which had become a refuge from plundering Vikings. The Staff of Bronach was kept there and, according to legend, God had hidden the house from the eyes of the marauders through the power of the precious relic. The MacOwens had been Keepers of the Staff ever since.

As Eamonn approached the Healing House it occurred to him that there was a lifeless feeling about the place, no smoke from the chimney, nor scratching chickens. Even the well seemed overgrown with weeds and uncared for. He tentatively called out, not expecting anyone to be at home. There was no reply. He pushed open the front door, only lightly latched, and called again.

'Mistress MacOwen? 'Tis Eamonn. Eamonn O'Lochlainn!'

'And what do you want of me, O'Lochlainn?' The voice which sounded from the top of the staircase came from a gaunt, empty face, a shadow of the one which Eamonn knew.

'Are you all right? I thought that there was no one in the house.'

'Are you trying to get your hands on it too?' Dervla MacOwen asked bleakly.

'No, no, of course not!' Eamonn tried to reassure her. 'I came to enquire after your son. He has not been at his lessons lately.' The voice of Owen spoke sheepishly from behind.

'There seemed no point. I have no head for learning.'

'You must and will learn! 'Tis what your father would have wished!' Dervla MacOwen descended the stairs slowly. She looked so frail that Eamonn thought she would collapse.

'Mother, there is the rent to be paid – this quarter's and last.' He turned to Eamonn. 'They say that the Agent Coyle has his eye on this house. That is why he keeps raising the rent.'

'Rent!' laughed Dervla. 'For the land of his father's fathers!'

'I understand your grievance,' replied Eamonn. 'But do not concern yourself with my stipend. There was many a time when my father could not pay, and Master Dunn passed no remarks. 'Tis only those who can pay should pay,' he said. 'I would be only too happy to think that I was helping you in your hour of need!'

'Charity? Is that what you came to offer? Charity from an O'Lochlainn!' cried the widow. 'You expect me and my son to be beholden to the brother of a whore? The Planter's Whore?'

❖   ❖   ❖

'You should have made no comment regarding her circumstances,' advised Father Mackey. 'If the poor woman would not make a plea for her rent, she could hardly accept your charity.'

'But I meant no harm. I only wanted to help her,' replied a perturbed Eamonn.

'I know you meant well. In time she will see that herself. In the meantime, pass no remarks. 'Tis best put aside for now.' The

Parish Priest shook his head. The lad had no sense of judgement. Besides, he agreed with the Widow MacOwen's description of Grace O'Lochlainn.

Father Mackey had been travelling the roads since he first set foot in Ireland after his ordination in Rome in 1745. The Catholic clergy, then staunch supporters of the Jacobite cause, were looked upon as the greatest threat to the peace and security of the Hanoverian kingdom, given their ability to rouse the simple natives of Ireland. The persecutions of the Cromwellian and Williamite periods had continued well into the eighteenth century, and it was only after the decisive defeat of Bonnie Prince Charlie in 1745 that the laws governing the movement of priests in Ireland were relaxed. By the latter part of the century, many had forsaken their former political allegiances and had spoken in defence of King George's right to rule. As a result, priests could live in the parish which they served and, if there were few Catholic churches, there were many Mass Houses throughout the Diocese of Dromore. Father Mackey resided in Knockbarragh, some distance from the village, but within reach of most of his mountain dwelling parishioners. He liked his stone cabin, built for him by his people on a spot near the river, sheltered by a small copse of ash and hazel. His nearest neighbours were Minnie the Fox and her son Mick, who kept an eye on the place while he was on his travels, as it was frequently raided by the men of the Welsh Horse, for what reason he was never told. The house had two rooms, one of which served as a small oratory from which he conducted marriages, churchings and christenings.

Eamonn O'Lochlainn was the most eager acolyte he had ever encountered. Many poor families sent their sons to serve him in the hope that they might prove worthy of the priesthood, and the subsequent comfortable patronage of the church. Since Bishop Lennon had ordained that a thorough education was a prerequisite for any young man to be considered, this ruled out most hopeful applicants. Eamonn was an exception. He had pursued his studies with Thomas Dunn for long after most children had been put out to work.

The priest looked closely at the worried young man who had arrived in a state of breathlessness after his encounter with Dervla MacOwen. If he entertained any doubts about his student's physical ability to withstand the rigours of priestly life, he was certain that Eamonn was motivated by the best of intentions. The lad had removed himself to the oratory to pray for guidance, which gave Father Mackey a chance to get on with the task of preparing his evening meal.

'Will you partake of a bit of supper with me, O'Lochlainn?' he called as he dished out the potatoes. Shortly afterwards Eamonn looked shyly through the doorway.

'Thank you, your Reverence, but I think my mother will have my supper ready when I get home.'

'Sit down lad! You can have two suppers.' Eamonn tried to protest but he was pushed onto a stool and a steaming plate was shoved before him.

'I have no great appetite...' he began.

'Eat up!' commanded his host. 'A man must nourish body as well as soul.' He lifted down a black shape dangling from the rafters and sharpened his knife on the hearth-stone.

'The praties are all I need,' Eamonn protested.

'Not another word lad! We'll both enjoy this! A fine lump of fat bacon from Morgan's of Drumreagh!' He threw a few pieces onto the waiting griddle where it hissed and sizzled. Then he leaned forward in a conspiratorial fashion. 'Being a priest has its advantages for you always know where a pig is being slaughtered.'

'The praties are very good.' Eamonn looked in despair at the plate piled six inches high.

'They should be. I got them from Murnion of Glenloughlan.'

'But I don't know how I'm to eat them all...'

'Enjoy them!' Father Mackey insisted, turning the bacon, 'for if there's one thing a priest should know, it is how to eat, and how to eat well. Now smell that bacon.'

'But your Reverence – about the priesthood...'

'Eamonn O'Lochlainn. What is the central issue of all religion?'

'God?'

'Apart from that.'

Eamonn looked perplexed. He had not expected an examination over a plate of potatoes.

'The central issue is food.'

'Food?'

'Is it flesh, or is it bread? Is it wine or is it blood? Men have killed and been killed over the head of it. Now don't say food isn't important, and let me see you enjoy this!' He placed two thick slices on Eamonn's plate and poured the remaining salt grease over his potatoes.

'Have you enough buttermilk there? That's good. Now, I'll say grace.'

A man who had to walk to the remotest places in all weathers had to know how to feed himself. Father Mackey prided himself on having never once failed to answer a sick call. He regarded the young man struggling with his bacon. He seemed to be in good enough health, even allowing for his faint appetite. He had a fine intellectual capacity and his knowledge of Latin and Greek was matched by his charity and compassion for all manner of men. Really, he was far too good to be a priest. Father Mackey put that ignoble thought from his head. He really meant that Eamonn, being blind to the evils of the world, was ill-equipped to deal with them. He saw no harm in people and trusted men at their word. Eamonn was not the man to send to the fair with a poor milking nanny or a litterless sow. The wily dealing men of Clonduff fair would surely dance for joy if they saw Eamonn O'Lochlainn coming their way with goods for barter.

When Eamonn had broached the subject of his vocation, he had talked about – of all things – the phantom Bell of Bronach. There was a legend in the mountains that the hearer of the Bell was destined for the priesthood. Not being from these parts himself, Father Mackey had heard a few garbled versions of the tale, all of which he had dismissed as foolish pishoguery. He was surprised to hear such a ridiculous claim from Eamonn's lips, for the lad was a firm opponent of the many superstitious practices which still prevailed in the countryside. 'Have you wax in your ears?' he had asked Eamonn, who protested that the sound could only have a celestial origin. Finally, he had decided to bring Eamonn before the Bishop to see if he could talk any sense into the young man. Doctor Lennon, the newly consecrated Bishop of Dromore, merely enquired after all his old neighbours in the parish of Kilbroney.

'I told young O'Lochlainn here, m'Lord, that the road to the priesthood is strenuous and costly,' Father Mackey had goaded pointedly, but to his chagrin the Bishop just gave his stock answer.

'Go away and pray about it! May God's will be done on earth and in Heaven.' To make matters worse, he confided to Eamonn that he, too, had once heard the phantom Bell. It was that which had set him on course for the Irish College in Paris, the priesthood, and, eventually, the episcopal See of Dromore.

Now, Eamonn told Father Mackey over his barely touched supper, God had sent another sign, and had shown him the way to France. In spite of the war, he knew that there were privateers who would break through any blockade for a price. All he needed was the fare.

'No small consideration,' scoffed the priest. 'I don't suppose you received any indication as to the whereabouts of a hidden trove?' He instantly regretted his remark when he saw Eamonn's face light up, once again. He was thinking of his sister, Grace.

They finished their meal and Father Mackey bade the young man goodbye. Most of the bacon lay untouched on Eamonn's plate. Father Mackey, an advocate of the virtue of thrift, sat down and enjoyed it himself.

❖ ❖ ❖

Owen MacOwen was concerned about his mother. She had become wan and listless, a shadow of her former self. She had displayed a spark of fight in the presence of Eamonn O'Lochlainn, but Owen felt now that it was no more than a dying kick, and that she had lost the will to survive. The Widow Fearon had told him her body was thin but otherwise healthy, and that it was her mind which was disturbed. He watched her sit upright by the empty hearthside, haunted eyes staring into dead embers for hour upon hour, neither moving nor speaking. In the corner stood the Staff of Bronach. Their old neighbours, many of whom themselves had been dispossessed, no longer believed in its reputed healing powers. It was impotent, a useless reminder of an age long gone. Owen looked at his mother's face, her eyes devoid of hope, and his heart sank in despair. No longer able to bear the sight, he left the house to gaze over the land which year after year managed only to produce less and less. Sobs wracked his body. This was his failure: they faced eviction now, and Clan MacOwen of Levallyclanowen would be lordless and lost.

Owen decided to call on Briony Fegan, his friend now, to talk over his problems, for the blacksmith's boy was never short on solutions, even if they were often impractical. Passing down the valley, he met Mick the Fox who had come over the Badger's Mountain from Knockbarragh. Mick, the only son of Minnie the Fox, was a large, ambling redhead who had escaped from under his mother's beady eye with a broken scythe which he was taking to the forge by way of Sammy Shields' alehouse. He listened to the young lad's tale of woe, shaking his head in sympathy. By the time Owen had reached the forge, he had received an assurance from Mick that 'they wouldn't get away with it'. To one clutching at straws, this was an uplifting sign of support. His heart gladdened when he heard the skirl of pipes outside Fegan's forge. Giddyhead Magee was rattling out a hornpipe while Murtagh mended the shafts on his cart.

Murtagh enjoyed grandiose gestures, like accepting a tune in payment for work, even if his wife was not in full agreement. Brigid's objection was that all the neighbours were able to share in the hearing of the tune, and so it was like throwing money out on the street. There was no doubt that Giddyhead was doing his best on the wheezy old pipes, for a merry crowd of dancers had gathered and Patsy Kelly was acting the goat, looking around for a partner. The little Fegan girls squealed and ran from Patsy's grasp, sending Owen and Briony into peals of laughter. Briony, seizing the opportunity to escape from his chores, told Owen to join him at his usual hiding place under the bridge.

'Come on Owen!' he urged. 'Once the piping stops, my ma will come after me.'

Eamonn O'Lochlainn spotted the two truants as he passed by the forge on his way to Rostrevor. Briony, he was sure, would lead Owen into some kind of mischief, as if there was not trouble enough on the plate of the Widow MacOwen. He winced at the sound of Giddyhead's pipes and was inclined to concur with old Father Pullein's assertion that dancing was the work of the Devil. He shied away as a toothless hag with shins like a chicken's tried to drag him into the medley of dancers. It was a commonly held view that Eamonn O'Lochlainn was too sober-minded for his own good, and his frantic protestations were greeted with laughter. As soon as Giddyhead paused for a breath, he made his escape up the lane, which was to all intents and purposes Rostrevor's only street. A central drain led down to the river where the women did their washing. On either side stood neatly thatched houses behind tiny allotments. These housed the Valentines' most privileged tenants: masons, a thatcher, bleachers and scutchers. At the head of the lane stood the village pump, where a reluctant lad was having his hair scoured by a cross matron.

'You should see this head of his,' she called to someone in the nearest cottage. 'Crawling with nits! He'll be wearing a pitch cap for a week.'

❖ ❖ ❖

On an elevated spot above the lane stood the Barrack and beside it the Flogging Tree. Five spreading oaks marked the Square, which the troopers from the Newry garrison regularly used as a drilling ground. Opposite the Barrack was the inn, two good lodging houses, and Cole's, the barber's shop. Sergeant Pollard emerged into the sunlight, his whiskers freshly trimmed. Taking note of a few repairs which needed to be carried out on the Barrack gatepost, he lamented the shabbiness of the building for which he was responsible. Less than half a dozen lightly armed rogues, he reckoned, would have no trouble in ransacking the place. And all they would send him was a few young brats still wet behind the ears, who called themselves soldiers. As he walked across the Square he saw the peasant schoolmaster, Eamonn O'Lochlainn, 'Her Ladyship's' younger brother. Very like Grace he was, in his appearance at any rate. A furtive movement from the upstairs window of one of the lodging houses revealed that both men were being clandestinely watched by a third party.

'The nosey bastard,' muttered Pollard to a bemused Eamonn. 'Why can't he mind his own bloody business?' He longed to make a more forceful salute in the Agent Coyle's direction, but managed to restrain himself.

Inside the Barrack, a sullen Trooper Davies carried another slop pail from the latrines. Pollard watched his awkward movements with a long-drawn-out sigh. Davies was one of a large family from Liverpool who had clearly lied about his age for the privilege of wearing a smart red uniform and holding a gun. The army was full of the likes of Davies, refugees from the poverty of city slums. So much for the Loyal British Fencibles, the regiment the rebels feared most. Pollard was ruefully aware that Davies would be on musket drill yet again this evening. The Sergeant winced as he watched him move.

'Watch it lad!' he bellowed, 'you're spilling the slops all over your boots!' The red-faced trooper straightened up and wiped his boots against the back of his breeches. 'Bloody hell,' said Pollard to himself, 'thank the Devil we never have much trouble these days.'

◇ ◇ ◇

Beneath the rocky crag which jutted above the shore stood the Parish Church of Saint Paul. It had once been the chapel of Rory MacAongus, a maverick chieftain who had broken off relations with his kinsmen in Rathfriland. Now the church, a sturdy thirteenth-century building, stood beside the ruins of Rory's castle, testament to a vanquished race. Long since stripped of the ornate symbols of Catholic occupancy, the church was guarded by the gravestones of Cromwellian soldiers. Nearby, in an unmarked grave beneath a yew tree, lay the last of the chieftains of Clan Aongus. There was neither cairn nor burial mound, and no descendants to mourn over the grave, for the ground had been desecrated.

By contrast, the imposing family crypt of the Valentines housed the mortal remains of the worthless George Valentine, a splendid monument built to last for hundreds of years, in memory of a man held in disrespect even by his wife, who had remarried within a month of his passing. It was here that Henry Valentine had been christened with great pomp by the Vicar of Kilbroney thirty-five years ago, and it was here, Grace told Eamonn, that he would marry.

Grace was both perplexed and pleased by her brother's decision. 'God bless you and guide you Eamonn, but are you sure? The priesthood?'

'This is what I want! Whatever else may happen, I know this is my destiny.'

Grace looked tenderly at the young man with the shining eyes and eager face. He, of all of them, had never stood in judgement over her. Thady had ordered his sons to stay away from her; Sosanna she had not seen for many years, and remembered only as a little girl. Through all this time Eamonn had been her only link with home. She had often met her brother here, below the crag; discreet meetings, away from the watchful eyes which surrounded them. This, however, was their first rendezvous in more than a year.

Eamonn thought his sister looked lonely. He had never thought of her as being vulnerable before. The way she was grasping his hand... he noticed her tremble.

'Are you cold?'

'No, Eamonn, I was thinking of the last time I saw home.'

It had been on a bleak winter's day with snow capping the mountain peaks and a blizzard threatening in the skies. Her father and Seán had been out settling the sheep in their hides, and she and her mother had been stacking up extra turf and dead wood by the sheltered wall. Eamonn had been the only one to watch her go. Grace pulled her silk shawl tightly round her as the memory was rekindled.

'I suppose Seán is still at the quarry?'

'Now and again the work slows up.'

'What about his eye?'

'I never hear him complaining.' Seán never spoke of Grace, and was even more bitter towards her than Thady.

'Mother – is she well?'

'Yes, she is. Looking forward to seeing Sosanna wed next week.'

'It will be lonely for her. I...' Whatever was on the tip of her tongue was left unspoken. 'Did I tell you,' she asked brightly, 'that I saw the Holy Father in Rome? From a distance mind! He was being carried along the streets...'

She laughed at the sheer amazement on Eamonn's face. While she talked of Rome and the splendour of Venice he listened hungrily, and she wondered how he could possibly comprehend what he had never seen. In his life he had never been more than ten miles from home, had never heard music other than the sounds of pipes and fiddle, had never tasted food other than potatoes and oats, or had never seen buildings bigger than the village Barrack. Her heart went out to him as she watched him struggle to understand her descriptions of the lavish spectacle, pomp and ceremony of Papal Rome. She wondered if her reminiscences of visiting the French capital had first put the notion of studying at the Irish College in his head. Yet, she decided, if there was one final act of goodness within her power, she would help her brother to achieve his dream.

It was getting late. She turned and spoke with greater urgency.

'I want to come home.'

Eamonn looked at her blankly, lost for words.

'Eamonn,' Grace repeated with determination, 'I want to come home to stay.'

Despite her firm tone, Eamonn saw fear in her eyes. Fear of the rejection which she might face.

Eamonn returned home by the village. The redcoats were practising their manœuvres on the Square, under the critical gaze of the ancient sages who perennially sat under the ancient oak trees. They marched up and down, occasionally taking aim at an invisible target. Dogs barked and chickens scattered as the old men commented none too kindly on the calibre of contemporary soldiery. There was unanimous consent that in the olden days men were a foot taller, a breadth larger, and a damn sight smarter.

Their attention was diverted by the sound of galloping horses from the Drumreagh road, the only highway leading into the village. A man of some stature, with pristine white wig and sober civilian garb, led a sizeable military escort into Rostrevor. These soldiers were better dressed and better armed than those parading on the Square. The Barrack Sergeant saluted sharply as their leader dismounted. His horse was massive, black and shiny, like a well-groomed battle steed. It shook its long mane defiantly before being led through the Barrack gates. A whisper of excitement and expectation ran among the villagers. This was no routine inspection visit. What did the stranger want?

Eamonn O'Lochlainn showed no curiosity whatsoever; his thoughts were elsewhere.

❖   ❖   ❖

Owen MacOwen's heart was breaking. The baillifs had paid their long expected visit. The two burly men had read out an eviction notice in English, which he barely understood. They proceeded to throw out on the sward the few personal possessions and pieces of furniture that remained. Their bedding, a cooking pot, a rude table and a spade lay in an untidy jumble. Last to go, without reverence or ceremony, was the Staff of Bronach.

'Give me that!' Owen cried. 'You have no right to touch that. No right at all!' He threw himself in fury at one of the men. The baillifs, used to encountering opposition, had been surprised to find only the young son of the house at home. He was easy to deal with and a slap around the ear left him crying alongside the remnants of his possessions.

'This is what I give for the rights of a woman who can't pay her rent, and leaves a child to do her fighting,' replied one of the men, and he dashed the ancient Staff against the corner of the building, the old wood splintering to pieces. Then they nailed planks over every window, upstairs and down, before leaving to report to the Agent Coyle another successful eviction.

Owen watched them go, laughing and joking as carelessly as men walking from the alehouse. With the terrible despair of the helpless he cried aloud. The shards of the revered Staff lay at his feet and he stooped to gather them up. The hand of God had not burst through the clouds to smite the perpetrator of the sacrilege. He had not been stopped, nor punished. The sky did not darken, there was no bolt of lightening. This was the final blow to the memory of Clan MacOwen. The power of the Staff had gone. It was impotent, a crumbling useless collection of sticks that could hardly kindle a fire. Now, he realised, he would have to find his mother, and take her to her O'Neill cousins in Clonduff. Then he himself would join the growing hordes of migrant workers, a poor despised spalpeen.

❖   ❖   ❖

The Widow Fearon ran for all she was worth, past Leckan and down the mountainside, tripping and stumbling as she went. 'Jesus, Mary and Joseph!' she repeated over and over to ward off terrible thoughts and visions. Her heart pounded as if all the demons in hell were chasing her. In the distance she saw two men walking up the valley. 'Seán O'Lochlainn!' she screamed. 'Come quickly in the name of God and the Devil!' Seán dropped his pick and shovel and bounded up the hill towards the agitated woman, calling the Buller to follow him as he went. The Widow was in a state of shock and almost incoherent, but they allowed her to lead them across Leckan towards the grey precipice called the Churn. Standing on the edge, she pointed downwards before falling to her knees in prayer. For there, on the rocks below, lay the broken and mangled body of Dervla MacOwen.

Chapter Nine

1762 - 1780

THE TIME PASSED slowly for Grace after her parting with the youthful Henry Valentine. In spite of her hopes, he did not come back the following year, nor the year after that, and it was ten years before she was to see him again. As the wounds on her back healed, so grew a deep contempt for those who had caused her such pain. After some time, and with the support of Mistress Dunn, she felt strong enough to put all thoughts of her humiliation behind her. She stayed away from Kilbroney House and avoided visiting the village. She felt, Grace told Mistress Dunn, as though she was under constant scrutiny, and, indeed, Tom Dunn was quite sure that Coyle would have her well watched. It was Dunn who eventually told the true story to Thady, and restrained him from attempting further vengeance. The O'Lochlainns, he knew, were too poor and vulnerable to lose their breadwinner, and Thady reluctantly agreed with him.

Grace lived with her bedridden grandmother until the old woman died, shortly before the girl's sixteenth birthday. Old Mistress O'Lochlainn was the only member of the family to whom Grace could speak about her ill-starred love affair. Her brothers were too young, and her parents always got too upset. She found the old woman sympathetic, despite her obvious detestation of the Whitechurch breed.

'God sends his angels to earth's darkest places!' the old woman reassured her. 'Maybe there was a purpose to it all, and some good may yet come of it.' Grace was lonely when her grandmother died, even though her death had been expected for years.

It was during the long winter following her burial that smallpox struck the Poorland community. Not a house in the valley was spared and small children were the most vulnerable. Grace feared for Sosanna and puny little Eamonn, the sickly changeling who had been hanging on to life by the breadth of a hair since his birth. But it was Donogh and Tadhg who died, both on the same night. Poor Seán, Grace thought, suffered the worst of this blow: usually kind and cheerful by nature, he became withdrawn and embittered.

Annie Dunn's baby was among the victims of the disease, and to help her through the days of mourning Tom sent for Grace. Eily had seen her daughter grow thin and pale through the ordeal and at one stage feared that she too might be lost.

'How often have I wished that my girl might have a better life than I had,' Eily cried, 'and now she may not even have that much.' She was comforted by Mistress Dunn's reassurances that Grace would be warm and well fed.

'I would be glad of her company, at least until the days get longer,' said Annie. 'She can help me with the two boys, and at least you will not have to worry about her safety.'

And so Grace left the close for a second time. She stayed until the summer, returning again the following winter. At Dunn's Hill she learned the meticulous housekeeping methods of Mistress Dunn, and kept the books for her husband, all the time regaining her confidence and self-respect.

By the age of eighteen all the promise of youth had been fulfilled and Grace had blossomed into a young woman of great beauty. She wore her hair closely braided around a shapely head, and soft curves had replaced the wraith-like figure of earlier years. She had grown taller than either Eily or Thady, and the few who remembered said she resembled her grandmother as a young maid. As far as the local lads were concerned she was cold and unapproachable, and Eily despaired of her ever finding a man.

'I can look after myself!' her daughter assured her.

Everyone compared her with her spirited little sister, Sosanna, who from the age of two had had the whole O'Lochlainn household jumping to attention. Grace did not have the same warm friendliness as the little girl. Annie Dunn, though, was proud of her protégé. Not only had she weathered the storm of the whipping at Kilbroney House, but she had progressed to a level of scholarship which no other woman of her acquaintance had reached. Writing by candlelight into the small hours of the night took its toll, and Grace's eyesight suffered. Master Dunn provided her with a pair of reading spectacles and privately attributed Grace's stand-offishness with people to her poor sight. Dunn valued her excellent handwriting and often asked her to make copies of legal documents for the merchants of Newry who were his most valued clients.

On a few occasions, under cover of darkness, Tom Dunn had hosted meetings of men from Newry and further afield. As they arrived, with great-cloaks stained from the dirty roads, Grace would put aside her quill to brush down their clothes and polish their boots. Annie Dunn always had a hot stew bubbling in the pot, so that no one ever left hungry. As they gathered around the fire with pewter tankards raised, Grace listened to the discussion, and her heartbeat quickened with the passion and intensity of their speech. Most of them were Presbyterians, angry men with a burning sense of injustice. They directed their wrath towards those who passed laws which were of benefit to few and caused suffering to many. They spoke in English, but they spoke of Ireland.

The discussion often became heated as the Cochrane brothers of Newry, tall men with fiery eyes, spoke of their impatience with a government which was elected only by men of the Established Church. The gentle Sam Lowans spoke quietly, but with just as much anger. John Mercer, a young East India merchant was the most widely travelled of the group and it was he who had first-hand news from the Americas, where there was also great discontent with the government and its punitive taxation system. Andreas Boyd often told the story of how his great-grandfather, a simple baker, had stood against Cromwell's advancing army by drenching his ovens and smothering his fires. If any changes were to be made, Boyd argued, they would be made by ordinary people like the baker. Dunn usually had to persuade these men to control their anger, and to convince them that though their time would come, the moment was not yet right.

Grace was enthralled by their visions of the future, but she never

143

gave her opinions on the subject. As a woman, she was never asked.

1772

GRACE WAS AT home with her mother when he came for her. The children, Eamonn and Sosanna, were the first to hear the hooves and went scurrying around to the back of the cabin where their sister was stacking up turf before the onset of snow.

'Excisemen!' they called exitedly, for these agents were the most frequent callers to the close since someone had tipped them off about Thady's still. They listened before deciding that no exciseman would ever travel alone and hope to return in one piece. The horse's hooves seemed to pick their way tentatively down the bohareen, as if on unfamiliar territory.

'Eamonn! Sosai! Stay where you are!' Grace bade the children before peeping round the front of the cabin. She closed her eyes in disbelief.

He was mounted on a great stallion with silver reins. He was taller and broader than she remembered, but with the same piercing green eyes. It was as if the past ten years had been wiped out and they were meeting again for the first time. He had come back to her, this time as landlord. As she watched, Eily timidly came out to meet him and he dismounted to speak to her.

'I have come for your daughter. Rest assured that she will want for nothing.'

Grace, without a tear or a backward glance, left her home, her family and her poverty to go with Henry Valentine.

Eamonn, a slightly built nine-year-old, watched them leave in disbelief. Running up the pathway, crying for all he was worth, he called, 'Grace! Don't forget me! Take me with you!'

Grace hardly heard him, so overcome was she. Henry turned and, in his happiness, threw a coin to the boy. Then they set off at a quick pace down the valley.

There was consternation at the news of the return of the scullion to Kilbroney House. The man who had administered the ignominious whipping had since retired, but several retainers who were implicated one way or the other were still in the Valentines' service. Mistress Cunningham, the housekeeper, struggled to contain her nervousness at the sight of the couple. Stammering a greeting, she was silenced by the look in his eyes as he gazed intently at the bedraggled upstart with something akin to adoration. The housekeeper clutched her ring of keys in mounting desperation as she considered her defence. She could say that it was not her fault. That she had merely carried out orders. She knew she was at the mercy of the former scullion. To her surprise, Grace O'Lochlainn showed no signs of having recognised her. Mistress Cunningham dropped a curtsy in her direction and began to make alternative plans for her own future.

Marriage was never a consideration. In Henry's eyes the great gulf of class, creed and race made such a union impossible, and, much as he loved Grace, he was overcome by an overwhelming sense of duty, inculcated from the cradle. Grace never suggested marriage either. From her cradle she had learned how to suppress her own wishes and opinions, and the stronger the view, the more deeply it must be buried. Freedom of speech was a luxury enjoyed, if not appreciated, by men of Henry's class, and appreciated but not enjoyed by Grace's. The opinions she held, masked by her grey eyes, had been moulded by years of poverty and deprivation and fired by the aspirations of Tom Dunn.

Although both saw only the boy and girl they had fallen in love with so long ago, they soon realised that the distance of ten years had produced two very different people. So, as strangers, they began to learn to love again, and this time, they resolved, there was no power on earth which would part them. If Grace had cut herself off from her family and friends, Henry also lost many of his county friends, and the couple soon found themselves cocooned in their own company.

Grace was fascinated by the warmth in the big house. The cold, stark winters of the Mournes did not exist in these heated rooms with their fat, overfed coal fires. There was no sickness here, none of the hunger or exhaustion that were bedfellows of life in the Poorlands. Madam Valentine's discarded wardrobe provided her with fur-lined cloaks and fine woollen gowns, not one of which she felt able to wear with ease.

They did not stay in Kilbroney long, for as soon as the roads were passable they travelled to Dublin in a comfortable closed carriage with luxurious rugs and hot bricks underfoot. Henry Valentine usually broke his journey several times along the route, staying with friends, but Grace recoiled from being paraded in front of his gentlemen friends as his mistress. In Dublin the atmosphere was more relaxed, as the servants in the townhouse were obviously well used to seeing lady guests come and go. At their master's request dressmakers and milliners called, laden with silks and satins, determined to transform this country lass into a lady of fashion. They soon found that Grace had her own ideas, spurning the elaborate wigs of the current mode, preferring to keep her own golden locks, coiled and dressed with a simple comb. To the greater horror of the modistes, she refused to be corseted, pronouncing their whalebone stays to be fit only for the torture chamber. Despairing glances were exchanged. With her unfashionable twenty-six inch waist, Grace O'Lochlainn would be instantly recognisable as a peasant girl. Peasant or otherwise, she had heads turning in the street as she passed.

When not with Henry, Grace spent her time exploring the little streets of the city around Dublin Castle. Most of all she enjoyed browsing through the many bookshops of Dublin, often spending hours choosing a purchase. Henry was surprised by this scholarly trait, for neither his sister Fanny nor his mother had ever shown the slightest interest in books other than the illustrated fashion plates from London. When Grace asked his advice on which books she should buy, he gave orders for anything which might take Mistress O'Lochlainn's choosing to be delivered to his residence without delay. Grace, far from expressing gratitude, was appalled to think that money mattered so little to him, denying his playful suggestion that she was perturbed because the pleasure of making a worthy choice had been taken from her.

If Grace was overawed by the great imperial city she never let it show. Every morning they went riding, acknowledging the nods of recognition from Henry's acquaintances. There were, however, certain social institutions and functions from which she was debarred, including the balls and assemblies of the Castle, for her company was decidedly unacceptable among the women of Henry's class. There was a more liberal companionship which frequented race meetings, fêtes and concerts amongst which any woman of beauty and charm was welcomed.

Henry Valentine lived in the shadow of two men, both now deceased. They were his great-grandfather, Colonel Whitechurch, and his father, George Valentine. One had been a firebrand puritan priest-hunter, the other a gambling, degenerate reprobate. Yet Henry felt that he was constantly being compared unfavourably with either one or the other. He recalled, as a child, his father making free with any of the servant women who took his fancy, and filling the orphan asylums with his bastards. Yet to Daphne Valentine such behaviour was acceptable, as long as certain rules of discretion were adhered to. George haunted the gambling dens of Dublin, losing more than winning, confident that all he had to do to replenish the loss was to instruct Agent Coyle to increase the rents of his tenants. Weak and cruel, violent and selfish, and yet George was fondly remembered as a lovable rascal who had lived life to the full.

Henry Valentine also had little interest in his estate. He left its administration in the hands of Coyle who had transferred his total loyalty to the new master on the death of Squire George. Coyle's instructions were to act fairly and at all times within the law.

Henry harboured a sincere belief in the ascendancy of his own class, and in one crown, one faith, one kingdom leading to the mutual prosperity of both the rulers and the ruled. He opposed the granting of parliamentary franchise to anyone other than those who knew how to wield power with responsibility and integrity. Some men were born to lead, others to follow, and that was the natural order. He equally abhorred the misuse of privilege by degenerate absentee landlords who left their estates and those in their care to the mercy of corrupt agents and middlemen. He did not doubt Coyle's honesty. His agent was inclined to be over-zealous, a little lacking in compassion perhaps, but never corrupt. Henry had inherited an estate which had survived the excesses of his father only due to Coyle's good management. Now the linen industry in Ulster was blossoming and things looked well for the future.

The new landlord accepted his other roles of magistrate, Member of the Grand Committee, and Member of Parliament with greater relish. He held strong views on the need for uniformity of religion, although he did not share the anti-Romish views of the demagogue Lord Clanbrassil, his father's friend. He was suspicious of those who defiantly offered their loyalty to what to all intents and purposes was a foreign monarch on a far-off throne.

With Grace by his side, Henry Valentine's views mellowed considerably. At first he could only rationalise his love for her by imagining that she was misplaced, a well-born maid fated to be raised in poverty. As time went on he was forced to recognise her for what she was, a daughter of the Poorlands race, and had to adjust his views accordingly. Only the most begrudging of those who knew the landlord from childhood could fail to acknowledge that he had become a warmer, kinder, happier person than the Henry Valentine of old.

They travelled widely on the continent, where a mistress had almost as much status and often more respect than a wife. There, Grace was treated as a woman of considerable wisdom and substance, earning the admiration of all who met her. Henry was a more reluctant traveller. Perhaps it was because he had Grace all to himself when they were at home, and he did not have to endure the envious glances of others, but he also had to acknowledge a new, growing love, the love of his home in Kilbroney. The more often he went away, the keener he was to come back. Every time he returned from his journeys, and the first faint outline of the Ulster mountains appeared north of Drogheda, he felt his heartbeat quicken. There, to the west, were the wild hills of South Armagh, and beyond them the Mournes. He felt a yearning for his home which was as deep as that of any of the native clans.

Grace knew of Henry's wish to stay at home, but life for her in Kilbroney House was often dull and lonely. As a magistrate, and member of the Grand Committee, he often had to be away for days on end, staying with friends who were considerably less tolerant of mistresses than their equals in France and Italy. She suspected that had she been French or Italian herself, no remarks would have been passed.

She never lost the friendship of Mistress Dunn, and although Annie would not visit the big house Grace was always welcomed at Dunn's Hill. There was a new baby girl in the house, and Grace loved the opportunity to nurse little Betsy. Once, Tom Dunn approached her with an expression of worry on his face.

'Mistress Grace,' he said tentatively, 'while you were in my employ, you met people... heard things...' He seemed embarrassed. 'It concerns me now that you might...'

'Turn informer?'

'No!' he replied hastily. 'Of course not! But sometimes one will speak out of turn, without thinking...'

'Don't worry, Master Dunn! I never speak without due consideration,' Grace reassured him.

Grace did realise, however, that her visits to Dunn's Hill might have far-reaching implications. The men from Newry with political views very much at variance with Major Valentine's might stop their meetings, something she did not wish to see happening. So she decided, with regret, that it would be best for everyone if she were to visit there no more. Her gilded cage was becoming ever more securely barred.

Henry, confident that Grace had every bodily comfort which he could provide, rarely noticed her loneliness. He never discussed matters concerning the estate, thinking that they might cause her distress. He never mentioned to her his fear that he, or she, might fall victim to one of the many agrarian terror groups which bred on perceived injustices. He considered himself to be a fair and impartial magistrate who quickly referred any serious cases to the Circuit Court at Downpatrick. Yet any suggestion of treasonable activity brought down the full force of his wrath. The King's law, he conceded, was not perfect, but it was the only thing which stood between peace and anarchy. He had, both in Parliament and in the Grand Committee declared war on these barbarous organisations with their ridiculous titles. There were many of them: Oakboys, Torchboys, the Houghers and the Steelboys. Each professed slightly differing aims, but used similar methods including the maiming of animals and burning of barns. There had been attacks on big houses and, on occasions, there had been murder. Such lawlessness, he determined, would never be tolerated in Kilbroney.

1777

WHEN HENRY'S SISTER, Fanny Ward, was widowed, fifteen years after contracting a marriage which was both childless and loveless, she decided to take her leave of Armagh, her brother-in-law who had inherited the family estate and, most of all, his haughty, disagreeable wife, Phyllis.

Her anticipated arrival back at her old home caused considerable interest among the servants at Kilbroney House. They looked forward to a sharpening of claws as the landlord's sister confronted his mistress. Not that Grace O'Lochlainn, who had assumed the title of 'housekeeper' after the sudden and unexplained departure of Mistress Cunningham, had ever mistreated any of them. It was simply that they could not regard her as anything other than an upstart scullion.

Henry greeted his sister with outstretched arms. They were genuinely fond of each other and Henry had been upset to learn that she had been unhappy with the Wards. Of course she must come home, he had written.

'Henry, dear! How well you look! I had thought...'

'You thought that I could not get on without you?' he laughed. For all her lack of height, Fanny looked very much the 'grande dame' in her pale mauve travelling cloak and bonnet. He ushered her into the drawing-room, where a mighty coal fire blazed a welcome. She asked him about his health, talked about their mother's recent remarriage, and suggested that, now that she was home again, she might set about having the place redecorated.

Then a tall, fairish woman, garbed in grey to match her eyes, entered the room. She could have been a servant, carrying a tray with muffins and a hot posset, but there was something different about her. Henry's face lit up as the woman bestowed on him a warm smile, and a still warm, but slightly more wary smile on Madam Ward. Fanny became aware of a strange intimacy between the two as he lifted the tray.

'Well, Henry. Who is this?' she enquired in the imperious tone which she reserved for servants. Stretching her diminutive body to its full height, she turned towards the woman and peered at her inquisitively.

'May I present Grace O'Lochlainn, the woman who has stolen my heart.'

❖   ❖   ❖

The two women lived without rancour under the same roof during the periods when Grace was not travelling with Henry. Fanny Ward was secure enough in her position to be indulgent towards her brother's mistress. She almost liked the girl, for she clearly brought out the best in her brother and was an exceptionally good housekeeper. They never had cause for disagreement, and Fanny was quite relieved not to have to worry about domestic concerns. She preferred to concentrate on her gardening, and on enjoying a lively social life with her old friends.

It was under Fanny's patronage that the house once more played host to hunting parties and evening soirées. For the first time Henry, when at home, felt obliged to fulfill his obligations as a host with his sister by his side. Grace was quite adamant that he should do so, removing herself to the housekeeper's room when 'the family' had guests. Sometimes she heard him laughing in the company of some young gentlewomen, and she wondered if he did not wish to take his place beside one of them as a husband or father. He had never mentioned children, but she knew that as time went on he would realise the need for a legal heir, and might grow to resent her for what she could not give him. It was with these concerns that she embarked on the ship which was to take them to Italy in September of 1779.

1780

HENRY HAD ALWAYS promised to take Grace to the city of Venice. They had spent Christmas in Rome, and early in 1780 he arranged for them to travel north to spend some time in the Venetian Republic before returning home, early in April. Grace was charmed by their luxurious lodgings near Piazza San Marco, overlooking the Grand Canal. Here, of all the cities of Europe, master and servant could at least masquerade as equals, and she was treated with as much deference as any aristocratic matron.

One man who professed himself to be her devoted admirer was Prince Cesare Steffani, a blatant master of courtship, connoisseur of women, and boastful father of a host of illegitimate children. His advances towards her provoked an exhibition of jealousy which quite surprised Grace, and almost involved Henry Valentine in a duel. Soon afterwards the prince extended an invitation to the Palazzo Steffani, a request which Valentine was at first inclined to turn down. When Grace suggested that such a refusal might be considered petulant, he reluctantly accepted. Steffani, he believed, had thrown down the gauntlet for another challenge.

Dinner at the Palazzo was followed by a performance of Signor Pergolesi's old favourite, La Serva Padrona, a light divertimento to aid the digestion. Grace had enjoyed the opera on several occasions since coming to Italy, and found the Venetians to be particularly keen enthusiasts, with even servants regularly patronising the public opera houses. The Prince's servants were permitted to join the family for such performances, a familiarity which would never have been tolerated in Ireland.

As a merry party of about twenty seated themselves in the Teatro Steffani, a small private opera house, Grace watched the story unfold. The other guests were obviously familiar with the work and hummed along with some of the catchier tunes. Hundreds of candles lit the stage as the current Venetian diva made her appearance, to a murmur of approval.

The plot, she realised, concerned a conniving maidservant who tricked her ageing master into matrimony. Valentine laughed loudly at the antics of the mute manservant who was the go-between. Grace felt slightly uncomfortable. She felt that the parallels with her own situation being obvious, people were staring at her and making their own comparisons. At one stage she noticed Prince Steffani trying to catch Henry's eye.

'That is their true opinion of me!' she thought. 'They think I am like that wily maid.' She blushed as the Prince leaned across her to comment to Henry on the soprano's ample proportions, and wondered if he would have done so had she been, indeed, Madam Valentine.

La Serva Padrona was short, and the soprano came forward to receive the customary adulation of the audience. Grace seized the opportunity to disappear into the shadows and savour the cooling night air. The plot of *La Serva Padrona*, although amusing, had served only to remind her of the differences between her station and Henry's. In Italy one could make light of an ambitious servant who aspired to be her master's wife. Not so in Ireland. Neither of them would ever be forgiven for flouting the conventions.

Grace walked out to the balcony overlooking the Grand Canal, where the night's coolness eased her burning cheeks. Below, in the darkness, the water rippled and the sound of more laughter floated up. A hand touched her shoulder and she jumped.

'You startled me!' she cried. Then she folded herself into Henry's arms. 'Take me home! Please!'

'Why, Grace, you wanted so much to come to Venice, and we have more yet to see!'

'Yes, of course, I was only thinking of myself,' she answered apologetically.

'When do you ever think of yourself?' he whispered, holding her close to him. 'You always have my interests at heart. Now, if you wish to return home we will do so as soon as it can be arranged!'

'Yes.' She disengaged herself from his arms and turned away.

'Grace!' he called her softly. His eyes in the dusk seemed luminous and pleading. 'Grace, I want you for my bride. I want you to bear my children!' Like a gallant of old, he knelt and kissed her palms. 'Come home with me as my wife!' Her hands seemed cold to his touch and he took her in his arms once again. He felt her trembling with laughter and tears as slowly she shook her head. She told him then why she would not. She loved him too much.

❖ ❖ ❖

'Major Valentine must marry!' Grace said. Fanny, who had been tending her flowers sat up in amazement. She looked at the woman in grey and wondered if she had heard right. 'You should find him a bride, someone who will take good care of him... and bring him credit.'

Fanny was startled. Even after two years, there was much she did not know about this creature.

'Why, Grace, I was sure that you loved my brother.'

'I have never known any other love. That is why I must leave him.'

'Well, what a noble sacrifice!' Fanny could have bitten her tongue, as the sarcasm in her remark hit home.

'There is no nobility in me. That is your birthright. Mine is to survive as best I can.'

'Ah! You are naturally concerned about your future. Do not give it another thought. This sort of thing happens all the time, and I can assure you that you will be better provided for than most... women of your station in life.'

Fanny had become aware of a coolness between her brother and Grace since their early return from Italy. She knew that he only travelled for the woman's sake, as he always talked about how much he loved his home beneath the mountains. Perhaps, she thought, Henry's infatuation had run its course. The girl was acting quite sensibly and must be duly rewarded for her discretion. Henry must have come to realise that if he were to produce an heir, he must have a wife, and a wife must be well-bred. She vaguely wondered if Grace would continue to be his mistress after his marriage. That would be a suitable and fashionable compromise. Yet she knew in her heart that Grace's personal honesty would forbid such an arrangement. The peasant who had lived for so long in the shame of an unsanctified union had a higher moral standard than many wives, who married only for position and wealth. She had also educated herself, Fanny was aware, building up the family library until it was one of the best in the county. It was the only subject on which the pair had ever been seen to quarrel, as Henry's tastes in literature were more restricted than those of his mistress. She thought that Grace, though speaking with determination, seemed saddened by the finality of her own decision. But then again, it was hard to tell with her.

Fanny got to her feet and shook down her skirts. She walked back to the house while trying to extricate a splinter from her fingertip. There was only one thing on her mind: who would be the new Madam Valentine.

Grace returned to her room, her calm appearance belying turbulent emotions. She wanted to stay as much as she wanted to go. She loved him and she resented him all at once. Their love had been dying a slow death since – she knew not when. Perhaps since his sister had arrived at the house. Then he had been forced to compare her with the young women of his own class, and had clearly found her wanting. They were poles apart on almost every subject, from George Washington to popular franchise. She disliked being censured by him, and a hitherto unrecognised feeling of rebellion stirred within her when she felt that her opinions were being suppressed. She felt like those cloaked men, meeting furtively at Dunn's Hill, desperately wanting to let their views be heard, but fearing the consequences.

Yet when they were alone her love for him was still strong. Since their return from Venice, she felt, he had been cold towards her. There was no doubt that he had loved her once, but she likened his demonstration of feeling that night at the palazzo to the last burst of blossom from a dying tree.

❖ ❖ ❖

'Letitia! Letitia Butler! Just the girl!'

'Yes. She will suit him very well,' declared Madam Hall. The decision had been made within hours of Grace's announcement during a cosy teatime chat at Narrow Water. Madam Hall had been only too glad to help Fanny Ward come up with a list of every eligible heiress in the county, while wisely staying clear of blonde hair and grey eyes. It would be a simple and enjoyable task to organise a round of social events which would throw the pair together. Henry Valentine would simply not know what was happening until he heard the banns read. Afterwards he would realise that everything was for the best. Madam Hall, who had just returned from Dublin, was *au fait* with all the latest genteel diversions and was, more importantly, the godmother of Miss Letitia Butler.

❖ ❖ ❖

An only child of nineteen with doe eyes and soft auburn curls, Letitia made it simple for everyone by falling madly in love with Henry. Her usual pale, forgettable countenance took on a new radiance every time the Major was present. They danced together, hunted together, and fell behind the party when out walking. Within three weeks of their first meeting and to almost universal approval, the dashing Major Valentine and the heiress Letitia Butler were engaged to be married.

Grace remained at the house at the request of Madam Ward, 'until something has been sorted out.' In truth, Fanny had become dependant on her housekeeper, and would be glad to hand over her keys to Letitia after the wedding. But Grace eventually found the situation intolerable and decided that it was time to leave.

She stood before the master of the house as any other servant would, although perhaps her head was held a little higher.

'I wish you would reconsider your decision! After I am...' he stopped, embarrassed.

'After you are married, your wife will not perhaps need a housekeeper. She certainly will not wish to have your former mistress in the position.'

'Let me set you up in that little townhouse where I could visit you from time to time. If you wished to see me.'

'Our time together is over. We both know that.' Grace stared ahead.

Henry could not bear her coldness. He loved her now just as he had always loved her, but she had changed. Once, when he had talked of his hopes for the future, she had listened, eyes shining. Now she challenged him, and questioned his judgement. It was as if she blamed him for the wrongs of the world. He had offered her everything that was in his power to give. For her, he would have faced the censure of his class, and would even have wed her in the nearest church, that greedy obsessive church of Rome which demanded everything and gave nothing. He had asked her to have his children even though his own noble blood would be thinned by that of Irish peasants. He had bared his soul to her when he had asked her to be his wife, but she had just laughed.

Now she stood there, content to leave him to a loveless marriage. He left his seat and went over to the window. The sound of female laughter in the rose garden below floated upwards.

'You must live as a lady,' he said, 'for that is what you have become. I will, of course, settle a generous income on you. You have earned it.' If his hurtful words stung her, she showed no response. He wanted her to turn on him, to strike him, to give any sign that she still cared something about his opinion of her. Instead she answered quietly, almost in a whisper.

'For myself, I want nothing. But what you – so generously – would have bestowed on me, I wish,' she faced him proudly and squarely. 'I ask you instead to give it to my brother, Eamonn.'

'Eamonn? The blond-haired lad? What use would someone in his station have for money?'

'He is destined for the Holy Priesthood and must travel to

France. I will do everything I can to help him.'

'France? We are at war with France. That is quite out of the question.'

'But that is the route which young men of this area have taken for generations. They are not going to fight! They study for the priesthood at the Irish College of Paris.'

'I have heard of these Irish Colleges. They will teach him how to be a subversive in his own country.'

'Eamonn? Subversive?' Her lips twitched. 'I would hardly think so. You will see for yourself if you speak with him.'

'The Roman priesthood!' Henry turned towards her in a temper. 'You belong to a race of fools, Grace – a poor, blind, beaten race. You would make beggars of your very children to support your indolent priests. I lifted you from that. I offered you an escape.'

'I ask for no escape. I ask only for the chance to help someone close to me. You must know that it will not be easy to go back to my own people. At least if I can give them something, it would be in reparation for my sins.'

The anguish in her tone shocked him. At once he saw how lonely and cold her future would be: no family, no friends, no love. The tenderness of years gone by swept over him.

'For your sins, Grace? Then let it be for mine also.' He held her for the last time and gently kissed her. Then she turned, left the room, and never once looked back.

Chapter Ten

May 10th 1780

THERE WERE MORE than the usual number of mourners come to pay their respects to the mortal remains of Dervla MacOwen. They came like ghosts over the Poorlands and the glen to Levallyclanowen where they hovered outside the tiny cabin of the Widow Fearon. She could not be waked in her own home, for it had been desecrated, looted and nailed up by the bailiffs. But no lament was sung, no keening was heard in the valley, for Dervla MacOwen had taken her own life.

Father Mackey, weary from his day's ministry in the Poorlands, felt only compassion at the pitiful sight of young Owen, his thin face contorted with grief as he knelt by his mother's body. Between her waxen hands he had fixed the black image of the suffering Christ, the Penal cross. Every family had such a cross, and this one, like the others, bore the scars and scorch marks of years of repression. It seemed symbolic of Dervla's suffering as it lay on her breast, below a face now serene and free from care. Two simple rush candles illuminated her body, while alongside lay the broken shards of the Staff of Bronach. Father Mackey picked up the pieces of wood and decided that, come what may, he would have it restored. It had always been an important object of veneration to the people of Kilbroney during times of trial, and the MacOwens had fulfilled their hereditary duty well. He owed it to the boy, as well as to the memory of Dervla, to see that the relic was repaired and reinstated.

As he looked towards the huddle of black shawls by the door he became aware of the mute question on all the faces. He faced a dreadful quandary, having to decide if this was indeed a suicide. If the deceased had passed to eternity in a state of mortal sin she could not be buried alongside her husband on consecrated ground. Crossing to Owen, he laid a hand on his shoulder.

'Your mother rests in peace, Owen. Whatever terrible accident happened to her, we can be sure that she is now safely in the hands of Almighty God.'

The boy at last gave full vent to his anguish, and threw himself over the corpse, sobbing wildly. Father Mackey let him cry before indicating to the Widow Fearon to lead him away. Opening his Missal, he began to intone the Prayers for the Dead.

Owen MacOwen listened as the priest chanted tunelessly. He wanted only to get away from the crowd. The Widow's small cabin was stifling and he felt as though most of the mourners were there out of curiosity, not sympathy. Where had they all been when the bailiffs were battering at his door? He was overcome with anger, and a burning desire for revenge.

❖   ❖   ❖

That evening Samuel MacIntyre, the Valentines' gamekeeper, was making his way home for his supper. His mind was on the roast hare his wife would be cooking, with potatoes and spring cabbage. He would wash it all down with a jug of ale, and then park himself by the fireside to log the incidents of the day.

Mick the Fox had been seen prowling around and no doubt would have filled his own larder, given half the chance. He had chased a few children from the river. This was an almost daily ritual, for they never seemed to learn that it was a dangerous stream for the very young. As MacIntyre reached the salmon leap where the river sounded like muffled thunder, he met the men returning from the quarry, with their picks and spades over their shoulders. He was wary of the quarrymen, suspecting that they were helping themselves to the odd coney. Only the village bleachers and other privileged retainers were permitted to hunt rabbits. The men were covered in quarry dust, giving them the appearance of walking statues. One of them stopped to wash the dirt from his hair under the falling water, but MacIntyre raised his gun provocatively. The quarrymen understood his meaning, and quickly moved on.

On the opposite banks, the bleachers' lads, hard-working, law-abiding boys, were industriously rolling up bales of flaxen fabric for overnight storage. MacIntyre gave them a friendly wave and continued his journey upstream towards his home. It was a good, fresh evening, and the river glen was thick with wild flowers. He forded the stream below Dunn's Hill and turned to cast a backward glance on the peaceful meadows.

His attention was caught by an unusual haze in the sky. The young May moon had risen behind the mountains, but this strange light did not emanate from the heavens. The bleachers' lads came running towards him, alerting him to the source of the orange glow. Major Valentine's barns were ablaze.

❖ ❖ ❖

Under cover of darkness two shadowy figures approached the pound below Dunn's Hill, where the animals of miscreants and those who had fallen behind with the rent were housed. One was armed with a cudgel, the other with a knife. A light shone from the Poundwardens's cottage, but the animals' building was in darkness. Within minutes, impounded goats, donkeys, a pig and two thin cows had been let loose. The noise of the animals alerted the warden who emerged with his gun, only to be cudgelled on the head by a figure in the darkness. The animals were spirited away, and by the time the keeper had reached the Barrack, with a garbled story and a sore head, there was nothing in the pound but that which the inmates had seen fit to leave behind.

❖ ❖ ❖

In a lonely cabin in Knockbarragh a group of men waited. The woman of the house pottered around, tossing a few sticks on the fire. No one spoke and no one slept. The woman occasionally opened the door to scan the darkness outside. Eventually she spoke.

'They are back.' She admitted a few dark-clad persons.

''Tis done!' one of them said. 'And the barns are in ashes by now.'

'Arrah! That will give them something to think about!' said the woman. They all looked at her, as if she had said too much. She busied herself with the dying embers. One man went to stand by the door as the others talked in hushed tones. The night outside was silent and peaceful, and now and then the night bird called. After a while, the watchman spoke.

'We'd best be on our way. 'Tis break o' day, boys!'

❖ ❖ ❖

Major Valentine had a visitor, a man whose reputation had gone before him as a ruthless hunter of men.

'I have no doubt that they are here! No doubt whatsoever.' Captain Walls paced the room in an obstinate mood.

Henry Valentine was becoming exasperated with the Captain's trenchant views but, as he was recognised as the henchman of one of the most powerful political cliques in the country, there was nothing to be done but humour him.

'You must be mistaken, Walls. There have been no strangers in the area for months. None fitting your description, at any rate,' he assured the Captain. 'I have an excellent agent who misses nothing! Nothing whatsoever. If Coyle has not seen them, then they cannot be here.' Walls listened and stretched himself in front of the fire.

'Perhaps they have taken refuge in the mountain lands. Do you have daily patrols there? No! I thought not. Surely even your capable agent would have his limitations in that vast wilderness. Unless the man can fly.'

'If they are hiding in the mountains, then natural justice will take its course, for they will certainly fall foul of some cut-throat tory. Those fellows all have strong territorial notions.'

'Outlaws! They are one and the same, Valentine, I have no doubt of that. I suggest that every house in the area, no matter who the occupants may be, should be thoroughly searched. Yes, even your own stables and outhouses. One can never be too careful.' He waved aside his host's objections. 'I caution you! I will get a direct warrant from Dublin Castle if necessary, for this pair must be apprehended.'

'For what purpose?'

'Treason! Against the King's rule in Ireland!'

'Treason, you say?' Valentine, as a loyal soldier and sworn magistrate, was not inclined to make light of this serious charge.

'The older man is a bookbinder by profession, and a Nonconformist Presbyterian preacher by election. These Dissenters,' Walls confided closely, 'are brigands of the worst type! I have reports that he has often hosted many unworthy characters with dubious political affiliations. Some of them Francophiles!'

'Really? What makes them think that Louis would be any better than George?'

'They don't! They are anarchists!'

'And the other? To whom does he give his allegiance?'

'Ah! MacArtain is the Dissenter's adopted son. He is the more dangerous of the two, a malcontent young upstart. The bastard son of a Papist whore!'

'A volatile combination indeed.'

'We believe he is destined for France with information of a kind which is a threat to the security of the realm. Names, locations, weaponry and the like. In short,' Walls paused dramatically, 'Donal MacArtain is an agent of King Louis of France!'

Valentine gave the problem consideration. The present undercurrent of unrest was due to the growing fear of an invasion. It was now four years since thirteen distant colonies of the Crown had united and brazenly declared their independence as the United States of America. He knew that such a phenomenon, a land ruled by the ordinary folk, was destined to fail, but he was concerned that the opportunistic French monarch, who had already sent a fleet across the ocean to the aid of the rebelling colonists, might avail of the chance to stir up trouble among the simple, easily misled peasants of Ireland. This was not the best time to deal with the threat of a French invasion. The Spaniards had again declared war against the United Kingdom and Holland had entered the fray on the side of the enemy. The Royal Navy had lost control of the Atlantic, leaving it a pleasure ground for pirates and buccaneers. Now, in 1780, the West Indies were under attack, the Rock of Gibraltar besieged, and even in far-off India the native princes were rebelling against the King. The invasion of Ireland seemed certain, and the only questions now being asked were when and where. The most likely landing places were on the west or south coasts, but there had been dangerous sparring in the Irish Sea of late, and no part of the coast could be deemed safe.

There had been many European monarchs who had tried to steal the island of Ireland with Papal approval. It was now exactly two hundred years since the Spanish had landed at Dún an Óir in County Kerry with their avenging Jesuits. Lord Grey de Wilton had wiped them out as a deterrent to subsequent invaders, and their wailing pleas of 'Misericordiae!' had echoed down the centuries. Yet the peasants still watched from the coastal mountains for signs of another Spanish fleet, or of the Fleur-de-Lys ensign, and as long as they held that hope Henry Valentine felt that he could not rest securely. But he wanted to impress upon the Dubliner his concern that there should be no excessive show of military strength in the village, and that the fragile peace should not be violated.

'Well, Valentine!' Walls pressed. 'I trust I will have your full co-operation in this matter. Local issues cannot take precedence over the nation's security!'

What he is really saying, thought Henry Valentine, is that his judgement takes precedence over mine. Aloud he declared:

'I must first consider the peace of this part of the realm which is within my stewardship. It lies uneasy, but all the same it is there and it was hard earned. Peace means prosperity! Crops are tended; harvests are gathered; commerce flourishes. Everyone benefits: you, me, them. We disturb it at great risk!'

Walls looked at his colleague in distaste. 'Of course, I understand your problem! But you, likewise, must appreciate mine!'

'If they are here, and I repeat "if", someone, sooner or later, be it for reasons of loyalty, jealousy or greed, will be sure to come forward. Just offer a suitable reward and then be patient. It will work. If they are around here, that is!'

Walls was losing patience with this county soldier. The local garrison was inadequate, but he had already organised the necessary reinforcements from Newry. It would be quite possible to scour the area straight away, and even if he did not find his fugitives a good purge would be sure to bring some other rats out of their hiding places.

'I will wait for one or two days at the most. Then I will send for the Fencibles.'

'Take your ease, Walls!' Valentine tried to change the tone of the discussion. 'You must stay with us! I will have your things brought over from the Barrack at once. The ladies are always keen to hear the gossip from Dublin, especially news of the latest fashionable modes.'

Walls knew all about county ladies. Horsey women with buck teeth and pimples. 'Thank you. I will, of course dine with you, but I wish to stay at my station. I am a soldier. I prefer a hard bed!'

After Captain Walls had taken his leave, Fanny accosted her brother.

'Did you tell Captain Walls we are expecting him?'

'He says he prefers a hard bed!'

'Hard bed indeed! Grandfather Whitechurch would have approved.'

May 13th 1780

THE BURNED REMAINS of the barns were a sorry sight. As Major Valentine picked his way through the charred timbers, the extent of the waste depressed him. Had the grain been stolen at least someone would have benefited. But as for this! He shuddered as his boot touched the black carcasses of two hounds, burned on the spot which they had so loyally guarded. No human life had been lost and the barns had not been full, and for that he was thankful. As he walked away from the scene he considered the implications of the incident.

'Arson! No doubt about it!' It was Fegan the village blacksmith who spoke. He was one of the many who had arrived too late to fight the fire on the previous night, but had at least prevented it from spreading to the adjoining byres and farm buildings.

'Arson? Why do you think that, Fegan?' asked Valentine.

'It looks like the work of the Oakboys. They've done this before in other places.'

'The Oakboys, in Kilbroney? Surely not! Do I not always treat my tenants fairly? Have I ever given cause for grievance?'

'No. Of course not, Your Honour.' Murtagh Fegan could hardly have given any other answer. He turned away.

'Fegan!' called the landlord. 'Have you seen any strangers around here of late? Two men perhaps?' For a fraction of a second he thought he saw the blacksmith's back stiffen.

'No! No strangers, Your Honour!'

'Well now, you will let me know if you hear or see anything? We don't want brigands or bandits terrorising our village, do we?' With a nod, Murtagh touched his forelock and rejoined the woodmen, who were already calculating the rebuilding requirements.

Valentine turned his back on the smouldering ruins. He had not slept since Coyle had alerted him to the blaze. And he had only this morning heard about the vicious attack on the Poundwarden, and the loss of impounded animals. It was unlikely that they would ever be recovered. He wondered if the two incidents were connected, for Fegan had definitely given him the impression that there was something amiss. It was only a matter of time, he thought sourly, before they would come to the attention of Walls, and provide added grist to his mill.

On impulse, he took his horse and rode towards Dunn's Hill. As a magistrate, Valentine knew that Dunn had often taken the part of the most undeserving vagabonds, arguing as passionately on their behalf as if they were the sons of a bishop. He knew, too, that Coyle held Dunn in deep suspicion, not only because he was a champion of the poor, but because of his school. Yet, more than anything, Valentine envied the esteem in which he was held by Grace. His Grace.

Dunn expressed what seemed to be genuine regret at the previous night's conflagration.

'I have been told it was arson, Dunn, a deliberate act of terror.'

'A dangerous and stupid act.'

'I have always been fair. You know that! Certainly no one has ever complained.'

'With all due respect, how do poor widows without much English, or frightened boys register a complaint?'

'They can always see Coyle. He understands the old tongue, and, why, he has been here for nearly thirty years.' Dunn felt that perhaps there was a question in the landlord's voice.

'Perhaps,' he replied cautiously, 'Coyle can be over-zealous.' He described the events leading up to the eviction of the MacOwens, the despair, the terror, and finally the suicide of Dervla MacOwen.

Valentine felt appalled. The MacOwens represented the ragged remnants of the old Gaelic order in South Down. He understood why she would never have begged for a second chance, or humiliated herself before someone like Coyle. Obviously the man's lack of sensitivity to her position had inflamed local opinion; nevertheless, he was only upholding the law as he saw it, and should not be made a scapegoat because of the actions of this poor, unstable woman. The Major decided to see to it that her son was provided for in some way, and to have a word with Coyle. Preoccupied, he bade farewell to Tom Dunn.

❖ ❖ ❖

'Requiem aeternam, dona eis domine...' droned the mournful chant of Father Mackey as Briony Fegan stood by his friend Owen's side. A dull miserable rain was falling on the ruins of Bronach's monastery as the mortal remains of Dervla MacOwen were laid to rest in the grave of her husband. Not many witnessed the burial. There were no remaining MacOwens, save for Owen, and some of the neighbouring men feared association with the events of the previous night. Others still held a superstitious fear of the burial of a suicide, believing that the ghost would be caught in a limbo on earth. Briony, young as he was, felt a great pity for Owen as he stood there, fighting the tears. As the rain spattered

167

the roughly-hewn coffin, Briony burned with helpless anger.

'When I'm a man, I'll wield a real sword and right every wrong,' he promised himself, as the muddy earth dropped over the coffin.

Seán O'Lochlainn gathered up the grave spades which were used for that purpose only and passed around from family to family. The mourners huddled together in small groups as the rain eased to a light drizzle. There was universal agreement that the attacks on the previous night had been because of the recent spate of evictions, and especially because of the Widow MacOwen. Briony hovered around, listening to snippets of conversation. He felt outraged by what he heard, yet everyone seemed to be afraid to speak out. In pensive mood, he followed Owen up to the Widow Fearon's cabin.

❖ ❖ ❖

'They were so far behind with the rent that they could never have paid it. It was my duty to warn them, which I did, and then to evict them, which I also did.'

'For heaven's sake, Coyle! A demented widow and an unshaven boy! Why did you do it? You could have given them a small cabin! That class of people are happiest in simple surroundings.'

'Had they asked me, I would have rehoused them in Doyle's old cabin up in Knockbarragh.'

'But they did not ask! And you did not have the sensitivity to offer it to them. Now, thanks to you, we have an outbreak of lawlessness on our hands. Something for our determined Captain Walls to enjoy dealing with.'

'They would not have moved,' Coyle continued defensively. 'As far as that woman was concerned the land they farmed was their own. MacOwen land. "Leath Bhaile Clann Owen" it has always been called in Gaelic. She had considered you to be a usurper, sir.'

'I see. I see.' The Major paced up and down. 'It would be best to change the name perhaps. They cannot live in a world that has long disappeared. Theirs is a sad story, but they deluded only themselves.' Valentine looked at his agent, tired and older than he had ever remembered him. Agent Coyle, he realised, must be over seventy years of age. After so many years of loyal service it would hardly be fair to remove him from his position, but perhaps when the current unrest had been subdued he could see about setting him up with a pension.

'I will have the maps altered, sir.'

'Nevertheless,' sighed the Major, for he had not yet dealt with the root of the problem, 'this unfortunate woman's death coming now... No, Coyle, no one could hold you to be directly responsible,' he halted the Agent's mumbled protests, 'but the last thing any of us want to do is to stir up ancient grievances. No doubt the occurrences of last night were isolated, unconnected incidents.' Coyle waited for his instructions.

'I think you must delay any confrontational decisions for the moment,' Valentine continued. 'Any impending evictions must be brought to my attention. No! I have no sympathy with the lazy or the incompetent, but sometimes there may be mitigating circumstances.' Coyle was not pleased to have his powers reduced thus, but he made no comment as he turned to leave the room.

'Coyle! One other thing. I must have a house for Mistress O'Lochlainn's use.'

The Agent never questioned his master's wishes. It would be quite normal for his mistress to have separate accommodation, now that the Major was about to marry. He quickly suggested one or two residences of character about the village, untenanted and within a discreet distance of Kilbroney House. Valentine interrupted his flow of suggestions.

'She does not wish to live in the village, Coyle. Any unoccupied cabin, however humble, will suit her needs.'

'Mistress O'Lochlainn?' Coyle was surprised. He had not realised that the woman had fallen so far from favour.

'The MacOwen house,' said Valentine. 'It is superior among the peasant homes, is it not? Let her live there.'

Coyle heard the bitterness in his master's voice, and hesitated. Then he bowed, and turned towards the door. Valentine wondered at his agent's preoccupation.

'What is it, Coyle?'

'The Healing House of Levallyclanowen, sir,' Agent Coyle said slowly, deliberating. 'Is it suitable for the mother of your child?'

Chapter Eleven

May 14th 1780

MAJOR VALENTINE LOOKED at the young man standing before him. Eamonn O'Lochlainn was tall and thin under his threadbare clothes. Bony wrists reached well beyond the cuffs of an ill-fitting coat, as if he had still some growing to do. Wispy blond hair framed a face which displayed neither fear nor obsequiousness in the presence of his landlord, yet there was no hint of sourness or mistrust either. The young man's eyes gleamed with hope and goodwill.

'I have been told that you want to go to France.'

'I wish to take Holy Orders.'

'Yes, so I have been informed, but why do you wish to pursue your studies in Paris? We are at war, you know.' He wondered if the boy was even aware of the present hostilities.

'The conflict will not last long,' Eamonn replied, 'for it is God's will that I should join the priesthood. Poor men from here have taken the sacred route to Paris before, and I wish to follow in their footsteps.'

'And you think that I, a Protestant magistrate, should help you?' Valentine asked drily. 'Do you know that I could have you arrested as a spy? You could be a French agent for all I know.'

'Would you expect a French agent to approach you on such a matter? No, sir. I know you will help me because...'

'Of God's will?' Valentine finished the sentence.

'No. Because you are a good man, and because you promised Grace you would help me.'

'Yes, I did, and Grace could not possibly be... a French sympathiser.' He wondered at the doubt in his own voice. Grace had gone from his life, without ever telling him about their child.

He looked at the boy shrewdly. He spoke English fluently, albeit in the uncultured tones of a peasant, and the fashionable idioms of speech were missing, but there was no doubt, Henry thought, that he had inherited the attributes of a gentleman. There was a certain amount of polish about Eamonn which he could not have acquired in the mountain wilderness which was his home. He felt his resentment of Grace's secrecy harden: the young man would have been well catered for had his parentage been known. Did she think that he would have packed the boy off to the orphan asylum in Newry?

Eamonn had stopped talking and was now looking at him expectantly.

Such a relationship could never be acknowledged, the landlord told himself, for the honour of the family name was at stake, and he recoiled from the idea that a child with Whitechurch blood would join that band of hereditary foes, the Papist priests. Yet Eamonn spoke with deep sincerity and conviction, like a young Galahad in pursuit of a sacred quest.

'I will challenge his beliefs!' Valentine decided, 'for he will meet worse than I on his chosen path!'

For hours he fired at Eamonn every weapon to which he could lay hand, scriptural, historical, political and philosophical, but the young man remained unmoved. He admitted openly that he did not know all the answers, and agreed that he was appallingly ignorant on many issues. He was not fully conversant with scripture or the writings of the church fathers, and insisted that the interpretation of scripture should be left to wiser heads than his. He seemed quite ignorant of church history and had never heard of the Borgias, although he agreed that they sounded fearful. He also agreed that they would all lead a more peaceful and comfortable life if everyone held the same faith. As for politics, Eamonn was barely aware of King George let alone Henry Grattan, and he seemed to have little interest in the Americas. But he asked Henry Valentine to admit that the Borgias in their time must have performed some good acts, and King George some bad. As they talked, Valentine poured Eamonn a glass of wine, which he refused. A sign, the Major concluded, of the puritanical Whitechurch temperament.

After the interview each man was a little wiser and more understanding of the other, but otherwise unshaken from their chosen stance.

'By God, I'll make a gentleman of you yet!' declared Valentine suddenly. 'You will go Trinity. Forget this notion of yours!' He could be a worthy son, this boy with the burning eyes and distant hopes. He had been reared in ignorance and poverty through no fault of his own, and now he would have the opportunity denied to him since birth. 'Now! What say you to that?'

Eamonn hesitated briefly before turning to leave. As he placed his hand on the door-knob, Valentine spoke again. 'If, after that, you still wish to be a Roman priest, I will not stand in your way!' The young man's considered reply startled him.

'I am grateful to you, but time is not on my side. I must go now.' He tried to put into words the overwhelming sense of urgency which he felt. 'I do not expect you to understand, but,' he faltered, as if trying to find the right words. 'I heard a heavenly summons, from the Bell. The Bell of Time. I can ignore it at my peril.'

'The Bell of Time? 'Tis but a legend,' Valentine laughed, wondering if his perception of Eamonn had been wrong. Perhaps he was looking for too much in him. A mysterious bell heard on stormy nights was a ridiculous, outlandish notion, fodder for fireside tales, and the landlord made no attempt to disguise his opinion. 'Of course,' he added hastily as the boy hung his head, 'I understand very well why you might be so deceived, for even I have experienced strange emotions amid the height of a violent storm, when the Bell is supposed to ring. Especially here, where every mountain and tree bears its own lore. And the wind – it will play fearsome tricks with a man's hearing.'

Eamonn thought of the wind, and the wailing howls which sounded nightly through the peat cabins of the Poorlands. Some believed that they were the cries of the souls in purgatory, asking for prayers for the dead. The wind, he was sure, was an instrument of God's purpose, there to remind men of their mortality.

'The sound which I heard was beautiful beyond description; so

173

pure and blessed that it could have but one origin. It could only have come from heaven and I was meant to hear it!'

Valentine stared hard at the boy. He felt like hitting him. For some moments he tried desperately to understand, to see things as this young man did. But he would never comprehend Eamonn's motivation. It was not God, for God was common to everyone. Neither was it a perfectly understandable attempt to escape from the grinding poverty of the Irish peasantry, for Eamonn had rejected his offer of a comfortable life.

'I have no desire to see you wasting your life in the service of the Church of Rome, but I promised Grace that I would help you, and for her sake I will be your patron. When the present hostilities have ceased, and with the approval of your bishop, you may go to France!' He silenced Eamonn's flood of gratitude with a request. 'No one is to know of this,' Major Valentine smiled wanly, 'for it would not help my family's reputation if word were to get about that one of Whitechurch blood was financing the making of a Popish priest.'

Eamonn O'Lochlainn left the house, more running than walking. Valentine watched until he had gone from sight, wondering if his first call would be at Grace's new home. He could hardly believe that he had committed himself to sending him to the priesthood. Yet he could not imagine Eamonn preaching treason or rebellion – the lad was too innocent, too unworldly. And this was the only way left for him to show Grace how much he loved her, and how much he would miss her.

◇ ◇ ◇

Grace O'Lochlainn was dressed like any other peasant woman in a homespun skirt and shawl as she set about hoeing the small plot of ground at the back of her new home. She had been shocked to find the MacOwen house in such a condition and was determined to reinstate it to its former fine appearance. The old Healing House of the MacOwen's had had a special place in her heart since childhood, when it housed the Staff, and she vowed that it would come to no harm during her occupancy. In time, she hoped that the young man of the house would be able to return, when he was older and wiser, and he would probably be relieved to know that his hereditary home was in good hands, and not in the possession of the Agent Coyle. She also hoped that her own family would welcome her back to the close, when that time came. Perhaps after Sosanna and Eamonn had left. Then her mother would be glad of her company.

Her hands and her back were aching for the first time in years, but she felt strangely content and at peace with herself. Her life with Henry Valentine had ended but she had learned many things while living under his roof and travelling with him. She learned what it was like to have a warm bed, a full belly and a dry roof. She had read many books, and had seen how the rich and poor lived in other nations and she knew, as few others could appreciate, the absolute poverty and misery of her own people which had few parallels anywhere in Europe. Henry Valentine talked about poorhouse provision for the old, and workhouses for the young, of the deserving and the undeserving, claiming that poverty was the result of stubborn refusal to comply with the law. Grace put some extra energy into her hoeing. She also could be stubborn.

As the sun began to set, Grace filled a pail from the well. The grass around it had been recently scythed, as if someone, she suspected Coyle, was preparing the house for his own occupation. For the first time she wondered how people would feel about her having stepped into the shoes of a dead woman. She was quite well used to living under the disapproving eye of the populace, and, she told herself, people had too many worries of their own to concern themselves overmuch with her. They would forget in time. As she worked she saw a woman approach the house. Grace had grown used to being alone over the past number of years, and now she felt strangely apprehensive.

'Good health, Grace O'Lochlainn!' called a voice which she recognised as Annie Dunn's.

'Mistress Dunn!' Grace's voice betrayed her relief. 'My sight is not the best! I did not know it was you!'

'Too many hours spent reading by candlelight will take their toll on the eyes,' scolded Annie. 'I suppose you have not changed your bad habits!'

'No!' smiled Grace, 'although I may not have the same selection of books as before.'

'The only book you need is the Holy Bible, and thankfully no shortage has yet been reported.' Grace did not share her friend's views, but their differences were amicable. She invited Mistress Dunn into the house.

'I came at Tom's behest to ask you to bide at Dunn's Hill for a while. He will clear out the small barn for your use.'

'Thank you!' Grace smiled her gratitude at their thoughtfulness, 'but this poor house is where I will stay until I can go home.'

'Do you think you will be safe?' Mistress Dunn sounded doubtful.

'Did not the lepers of old find sanctuary here? Why not an outcast like myself?'

May 15th 1780

'MY FATHER SAYS it was a good sign that your mother was buried in the rain. It means her sins are washed away.' Briony offered Owen this small comfort as they settled into their hiding place.

The three-arched bridge below the forge was a popular rendezvous point for many, from courting lads and lasses to the men of the Welsh Horse. It was also a hidden playground for the children of the village, who could give their parents the slip for hours on end as they hid under the arches. Here small pebbled islands like miniature beaches had formed around the stone pillars, and the ivy hung down so thickly in places that three eerie green caverns, like witches' dens, were formed. Only the most intrepid adventurers, like Briony and Owen, ventured under the middle arch. Briony, who should have been making his way up to Kilbroney to weed his great-aunt's potatoes, had persuaded his grieving friend to join him.

'He says that it was hopeful, that it rained,' continued Briony, 'for now you can be sure your mother will rest in peace.'

'Murtagh Fegan knows more than his prayers,' Owen replied sharply. His sense of helplessness and grief could not be understood by his companion, yet he was glad of his company. The Widow and the other women of the valley fed and cosseted him but they were forever praying and lamenting and telling him to keep his heart up. At least with Briony he could express his anger, and his desire for revenge.

'Do you know who is living in my house now?' Owen asked Briony. 'Grace O'Lochlainn. My mother always called her the Planter's Whore! And now she's the mistress of MacOwen land!'

'She is Master Eamonn's sister!' Briony replied cautiously. His father and mother always talked about Mistress O'Lochlainn in hushed tones, especially in his presence. Murtagh had warned his son to keep his mouth shut when it came to subjects about which he knew nothing.

The attention of the boys was diverted by the sound of thudding hooves on the bridge above. Briony stuck his head through the fronds of hanging ivy to see who the riders were. He heard voices, and motioned Owen to be silent.

'Who is it?' urged Owen.

'Soldiers! 'Tis the Welsh Horse.' Briony cocked his ear, listening intently to what was being said.

The voices on the bridge sounded urgent. Then they ceased. Briony returned to sit beside Owen, and his eyes were wide with excitement.

'They are leaving, Owen! The bold rapparees are leaving for France! And I am going with them!'

❖ ❖ ❖

The time was approaching for Makepeace and Donal to leave the close, and both had reason to regret their impending departure. Yet news of the arrival of Captain Walls at the Barrack soon dispelled any notion they had of lingering. Makepeace was well prepared for the voyage, and had added a few new items to his belt.

'You never know,' he warned Donal, 'what 'twill be like in France. It could be hard enough to put your hand on a decent nit comb.' He had spruced up his boots and hat and put on his newly laundered breeches, declaring that there was no sense arriving in a foreign land with the look of a beggarman.

On the eve of their departure, he looked around for Donal, who was nowhere to be seen.

'Away like a tomcat!' said Makepeace crossly. He was annoyed at his foster son's indiscreet attentions towards the betrothed daughter of the house, and if Donal thought that no one had noticed those exchanged glances and contrived meetings, he was wrong. Makepeace was painfully aware of them, and, he suspected, so was Mistress O'Lochlainn. It was clear that Thady was particularly sensitive about Sosanna, which made Donal's behaviour all the worse. Makepeace hobbled to the doorway to see if there was any sign of the young man. He still walked with a limp, but he had discarded his crutch. A stout blackthorn stick was all he needed now. It would also be useful, he said to himself, for fending off attackers. Makepeace had never in his life struck a man, but he maintained darkly that God's holy wrath could be a fearsome sight.

He had the Widow Fearon to thank for his present state of good health, and though she dabbled in ancient rites more decadent even than Popery, he was grateful for her healing touch. She had shouldered him around for an hour or so every day until he had got the feel of walking without his crutch. They were an unlikely pair, the preacher and the half-witch, but he enjoyed her company and the banter which passed between them. His evangelical seeds, however, fell on stony ground.

'Salvation?' she had cried, 'you daren't talk to me about salvation! I had one bad dose of it last Christmas after swallowing a clocked duck egg. Talk about churning my insides! They were running out of me from both ends. No harm to you, but I wouldn't thank you for another duck egg.'

Makepeace, confused, resolved that he too would leave the duck eggs to the ducks, but felt that he should soldier on with his appointed task. 'Scripture tells us,' he persisted, 'that a man must be born again!'

'Well, if that same man had got the dose I'd got, he would have been wishing he never had been born at all.'

'You're a hopeless case, woman! I am talking about your soul, not your body!'

'Let me tell you, 'tis the smart boy as can separate one from the other without getting himself hanged. I'll thank you, but 'tis my wish to hold both together for the time being.'

Having given up on finding Donal, the Dissenter took off his spectacles to polish them. A familiar voice called.

'Damn it, if you're not a good-looking man without them things on your nose!' The Widow was paying a last visit.

'I cannot see without them,' he explained to her. 'You're a fortunate woman to be blessed with such good sight.'

'Good sight?' she exclaimed. 'I could see the toe-nails of a goat in Cooley. But 'tis not your sight or the lack of it that worries you now, is it? I know when there's something ailing you, for you have a quiet look about you.'

Makepeace wondered what she meant by 'quiet', although he was touched by her concern. He asked her to step into the cabin as he had a proposal to put to her, and it would not be easy for him.

'I have thought it over,' he said, 'and there's no doubt left in my mind, that you're the only woman that will do!'

The Widow listened attentively as the Dissenter continued. Her face softened, and tears welled up in her eyes. Then she blew her nose loudly into her kerchief.

'Please tell me you'll agree,' Makepeace coaxed, 'and when I come home from France with my fortune made, yours will be the first door I'll head for!'

The Widow considered his tender request before replying.

'You didn't even have to ask me! I'll take care of your wee dog like he's my own flesh and blood!'

❖   ❖   ❖

In a quiet corner of the inn at Hill Town, Ned Maguire picked his teeth with a quill as he contemplated his plan of action once again. He had already been well paid for his services, but looked forward to increasing his profit before the night was out. Then flouncing up his soup-stained lace jabot, he paid the innkeeper for his meal and left by the back door. His straggly whiskers thinly camouflaged a face disfigured by the scars of a smallpox epidemic which had wiped out the rest of his family. Ned Maguire considered himself one of life's survivors, for the luck which had spared him then had never left him, as he steadily gained a reputation among the smugglers of Iveagh as a trustworthy middleman. It was unfortunate that the price of his survival was often the liberty of others, but Maguire had little sympathy for the weak or the foolish. He saddled his horse in the yard, where the innkeeper had provided him with stabling for his beast in return for services rendered. The inn was well used to the coming and going of shady characters and to the subsequent visitation of the law officers, for Hill Town, situated on a crossroads between Newry and the coast, was a recognised centre for contraband. As the inn benefited both directly and indirectly from this illicit trade, Maguire was always facilitated and no questions were asked.

The smuggler's sharp eyes scanned the sleepy square, empty except for an old women smoking, as he prepared to ride to Kilbroney. He liked to vary his route as much as possible for he trusted no one, and the beggars around the Bolie would turn him in for the price of a draught of ale. This time he chose to travel through the small tracks and sheep-paths out onto the Poorlands, for he had an important mission to carry out, and if everything went well, he could afford to lie low through the following winter. He galloped over the open ground past Rooslieve before turning to descend into the valley where lay the O'Lochlainn close. He reined in quickly as he noticed, in the distance, a small group of people outside Thady's cabin. Dismounting, he continued on foot to where he would have a clearer view of the close.

'Revellers!' he groaned in exasperation. 'The wedding must be in the morning.' On closer inspection he decided that they were only the neighbour's children, out for some diversion. He paused for a moment before continuing onwards. No one would pass any remarks if another body joined the party.

In the byre below the close the fugitives listened as Ned Maguire outlined his plan. They would be picked up by a French ship shortly before dawn, which would have them safely in La Rochelle within a week, weather permitting.

'But how will they know where to pick us up?' asked Donal.

'Commodore O'Farrell will be waiting beyond the bar. When he sees the beacon flash on Knock Shee, he will send in a dinghy to pick you up at the cove of Ballyedmond. He has been there before, to deliver certain goods which would be otherwise hard to obtain,' answered Maguire.

'And he has never been caught?' Seán queried excitedly. Foreign privateers and contraband agents were not his usual fare.

'O'Farrell? There is a price on his head that would tempt a less honest man than myself!' answered Maguire airily.

'And the beacon? Who lights it?' put in William Dwyer, who had appeared in the doorway. Maguire was irritated by the merchant, whose presence was not necessary to the operation.

'We'll leave that aside for the minute, while we come to the small matter of payment,' said the smuggler. 'You realise of course that this will be an expensive undertaking.' He whispered a figure in Donal's ear.

'Fifteen sovereigns?' cried Donal. 'Where would we find that amount of money? 'Tis a king's ransom!'

Ned Maguire coughed discreetly. 'That's my price, MacArtain. Why, 'tis a risky business dealing with the French! I could hang for it yet!'

MacArtain looked coldly at the smuggler, knowing that they had no choice but to meet his terms. They haggled over the price and eventually Maguire agreed to accept twelve sovereigns, 'being sympathetic as I am to your cause.' Between them Makepeace and Donal could raise no more than eight, which the Dissenter had sewn into his coat lining. As Maguire rose to his feet in a symbolic gesture of farewell, William Dwyer spoke again.

'Twelve sovereigns? I'll make up the difference!' The merchant produced his fat purse. The bartering continued for a while before Dwyer spat on his hand and they shook in agreement.

'Thank you, William Dwyer!' said a humbled Donal. 'I will be forever in your debt.' He bowed gratefully while Makepeace murmured a prayer of thanks.

'You will never know how relieved I'll feel just to know that the two of you are safely on your way to France!' declared William with such feeling that Donal wondered uncomfortably if he had an inkling of his affection for Sosanna. He wished that things had been different, but he knew that he would never forget the girl, no matter how he tried. Makepeace, his faith in human nature restored, shook William Dwyer's hand with fervour and congratulated him on his fine patriotic gesture. He, too, suspected that the merchant would be glad to see the back of his rapscallion of a foster son.

'We leave in about four hours time,' declared Ned Maguire, after carefully counting his money. 'You may as well take some rest now, for you sail on the morning tide.'

❖ ❖ ❖

Sosanna hugged her knees by the fireside as her mother brushed her tousled hair. It would be the last time she would enjoy this nightly ritual, for the next night would be spent under the roof of William Dwyer, her husband.

'Young Mistress Dwyer! That's what they'll be calling you!' mused Eily as she admired the sheen on her daughter's hair. 'When you walk down the street on a fair day they'll be stepping aside to give you room to pass! And when you go to your feather bed at night, you'll have a real lamp to light your way, and won't be depending on the starlight through the thatch.'

Suddenly, and without explanation, Sosanna leapt to her feet and ran out of the cabin. Some neighbours were arriving at the close to wish her well on the eve of her marriage, as was the local custom, but she paid no heed to their greeting. She found her favourite spot behind the well, where she could nurse her sorrows in private. The girl had made her decision to marry Master Dwyer and was not inclined to change her mind. The O'Lochlainns had never known anything but poverty and living from one season to the next in fear of a failed crop and consequent eviction. She knew how Thady had struggled to keep his family together, working night and day to raise the means to pay his Hearth Tax. She knew that he had never recovered from the shame of losing his elder daughter to the landlord. For all these reasons, she was determined to embark on a loveless marriage with a man three times her age. Yet when her mother had mentioned the starlight through the thatch...

At first he had seemed to be the answer to her prayers, but that was before she had met Donal MacArtain. Then Sosanna began to notice things about William Dwyer, and to make unfavourable comparisons. His breath stank, while Donal's was sweet. His flesh was soft and flaccid, while Donal's was firm and muscular. But most of all, there was the contrast between their hopes and their dreams. The older man wished for nothing more than a warm bed and a docile wife to nurse him into old age. The younger had opened her eyes to visions of a new life in a new world. All in all, it would have been easier if she had never met Donal MacArtain.

❖ ❖ ❖

Thady was in his element as Giddyhead Magee arrived at the close at the request of his intended son-in-law, William Dwyer. The piper was settled on a three-legged milking stool at the cabin door, where he began to pump up the bellows on his pipes. The Buller was among those who claimed that Giddyhead had no rhythm, but it did not stop him appearing on the scene at the first skirl of the pipes. For people who led dull and weary lives, day in, day out, any diversion or excuse for a celebration was welcome. Minnie the Fox of Knockbarragh had made the trip over the mountain, 'just out of nosiness,' Eily confided to the Widow Fearon. As the 'Foxes' had a reputation for being light-fingered, the woman of the house resolved to keep her eye on Minnie until she saw the back of her.

As a few dancers stepped forth outside the cabin the Buller voiced a complaint to his host. 'Can he only play the one tune? Reels, hornpipes – his all sound the same to me.'

'If he was any good,' replied Thady, 'what the devil would take him up Kilbroney?'

The old women shuffled into the house to vie with each other for a place at the hearth, where they lit up their clay pipes and spat into the fire. There they discussed a range of medical ailments concerning parts of the body never mentioned when the men were around. Silence descended as Thady made an appearance in the doorway. 'I'm like a stranger in my own house, for I can get neither next nor near the fire. Move over there till I get my arm around you!' The laughs and chirps changed to delighted and unconvincing protests as Thady produced yet another gift from the worthy merchant of Clonduff, a bottle of sweet brown Spanish wine which he slopped into a bowl so that everyone could partake of a sip.

Outside, a paler liquid, synonymous with such occasions, was being furtively passed around from mouth to mouth in a crude earthenware jar. Young lads in ill-fitting breeches gathered by the ditch, sharp-eyed as a line of crows, some waiting for the opportunity of having a sup of poteen when their mothers were not looking, others waiting for a beguiling smile from one of the colleens around the piper. The same lasses did not seem to be aware of the presence of any other than themselves and the seventy-year-old piper.

As darkness fell Seán attempted to light a warming fire in the yard of the close, while Cáit Murphy and other mothers dragged their offspring kicking and struggling off to bed. ''Twill be a good fire when it lights!' he informed the Buller, who had little faith in Seán's attempts at kindling.

'Stand back and leave it to me! I wonder at you wanting a fire on such a night. It's the warmest so far this year.' Seán did not reveal the real reason for the fire. He had been asked to divert the company's attention, to make way for the departure of Makepeace and Donal.

Giddyhead Magee had fallen asleep, but the dancing, accompanied by an impromptu orchestra of seasoned lilters, the beat of an upturned cooking pot and many tapping feet, was livening up. Eily was coaxed into a burl around the yard with the Buller. Carried away by the euphoria of the evening, Thady, the magnanimous host, decided on the spur of the moment to kill the rooster for soup. The unfortunate bird had had its neck pulled and feathers plucked before Eily, who personally tended the fowl, knew what was going on.

'That's what I get for dancing at my own front door,' she snapped at Thady, angrily snatching the bird from his clutches. 'This was the finest rooster in Kilbroney!' she lamented. 'We'll never see as good as his like again.'

'Not at all, woman,' admonished Thady. 'That old bird was crowing cock-a-doodle before I married you.'

An hour later broth was bubbling in the pot. By then the mood had changed. Someone was singing a song about his dead mother; many were crying, including those who did not know the singer's mother. It was a fitting climax to a great gathering, thought a tearful Thady as he joined in the dolorous refrain. Almost no one noticed Sosanna return to the cabin and ascend the ladder to her loft.

❖ ❖ ❖

The Dissenter sat uneasily astride the Buller's donkey, nervously clutching the makeshift reins.

'I'm grateful to you, man!' he said to Seán. 'I'm grateful to all of ye. Tell the Buller I will tether him by the shore and he will find him there tomorrow.'

'Don't overly concern yourself about that donkey,' Seán assured him. 'The Buller would tell you himself that he couldn't give the beast away. I don't know how many times he sold it at Hill Town fair and it made its own way back every time.'

'I didn't think there were men as soft as that around here!' declared Makepeace, doubtfully considering the Buller's methods.

'Oh, we're all hard men in Kilbroney. The trouble is that we have our soft spots.'

Ned Maguire, who had not a soft spot in his body, was growing impatient. It was time to go, but there was no sign of Donal MacArtain. There was some singing in progress above at the close, and he hoped that the young fugitive would not be so foolish as to show his face to the gathering.

'I suppose he's out bloody whoring somewhere,' Maguire seethed. He did not like any impediment to his carefully laid plans, and certainly not at this stage. It was an otherwise perfect night for their journey, with a young moon in the sky. Marcas Brennan would have the beacon ready to ignite and the French ship would be waiting for the signal from Knock Shee. They would then be set to sail on the morning tide. The operation had been carefully planned and now this young upstart was holding everything up! Maguire saw a figure coming from the direction of the river and he gritted his teeth. He was sorely tempted to abandon the whole plan and to ride back home, but he had twelve sovereigns in his pocket and did not intend to part with them yet. To his further exasperation he found that it was not Donal MacArtain who approached, but Thady O'Lochlainn's scholarly son, Eamonn.

'God save you Eamonn, lad!' called Makepeace. 'Did you see any sign of that rascally MacArtain?'

It was clear that Eamonn neither knew of nor cared about the whereabouts of Donal, for his eyes were glazed and his breath was short.

'If I didn't know better,' muttered Seán, 'I would say that he's been drinking.'

'What ails you, son?' enquired a concerned Makepeace. 'You look as though you've seen a ghost!'

'I have been to see the Bishop, brother Makepeace!' answered Eamonn. 'By the will of God I will soon be joining you in France, for He has seen fit to provide the means.'

'Ghost? 'Twas a fairy he must have seen,' scoffed Seán, 'with a full crock of gold!'

'Do not mock,' reprimanded Eamonn in a stern voice, 'for God has seen fit to work through the least of men.'

'I wish you good fortune, Eamonn,' said Makepeace warmly, 'although if 'twas I who had come by a fortune, there is many a use I would have for it without bursting the coffers of Rome!'

'If your young man does not come soon, you'll be leaving without him,' Ned Maguire butted in sourly. He was beginning to get distinctly unfavourable forebodings about the whole operation.

To his and the Dissenter's immense relief, Donal appeared out of the darkness. A meagre bundle was flung over his shoulder as he took his leave of the brothers O'Lochlainn.

'God save you all!' he cried. 'I will never forget you!' Maguire had started off, and there was nothing to do but to follow him.

❖ ❖ ❖

Eamonn stood in the shadows watching the last of the revellers leave. Later, he walked past the ebbing bonfire, stepping over the snoring piper, who had fallen asleep in the doorway. The Buller and Paddy O'Linden were still with his father, muttering in subdued tones about past ages and the easy times young folk had compared to the youth of the hungry thirties. He bade them goodnight, and kneeled to say his night prayers. After a few moments his rosary was interrupted by the sound of sobbing from the loft above. He softly called Sosanna's name, and when no reply came he climbed the ladder to where his sister slept. Reaching out to the trembling form huddled in the shadows he spoke.

'Sosaí, a chroí, what ails you? Did anybody...'

'No!' she sobbed, moving away from him. 'Nobody touched me!'

'Well, did anyone throw a cross word at you? I would not see you crying like this, and you to be a bride!'

'I don't want to be a bride,' she choked, 'and I'm not crying!' She turned to sob on his shoulder. He hated to see her so unhappy yet was unable to offer any comfort.

'Hush!' he said helplessly. 'Your eyes are swollen and it spoils your good looks.'

'I don't care about my looks!' she answered crossly, pulling herself away. Then, being aware of Eamonn's injured expression, she reassured him. 'No, Eamonn, nobody offended me! I have only hurt myself!' He looked puzzled. 'Oh, I would not expect you to have noticed anyway! You're only concerned with your own ambitions. No, I am sorry...'

'You are right, Sosanna! I always say the wrong thing. And I did not notice how unhappy you had become!' he whispered.

In the end, it was she who ended up offering reassurance and comfort to her brother.

'I suppose,' she sighed, 'that all brides get a bit forlorn on the eve of their weddings.'

'If you like,' he offered, 'I'll sit by you till you fall asleep.'

They were close in age, Eamonn and Sosanna. She had always been the more robust of the two, the one who would brave Murphy's gander while he would cower in fear. He had no doubt that she would make the best of things and in time forget her sorrows once she had been installed as the merchant's wife. He would miss her when she had gone, but then, it would be but a short time before he too left home. His thoughts returned to the miracle of Major Valentine's offer, and his heart rejoiced once more. He wished that he could share his news with Sosanna, but he would remain faithful to the promise he had given to his benefactor. Only Father Mackey, his confessor, and Grace, of course, could share his secret.

'They say that it is as well for us that we never know what really lies ahead,' he said to his sister, but Sosanna had fallen asleep.

Chapter Twelve

May 15th 1780

SERGEANT POLLARD WATCHED his informant leave and grinned wryly. This was his opportunity to win a few honours to take home to Wales. It would not be easy, as there was no knowing how Major Valentine would react to the news, but it was his duty to report to Captain Walls, a man he did not like, but respected as a good soldier. Walls would know how to handle the matter.

There were a few details yet to be ascertained, such as when the traitors were to leave and who had assisted them, but one thing was certain: Thady O'Lochlainn and his family were involved in treasonable conspiracy. Sergeant Pollard chuckled to himself. Everyone knew about Grace O'Lochlainn, everyone, that was, except for the Major's bride-to-be and Captain Walls. It would not be easy for Valentine to hear that the woman who had shared his bed belonged to a family of rebels. He wondered which of them had fired the barn; that information, the Sergeant decided, would come out in time. He gave his boots a quick wipe and went off to report to the Captain.

❖   ❖   ❖

Fanny Ward was in a panic. Half the county had been invited to Kilbroney House to meet Henry's future wife, yet he was taking little interest in organising the household for the party. Grace O'Lochlainn had departed, most disloyally thought Fanny who had been left to cope with the arrangements all by herself. On Madam Hall's advice a band of 'gentlemen fiddlers', as they called themselves, had been hired from Newry, as well as Lord Bristol's favourite bard, the harper Hempson, although one never knew how reliable such people were. Her biggest problem concerned the kitchen. Madam Hall had insisted that a country cook simply

189

could not be entrusted with such a task, and had recommended a Dublin chef. Now there was pandemonium below stairs with raised voices and unpleasant odours. And on top of everything, Henry was nowhere to be found.

Fanny stood outside the kitchen door trying to summon up the courage to face the affray within. Clouds of steam hit her in the face as she confronted the protagonists. The cook, her face beet-root, pushed past her to pick up a large soup cauldron which she wielded like a battle-shield. 'There! Will that suit you, you gob-shite?' she yelled at a white-clad male who wore a Gallic mous-tache. In response, the chef raised a butcher's cleaver menacingly. Fanny watched in despair; her presence seemed to have little effect on the confrontation. What was most humiliating, though, was the disproportionate number of minions turning the spit, stirring the pot, or otherwise standing witness to her humiliation.

'God damn it!' Fanny cried suddenly, 'we will be the laughing stock of the country by now. Get about your business! All of you!' She shooed away the onlookers as if they were straying poultry. Fanny considered for a moment how best to handle the situation. She had a niggling feeling that these people were laughing at her discomfiture, so she dispatched a lad to fetch the Agent Coyle. Mention of the Agent's name took effect, as there was an imme-diate buzz of industry about the kitchen.

As she closed the kitchen door behind her, she breathed a prayer of thanks for Coyle. And all this chaos was because of Doctor Butler. The bride's father had lofty gastronomical expecta-tions which were unlikely to be met by Cook, an excellent provider of everyday fare who undoubtedly baked the best bread in the land, but quite out of her depth when it came to soufflés, flummeries or galantines.

Shrugging aside the problem Fanny removed herself to her boudoir, a haven of scent and silk. Her maid had prepared her best wig for the evening party, with a sprinkling of lilac butterflies to compliment the lilac satin gown of French design.

'We are supposed to be at war with the French, and yet we copy their clothes, their food, their hair,' she mused, while the maid, who lived on a diet of potatoes and oats, agreed.

❖ ❖ ❖

Briony Fegan was going to France to join the Irish Brigade. The little boy had listened in awe to the bold Dissenter's tales of bravado and stirring feats, and was determined to follow in his footsteps. He watched the guests arriving at the gates of Kilbroney House. A plan was ticking over in his mind as he opened the gates for the coaches in the hope of getting something in return, for he would, after all, need some money for what he had in mind.

He had thought of leaving his mother an explanatory letter, but she could not read. His father had not learned anything beyond copying his own name and, besides, there was always the possibility that he might ask some untrustworthy person to translate. He imagined Sergeant Pollard and his men being dispatched to France to bring him home. Another war could start on account of him.

The boy leapt to his feet and straightened his back as he pictured the consequences in his mind: Briony Fegan the returning hero, being led through the village in chains, for that was what happened to all Irish heroes. He would be riding a great white horse, for a hero deserved at least a horse, while his mother and sisters wept along the road. He would make a noble speech before they hanged him. The trouble was, they did not hang people in Rostrevor these days, and he would have to be taken to Newry or Downpatrick where nobody would know him. In Rostrevor a man would only get a hard flogging, and that did not appeal to Briony at all. There was little glory in a flogging, for he had once been a witness to one, before his mother dragged him away. The victim had squealed like a pig for slaughter, and had wet himself like an infant. In the stories Briony had been told, heroes endured pain without flinching.

On further reflection, he decided that there was much to be done before he joined the ranks of dead heroes. He would inform Owen MacOwen of his plans – he could consider Owen a comrade-in-arms of a sort, and would extract a promise bound by some terrible oath. He left his post by the gates in search of Owen so that he might finalise his plans.

❖ ❖ ❖

Another man who knew about the departure of Donal MacArtain and the old Dissenter was Father Mackey. Eamonn O'Lochlainn had insisted on telling him, even though he would rather not have known. Some Protestant military men did not understand the sacred nature of the confessional, and assumed that a priest's refusal to give forth its darker secrets amounted to treasonable behaviour. People were forever coming to him with their secrets, even though he did not always want to hear them. He had found out about the fugitives in O'Lochlainn's from Eamonn, who was earnestly trying to convert the heretic Agnew.

The Parish Priest had fed and watered his exhausted grey mare which had carried him to Newry and back that very day, and now he finished off Compline, meticulously reciting every last intercession of the Divine Office. Since his ordination, Father Mackey had been as attentive to his Office as any Benedictine monk, and in spite of the weight of parochial duties never retired to bed without having said his night prayers.

Following Eamonn O'Lochlainn's revelations concerning his generous new benefactor his meeting with the Bishop had been most urgent. He had had to wait for some hours while Bishop Lennon met with the Town Seneschal to discuss the siting of a Catholic church outside Newry. The wily prelate had used every possible resource to soften the resistance of this influential town official, and Father Mackey had sniffed the fumes of something stronger than communion wine when the red-faced Seneschal emerged from the modest episcopal residence. A diminutive chaplain who had been providing the Kilbroney priest with a running commentary of the proceedings, as overheard from the keyhole, ushered him into the Bishop's presence.

Dr Lennon listened to Father Mackey's story. A planter – no, worse than a planter, a Whitechurch had declared his intention of becoming the benefactor of Eamonn O'Lochlainn. The fact that the boy's sister had flaunted her immoral relationship with the same benefactor for many years was a terrible scandal in the eyes of the priest. To accept Major Valentine's patronage without question would imply acceptance of her sinful behaviour, and allow other innocent young girls to fall foul of such philanderers.

'And you say he is prepared to finance young O'Lochlainn's education entirely?' asked the Bishop. Father Mackey smelled defeat. The Bishop was a hard-nosed church diplomat who would not risk offending such an influential landlord as Henry Valentine, nor would he turn down such a sizeable donation for the sake of the morals of a few hypothetical Kilbroney girls. Besides, the priest noted sadly, his lordship had a soft spot where Eamonn O'Lochlainn was concerned, perhaps because they both came from the same background. He should have felt reassured by Dr Lennon's approval, but the feeling of unease which dogged him whenever the matter of Eamonn's vocation was raised simply would not go away.

Father Mackey concluded his nightly litany and prepared for bed, remembering that Thady O'Lochlainn's younger daughter was to be wed in the morning. He would be glad to see her safely out of the parish and in the care of the Parish Priest of Clonduff, for the O'Lochlainn women brought trouble with them. Then, regretting such an uncharitable thought, he sank to his knees once more and prayed for the salvation of Grace O'Lochlainn.

❖ ❖ ❖

As the carriage rolled out from Narrow Water, destined for the party at Kilbroney House, Letitia Butler silently contemplated her future as the wife of Henry Valentine. Sitting beside her, her mother chatted incessantly with Madam Hall about arrangements for the wedding at the end of the month as if she, Letitia, were an optional decoration for the event. She looked blankly at the ivy-clad medieval fort which had once stood sentinel over the narrow strait at the head of the lough. A few urchins, ankle-deep in the mud flats, were collecting shellfish in reed baskets, and one little girl caught her attention as she balanced an enormous load on her head. Letitia smiled wanly at the child and was rewarded with a curtsy which failed to topple the basket. Natural grace had come so easily to that simple child while she, a descendant of the noble house of Ormonde, had suffered long hours of deportment lessons to the same end.

Letitia was the only child of aging parents, who had grown quite used to having hopeful suitors ejected from the house. Henry Valentine was different. She had fallen in love with him seconds after their first meeting, attracted by his handsome looks and a smile which seemed to hide some secret sorrow. He was less exuberant, more distant than her other suitors, and beside him she felt clumsy, gauche and unworthy. She had been overwhelmed when the gallant Major had asked for her hand in marriage, and had vowed to do everything in her power to make herself worthy of his trust.

'Doesn't Letitia look so pretty this evening!' remarked Madam Hall in a kindly fashion, leaning over to rearrange a few curls on the young girl's coiffure. Letitia blushed and tried to draw the folds of her gown so as to hide a muddy mark on the creamy fabric. She must have brushed against a wheel while entering the coach. These things seemed to happen to her.

The coach took the main road past Clonallon Church into the townland of Moygannon, and in less than fifteen minutes had reached the entrance to Kilbroney House. A little boy opened the gates before the Narrow Water party and coyly reached out his hand in expectation of a gratuity.

'Drive on!' ordered Madam Hall. 'I think it is unwise to encourage begging.'

Letitia had noticed a few old crones along the roadside bent double under the weight of their burdens. This was the closest she had ever come to the ugliness of poverty and she did not like what she saw. She resolved to keep such people well away from the house when she returned as mistress.

The party was warmly welcomed by Fanny Ward, who, in between complimenting Letitia on her exquisite new gown, offered embarrassed apologies for the absence of her brother.

'I can't think what has delayed him!' she kept repeating to Dr Butler, who, having napped on the journey, seemed somewhat unsure of his present whereabouts. Letitia thought she noticed her future sister-in-law and Madam Hall exchange meaningful glances.

'For God's sake smile, Letitia!' her mother hissed. 'If anyone knows where his duty lies, Major Valentine does.'

❖ ❖ ❖

Henry Valentine rode hard against the wind in an effort to rid himself of a deepening melancholy. His horse galloped across the shore sending a spray of seawater in all directions. He turned to ride past Crag field towards the cherry plantation on the hill behind the Barrack. He did not want to be seen and the blossoming trees afforded him some cover before he emerged on the open ground above Dunn's Hill. In the distance lay the mountain of Leckan, but before that, the townland of Levallyclanowen.

'The Park,' he corrected himself. He had rarely visited this part of his property, but curiosity had induced him to see the MacOwen home, and to find out where Dervla MacOwen had died. The valley behind him was clothed in woodland of various hues, through which the distant chimneys and turrets of his own house protruded. As he passed, curious eyes peeped out from tiny cabins, and toiling men stopped to wonder at the sight of the gentleman rider. Henry brushed aside the notion that he could feel their hostility and spurred his horse onwards towards Slievenabroc and Leckan. He rode past the cairn of the first Owen, a pre-christian burial mound where the clans of Iveagh had often met to settle disputes. The southern slopes of Leckan were thick with bracken and heather and the horse made slow progress upwards, slipping now and again on loose gravel. To the east of the mountain was the distinctive two-storey Healing House, where Grace O'Lochlainn now lived.

He watched a thin trickle of smoke ascend from the chimney. It was a small miserable hovel by his standards, marginally better than the peat cabins of the Poorlands but in need of re-thatching.

Try as he might, he could not dismiss Grace from his mind. The residence might be of her own choosing, but he could not stand the thought of her living in damp miserable conditions as did the majority of his tenants. For the first time, he forced himself to think seriously about his stewardship. Somehow he had always imagined the simple peasants living in squalor through choice; they did not have the same delicate feelings of gentlefolk and were happier in such rustic surrounds. Yet Grace deserved to live in dignity, even though she chose to live with him no longer. He would have a word with Coyle about the thatching of the Healing House, and perhaps other cabins...

The precipice came on him quite suddenly, a sheer rock-face on the mountainside, a trap for the unwary in a God-forsaken place. Looking down from horseback it seemed particularly forbidding, a chasm between Leckan and Slievenabroc, undoubtedly the place where the unfortunate MacOwen woman had lost her life.

'It could have happened accidentally,' he told himself with a sense of relief. 'She could have lost her way, or strayed here unawares...' It seemed a hollow excuse, for the woman would have known the area well. Perhaps, he thought, she was too distracted with worry to take due care. He realised that it was difficult for him not to accept at least some responsibility for the poor woman's death.

'Coyle should have informed me,' he said aloud. But when had he ever shown such interest in running the estate? He had always left things in the Agent's hands, relying on his superior local knowledge and judgement of the situation in hand.

The horse reared in panic as a stone struck his hindquarters. Hooves slithered and stumbled on the shelf of the cliff. The desperate rider struggled for control; he pulled at the reins and tried to soothe the beast as sods of loose turf and stones tumbled down the precipice. In spite of his efforts Valentine felt the ground disintegrate under him. The horse whinnied and snorted in terror.

'Whoa! Steady there!' he urged the frightened animal, finally hauling it back from the edge. Dismounting, he rubbed the sweat from his brow; he could not recall ever having been so frightened.

'Hush; you're safe now,' he soothed the horse, although his own heart was hammering. A sudden movement made him look to his right. There stood a boy on an elevated rock. The spindly youth with wild black hair watched him in silence.

'Damn you to hell, you rogue!' Valentine roared angrily. He raised his whip towards the boy. 'You might have killed both me and my horse!'

He expected the boy to run away, but Owen MacOwen stood his ground and stared back, his shoulders stiff with defiance. He was not to be intimidated by anyone, for he stood on the land of his fathers.

Valentine was shaken. He turned away from an encounter with the boy, whose identity he had guessed. He knew he could have him arrested and hanged for attempted murder, but there would be little satisfaction in that. The youth would become an innocent martyr, dying to avenge his mother, and the peasants of the Poorlands would only see another injustice, another wrong to be righted, and another cause to be fought for. He would send for the boy later and question him thoroughly, though, because he would almost certainly have been involved with the destructive acts of recent weeks. He might have to lock up MacOwen for a long time. The Major felt a certain amount of pity for the young lad, but this feeling was overruled by his belief in law and order.

The recollection of duty made him reach for his watch. He knew he should return home immediately, but an impulse made him turn from the direct route along the river and ride once again towards Levallyclanowen.

The Healing House wore an air of mystery in the half-light. A rush candle glimmered weakly from within as a shadowy figure stepped away from the open door. Valentine reined his horse to a halt.

Had Grace come out at that moment he would have gone to her, given up everything for the love of her, if only she would come to him with open arms as in the old days. His life, his future, hung in the balance. Would she come?

He watched until he saw the door close and the candle's glow extinguished. A chill numbed his heart as he rode back to Kilbroney House, to his duty.

From the Healing House, Grace had seen the approaching rider. Memories flooded back of their first meeting on the flaxfield so many years before, when he had singled her out from the other women. Now he was coming for her again, and everything would be as before! Her heart leapt as she removed her coarse overskirt and tidied a few wisps of stray hair. She saw him stop before the house. Had he come to her then, she would have broken every vow she had ever made and gone with him, be eternal damnation the price. She waited, heart pounding, hoping against hope, but he did not come to her. She closed the door and listened to the dying sound of retreating hooves. He had gone.

Chapter Thirteen

FROM THE COUNTY of Derry, by way of Armagh and Newry, through Ballyholland and the Bridge of Mayo where he was treated like a king, and finally through the townlands of Drumsesk and Drumreagh came the renowned harper, Denis Hempson. The bard's sightless eyes stared vacantly ahead as the guide led his ancient pony, a scraggy piebald which was almost as blind as its rider. The guide was a one-armed army veteran with red hair and a nose to match, the result of the excessive hospitality which they enjoyed along the road. His cheerful, gregarious nature rendered him incapable of remaining silent for more than a few minutes of his waking day, thus limiting his circle of friends but proving invaluable to a blind man. Hempson's guide kept his master in constant touch with the surrounding world, describing in cheerful detail the rolling countryside, the predominant foliage, the curious expressions on the faces of bystanders, the gait of passersby and other minutiae which most sighted folk would consider too trivial to mention. Plodding along the winding lane leading towards the village, the guide was at pains to describe the size and shape of the family who were sitting down to a feed of stewed cabbage in a roadside cabin.

'You did not have to mention the cabbage,' declared Hempson somewhat tetchily. 'I can smell it from here.'

The guide took no notice of his master's moods. He was always as cross as a weasel towards the end of a day on the road. He looked around for something else to distract Hempson's attention.

'Bedad! A big stout girl in a green skirt with an armful of turnips and she's wondering whether or not to pass us. You may take my word for it that they're fine turnips. As big as ever I've seen. Good day to you, ma'am. Brave looking sky!'

The shy girl passed them by without comment, her eyes trained on the path beneath her. Unfortunately, curiosity prompted her to cast a backward glance at the strangers. The guide had been expecting such interest.

'So one of the two of us has taken your fancy? Which is it to be? The blind bard or the armless soldier lad? You're lucky the rest of my bits are oiled and working, so don't be passing me by! Ah now, don't be so proud! The women flock round us every step along the way, from the Bridge of the Bann to the Bridge of Mayo. Musha! You'll not meet the like of us again in all your born days.'

Hempson usually enjoyed such encounters and would often throw in a few saucy remarks of his own, but with his journey's end in sight he was impatient to proceed. His back ached and his fingers were stiff in their woollen mitts.

'Move on there, and quit your nonsensical chatter!' he demanded.

Denis Hempson, now aged eighty-five, was held in high esteem, respected both by native and planter as a skilled practitioner of his art. He was one of the last of the ancient school of harpers, a distinguished performer, composer and poet. Like many of his colleagues he was old and blind, and had been an itinerant for most of his life. Tall and thin, Hempson's figure seemed moulded to the wire-strung harp which he kept by his side at all times, even in sleep. His long spindly nails were the badge of his profession, and he despised the younger generation of harpers who played gut strings with fleshy fingers. For those who suggested that he should discard the wires and restring his harp he had ready a sharp rebuff.

'I will play no other way, for there is no other way.'

Known widely as 'the man with two heads' because of an enormous growth on the back of his neck, Hempson was on the verge of marriage to a woman from the Inishowen peninsula in northernmost Ulster. For a man of eighty-five this was a brave step, and his friends had some doubt as to the suitability of his crippled bride. Hempson himself suggested that only the Devil could buckle together a lame woman and a blind man.

"Tis a pity you can't see the Cooley Mountains before you,' the guide was speaking still, 'for that profile is most certainly that of Fionn of the Fianna, God rest his soul.'

'How far have we to go?' interrupted the impatient master.

'We are about to enter the old town of Rory's Castle, where the bold Rory MacAongus lived and died. Rostrevor, they call it now. I can tell you in all honesty, Master, I've seen livelier graveyards. Before us is a brave size of a street with five green oaks in a row...'

'Never mind the trees. Can you see anybody about their business?'

'Aye, surely. There's two old boys under one of the trees. I see the smoke rising from their pipes so they must be awake.'

'Then quit babbling and ask them, as civilly as you can, the direction to Major Valentine's residence. And only the front approach, mind!'

The invitation to play in Rostrevor was one of a series which the old itinerant was pleased to accept. Although Lord Bristol had graciously provided him with a warm stone house near Magilligan, travelling had been in his blood since childhood and the acclaim of a new audience was food and drink to him. He was well paid for his efforts by the gentry and was currently benefiting from a nostalgic revival, as families of fashion tried to recreate the ways and customs of the chieftains of old. Neither was he averse to catching a penny or two at the crossroads along the route, throwing out a few tunes just for the fun of it.

In his youth, Hempson had travelled widely throughout Ireland and Scotland, and would recall, with considerable pride, his performance before Charlie the Pretender. He often mimicked the clipped English voice of the man for whom so many Scots and Irishmen had given their lives. He would not tell that story tonight, however. He expected the Valentines to be fiercely loyal to the Hanoverian throne, and experience had taught him that such folk possessed a poor sense of humour.

❖ ❖ ❖

Captain Walls grunted with satisfaction as he donned his silk evening hose and satin slippers. His military decorations had been laid out in the correct order and he surveyed them proudly. Yes, they would impress the country ladies and undoubtedly give him the chance to relate a few anecdotes concerning his exploits on the battlefield. The ladies usually quizzed him about the ceremonial behind the medals – what had the Lord Lieutenant said, and what had his lady worn? Women, he observed, were always impressed by a military uniform; women of every class, from Madam Ward's guests to the bands of camp followers who serviced the barracks. He did not object to the common soldiery keeping their women in tow, for the local peasant girls could be dangerous sirens.

He considered the news Sergeant Pollard had just delivered. Everything was working out to his satisfaction. He was particularly pleased to have the opportunity of shaking up that complacent Henry Valentine. If there was one type of person he despised, it was a soldier who neglected his duty. Captain Walls had one last glance in the mirror before his man sprayed a mild scent over his person.

'Henry Valentine, the crafty devil!' he chuckled to himself. 'I wonder what he'll say when we arrest his mistress!'

❖ ❖ ❖

A neat band of gentlemen fiddlers had been hired from Newry for the occasion, under the baton of a dapper Flemish organist who had recently settled in the town. Madam Ward personally supervised their positions behind the balustrade at the top of the stairs, directing the footmen to place the candles in a way which made the best display. When one of the fiddlers respectfully suggested a change, Madam replied, 'Nonsense! We can see you much better if you place the candles... thus!' The diminutive maestro raised his eyebrows to silence the protests of the band.

'Wait until she has gone!' he whispered, 'then we can put them where we can read the music.'

'Now maestro!' instructed Fanny. 'You will play as the guests arrive and for some dancing after supper. Please keep it lively. Yes, I suppose Herr Handel's music is quite acceptable but I would prefer something more "a la mode". You know that man from

Vienna everyone keeps talking about? No? Well, I didn't think you'd have heard of him...'

Fanny was disturbed by a commotion down in the hall, where the butler was refusing to admit a shabby looking old man. Fanny swore in exasperation. 'Oh, for God's sake chase him around to the back door, Donnan! If he waits, he may have a few crusts later on. Tomorrow perhaps! Oh, what an insensitive time for anyone to come begging. This sort of thing would never happen in Armagh.'

'Madam!' One of the gentlemen fiddlers attracted her attention by waving his bow.

'Yes? What is it you want? You have been told what is expected!' she barked crossly.

"Tis Hempson, ma'am!' the fiddler whispered urgently. 'That old man at the front door you have just ordered out. 'Tis Denis Hempson, the bard!'

'Bother!' she muttered, 'how was I to know? He looks like a tramp!' Changing her tone of voice and increasing its volume she descended the stairs.

'Why, Master Hempson!' she cried, 'welcome to this humble house!' She had been assured that such was the greeting to impress a bard. Old Hempson, totally blind from the age of three, was not so easily fooled. His eyes were useless, but his hearing was unimpaired.

'I thank you, ma'am!' he replied curtly. 'And I hope I do not have to wait till morning for those crusts you promised me!'

❖ ❖ ❖

Samuel McIntyre bolted his gate. Then he barred his cottage door and shuttered the windows. His wife, who was frying oatcakes in sizzling bacon fat, looked up from her task in concern.

'Why, 'tis not you they're seeking, lad!' she said.

'I'll take no chances!' replied the gamekeeper. He sat down at the table with his firearm and proceeded to rod the bore.

'Whoever burned the barns could be after me next! I've heard tell of baillifs and gamekeepers, good decent men and all knifed while abed!' He peered down the muzzle as his wife set a plate of oatcakes on the table in front of him, where a brimming jug of buttermilk sat in readiness.

'Here!' she ordered. 'Get that into you! I've heard enough talk about barns. Sure what was in them at this time of the year other than mouldy meal and a few rats, and who would mourn their passing?' She took off her greasy apron, pulled up a stool by the table and continued scolding. 'Now put that weapon away until you've thanked the Good Lord for the bountiful provision he has laid before us.'

McIntyre bit back the retort that he had worked bloody hard for those oatcakes without much help from the Good Lord, who tonight was providing the finest salmon and wild game for the table of his master. As his pious wife bowed her head in prayer, McIntyre's thoughts returned to his gun. This was not the first occasion on which he had felt vulnerable; at the best of times, he knew, he was an unpopular figure among the people of Kilbroney. He began to oil his gun while Mistress McIntyre sniffed in disapproval.

'Enjoy your oatcakes, girl, while you still can!' he advised.

◇ ◇ ◇

Denis Hempson was retuning his harp. To the average ear the instrument was at pitch, but Hempson could detect the smallest inaccuracy, to a fraction of a tone. For that reason, most bagpipes, fiddles and 'those perfidious harpsichords' offended his sensitive ears, but nothing compared with the high-pitched social chatter which made his present task so difficult.

'The squireens!' he muttered to the guide, who had so far resisted all attempts by Donnan the butler to remove him to the kitchen. 'They think that, because they have me here, it puts them in the same class as the chieftains of old! Yet the whole breed of them herded together would not make one of the least of the O'Neills.' Hempson cherished the memory of Owen Roe O'Neill, and took inspiration from his illustrious predecessor, the Derry harper Ruarí Dall Ó Catháin, who had defended the name of The

O'Neill before James of Scotland.

An unfamiliar sound interrupted his thoughts. 'What's that noise I hear, like pigs' crackling?' he snapped at the guide, who was crunching a mouthful of titbits.

'Nuts, Master Hempson,' came the answer. 'They're delicious! I'll steal a handful for you.'

'And what use has a man with no back teeth for nuts?' asked the irate bard. 'May they give you the devil of a belly-ache!'

The guide downed his mouthful, not because of his master's threatening tone but because of the close proximity of a glowering butler who could not accept that the bard, who was stationary, had any need of his guide for the remainder of the night. Hempson, meanwhile, contemplated a suitable programme for the evening. He liked to study his audience before making any firm decisions, and for a blind man that meant listening to the passing chatter. He was not impressed by what he heard. He was not fond of playing the music of Turlough O'Carolan, preferring instead his own compositions and arrangements. Tonight, he decided, he would make an exception, and begin with Carolan's 'Fanny Power' in honour of his hostess, who had been forgiven for her earlier *faux pas*. He would follow that with his own favourites, 'The Dawning of the Day' and 'The Coolin'. Then, depending on the response of his audience, he would offer an improvisation of his own, or a few lively dance tunes. There was no word yet of his host, Major Valentine, who might after all have his own requests to make. He swore loudly, to the distress of an ageing maiden nearby. A string had snapped and would have to be replaced before he could play anything at all.

❖   ❖   ❖

'Where have you been? I am mortified making up excuses for you!'

'I am sorry,' Henry Valentine replied, 'I was delayed.'

Fanny looked at her brother closely. 'You look wretched!' she exclaimed. 'What can have happened to you?'

'I will speak of it later. Do not distress yourself!' he urged. 'I must go and change.' He entered the house and marched up the stairs, past the fiddlers who were now going through their repertoire for the third time.

'Back to the *Allegretto Moderato!*' hissed the Flemish maestro, as all heads turned in curious pursuit of the Major.

Major Valentine's valet, who had been reduced to a nervous wreck while waiting for his master, all but lunged at him as he entered his dressing room, tearing off his hunting coat and pulling at his boots. Within a frantic ten minutes the riding garb had been replaced by evening dress; the valet charged around the room with a looking-glass before pronouncing Major Valentine ready to join his guests.

❖ ❖ ❖

The fare, at least, was excellent, mused Fanny as one remove followed another, with a splendid assortment of whimsical side dishes such as goose and winkle pie, tiny woodcock stuffed with spiced liver, and a delectable moulded brawn bearing the Whitechurch crest. There was the usual array of giant salmon, roast venison and a local speciality, succulent baby mountain goat. Denis Hempson, by choice, declined any fine dishes and ate only potatoes. Buttermilk was procured from the kitchen, to the disgust of the visiting chef, for it was the only beverage ever to pass the lips of the ancient bard. No one, he claimed, had ever died of poisoned buttermilk. His tastebuds were as sensitive as his hearing and he claimed the ability to tell the age and state of health of the cow from which the beverage originated.

In contrast to the bard, Dr Butler, Letitia's father, could not get close enough to the table. He was a man of ample proportions who had all the appearance of an elaborate confection, with a lavish, slightly *démodé* periwig, and a belly girded with a yellow satin waistcoat. It surprised no one when, during the course of the evening, the tortoiseshell buttons began to pop, one after the other.

After the supper the fiddlers commenced a medley of country dances, and a few game revellers formed a set in the hall. Letitia, encouraged by the many compliments her appearance had provoked, sought out Major Valentine to join her on the floor, and found him engrossed in conversation with Captain Walls. She asked her father to disengage him, but Dr Butler was polishing off the remains of a quivering blancmange on the sideboard. An exasperated Madam Hall quickly came to her rescue.

'Come now, Captain Walls! We ladies are simply dying to hear all the latest gossip from the Castle! Is it true that m'Lord Deputy has a new paramour?'

Walls, finding himself surrounded by several spotty adolescents and pasty dowagers, realised that all his military training had not equipped him to deal with the field manoeuvres of the county ladies of South Down. Raising his hands in a gesture of surrender, he was firmly ushered to a corner from which there was no visible means of escape. Letitia, detaching herself from the bevy, looked around for her fiancé, but he was nowhere to be seen.

❖ ❖ ❖

Henry Valentine stood on the terrace overlooking the dark waters of the lough. He quickly downed a brandy and called for another. Walls had to be wrong about the O'Lochlainn family's involvement with the outlaws. Grace, he knew, had had little contact with her people. That had been her choice, and theirs. At first he had liked to think that she had nothing in common with them any longer; now he knew better. Yet surely they would not harbour dangerous traitors...

He felt that Walls was mistaken, and yet doubt remained in his mind. The only time that Grace and he had ever quarrelled was on the subject of the seditious literature she had been reading, and her association with that fellow Dunn, who was clearly a radical. He knew little about the other O'Lochlainns except that they were simple peasants, and sadly the simple peasantry of Ireland accepted the authority of King and parliament in a very piecemeal fashion. Good laws were upheld, bad laws ignored. Valentine saw such discrimination as dishonourable, for the law was above everyone, and both good and bad laws – of which, he conceded, there were many – must be obeyed for the common good. There would be total anarchy if everyone recognised the law only as it suited himself, and rigid enforcement would become an unfortunate necessity.

A footman arrived with the decanter and placed it on the ballustrade before him. The music from the house stopped, and he heard someone call his name. He poured himself another glass of brandy. Not for the first time, his inbred sense of loyalty was in conflict with his devotion to Grace. He knew, of course, that she was innocent, but guilt by association worked two ways. She was associated with them, and he with her. He was a magistrate, and must be seen to administer the law impartially, and, above all, to distance himself from any treasonable action. He had no doubt whatsoever that any jury would find her innocent – if innocent she was. At this stage, he could not be sure of anything.

The moon came out from behind a cloud to illuminate the ghostly shape of Letitia in her white satin gown. She looked puzzled and a little apprehensive, but very beautiful. Henry looked at his nervous young bride. She timidly removed the glass from his hand, and he raised her fingers to his lips. Then he took her in his arms and kissed her. He felt her heart beating wildy as she returned his embrace, and he told himself that here was his future, with a woman who loved him, one of his own kind. Together they walked back into the house under the doting gaze of friends and relatives, relieved to see that Henry Valentine had at last found the happiness he deserved. As Fanny approached them, her face beaming, he made up his mind. Tomorrow he would order the arrest of Grace O'Lochlainn.

Out in the hall the gentlemen fiddlers had commenced a cotillion and there were calls for the betrothed pair to take the floor. Fanny roused a few reluctant squireens, pairing them off as best she could with simpering neighbours' daughters.

'Why do any of them bother coming?' she asked Madam Hall crossly, 'when they make such a fuss about complying with the slightest civility.'

'You will know to trim your guest list in future!' replied her friend, well used to Fanny's less than genteel outbursts. The hostess walked into the dining-room where mouse-like maids were quietly gathering away the debris. As she had expected, Dr Butler was back at the table, about to engorge himself with a virgin wine jelly.

'My dear Dr Butler!' Fanny cried gaily. 'They are waiting for the two of us to start the cotillion!' Deftly removing his bib, she ushered him into the hall, all the while praying that the lively dance would not disgorge the contents of his belly. Joining the set, she was relieved to see that her brother appeared to be enjoying himself.

'He is so handsome when he smiles!' she said vaguely to Dr Butler, who was belching unashamedly.

❖　❖　❖

'I've said it before, and I'll say it again! You'll not find better servants than the Irish anywhere in the world! They know their place!' proclaimed a patriotic lady for all to hear. A murmur of approval greeted this pronouncement, though there were one or two voices raised in dissent.

'I really don't know, Leontia!' someone replied. 'Their talent for mimicry has made me, on occasion, feel most uneasy.'

'Forgive me,' intervened Captain Walls, intent on stirring up some further dissension during this sleep-inducing conversation. 'I may be ill-educated, but how does one tell the difference between a genuine lady and her humble impressionist?' He delighted in the horrified expressions on the faces of his audience.

'Breeding,' declared a big-boned lady in a wig reeking of camphor, 'is something which cannot be imitated!' As murmurs of assent passed around the room, Fanny choked on her Madeira wine. Grace O'Lochlainn certainly had little in common with this critic of her class.

'I think,' she interrupted, 'it is time to call upon our bard for some pretty Irish tunes!'

Walls did not like harp music. He liked even less the caterwauling string band from Newry. But at least, while everyone else was otherwise occupied, he had time to think about more important matters. Valentine had not vetoed the arrest of his mistress, to Walls's disappointment. She could not, after all, be of any great importance to him. But he was taken aback at the Major's insistence that Eamonn O'Lochlainn was not to be touched. Walls could not yet afford to go against the wishes of such an influential man, but, all the same, he resolved to find out why he was going to such lengths to protect a peasant boy.

❖ ❖ ❖

Samuel McIntyre ignored his wife's order to put down his gun and get into bed. He decided instead to have a quick scout outside. Pulling on his boots to the accompaniment of Mistress McIntyre's studied insults, he declared his intention of walking up to the big house. His wife huffed and rearranged her large form in a tight ball beneath the sheets. The gamekeeper hardly noticed her petulance for something was disturbing him. There had been drill on the square this evening and perhaps all the troopers had been assigned to the protection of the guests at the big house, but, all the same, McIntyre, a creature of habit, felt uneasy. In the distance, every window in Kilbroney House was ablaze with light, a sight not seen since 'old madam's' day. Even his thrifty wife had marvelled at the sight of so many lamps. It was good, she had told him, to see the back of the O'Lochlainn woman. She had always predicted that good would, in the end, overcome evil.

McIntyre stepped cautiously through the trees. He passed a fresh-faced young weaver out walking with his girl. Both seemed embarrassed to see him but he nodded a curt greeting. What folk did in their own hours was none of his concern. By the looks on their faces they had been up to no good, but he did not think it likely that they had been setting fire to barns! Pushing aside the branches he stepped into the meadow. Everything, he decided, was as it should be, peaceful and quiet. Satisfied, he prepared to return to his wife, when something in the distance caught his attention. It was a flickering light. McIntyre lifted his gun.

❖ ❖ ❖

Hempson, having assigned his audience to the lowest rung of the ladder of musical appreciation, decided to perform a series of technical stunts with a generous sprinkling of trills and turns, his spidery nails shimmering over the strings. Dr Butler, who had just awakened from a nap, applauded loudly.

'Bravo! Bravo, my good man!' Turning towards Hempson's guide he asked, 'I say! Can he play any Scottish tunes?'

The incensed bard answered sharply: '"He" can play in any language from any land beneath the sun! What "he" chooses to play is quite a different matter altogether!'

Henry Valentine stepped forward in an effort to repair the damage done. There was once a time when it was dangerous to insult a bard, but it was sympathy for the old man, the greatest exponent of his art any of them were ever likely to hear, that prompted the landlord to offer him a gracious apology. Suitably mollified, Hempson bowed and replied, 'Now, perhaps you, sir, will honour me by naming a piece of your choice!'

Letitia placed her arm on Henry's. She was anxious to hear the last of the harp music and to get on with the dancing. 'And what would you like Master Hempson to play, my love?' he asked her.

'Oh, anything; something short!' Sensing Henry's disapproval she added, 'Perhaps something by that man, what is his name... Carolan!'

'Turlough O'Carolan!' Hempson sighed. He had offered them the choice, and there was nothing to be done but comply. 'A short one, you said?'

'That will be quite adequate!' smiled Letitia.

'Then I shall give you a fine air composed in honour of the lady, Grace Nugent! I cannot see your face, Madam, but if it is half as fair as that of Mistress Grace, then your future husband will indeed be a fortunate man!'

❖ ❖ ❖

'Can't this wait until morning?' Madam Ward demanded. The messenger looked uneasy. ''Tis Samuel McIntyre, ma'am. He needs to see the Major with all speed!'

'Oh! Damn them all!' Fanny was loathe to have her brother interrupted, but had to admit that McIntyre was unlikely to take such a course of action unless he felt it necessary. Henry Valentine had just finished dancing when the messenger whispered the news.

'I did not wish to alarm the ladies, sir, but Samuel McIntyre is waiting for your instructions back by the stables.'

'What is he doing there?'

'He has caught one of the Oakboys, sir!'

Captain Walls was by his side. He looked triumphant.

'It is no less than I had anticipated. This is the night for them to strike!' he cried.

'I do hope there will be no more trouble,' said Fanny anxiously, hoping that her other guests would not be disturbed.

'No more trouble!' Walls reassured her. 'By morning we will have routed a den of traitors, cocked a snook at the French and,' he beamed, 'showered ourselves in glory!'

'You have nothing to worry about,' said Henry.

'Nothing to worry about? Why are there so many damn soldiers about the place? They are not here for a picnic, I'll be bound!' replied a peevish Dr Butler.

Valentine looked at his yellow waistcoat with distaste. 'Just some local disturbance, sir! It will be quickly dealt with!' he said coldly.

'And what are we supposed to do now?' cried Dr Butler in a high pitched wail. 'With the countryside amok with brigands and bandits?'

Fanny Ward felt like slapping him hard. It would be bad enough for a woman to be causing alarm. But for the father of Henry's bride...

'Please do not distress yourself,' she soothed. 'We have the gallant Welsh garrison to protect us!'

'Clanbrassil was right! I should have listened to him. There is nothing but madmen up here in the north! Complete lunatics, I call them!' Dr Butler removed his wig and began playing with it.

Valentine rushed into the darkness with his ceremonial sword drawn. 'Hurry man!' he called the lad who had delivered the message. 'Who knows what these rascals could be up to next!' He shuddered at the thought of a few lighted torches flung through the window of his home. Half the county might have been roasted alive were it not for McIntyre's vigilance. Two soldiers on sentry duty joined him as he entered the stable-yard where a small group of stable-boys had gathered to help McIntyre. Grabbing a lantern, Valentine thrust it forward, illuminating the frightened face of the village blacksmith, Murtagh Fegan.

❖ ❖ ❖

Fanny, having said goodnight to most of her guests, was forced to accommodate the squeamish who were reluctant to venture out in the face of the evident local unrest. She would have been stuck with Dr Butler had not Squire Hall pooh-poohed his objections and pushed his large posterior into the Narrow Water coach. The gentlemen fiddlers with their maestro were being accommodated in lodging houses in the village, while Hempson had since retired to a small attic room which Fanny presumed would be good enough for him. At this point in the proceedings she did not care if he complained or put some dreadful curse on the family. She was about to retire herself when the fear suddenly hit her that all had been in vain: the Butlers might now change their minds about Letitia's nuptials. Then she remembered the tender scene she had witnessed between the two, and went to bed satisfied that everything would sort itself out.

❖ ❖ ❖

'All right, McIntyre!' Valentine indicated to the gamekeeper to drop his gun. The distraught face of Murtagh Fegan puzzled him. He had expected some defiance, perhaps protestations of innocence, but the big man looked strangely agitated, like a helpless bear surrounded by dogs in a pit.

'My boy!' Fegan blurted out all at once. 'I was out looking for Briony!'

'With a torch?'

'Aye! We feared he'd met with an accident, or got trapped in a snare. That is why I carried the torch. God knows, I bear this house and your good self no grievance.' The smith's tone was anguished.

'Now tell me, Murtagh Fegan,' asked Valentine sternly. 'How can anyone be expected to distinguish between yourself and one of the Oakboy rebels?'

'The Oakboys? They are the least of my concerns; Briony is missing.'

Valentine rarely encountered disobedience and did not take kindly to it.

'Lock him up!' he ordered, turning away, but the big man fell to his knees, crying pitifully.

'For Jesus' sake, if there's a spark of mercy in you, let me go and look for Briony! He has never been out at night before, and for all his bravado he's only a child! He could be lying injured somewhere and in pain! You can lock me up for as long as you like after I've found him!'

Valentine realised he spoke the truth. 'Let him go!' he said shortly. 'I do not suppose his intentions were harmful.' To his surprise, Samuel McIntyre spoke up.

'I was hasty, Murtagh Fegan. I did not listen to your story and have delayed you,' he said. 'Let me help you find your boy!' With a brief nod of gratitude the blacksmith left, followed by McIntyre.

'I trust you will find the lad is safe,' called Valentine, as the two men disappeared into the night.

Chapter Fourteen

SOME DISTANCE OUT, in the dark waters of the Irish Sea, a small cutter, sails tightly furled, had put down anchor. From the poop-deck, an eyeglass was trained on Knock Shee, the Fairy Mountain of Kilfeighan, which flanked the southern Mournes. Commodore Thurot O'Farrell watched for some time before he slowly lowered the eyeglass. He would allow them another hour, but no more. It was a good clear night for such a rendezvous, with a young moon and calm sea. So calm was it that the snores of the crew rumbled in the depths of the ship like the purring of some great sea monster. O'Farrell smiled: legends were inspired by less than this. From the little offshore island of Seal Rock a barking noise startled him. The curse of local fishermen, the seal population was forever in the act of multiplying itself, and this, O'Farrell assured himself, was the cause of the noise. More worrying was the rasping cough of his gunnery master. The little cutter was well armed, the single row of gunports housing six-pounders and a few twelve-pound cannon. It was well able to engage a naval frigate, if necessary. The Commodore hoped that that would not prove necessary.

O'Farrell was the son of a French naval hero of the same name, and wore the distinctive hat of a Commodore, which sported the white cockade of the Bourbons. It was not the only hat he wore. He had a variety, to suit the occasion, just as his vessels carried a number of ensigns for the top mast. His unlikely name came from his great-grandfather, an O'Farrell of Longford, one of the Wild Geese who had faced exile in the wake of Ireland's defeat. For many years he had eluded both the Royal Navy and the King's excisemen, landing on hidden coves and lonely beaches with his cargo of contraband. He often returned with passengers, grateful fugitives and rebels, and he had been wounded during skirmishes both on land and at sea. His father had died in a sea battle off the Isle of Man after holding the fortress castle of Carrickfergus for a week, and had been posthumously decorated by King Louis for his valour. His son had inherited both his hunger for adventure and his reputation as the 'Phantom of the Seas'. O'Farrell's seamanship and daring had so far saved him from being caught and executed for piracy.

Recently his little fleet of ships had put into La Rochelle for repairs after a year's running with sulphur and molasses between the West Indies and the rebel government of America. He had scarcely been on dry land for more than a fortnight when he was called upon to carry out a new and highly sensitive mission, financed directly from Versailles, he was given to understand. This could only mean that the King himself had taken a personal interest in the mission, and it was therefore wise to accept the commission. Besides, O'Farrell had recently had quite a few encounters with the authorities on the subject of unpaid taxes and confiscated loot.

He was required to return to his old haunts along the northeastern coast, and Carlingford Lough in particular, which he knew better than most men. An old pirate had told him once that there was buried treasure on the island, and O'Farrell had been determined then to find it, but he had long since abandoned the hope as there was such a price on his head that he could rarely risk going ashore. He did not trust his crew, for although they had always been loyal to him in the past the temptation of a big reward was great.

The pain-racked cough sounded again from below, reminding O'Farrell that betrayal and capture were not the only dangers faced by a mariner. Years of exposure to the bitter cold and constant damp took its toll. He would soon be seeking a new gunnery master.

❖ ❖ ❖

Having taken their leave of the O'Lochlainns, the travellers set forth in the darkness, with Donal MacArtain leading the Buller's

216

sure-footed donkey. Makepeace was glad of his mount, for the steep climb before them seemed daunting. Ned Maguire had impatiently ridden on ahead, all his smuggler's senses on full alert; then, satisfied that all was well, he rejoined the fugitives at the river ford.

'This track takes us straight up through the forest,' he explained. ''Tis narrow in parts, but otherwise safe. I have used it before.'

Donal's eyes, well accustomed to travelling in the darkness, were drawn towards the hill which stood between them and the coast. Once they entered the forest the familiar outline of the peaks would be lost. The forested slopes were perilously steep in parts, and at the summit was the promise of several miles of rolling bog and grassland. Maguire was in a surly mood, and had called Donal all the stupid curs of the day for his tardiness, but the young traveller was happy to forgive his insults as long as he led them safely past the hazardous bogholes and trenches which scarred the mountains. At any rate he had no choice at this stage but to trust and follow his guide.

Makepeace, in a buoyant mood, chatted happily away. When he received no response from his companions he began to hum the tune of one of the metrical psalms.

'Do you want to bring the watch down on us?' Maguire hissed crossly. 'You shut your mouth and keep it shut!'

'If they have not caught us by now, they'll not catch us at all. The Lord protects his pilgrims!' answered the Dissenter with confidence. Maguire was disturbed by such foolhardy complacency.

'Never you underestimate any man,' he advised cautiously. 'Not even your own grandfather, should he be bedridden, blind and deaf!' Maguire's success as a smuggler rested, to a considerable extent, on the respect he had for the intelligence of other human beings. To assume that other men were fools was in itself the height of foolhardiness, and just as he respected all men, he trusted no one.

Many types of contraband had made their way from the beaches along the coast of Down, up the smugglers' route through Attical and into Hill Town, and from there to a myriad of secret destinations. Maguire also conducted a flourishing trade in poteen, which he referred to as 'the whey of the mountain goat'. He never touched the liquor himself, for he knew its power, and others who shared his profession but not his abstemious conduct had eventually found themselves in gaol, awaiting the hangman's noose. He had used this particular route once or twice in the past and had no apparent reason to feel as uneasy as he did now. He wondered what was the cause of such an unlikely pair taking flight, and decided that perhaps they were not as poor as they made out. Perhaps it would profit him more to slit their throats there and then.

'Tell us, Maguire,' Donal suddenly interrupted the smuggler's dark thoughts. 'Are you at liberty to say who or what will be taking us to France?'

Maguire looked around at his companions. 'You are an infamous pair of boys, I gather!' The question of their value was still lurking in his mind. 'They're putting you in the care of one of their best sea captains.'

'Infamous indeed,' chuckled Makepeace. 'Don't we look like a right pair of rapscallions?'

Maguire agreed that the old Dissenter in his threadbare black clothes and straggly white hair was a most unusual fugitive. Yet he could be a cunning military spy in disguise.

❖   ❖   ❖

Thurot O'Farrell helped himself to a plate of salted beef with fried potatoes in the galley; a pot of hot chocolate simmered on the stove. The Commodore sat back and considered his next move.

For this undertaking, Monsieur Rochard, the emmisary from Versailles, had instructed him to display the greatest possible caution, and had paid half of the sizeable commission in advance. O'Farrell had carefully chosen his best seafarers for the task, especially Jupiter, a branded slave, and a Kerryman from the wild coast of Dún Chaoin. Jupiter had always shown himself to be fiercely loyal to the man who had defied his stalkers in Louisiana and given him asylum on board his ship. The Kerryman, who was generally known by that title, was a skilled oarsman who contemptuously regarded the waters of the Irish Sea as little more than a fishpond compared to the mighty waves of the Atlantic which had borne him since childhood. O'Farrell felt that they would suit his present purpose admirably.

His belly filled, the Commodore went out on deck where the watchman, Duffy, was keeping a conscientious look-out for the signal from land.

'Have you seen anything, Duffy?' he asked.

'Not a thing, sir,' Duffy replied. 'The wind has risen a fair bit though.' O'Farrell was impatient. He wanted to be well on his way before dawn broke, and that could not be long away. He knew that there were no naval ships in the area just then, as he had received word from a Manx merchant that the English fleet had mustered at Bristol for a royal review, and he intended to make the most of this opportunity.

'Away with you,' he told Duffy. 'You will find some potatoes on the pan below.' The last thing that Duffy wanted at that moment was a feed of greasy praties, but he thanked the captain for his consideration and went off to his hammock.

'Duffy!' The Commodore had one further instruction. 'Rouse the Kerryman and Jupiter. Tell them they may make ready to jump, and put the gunnery master on alert. We'll be away on the north wind as soon as we can.'

O'Farrell resumed his watch.

❖ ❖ ❖

As the trio emerged from the forest into the clearing, Maguire took them on a winding route, skirting the Red Bog and the treacherous 'eel holes'. Belted Orion in the sky above was the only familiar sight to Makepeace and Donal, the latter having maintained a depressed silence for most of the journey. Makepeace also began to feel lonesome for his dog and concerned for its welfare. Once or twice he called the party to a halt.

'Wheesht!'

'What is it now?' whispered Maguire.

'Did you hear something there?'

'Hear what?'

'Listen. There you are...'

'God Almighty!' exploded the angry Clonduff man. 'If we have to stop every single time you hear a rat scurry we might as well go back to where we started from.'

''Twas no rat I heard,' replied Makepeace with certainty.

'Do you not know,' insisted Maguire, clearly at the limit of his patience, 'that wild beasts get up to the same line of activity at nights as most men do? And if I had any sense, that's what I'd be at too, instead of risking my neck for the pair of you.'

'I'm not speaking to you of wild beasts,' censured Makepeace.

'Then what are you talking about? For I'm no wiser now than when you started,' snapped Maguire.

'Why, my dog, of course. He's followed me many a time before, you know.'

Donal spoke up at last.

'Don't fret yourself. The brave Widow Fearon will be glad of his company. He'll soon forget about you,' he reassured his friend.

'Do you suppose so?' The old man sounded dejected. There was little comfort in the thought of his dog transferring its affections to someone else so readily.

'Anyway,' continued Donal, 'we'll be sure to find a good pup in France. You can train him to your liking.'

'I still hold that my dog's following me,' the Dissenter persisted.

They carried on, lapsing into silence, neither traveller caring to share his thoughts with the other. If Donal was pining for his girl, and the Dissenter for his dog, Maguire was sorely missing his bed. He knew a friendly woman at Ballyedmond who would put him up for what was left of the night; he tried to remember her name as he rode. They traversed the Killowen mountains with relative ease, Maguire having located a goatherd's path. Suddenly the soft whinny of a pony startled him. Maguire lifted his pistol, cursing a prayer under his breath. A dark figure loomed above them.

'I was just about to give you up!' a voice spoke in the darkness.

'Marcas Brennan! I thought you were the redcoats!' Maguire exclaimed, putting his pistol away. 'Isn't it as well you spoke before I blew your head off.'

'Isn't it as well for yourself that you didn't.' The Kilfeighan goatherd added that he had been waiting for the trio for some time. 'I was beginning to think you'd lost yourselves,' he said.

'Devil the fear of me losing my way,' replied Maguire, 'although if this here Dissenter had had his way, we wouldn't even have got as far as this.'

'You've little time to lose,' urged the Kilfeighan man. 'Follow me and I'll set you on a path that will take you straight down. If you'd continued the way you were going, you'd be in the river by now.' They started off again, with Marcas Brennan leading the way.

'Who is he?' Donal asked Maguire quietly.

'If you had been paying heed to Maguire in the close instead of sneaking off you would have heard all you needed to know,' snapped Makepeace.

'Isn't it fortunate for us both that your memory serves you so well,' said Donal mildly. 'No doubt you listened carefully to every word he said.'

'Yes, indeed!' Makepeace was proud of his reputation for remembering obscure tracts and biblical verses. 'No pilgrim should set forth on his progress without thinking of the whithers and the wherefores. That man is Marcas Brennan of Kilfeighan, the townland around Knock Shee, so I'm told. He lights a beacon there in foggy weather to guide ships past the bar.' Brennan, he continued, would give the signal to the ship which, hopefully, now waited in the darkness.

Brennan spoke again. 'You'll find your bearings again in a while, Maguire, if you keep to the path on this side of the stream and never stop till you arrive at the cove of Ballyedmond. You'll be expected.'

Marcas Brennan bade the trio farewell and prepared to depart. He stopped for a moment and listened. His keen ears had picked up an unfamiliar sound, and he watched and waited. Satisfied that there was no one there, he rode off at a gallop towards Kilfeighan. It was less than an hour to sunrise and he had a job to do. In a short while he had reached the brow of Knock Shee and produced a tinder box. He had prepared the kindling beforehand, and all that was needed now was a spark to ignite the wood. Within minutes flames were leaping into the night sky; then almost immediately, the blaze was extinguished with damp hides. The signal was meant for one pair of eyes only.

❖ ❖ ❖

Briony Fegan had followed the outlaws all the way from Kilbroney. A few precious possessions had been packed into a rag tied to a stick, and with a merry step he had set out on the greatest adventure of his life. He was determined to follow in the footsteps of Master Agnew, and find treasure on sun-drenched isles far from the humdrum life of the forge. It had been good fun to start with, and Owen had been very impressed with his bravery. He had earlier confided in Roise, one of his little sisters, but not before she had taken a hideous oath and promised never to reveal his true whereabouts. She had pleaded with him to take her with him, but he had been contemptuous of her offers to carry his pack. Now he rather regretted having dismissed her so quickly, for it was hard work climbing mountains with a burden on your back. He had to admit to himself, too, that he would have enjoyed a little company, even Roise's.

By the time the men had caught up with Marcas Brennan he was cold and hungry and very tired. He was relieved when they stopped to talk to the Kilfeighan man and he ate the last of his rations, a ragful of cold potatoes, as he rested. When they moved on again, his legs felt heavy and his eyes were sore from trying to focus in the dark. As the travellers turned down into the trees once more, Brennan looked around as if he knew Briony was following; the little boy lay still. When eventually it seemed safe to follow the band he ran down the slope, tripping over a curling root and gashing his hand. He wanted to cry out, but dared not, so he picked himself up and tried to stem the flow of blood as best he could. A wave of panic overcame him as he looked around to see only the dark trunks of trees, and behind them, tree upon tree.

The starlight far above seemed to recede before his eyes. He could hear nothing – no voices, no plodding hooves... In consternation he ran forward, but once again tripped and fell. He lay there sobbing.

Somehow his notions of dashing buccaneers and palm trees seemed faded and unreal, here alone in the damp darkness. Maybe in another year or so, when he was bigger, he would try again. In the meantime, he would go home to his warm bed. What a welcome his mother would have for him as he arrived in the village. His sisters and Owen MacOwen would be enthralled by his adventure stories! Nothing much had happened really, but Briony was not averse to a little exaggeration. For the first time he began to wonder if Master Agnew had also embroidered the tales of his exploits. With such doubts in his mind, he prepared to find his way home. That would be a simple matter. If he veered to the right and kept going downhill he would soon reach the shore. Then all he had to do was to walk along the beach until he reached Rostrevor, where a steaming pot of porridge awaited him.

Briony fought his way through a sea of ferns and bracken. He was accustomed to the darkness by now, but already the promise of dawn was in the air. An unexpected sound caused him to stop in his tracks. It was a voice, nothing more than a fleeting murmur, but certainly a man's voice. He listened, but heard only the sound of the incoming tide. He was about to move forward once more when the voice barked a sharp order. The terrified Briony realised that he had stumbled on a military exercise. Perhaps someone had alerted the troops. Perhaps Roise had broken her vow and they were coming to arrest him! Fragments of information he had gathered tumbled through his mind – the voices on the bridge, the involvement of Tom Dunn, the secret journey through the night. With mounting alarm, he realised that he had accidentally come upon an ambush party. These soldiers were setting a trap for the outlaws and anyone who was assisting them. He must find the travellers and warn them.

❖ ❖ ❖

The rowing boat skimmed over the choppy waves at the entrance to the lough, picking out the deep channel between rocks and sandbanks. The two strong oarsmen made light work of their course and they were soon inside the mountainous inlet.

'There they are! I can see them,' said the Commodore, a note of urgency in his voice. The Kerryman asked him how many he expected to take aboard, having spotted what looked like a small menagerie on the shore.

'Two!' he answered. 'A young man and an aging preacher.'

'*In ainm an Diabhail!*' exclaimed the Kerryman 'A preacher? *Íosa Críost!*'

'What did the Kerryman say?' asked Jupiter anxiously.

'He said that he would have to be careful about his choice of language with a preacher on board,' grinned O'Farrell.

❖   ❖   ❖

Makepeace dismounted on wobbly legs, glad to feel firm ground under his feet once more. He retrieved what few possessions his belt would not hold from the donkey's back, and slapped his rump to send him back home to his master in Kilbroney. The Buller had said it might take him a few days, but he would surely find his way home for the wily old animal had never once been impounded. After a few steps on the shingle, Makepeace began to feel the blood circulating once more, and reassured himself that the sea journey would be safe and short.

'I see them!' cried Maguire. 'Ahoy there! We're here, ye boys!' He ran forward waving to the incoming dinghy. He wanted to go through the motions of paying the fare, though in reality the entire sum which William Dwyer had subsidised was his, for the voyage had been financed from France, but Maguire did not wish his clients to know this until the ship was safely out on the high seas.

Donal was busying himself with his belongings as the rowing boat approached. He could see a man, obviously the captain, salute Ned Maguire from the water. The two oarsmen had their backs to the shore.

'We'll not get as far as France in that,' jested Makepeace. 'It would not hold the two of us.'

Without warning, the shrill voice of a young boy broke through the air. 'Donal! Master Agnew, go back! 'Tis a trap! The troopers are awaiting you!'

The small figure of Briony Fegan came racing towards him, waving frantically.

'Briony!' Donal called. 'What brings you here?'

The little boy came panting and stumbling as if the devil were on his tail. 'Go back! Save yourselves!' he was crying.

The words were no sooner out of his mouth than a dozen redcoats appeared from the trees, bayonets at the ready. The ambush party.

'Christ!' screamed a furious Ned Maguire. 'Some bastard's informed on us.'

The crew of the boat, their own instincts for self-preservation paramount, turned the vessel with the speed of lightning. Guns were pointed at the retreating dinghy as Makepeace, the truth of the situation hitting him like a stone, used his own, very different instincts.

'Run now, Donal!' he roared. 'Away like the wind, for 'tis the only chance you've got.'

For an indefinable moment, Donal looked at the pleading face of his beloved foster father. It was as though he was a small boy again, being challenged to run faster than the other boys.

'Run lad, like the wind!' The voice was strong and sure.

Donal looked at the advancing line of redcoats as though they were toy soldiers. The blast of a gun resounded, shocking him into action. He turned, racing with all his might towards the trees. The gunfire followed him as he ran, accompanied by a cacophony of venomous oaths and shouts. Above the noise he heard a cry. Makepeace, brave Makepeace was roaring in agony. Donal ran all the faster as though he could not bear the sound, tears stinging his eyes, darting in and out through the trees, putting as much distance as he could between himself and his pursuers. Shots splintered the wood around him as he ran in the dimness of the morning light. Fear whipped him on as he scrambled up the steeper inclines, lungs bursting with the pain of the chase. He finally collapsed in the bracken and for one tortured hour lay motionless as the troopers hacked at the undergrowth with their swords. Twice they passed within an inch of his head, roaring threats one moment, and offering deals the next.

'Give yourself up MacArtain!' the voices called. 'You have a life ahead of you yet! Just tell us the names of your comrades, and escape the noose.'

Some time after the last sounds had faded, he dared to look up. He was certain that they would be back soon, and this time they would have their bloodhounds with them.

❖ ❖ ❖

The old women scavengers, bent under the weight of their creels, were already out combing the beach for discarded coal cinders and flotsam from the sea as the mid-May sun rose in the east. The tide had turned as a strange procession appeared from the Killowen direction, moving along the beach at funereal pace. One woman nudged another and they crossed themselves in fear as the curious spectacle approached, winding towards the village. Two men were bound in chains, heads bowed and shoulders stooped in defeat. The older of the two was clad in black, and his white hair was caked in blood as he limped painfully over the stones. No one spoke; a sombre air hung over the whole entourage. A small group of troopers guided their prisoners, now and then lending a steadying hand to the old man. The women recognised the soldier following behind. His large frame was bowed in grief.

'Sergeant Pollard!' someone murmured. 'What is he carrying?'

The women clutched each other in distress, for in Pollard's arms lay the lifeless body of little Briony Fegan.

Chapter Fifteen

I N THE DAYS that followed the killing of Briony Fegan, it seemed that the past twenty years of relative peace had been wiped out with a vengeance, and the worst of the Penal Laws reinstated. Old wounds were re-opened; whispered suspicions of old were now shouted openly, as children asked their grandparents about the terrors of their childhoods and the massacres of the troubled years. Hard-won friendships between native and planter dissolved in a wave of recrimination.

Old Mistress Brennan walked along the shore from Ballyedmond. Someone had already planted a tiny wooden cross at the place where the blacksmith's young son had fallen. She felt the sorrow weigh her down, like an invisible chain. It was a rare thing for her to visit Rostrevor, as the only times she was known to leave Kilfeighan were for the twice yearly Ram Fair at Greencastle, but she was desperate to find out what had happened to her son, Marcas. The sea was grey and empty, and even the gulls were silent for once. The little fishing vessels which they always followed were moored tightly to the quayside, where a few women and children huddled together, shawls masking their frightened faces. They scurried into their cabins at the sound of approaching hooves, and Mistress Brennan wondered for a moment if she too should beg shelter. The men from the fishing families, White Matt McVeigh and his brother, and the McAlinden boys, had disappeared through the Barrack gates three days previously and had not been heard from since. It was with some relief that the Kilfeighan woman recognised the rider as Thomas Dunn. Running towards him she cried out.

'Master Dunn! Have you word of my son?'

Dunn dismounted. It was a week since Marcas had been arrested.

'I have just left his side. He asked me to tell you that he is in good spirits, and he's saying his prayers,' he replied.

Mistress Brennan was relieved, but knew her son was still in very great trouble. 'And what do you think? Will they let him go? I know he lit that beacon, but he's often done so in the past, if it was a bad night. For the boats. I don't know what those men were doing, for he didn't tell me.'

'I know that he always lit the beacon, like his father before him. That's his best defence,' said the lawyer cautiously.

'The lough was always treacherous,' sobbed Mistress Brennan, 'and the fire helped the ships, big and small, past the rocks. We never enquired as to who owned the ships. We didn't care. Then he got word to meet the northern men and to light the beacon.'

Dunn knew that Marcas Brennan would be lucky to get away with a flogging.

'And how am I going to till the fields and mind the goats all on my own?' the woman was wailing. 'Surely they wouldn't leave me without my son.'

Dunn could offer little comfort. 'They're frightened,' he explained, 'and like the rest of us, they panic when they're frightened. It might have been put down as an isolated incident were it not for the burning of the barn, and that stupid attack on a poor woman the night after the boy was shot.'

'Grace O'Lochlainn?' Mistress Brennan replied angrily, 'she deserved what she got. It was owed to her this long time.'

'That is unworthy of you!' Dunn was angry at the woman's spite. 'She was an innocent woman, and deeply wronged.'

The lawyer took his leave of her, acknowledging the white faces peering from the smoky quayside cabins, and rode into the woods. He regretted having spoken sharply to the poor woman, but the subject of Grace O'Lochlainn provoked strong feelings in him. Grace was very much on his mind, as it was indirectly on her account that he himself had been released from custody. Yet few others would feel that they owed her any gratitude.

❖ ❖ ❖

It was on the evening after the ambush that anger over the death of Briony Fegan reached its most intense. Thady O'Lochlainn, his son Seán, Thomas Dunn and Marcas Brennan of Kilfeighan were among the first to be arrested, but many others followed them. Under the direction of Captain Walls an intensive search of the area was quickly underway, with troops carted in from Newry and Castlewellan to assist the local men.

All holdings and peasant homes in every townland of the parish were thoroughly searched, from the meagre peat cabins of the Poorlands to the stone cottages of the bleachers and weavers in the village. Rumour fed panic as the sight of advancing redcoats flooding through farm and field with bayonets at the ready reawakened sleeping folk-memories of rampaging Vikings, Cromwellian zealots, and the more recent slaughter of the innocents at the Priest's Mountain. Frightened mothers packed small bundles for their sons and sent them scurrying into the mountains as those who had no English heard the news from those who spoke a little. Annie Dunn found herself reassuring a group of nervous women, although she herself feared for her husband's safety.

'They are hunting down an escaped prisoner,' she explained. 'You need not worry for your sons, 'tis only the one man they want.' But there was little conviction behind her words.

The military exercise was not quite the dispassionate operation that many in authority believed it to be. Energetic young soldiers unleashed from the boredom of the barracks revelled in their newfound freedom. It was not quite the excitement of battle, but it was preferable to policing the occasional Volunteer parade. Their orders were to hunt down the outlaw Donal MacArtain, and to collect evidence pertaining to the existence of a secret agrarian organisation known as the 'Oakboys'. The occasional pocket of resistance from scythes and pitchforks was quickly dealt with as defiant cottiers tried to protect their newly sown crops. Those who resisted fared worst of all, for their homes were taken apart, their wells filled in, and their farm implements confiscated. The women could only watch as their husbands and sons were marched away.

In his headquarters at the Barrack, bare and cramped by military standards, Captain Walls received an account of the ambush, a badly bungled job in his opinion. Sergeant Pollard, nursing a hand injury and weary from the night's work, was the object of his interrogation.

'By God, Pollard! You let that young lout escape again? Having staked out the place for hours? What the hell were you doing?' The Sergeant did not answer. 'And the men in the boat?' Walls continued with added venom. 'Did you manage to make any kind of identification?'

'It was quite dark, sir, and I was not in a position to see their faces,' Pollard stumbled, 'but according to Ned Maguire one of them was the French pirate, Thurot O'Farrell!'

'O'Farrell?'

'So he said.'

Walls grew crimson in the face. 'A pirate with a price on his head, within an inch of our shores? He escaped, I take it?'

'We engaged them when it seemed that they could not be captured. We shot one of the boatmen, I feel sure of that.'

'And they shot you?'

'Just a hand wound, sir.' Pollard tried to make light of his pain.

'And yet they were able to escape unhindered? How will that look on paper? I hope for your sake, Pollard, that you've a sound record.'

'Thirty-five years...'

'And all we have got is that rascal Maguire, a weasel who could have been picked up at any time, and an old half-blind preacher who can barely walk unaided. But O'Farrell's presence confirms my worst fears. There must be a major alert. I want every man in the valley questioned and I have ordered the Fencibles in from Newry. Let them work for their money, for a change. This place needs a hell of a shake-up, and that includes this flea-hole of a Barrack, Pollard.'

'Sir?'

'Yes?'

'The boy's death,' Pollard spoke hesitantly.

'Oh yes, the boy!' Walls seemed more concerned with his paperwork, but Pollard had been deeply moved by the tragedy. He knew Fegan the blacksmith and had delivered the body himself to the forge. 'It was one of the lads,' he began to explain, 'not much more than a boy himself...'

Walls stretched impatiently. The boy's death was unfortunate, but he had more pressing concerns than the feelings of one family.

'He lost control. He had been well drilled in the use of firearms,' Pollard continued sadly, 'but this was his first time...'

'It was unquestionably an accident!' Walls cut in. 'Of course these things happen.' He strode to the window to observe the comings and goings at the inn. He saw Coyle leaving his lodgings, no doubt to learn a blow by blow account of the night's events which would subsequently be relayed to his master, Henry Valentine. 'Yes,' he continued, 'these things happen all the time in this country, and naturally it is highly regrettable. We'll put our sympathy on record.' He picked up his quill again as though to close the incident. 'Although personally,' he said as he wrote, 'I would be inclined to place the blame firmly on the parents of the dead boy. They should not have allowed him to be out at such an hour in the first place.'

'He was very young – Davies, the lad who fired the shot. I should never have allowed him to handle a live firearm so soon, for he just wasn't ready. You know, it was his first shot in uniform, and his first death. It upset him badly. It upset us all.'

'Good God man!' Walls thundered, 'you must have seen many an unpleasant sight in your career. I know I have. I can recall seeing a whole family...'

As Captain Walls embarked on his reminiscences, Pollard listened with deaf ears. His sorrow at the incident extended to more than just grief for the loss of a small boy. Never again would he be able to exchange a friendly word with the native people, many of whom he had grown to know and respect. Any goodwill which had been built up over the years had been wiped out with this single incident. None of them, he felt certain, would ever believe the official account, that the shooting was an accident. In time the story would become distorted, and eye-witnesses would present themselves who would swear to having seen an unprovoked attack on the child. Sadly, some of his own men would, in the wake of wild accusations and misapportioned blame, convince themselves that the boy himself was armed and guilty as sin.

❖ ❖ ❖

The Agent Coyle wasted little time in bringing a detailed account to Kilbroney House. Major Valentine listened grimly to his report of the incident, shocked by the news of young Briony's death.

'Poor Fegan!' he said quietly, thinking of the anxiety displayed by the blacksmith on the previous evening. 'I do not doubt but that he will be heartbroken.' He listened impassively to the news about the morning's arrests.

'As to that, Coyle, justice must take its course. I pity the simple-minded men who allow themselves to be misled so easily. Any treasonable action must, of course, be severely punished.' He tried to put from his mind the fact that he was referring to the family of Grace. She was no longer part of his life, and if she had betrayed her country to the French, she had also betrayed him. He could certainly not excuse her on the grounds of being feeble-minded or ignorant.

'Eamonn!' he realised suddenly. 'Was he..?'

'Not from what I saw. Only the father and the elder son.'

'Thank God for that. Coyle?'

'Sir?'

'Make sure he is safe.'

Valentine's head ached from the revels of the previous night. He called for a drink to settle himself as he saw from the window Captain Walls come riding towards the house. He resented the fact that the man had proved to be right in claiming that the traitors were being harboured in the area, and that more unrest would inevitably follow.

'If I had acted according to my own judgement in the first place,' Walls was adamant, 'that child's death would have surely been avoided.'

'It was not our problem to begin with.' Valentine was defensive.

'So you always said! But that is not the case now!' Walls looked at him coldly.

'Those outlaws were not from here. That they received temporary shelter here does not prove collaboration on the part of people who are naturally guileless.'

'They are undoubtedly part of a larger network,' the Captain insisted. That Pollard was lamenting the child's death was bad enough, but he had not expected a similar reaction from the landlord.

'Can you not see?' Valentine was appealing. 'For the first time in years, if not in generations, we've had a semblance of peace. In Whitechurch's day, the house was as heavily fortified as any arsenal. Now, at least one can walk unarmed without fearing for his life.'

'Oh, really? I have heard differently.' Walls's eyes narrowed as he looked at the Major shrewdly. 'I wonder how well you really know your tenants, Valentine. After all, let me remind you that we are talking about treason.'

'Treason bedamned!' Henry Valentine looked distastefully at the smug face. 'I have heard about your valiant capture of a pathetic old cripple. Is the realm so unsafe that any action of his could shake it?'

'As I said, he is only one of many. Part of a widespread network of villains. This sort of thing goes on all the time, Valentine, and the reason you never hear of many of the plots against authority is because of the vigilance of men like myself.'

'I suppose we should be grateful!'

'Yes! And I also know who some of the others are!'

'If you know who they are, why did you not have them arrested in the first place?'

'I intend to! You did agree, did you not, that Grace O'Lochlainn is a dangerous woman?'

Valentine rose to his feet in anger. 'No! I have changed my mind! You are wrong in this instance!'

'As I have said before,' Walls was derisive, 'you do not know your own tenants half as well as you think you do.'

'Grace had no reason to be involved. She has always kept her own council. And she has less motive than those who live in poverty.'

'A discarded mistress? No motive?' Walls watched the shadow of pain drift across the green eyes. He despised the man's weaknesses.

'I can tell you in truth that she has been loyal for many years.' Henry found his anger once more replaced by a feeling of deep melancholy and hopelessness. He sat down and buried his head in his hands.

'Loyal?' Walls repeated. 'Loyal to whom? And you Henry Valentine, where does your loyalty lie?' He did not try to hide his contempt for the landlord of Kilbroney. He, a poor younger son, a career soldier, begrudged Valentine his inheritance, his land and his comfortable life. Nothing was earned, everything had been given to him; he was, like most of the 'squireens' of Ireland, '*fruges consumere nati*.'*

Not only did Henry Valentine not have to cheat, to lie, to betray his friends to gain recognition, but this handsome well-built man had power and influence handed to him on a platter. And yet the Major seemed incapable of using power, but was content to leave his authority in the hands of agents and baillifs. As Walls left the room, he had one more thing to say to Henry Valentine.

'I will flog the lot of them – to death if needs be.'

❖   ❖   ❖

The O'Lochlainns had been lifted during the night. The Buller heard the women screaming and lifted his scythe from behind the door without a second thought. He always kept it well sharpened for such an eventuality and fearlessly scrambled over the ditches, taking the shortest route to the close. Sosanna was crying as Thady and Seán were dragged out, the former kicking and wriggling as his assailants bound his arms to wooden stakes. Eamonn looked

---

*Born to eat the fruits.

on helplessly while his mother swore and :pat at the redcoats; the soldiers, having no Irish, did not understand a word she was saying. Seán offered no resistance, bowing his head while his arms were bound like his father's.

'Unhand him, you red bastards!' called the Buller, charging across the field wielding his scythe. A shot rang out and the old man dropped to the ground, clutching a bleeding shoulder.

Sosanna ran towards him, crying. 'Have a bit of sense or they'll take you too!' Throwing her arms around him she continued, 'Leave your scythe there or they'll shoot you again.'

The Buller, accepting the better judgement of this skit of a girl, did as he was told.

'Stay with the women!' Thady called to Eamonn as the prisoners began the long march down the valley. 'I don't know what will become of us now.'

Sosanna watched them go, not in sadness but in anger. How did they know, she asked herself. A terrible new thought suddenly struck her.

'Eamonn!' she cried. 'The outlaws! Could they have been ambushed? Could they have captured Donal?' As she bathed the Buller's wound, all concerns about her imprisoned father and brother left her mind. She had to find out if Donal was safe.

Ironically, it was William Dwyer who brought Sosanna the news, well into mid-morning. He had arrived at the priest's house in Knockbarragh for the nuptial ceremony along with his mother and two old aunts. They had arranged to meet the O'Lochlainn party at the house and were surprised to see neither sight nor sign of anyone, not even Father Mackey. The nearest cabin was that of the 'Fox' McCann across the stream, and William decided to make enquiries of the woman of the house. To his further annoyance no one answered his greeting or opened the door to bid him good day, yet he felt sure that there was someone hiding in the cabin which Minnie the Fox shared with her son, Mick.

The truth was slowly dawning on the merchant. 'Pollard!' he whispered. 'He has not kept his word. The O'Lochlainn's have been taken too.'

William turned to try to pacify his scolding mother. 'I knew no good would come of this!' she insisted. 'They have you for a clod-pate, William Dwyer!'

In spite of his mother's dire prophesies, William knew that there was nothing to do but wait, for appearances sake. To his relief, the sound of hooves heralded the return of the priest.

'Look,' he told his mother. ''Tis Father Mackey.' Mistress Dwyer and the other old women had been saying a Rosary in the back of the cart, and seemed annoyed by the interruption.

'You may go back to Clonduff, Dwyer!' the priest began as he dismounted. 'There will be no wedding for you this day!' William listened silently as he heard the priest's tale of how Samuel McIntyre, of all people, had come in search of him with the news that the blacksmith's lad had been killed.

'There had been an ambush! It appears the boy knew of it. He heard someone talking while he was playing under the bridge and decided, as young lads will, to run away to sea with a pair of foot-pads. Ah! 'Tis a sad day for his people.' The priest shook his head. It had been a hard task trying to convince Murtagh Fegan that his son's death was the will of God. He could hardly believe so himself.

William listened without comment as he heard about the arrest of Sosanna's father.

'Thady!' he exclaimed. 'That should never have happened!'

He heard a sharp intake of breath from his mother. Now she knew. She knew that her son was a traitor. Some day he would explain to her, if he could, how jealousy of his rival had overshadowed all reason. He was just beginning to pay the price of his deceit.

'And the irony of it all,' the priest was saying, 'is that he escaped. The young man they wanted so much to apprehend managed to escape!'

❖   ❖   ❖

That evening, a lonely Grace O'Lochlainn looked out from her new home. She had noticed increased military activity during the day, with small bands of redcoats advancing up the valley, and a few ragged figures disappearing over the hillside. Sensing the growing unrest she abandoned her patch of tillage and ran down the mountainside towards Dunn's Hill. As she neared the house the dogs began to bark frantically.

'Mistress Dunn!' she shouted. 'Are you there?' The dogs, recognising her voice, rushed towards her.

'Down, Bran! Good dogs!' she shushed them. She called a few times more and then entered the house.

The Dunn's home had been ransacked. Furniture lay in a heap on the floor along with broken dishes and jugs. The feather mattresses in the bedroom and in the loft where the Dunn boys slept had been ripped open. The sight disturbed Grace deeply, for this haven of warmth had provided her with comfort and security when she had most needed it. Grace felt a chill as she realised that some dreadful harm could have befallen the family. A sudden loud noise frightened her and she ran outside, expecting some other calamity, but it was only Annie Dunn's milch cow lowing pitifully in the byre. It was an old cow and her milk was dripping, forming a pool on the ground. Grace lost no time in relieving her of her load as she had often done before.

'They've been here too,' she whispered, looking around the little cobbled farmyard which had always been a model of neatness. Doors had been kicked in and bales slashed; chickens rushed helter skelter over the debris. As she picked up the milk pail to bring to the churn the Widow Fearon appeared in the yard.

'Grace, dear!' she wheezed, 'away back to your house with you! These are dangerous times for you to be abroad by yourself with them bloody soldiers out on the tear.' It had been years since Grace had seen the Widow and yet she spoke as if their last meeting had been only yesterday.

'I was looking for Mistress Dunn!' Grace explained.

'Ah, Merciful Mother, did you not hear the news?' The Widow turned to let Grace assist her in removing a large pannier of weeds and herbs from her back. 'Let me sit down to get my breath!' she croaked.

Grace blanched as she spoke of the death of Briony Fegan and the arrest of Tom Dunn, and then she told her that Thady and Seán had been taken too.

'I'm going up to Kilbroney to make sure my mother's all right.' Grace said immediately, but the Widow stalled her.

'You'll do no such thing,' she scolded. 'You go back to the Healing House and bar the door, and I'll join you there when I've seen the woman of Dunn's Hill and got this place cleared up.'

'But my mother! And what of Eamonn?'

'They will be all right. And the neighbours will all rally round. But they won't want you!' The Widow did not mean to be unkind, but her words stung Grace.

'I understand,' she replied sadly. 'I'll go back to the Healing House.' She turned to go; but then, in a decisive gesture, she turned back, rolled up her sleeves and started to tidy the disarranged home. The Widow, still claiming shortness of breath, got out her pipe and was happy to council Grace from a stool in the corner.

'I wish I was your age again,' she remarked wistfully. 'I could have done that in half the time.' Grace smiled as she sewed up the mattresses as best she could. At least Annie Dunn would have a bed to lie on. As she worked she thought about the tragic death of Briony Fegan. She longed to comfort the family in their grief, and said as much to her companion.

'You'll take my advice, girl, and away home now,' replied the Widow. 'I'll be up to join you when I can!' she reminded Grace.

Grace did not heed the Widow's warning. Pulling her shawl up around her face she hurried down towards the village. She met several women heading the other way, carrying fractious children in their arms and loaded panniers on their backs. Everywhere was the sound of crying and marching feet. Yet she had to visit the forge. It was one thing when grown men took their chances with the law, but a child had been killed. He was innocent – and he was one of their own. Grace joined the keening women outside the forge. She looked like any one of them in her dark skirt and shawl.

Once inside the cabin she saw Murtagh crouching by the body her heart went out to him and she moved forward, throwing back the shawl from her face. The keening stopped as all eyes turned on her. Her grief turned to fear when she saw Murtagh's expression – his face was a mask of bitter resentment, as though he was blaming her for his loss. She turned and ran from the room.

She raced homewards as though bloodhounds were on her trail, although no one was following her. Her gown caught in the brambles as she stumbled; she pulled at the thorny stems, the barbs embedding themselves in her palms. She hurried past Dunn's Hill, fearing to stop lest her imaginary pursuers would catch her before finally finding sanctuary in the Healing House, her hair and clothes dishevelled and her cheeks flushed red. There, in solitude, she wept for Briony, for her father and brother, and for her lost love. Darkness had fallen before she crawled to her feet and went out to the well to tend her abraded hands.

The softness of the night air soothed her burning cheeks, and the water was cool and sweet. She drank a long clear draught, wishing that it had the power to wash away memories, and the doubts and guilt which accompanied them. Not for the first time she questioned the purpose of her own existence, and envied Dervla MacOwen who had put all her cares behind her. The well looked deep and inviting. She rose to her feet with a sudden determination to stand firm. If there was a reason for her to continue, she would find it. An unfamiliar sound disturbed her dark thoughts.

'Is there someone there?' she called, hiding her nervousness. There was no answer. Apprehensive at the silence she returned to the house, bolted the door and prepared to retire to bed. She undressed and slipped on a fine linen nightgown, a reminder of her former life and a luxury she had found difficult to abandon, and ascended the stairs. She lay uneasy, tossing and turning, but sleep evaded her. She rose and went downstairs, throwing a few sods and dry sticks on the dying hearth. She would read for a while, although the dim light did her eyes little good. Before she had commenced her book, there was a loud banging on the door. She opened it and peered out.

A few shapeless figures stood outside the Healing House, and although Grace could recognise no one in the darkness, they seemed to be mostly young boys and a few women.

'What is it?' she called from the doorway, trying to sound unruffled, 'What do you want? I have nothing here I can give you!' In answer a stone flew past, shattering an earthen crock behind her. She slammed the door shut, drawing the bolts, then barred the shutters on the tiny downstairs window. She cowered in the corner, fists clenched. The voices outside increased in number and volume, and a barrage of stones and sods resounded off the door and wooden slats.

'Come out, you whore!' they yelled as she stumbled through what prayers came into her head, her skin cold and clammy with fright, the words jumbled and ridiculous.

A roar from outside sent a new wave of dread through her body. She struggled to her feet. A few blackthorn sticks lay by the hearth and she armed herself with the stoutest one. She waited for the door to break down and for the screaming mob to invade her house. 'This is the Healing House!' she whispered to herself, 'even the Norsemen did not dishonour it!' So, she thought, the young braggarts outside can have no more than scant regard for their history. She wondered what they had in mind for her. Would they beat her up with rocks and cudgels? Or would they throw her in the river as they used to do to witches in Cromwell's time? Or worse, Grace realised, as the acrid stench of smoke and burning reeds wafted down the stairs. They intended to burn her out! She screamed hopelessly, knowing that there was no one to hear or to help.

✧ ✧ ✧

Coyle was most unhappy as he rode through the village. The extra troops had been billetted in houses around the town, and he had almost been thrown out of his lodgings in order to make way for some chinless officer from Newry who seemed more interested in doing 'a spot of fishing' than catching his man. The additional horses about the village had churned up the main street with their hooves and had left such a sea of muck that pedestrian access to some buildings was difficult in the extreme. None of the troopers seemed to know who the Agent was, or to accord him the respect due to one in his position. Even his weekly lady visitor had not turned up at the appointed time, for fear of the soldiers.

Earlier, he had bade farewell to the harper Hempson and his guide, grudgingly admitting to himself that the bard, unlike his gentle patrons, was completely unperturbed by the night's events and had declared his intention to return at the end of the summer for some medicinal goat's milk. The guide, an odd fellow who would not shut his mouth, had thanked Coyle grandly, as though he owned the town, a civility which pleased the Agent.

He had encountered more insolent behaviour later in the day from the village children, many of whom were free from the restraining influences of their fathers, now locked up in the Barrack. Coyle deeply regretted the breakdown of order, and was bemused by the number of strange faces. The old men who usually sat under the trees during the day had gone to ground, and even Napper Donnan had not been near the alehouse. He met Samuel McIntyre, who declared that he was going home, but intended to have his gun at the ready.

'I'll not sleep tonight, Master Coyle,' he said. 'You know 'tis always the likes of ourselves that come out worse at times like these, for each side looks on us as being in the pay of the other.'

'Aye!' agreed Coyle morosely. 'Of one thing you may be sure, McIntyre. There will always be a scapegoat found. Always!'

As though stung by the truth of his own words, he abruptly left the gamekeeper's company and went in search of the Major.

❖ ❖ ❖

Annie Dunn arrived home on the mare with little Betsy, weary from the day's vigil outside the Barrack. The Widow Fearon had taken her cauldron of weeds from the hearth and boiled up a pot of porridge. It was not quite as good as that of the woman of the house, but it was warm and lined the child's belly for her. As the little girl dozed off in her cot by the fire, Annie took stock of the house. Her good delft had gone, the furniture was broken and scarred, the face of her clock was shattered. Worse than that, she noticed that all her husband's books and documents were missing, and were no doubt now being perused at the Barrack. She was told that she had Grace O'Lochlainn to thank for the relative order in her home, although the Widow tried to claim some part of the credit.

'Did she not stay?' she asked the Widow.

'I told her to run on home and bar her door. She would have got a bad handling if she'd gone back to Kilbroney after what happened the father.' The Widow seemed confident that she had given the right advice.

'But she will not be safe on her own! With the soldiers, and...'

'And who would sully their good name by taking in the Planter's Whore, although mind you,' declared the Widow with sincerity, 'I always liked her well.'

Annie buried her head in her hands. Her mind was already overburdened with worries, and she could not add Grace's safety to the load. The latch rattled and Owen MacOwen presented himself. He was flushed, excited.

'Did you see the boys?' he asked, his eyes wild. 'They're going to burn the bitch out!'

Annie pushed past him to look up the mountainside. In daytime she could see the Healing House, but all was now in darkness. Casting a cold look at the boy, she left her house in the Widow's care and rode to the Barrack to inform the Major. She found him at the Barrack gate.

Henry Valentine listened grimly as Annie Dunn, a tiny woman who obviously felt she owed him no deference, described the dangerous situation at Levallyclanowen.

'I will go at once,' he said. Just then a third voice spoke up. The Agent Coyle reined in his mount alongside the couple.

'No, sir!' advised the Agent. 'You must not be seen to intervene. After all, the present troubles are not of your making.'

'I must protect her!' He brushed Coyle aside, intent on rushing to Grace's aid whatever the risk.

'And what good can you do? Your loyalty will be thrown into question!' insisted Coyle.

Valentine was unswayed by these arguments. Then Annie Dunn spoke again.

'Let my husband go free! He is devoted to Grace O'Lochlainn as I am. Let him intervene with the crowd. You see,' she explained, 'they are leaderless and frightened. And very dangerous. They might kill you as well as Grace. If you carry her off, that will merely confirm in their eyes that she is a collaborator, and then she will have nowhere to go.' Valentine paused; Mistress Dunn's voice was calm and sensible as she outlined her plan.

Rushing to the Barrack he demanded to see Sergeant Pollard, who had just retired.

'Well, tell him to get out of his bed!' he shouted at the soldier who had just delivered the message.

'I'm here, sir, I had not retired.' Pollard was trying to button his coat with his left hand.

'Pollard, I need your help. Release the lawyer, Dunn, into my custody.' Pollard looked wary, but the Major was emphatic. 'I personally will take full responsibility. And I have a further mission for you!'

The Sergeant sighed wearily. It was going to be another long night.

❖ ❖ ❖

Grace choked into her shawl as the thick black smoke filled the house. The air along the ground was less dense, so she crawled, trying to breathe what fresh air she could from under the door. A blazing board from the ceiling came crashing down beside her, setting the hem of her nightdress on fire. She rolled around in desperation to extinguish the blaze. Then, clawing at the bars on the door, she fell out into the night. As the cold dark air rushed at her, searing her eyes and her lungs, she coughed and gasped. Hands grabbed at her burning nightgown and dragged her by the hair across the grass. Despite her pain she was aware of the voices,

243

the accusations. Her body froze under the remains of the thin fabric as heavy blows rained on her. Finally, she screamed.

'Help me! God help me! I've done nothing! Nothing at all!'

She could see that most of her tormenters were not much more than children, like evil imps out of hell. A few adults swelled their ranks, but none were recognisable. The Healing House was now burning fiercely behind her, lighting up the night sky. Everything – her clothes, her books, her few treasured possessions – was being destroyed.

All of a sudden, the familiar figure of Tom Dunn stood before her, his face taut.

'Get back to the shadows, you fools!' he roared above the frenzy.

The crowd retreated, but did not disperse. Most of them, as Grace had guessed, were young, no more than sixteen years old. Over the years they had heard their elders gossip and whisper about the 'Planter's Whore' and had learned to blame Grace O'Lochlainn for every evil that had ever befallen them. Dunn recognised some of them, the children of fathers who had been arrested during the day.

'Go home now, I tell you! You'll get your revenge some day. Not here; not now! And not against this poor woman.' He looked at Grace shivering on the grass, her back bare. He thought of the whipping she had received in her youth. One of the crowd, a young girl, handed Grace's shawl to him. He helped her to her feet.

'She doesn't belong here!' called a voice amid renewed murmurs of defiance. 'She took the house of the Widow MacOwen! She caused her death.'

'She's the Devil's own!' cried another.

'Look around you!' Dunn shouted angrily. 'The Healing House has gone! It is no more! Yet it stood through worse times than this! It wasn't the heathens or the invaders that destroyed it. It wasn't Grace O'Lochlainn. It was yourselves!'

Many of the shadowy figures drew back, tossing aside their weapons. Others remained, hungry for more sport, and unheeding of Master Dunn's words. Those who had led the mob were unwilling to surrender their power without a further show of strength. Then without warning a shot rang out, and the crowd melted like ghosts into the darkness. Grace clung to Tom Dunn, still coughing and wheezing from the fumes and smoke. He stroked her hair gently.

'There now! No harm will come to you, Grace. You are quite safe.' The tears began to flow with relief and gratitude as she accepted the comfort he offered. From the darkness, the burly figure of Sergeant Pollard appeared.

'Grace O'Lochlainn?' he spoke loudly. 'I have here a warrant for your arrest!'

'My arrest?' she gasped, eyes wide in her tear-stained face. 'What have I done?'

'The charge is treason, ma'am! We have evidence that you willingly assisted persons who are declared enemies of His Majesty, the King!' This speech was delivered with unusual volume and drama. Was it, Tom Dunn surmised, as much for the benefit of the listeners in the shadows as for Grace?

'Does Major Valentine know of this warrant?' she asked quietly, as Dunn draped a shawl over her shoulders.

'Major Valentine?' echoed Pollard. 'He has signed it himself!'

Chapter Sixteen

May 17th 1780

T HE EARLY MORNING birdsong was a cruel, tormenting chorus to Donal MacArtain as he woke to his first day without the company of Makepeace Agnew. He was cold and damp, for the mountain mist and the drizzling rain had made little of his great-cloak, his only shelter from the night. Intense as his physical discomfort was, the pain of guilt taunted him more harshly as he relived, over and over, the moment when he had left his old friend. Somehow, he had always imagined that if the worst were to happen they would at least die together, be it on the scaffold or the battlefield. He was young, fit and strong, handy with pistol and sword alike, with enough vitality for the two of them. Yet Makepeace was wise, sagacious and true, and these traits more than compensated for his lack of physical ability. Donal hung his head in shame when he realised that, at the moment of reckoning, his foster father's first instincts had been to save his son, while his had been to save himself.

As he grieved, the fugitive felt an inner voice urging him on; one moment it was that of Makepeace, another it was that of Sosanna. He stood up, realising that if he stayed put, it was only a matter of time before the dogs caught him.

He had spent most of the previous day lying low, waiting until nightfall before moving on, scrambling through bracken and over bog until he dropped from exhaustion in a hollow. There he slept until the chilling rain disturbed his rest. Climbing to a small clearing in the trees, he could vaguely make out, far below, the little syenite quarry where Seán worked, and beyond it the meadow and the bridge leading to the village. The Barrack on the Square he recognised, with its orderly outbuildings and well-cobbled yards, and the scene restored some of his shattered confidence. The Barrack looked tiny and insignificant beside the vast mountains and forests which had sheltered bands of rapparees and fugitives from the law for years. The rain, too, unwelcome as it was, would serve as a deterrent to the bloodhounds, which would have trouble in picking up the scent. Yet a life alone, forever walking in fear was not what he had envisaged for himself, and he still had a mission to fulfill. He still had to reach France.

Not caring to look beyond his immediate future, the young man made his doleful way upwards, towards the moorland plain, wishing only for a hole into which he could crawl to hide his wounded heart. More than ever he missed his mentor.

❖ ❖ ❖

Sosanna folded the fine wool skirt which she would have worn to her wedding. It had been a gift of old Mistress Dwyer's, the one in which she had been wed, and Sosanna had no great love for it. Beside them she had placed a pair of brown brogues, her first real shoes. Stretching herself out on her bed, her body felt liberated, and even her toes wriggled, newly released from their leather confines. The relief of not having to lie with William Dwyer overshadowed all other issues. Now that she knew Donal was free, she would find him and run away with him, and to hell with milch cows and feather beds.

The sound of her mother's sobs brought her back to reality and she climbed down the ladder to lay her head in Eily's lap, as she had done from childhood. Worn hands stroked the silken head as Eily crooned. She had just been told of Grace's arrest and all hope had drained out of her. She had nurtured a lingering belief that her wayward daughter would intervene on her father's behalf. If she was beloved of Major Valentine he would surely have protected her. Now Eily's worst fears were realised and she stood to lose three of her family – her beloved husband, her son and her daughter. As if contemplation of the present was too much for her, she cradled Sosanna as if she were a child again.

'My poor wee girl,' she moaned, 'and you should have been a bride by now, young Mistress Dwyer...'

❖ ❖ ❖

247

Grace O'Lochlainn refused, for the second time, the food offered. She wanted to die. She wished she had remained in the house and roasted, for it would be preferable to the pain of knowing she had been betrayed by the man she loved. She had been terrified by the sound of the cat-o'-nine-tails being wielded at the flogging tree outside her cell, and the painful moans and cries of the ignorant and innocent alike. Most distressing of all was the sound of her own father's voice.

'Father!' she cried. 'Hold firm!'

She willed him through the ordeal. She wanted to suffer with him; sharing his pain, she was once more his daughter.

During the day, she endured the mockery of the young troopers as they passed the cell which she shared with one other prisoner, a drunken hag who was regularly locked up for abusive behaviour. The hag complained about having to share with Grace.

'I'm used to better than the like of you!' she spat. 'He didn't think much of you in the end, did he? And I suppose you thought you were better than the other whores?'

Later, Grace was taken to Captain Walls for questioning.

Walls had been looking forward to this confrontation with Henry Valentine's mistress, knowing he had scored a victory over the local man by forcing his hand. Walls was suspicious of everything and everyone, and felt he had good reason to be wary of a magistrate, sworn to uphold the law, who had had such an open intimacy with a peasant, especially the daughter of Thady O'Lochlainn who, but for his advanced years, would be in the condemned cell by now.

The girl who stood before him was dirty and dishevelled, her skin and hair blackened with smoke and her pauper's gown reeking of vomit, yet she stood with poise and confidence. Her aloof demeanour angered him and he vowed inwardly to break her composure, but she listened dispassionately as he raked over her past, goading her about her intimacy with the landlord class. Even the mention of Henry Valentine's name provoked little response, although Grace burned with anger at the man who had shared memories of their most cherished moments with a brute like Walls.

'Now tell me, O'Lochlainn,' he goaded, 'tell me about these traitors. What dealings did you have with them?'

'I have never seen these men you speak of.'

'Yet they shared a roof with your father, your mother, your brothers; or perhaps you, in your exalted position, have no truck with your family? Perhaps you despise them? Your father certainly squealed like a pig under the lash! Oh yes! He is guilty of harbouring criminals, although I have decided to be merciful on this occasion.' He looked to see if she would respond, but she merely shrugged indifferently.

'I have not seen my family for many years. They have little in common with me, 'tis true.'

'And Eamonn, have you seen him lately?'

'Eamonn! You have arrested Eamonn?'

'Should we?'

'No! He is very gentle! He aspires to the priesthood.'

'I see. And he will pursue his studies in France.'

'No – I mean yes, God willing.'

Walls leaned forward, satisfied that he had shaken her. 'God has nothing to do with it, and well you know! I am talking of treason. I wish to ascertain whether or not you share your father's views.'

'I cannot say. I have not spoken with him for such a long time.'

The Captain paused for thought. This woman, for all her apparent composure, was holding back a well of feeling which he was determined to breach.

'Really? And you did not speak with him this morning while he was co-operating with our investigations?'

'While you were flogging him!'

'A distasteful necessity in many cases. You see,' he leaned forward, 'we had to make an example of your father, lest it seem that we were favouring the family of Major Valentine's whore.'

'You curs! I salute any man who by fair means or foul has tried to rid this country of your rotten breed. I have seen the poor of other lands, and nothing begins to compare with the anguish and suffering of my own people. And do you know the worst of it?

They think they are well off if they have a hearthstone they can call their own, for they are comparing their lot with that of their forefathers.'

'And you think that by helping these brigands your people will prosper?'

'What choice do they have?'

'Do you know, Grace O'Lochlainn, we should have left you to your roasting at the hands of these peasants who cause you so much concern.'

Grace stood white and trembling, goaded beyond fear. Walls picked up his quill, satisfied that he had a provocateur on his hands. People like Grace O'Lochlainn, who had tasted privilege, were more dangerous by far than those who had only ever known potatoes and oatmeal.

❖   ❖   ❖

Fanny Ward rode out to Narrow Water only to find that the Butlers had returned to Dublin. Dr Butler had taken one of his 'turns'.

'Biliousness from overindulgence, if you ask me!' declared Madam Hall crossly. She felt rather let down by her friends, although Letitia had been genuinely upset at having to go with her parents. Fanny was not unduly worried by their departure, engrossed as she was in the chaos of her domestic situation. Her other guests had departed in unseemly haste and only a few inexperienced maids from Newry were left to serve the house. The cook had taken to her bed for the first time in twenty years with a 'bad bellyache', which Fanny recognised as retaliation for her having allowed a strange chef into the kitchen. Donnan, a nervous sort, had also abandoned his post and fled to his brother's in Waring's Point. The result was miserable meals prepared by the kitchen maid and shabbily served with all the wrong cutlery. Fanny had, in desperation, sent for Samuel McIntyre's wife, only to be informed that she too was 'bad with her nerves', and refusing to set foot outside the door.

'Such a to-do about nothing,' the vexed Fanny commented to

Madam Hall.

'I would not say "nothing", my dear,' the Squire corrected, 'these agrarian outrages must be taken seriously. One night your barn is burned down. Next night it could be your house!'

'Oh, but that's not what it's all about!' Fanny protested. 'They are looking for a French agent. Our own peasants would not harm any of the family. I'm sure of that! And I told Captain Walls so!'

'Be careful what you say to that fellow,' advised Squire Hall. 'You know what these Castle men are like! Can get hold of the wrong end of the stick. Doesn't like northerners. Of that I'm sure. Doesn't understand us.'

Fanny did not mention to the Halls her real concern – her brother, Henry. He had begun to drink heavily; indeed, due to the shortage of household staff, he was imbibing brandy quicker than the glasses could be cleared away.

'Of course it's none of my concern,' Fanny rambled on as they rode through the woods of Narrow Water, 'but Henry and Captain Walls... He's not our sort really.'

'It's really up to Valentine to see that Walls doesn't go beyond the bounds. Perhaps I should pay him a call,' mused the Squire.

Fanny was barely listening. Her brother's melancholy, she suspected, had less to do with the military presence in Rostrevor than the loss of his mistress.

❖   ❖   ❖

'There is nothing innocent about her. We are dealing with a dangerous woman. I cannot consider releasing her!' Walls said stiffly. 'If you wish, I will have her transferred to Newry where at least she may be safe from the other prisoners.'

'I demand her release!' Henry Valentine insisted sharply. 'I only agreed to her arrest for her own safety! She was safer in custody.'

'And it will be safer for all of us if she remains in custody.' Walls was angry that the Major had taken it upon himself to order Thomas Dunn's release, for the lawyer could have provided him with some useful information. Not that he was the type to be involved with the mindless Oakboys, but he was certainly well informed on other more political matters. Besides, he knew the law, and it would not be easy to re-arrest him without due cause.

'All these prisoners, they are entitled to a fair trial if there are grounds for suspicion. And I don't see how excessive use of the whip will help. People will confess to anything to escape that,' Valentine protested.

'What? In order to be hanged, drawn and quartered? That is the fate to which the old Dissenter has condemned himself, a man who should be whiling out his remaining years by his fireside. Getting involved in French plots! Any man who has taken an illegal oath will face transportation at the very least.' Walls was convinced of the effectiveness of flogging, and did not feel that his measures were in any way excessive. 'Besides, I warned you that it would be unwise to interfere. This is no simple local matter. If anyone is harbouring MacArtain he must expect the sternest punishment, for it is no less than he deserves. Those fools in their bog cabins dream of the French, when some of them don't even know where lies that land or how Louis would govern them!'

'That reflects sadly on us,' Valentine responded, 'that they would be prepared to take their chances with someone like Louis, who could be a demon incarnate for all they know. If those traitors – and yes, I want to see them hanged as much as you do – but if they were given food and shelter it is merely because hospitality is second nature to the folk in the Poorlands. They survive by helping each other. They would not turn a stranger in need away. Call it, if you like, the shreds of an ancient dignity not yet lost to this poor beaten race.'

Walls did not reply. He suspected that the local man's education had been too liberal.

❖ ❖ ❖

Henry Valentine was relieved to find himself with an unexpected ally. Squire Hall rode in from Narrow Water, demanding to be informed of the situation. He was concerned for the general peace and stability of the area, and was unwilling to sanction any extreme measures to recapture the outlaw.

'As I see it,' the Squire observed bluntly, ''twas your own fault that the blackguard escaped in the first place.'

Captain Walls, confronted by two influential landlords and magistrates, was forced to make concessions.

'It's all jolly well for you,' continued Squire Hall, 'but crying women and untended flocks don't pay the rent. And there are enough bitter memories to feed the peasant's anger never mind adding to them. I warn you, Walls! Any excessive act which reaches my ears will be personally reported at the highest level.'

Walls knew that this was no idle threat, for Madam Hall was related to the Lord Lieutenant. 'That will not be necessary,' he replied. 'I have already given orders for most of my prisoners to be released, although,' he cautioned, 'further charges may be brought. At least you may be grateful that I have given your local agrarian bully boy's society a good shaking up. They should be left in no doubt about who is master here.'

❖   ❖   ❖

Donal, cold and wet, plodded over the boggy ground, his boots sinking in the mire. The baying of bloodhounds quickened his step as he clawed through the mist, knowing not where he was going, nor whence the baying came. He was numbed and exhausted when a different, more welcome sound attracted his attention. It was the ring of a goat bell.

'Sosanna!' he cried. There was no reply. 'Christ!' he breathed, 'Now they'll surely know where to find me.' He stumbled as the ground fell away beneath him, staggering downwards, clutching wildly for something to hold. With a splash he landed in a stream, one of the many which cut its way through the mountain turf. Cursing his lack of judgement, he picked himself out of the freezing water and tried to recover his bearings. Slightly upstream his eye alighted on an overhanging shelf which looked familiar to him. It was the place where he had first kissed Sosanna.

Dusk was falling, and he had to find refuge from the biting cold of night. At the back of his mind was his meeting with Sosanna, when she had mentioned something about a booley hut. At the time shelter against the elements had not been his first consideration, but he realised now that if he was to survive another bitter night he would have to find the hut. The barking of the dogs had ceased, and only his rasping cough broke the silence as he stumbled over the turf in search of a place of refuge. It took him some time to find the booley in the darkness and mist. It was a partly hollowed out cave with two walls and a roof of sods and thatch, so overgrown that it blended in with its surroundings to the point of being invisible.

Donal's eyes and nose were streaming; his aching throat longed for the soothing potion which Makepeace kept for such emergencies, and this reminder of his loss only served to deepen his misery. Closing the hurdle door behind him, he blinked in the darkness. The hut was chilly and damp and all his garments were soaked through. He would have chanced kindling a fire, but there was nothing to burn. The cowherd who built the booley had a makeshift litter in the corner, and the young man stumbled towards it, his feet squelching in his boots. He was overcome by another spasm of coughing as he prised his icy feet from his boots. To his astonishment, he discovered a few thick fleeces and a dry blanket folded on the bed. Clearly the booley was in use, but as there was no sign of anyone coming to claim his bed, Donal made himself as comfortable as he could. As he did so his feet knocked against a reed basket containing a can of buttermilk, cold potatoes and an oatcake. In a moment of panic he scrambled to the door and peered into the night to see if there was anyone outside. There was only darkness. As he wolfed down the food and milk, he looked hard at the basket. There was a scrap of ribbon tied to the handle... Memories flooded back of the sunny fair day at Clonduff – Sosanna had sported a ribbon then. He smiled and pulled the fleeces around him. Somehow he did not now feel so alone and forlorn.

❖   ❖   ❖

'What more do you want of me?' Grace snapped at Sergeant Pollard as he entered her cell.

'I came to tell you that you will be shifted to Newry soon. We cannot keep women here for long,' he replied shortly. 'You will be provided with clean garments,' he added, looking at her filthy skirts.

"Tis of little matter to me,' she shrugged, running her fingers through her hair. Now, thought Pollard, she would have to answer for her bravado, abandoned and alone. He hesitated in the doorway before turning to speak again.

'He did the right thing by you, you know.'

'What are you talking about?'

'Think about what that howling mob would have done to you, if it wasn't for him.'

'I presume you are speaking of Master Dunn. 'Twas he who saved me from injury at their hands.'

'But Major Valentine himself sent Tom Dunn. And had you arrested. What better way to convince the crowd of your innocence?' Pollard hesitated and looked out to make sure he was not being overheard. 'I only say this, ma'am, so that you'll know. He, the Major that is, had to be stopped from riding to rescue you himself. Then you both would surely have been killed.' He looked at her sitting motionless, showing no sign that she was listening.

'I'll see to those clothes then, ma'am,' Pollard bowed and prepared to leave.

His bandaged hand fumbled so awkwardly with the latch that Grace herself opened the door.

'None if this was your doing, Sergeant Pollard,' she said.

'What was my doing was not to my liking.'

That evening Pollard returned with some clothing and a pan of water. This time it was Grace who initiated the conversation.

'Why do you think he had me arrested? Did he think I wished for the indignity of a prison cell?'

'I cannot say, ma'am. I should think he was convinced, as we all were, of your innocence.'

'Were? Are you no longer convinced?'

'I don't rightly know what constitutes innocence and what guilt. Wiser men than me will ponder on that question. You know,

Mistress O'Lochlainn, when you walk free, you will be absolved of guilt in the eyes of the law, and you'll be well thought of by your own folk for having shared their troubles. As for the Major, he risked everything for you.'

'Henry Valentine? Risking everything?' Grace laughed scornfully. She looked at the soldier. 'Oh, have you not been here long enough to know how "proper" they are!'

'Not long enough? Too bloody long, if you ask me!' They both smiled.

'How long have you served in uniform?'

'I enlisted when I was fourteen, give or take a few months,' the Sergeant answered. 'Of course I lied about my age when I took the King's shilling, but no questions were asked. Ach, they were desperate for men to put down the rebellion in Scotland, and I was big enough – that's all that mattered to them.'

Grace listened quietly as he spoke of his childhood in Wales, and how he had given his mother the slip to listen to the promises of the recruiting band. From there he had been swept into wars in lands he had never before heard of, against enemies he did not know he had. It was many years before he was allowed home again to his valley, 'in ways,' he said, 'like this valley, except it was home...' His mother had run to meet him, crying and scolding, her small frame even tinier than he had remembered. She had been working the farm alone, for his father was dead and brother Glynn sick; yes, it was hard for him to tell her that he had already signed up for another term. In the end she just smiled and told him she knew he'd make her proud of him.

Grace had somehow never thought of these faceless redcoats as having mothers, sick brothers and worries of their own.

'She must be elderly now,' she said, as she washed her grimy face in the water pan.

'Aye! Eighty years old next winter,' he said proudly 'and you wouldn't take her for seventy. Still dresses up on a Sunday and visits the graves with my sister's sons. Blind as a bat, she is, but she has a wit like a sickle.' He held up his right hand. 'I usually write to her. Once a month, so that she can tell all's well. I hope she won't take it that there's something amiss this time.'

It did not take Grace long to write his letter. She was doing him a kindness, and while there would be those who would criticise her for it, Grace had had acquaintance with many different types of people in her life, and the Sergeant of the Barrack was no worse than many of them.

'The minister will read her the letter, so she won't know it isn't my writing,' said Pollard.

'And is this all you want me to say?'

'Read it out to me. Just to make sure. You have a lovely flow of the hand.'

Grace cleared her throat and began to read.

'Dear Mam,

'I wish you to know that I am in good health. The rations here are plentiful. Look after yourself and do not worry about me,

'Your loving son,

'Aeneas Pollard (Sergeant)

'May 19th, 1780.'

❖   ❖   ❖

Donal shivered as he pulled the blanket around his shoulders. The falling rain thundered down on the booley. He was too unhappy and miserable to form any plans for the future. He sorely missed his beloved Makepeace, and recalled over and over the last cry he had heard him make.

Tears streamed down his face as memories came flooding back. The rough black shoulder which had comforted him as a child; expeditions to the tanners' yards, where Master Agnew picked up the raw materials of his bookbinding trade; visits to the port of Larne, where Makepeace liked to minister to heathen seafarers and backsliders. Donal had often thought that the real purpose of these visits was because the Dissenter shared his fascination with tall sailing ships and the smell of tar and rope. He asked himself if it was there that he had first acquired the cursed wanderlust that had got them into their present predicament, and dejectedly blamed himself for following his own selfish ambitions.

Now, here he was; the sunny climes Makepeace had talked of further away than ever, impossible to dream about let alone reach. Hunted, helpless, he knew he should try to move on once darkness fell again, but where to go, he knew not. The fugitive shook out his sodden great-cloak, clutched his blanket close to him, and returned to the bed.

'Donal!' a voice called from outside. He stiffened. It was Sosanna! He choked on his tears but did not answer. He heard her call again, timidly.

'Donal, *a chroí?*'

Instead of opening his arms to her, wretchedness and shame overwhelmed him and he hid his face.

'Go home, Sosanna. Go home now!' he choked.

'I've brought you food, and some dry clothes. I stole them myself.'

He lifted his heavy streaming eyes towards her and a coughing fit overcame him once more. She dropped her burden and ran towards him, cradling his head and crooning as she would to a sick animal.

'You will feel better when you have changed your clothes,' she whispered, 'for then we must leave.'

'We?'

'You surely didn't think I'd let you go without me!' she said, and her eyes shone like stars in his darkened world.

❖ ❖ ❖

Commodore O'Farrell put into port at La Rochelle as he had often done before. A warm evening sun gave the French town a welcoming glow as a few women with their children and babies waved to the berthing ship. It was a happy homecoming for most of his crew, but O'Farrell was deeply concerned for the welfare of Jupiter who had been hit at Ballyedmond cove. The man had bled freely and was very ill. The voyage had not been one of O'Farrell's more successful missions, but at least the ship was undamaged and he still had all his crew. Had it not been for the skillful oarsmanship of the Kerryman they might all be lying in some stinking

Irish prison by now. He knew that the hopeful little party on the shore had been impossibly outnumbered and now stood no chance of being rescued. The wounded Jupiter would not have been the only casualty.

'What takes you back there, again and again, Seigneur?' asked the black man from his bed. O'Farrell thought for a moment before answering.

'I think, Jupiter, I will not be returning to Ireland,' he said. Picking up his quill he added two words to his log book.

'Mission abandoned.'

Chapter Seventeen

S EÁN O'LOCHLAINN stirred in his sleep on the gaolhouse floor. There were not many of them left now; some, including Brennan of Kilfeighan, had been transferred to the Assizes at Newry or Downpatrick to face the mercy of the circuit judge. He had kept his head and had confessed to nothing, although he had been at different times beaten, or cajoled with promises of instant freedom. Tom Dunn had prepared him for such an eventuality, and he knew that it was wisest to keep pleading ignorance. He could in all honesty say that he had nothing to do with the Oakboys.

Seán had assumed the mantle of leadership of the prisoners once Dunn had been released, and Father Mackey, allowed one visit to his imprisoned flock, had exhorted the Kilbroney man to 'look out for the foolish younger lads'. Seán felt he himself was the foolish one for getting caught in the first place. He wondered why Eamonn had not been arrested like the others, for although his brother was a guileless lad, how were the authorities to know that?

'O'Lochlainn?' A clipped unfamiliar voice sounded in the doorway. 'No charges. You can go.' Seán struggled to his feet. He would be glad to get home, but he felt guilty about those he had left behind, who were to face the magistrate on petty charges. The way Squire Hall doled out sentences depended, they said, on the turn of the moon.

'You may take your father home with you,' the same voice added as Seán's eyes adjusted to the light.

Thady was still manacled to the flogging tree. His back was stretched and raw, flies alighting on the suppurating wounds. Seán looked away. He wondered if the old fellow still had a breath in him. The trooper who unlocked Thady's chains reassured the younger man: 'He's been well salted. I'd say he's in with a fighting chance, if he doesn't die of the shock.'

Seán gingerly eased his father onto the sward of the Barrack Green. He looked around for help, but folk appeared to be going about their daily business as if nothing untoward had happened.

'Mother of mercy,' he wept softly, 'how could they do this to you?' The villagers were too frightened to come forward to help them. They kept their distance out of fear of becoming embroiled with, or of being seen to help suspect men. The old man groaned weakly; he had clearly lost a lot of blood during his ordeal.

'You're all right!' Seán reassured him. 'We'll get you home.' He lifted his father over his shoulder and staggered up the hill under his burden. Thady whimpered with pain. 'I'm going as steady as I can,' Seán soothed him anxiously. 'We're almost at Mistress Dunn's.'

❖ ❖ ❖

Dawn rose over Dunn's Hill as the master of the house prepared to ride to Newry. 'I am not happy leaving you at a time like this,' he told Annie.

'Can't your business wait?' his wife asked.

'No. There are men I must speak with. I have to see if there is any protection in law for the men facing the circuit court. I may call on Squire Hall.'

'I never heard you speak well of him before.'

'No. But I have heard that he hasn't taken kindly to Walls exerting his authority in his area. They're like dogs defending their own patch, all of them. Perhaps Hall will extend his protection to humbler men.'

'He'll more than likely sentence them to transportation – and you too, Tom, if you're not careful!'

'Am I not always careful?' He sat down to break his fast, noticing that her face seemed thinner and more apprehensive than before. Taking her hands gently in his, he spoke softly.

'What is it, love? Will I arrange for you and Betsy to have company? 'Tis a pity the boys are at school at such a time.'

'Thank heaven they are at school. Had they been living here, they might have been taken away too,' she answered angrily. 'Did you see Thady? Did you see how they left him? If anything like that ever happened to you, I don't think I...' She raised a fearful hand to her mouth. He made to take her in his arms, but she shrugged him off.

'Do you not see, my love, that if they had any real evidence against me they would have moved long ago. They don't, so they can do nothing. Annie,' he silenced her protests, 'if I know anything, it is the law of the land. For the greater part, the law is fine and just, and by punishing me without evidence they would only belittle that which they claim to uphold.'

Annie listened to him patiently as she always did. He was so sure of himself, and, despite her misgivings, all she could do was nod in agreement. She was a good Presbyterian, and attended the Meeting House in Waring's Point when she could. She knew that Tom was not the most pious of Papists, but he had strong political beliefs which she respected, even if she did not share them.

'And are they French agents?' Annie asked.

'Agnew and MacArtain? An unlikely pair, by any standards. An impulsive youth who talks when he would be better remaining silent. The other an ancient cripple. No, I don't think so. Perhaps their mission was to join the Irish Brigade. Who knows?' Dunn wiped his bread around the bowl.

'You mean,' asked Annie, 'you became involved with this pair to no purpose?'

'Do not quiz me too hard, Annie! You are worse than Captain Walls. Mark what I say, for then you, too, will know what to say. I repeat, it is my belief that Agnew and MacArtain were not French agents. The young man's a braggart!' He rose to lift down his travelling cloak. 'Now tell Betsy to come and give me a kiss before I leave,' he coaxed. For once Annie was determined not to let him away with his explanation.

'What do you mean, a braggart?' she enquired.

'Boyd told me the story as he heard it. It seemed young MacArtain had some whimsical notion of fighting under the

262

banner of the Irish Brigade in France. Well, to me, one band of mercenaries is much the same as any other, but he was adamant that he was going to France, and nowhere else. One night he accompanied some other young bucks to a tavern and declared, for all to hear, that his father was a Frenchman. No doubt he was under the spell of Bacchus, for he added that his father had the ear of King Louis. Well, you know how rumours spread, and the words were no doubt exaggerated, so, in a short time both he and old Agnew were arrested.'

'And was there any evidence against the pair, apart from his drunken prattle?' asked Annie.

'None that I know of. At any rate, the old Dissenter was sent home with a stern warning, and Donal was detained, to cool him off, perhaps. The whole thing would have blown over had not the young fool escaped from custody. Then the hue and cry really went up. The incident reached certain paranoid ears at Dublin Castle and there was a full-scale alert.'

'And how did they end up here, I wonder?' Annie was not impressed with tales of drunken louts and gaol-breakers.

'In desperation Agnew sought the help of my friend Russell, for whom he had bound books in the past. Russell concurred that recapture meant, at the very least, long years in prison, so he agreed to help. The old fellow would have given anything to save the unworthy lad, I believe, and perhaps Russell had earmarked him for some future role. Russell has French contacts, so they say.'

'And Captain Walls obviously had no doubt that the whole parish was in it with him,' added Annie.

'Certainly! He was sure that the agrarian society reprobates were in collusion with the enemy, and he did not like Valentine's placatory attitude. It did not go down well with a government which has armed militia marching and drilling all over the land. And then, to cap it all, he finds a connection with Valentine's discarded mistress.' Dunn picked up his daughter Betsy, mindful of Annie's warning to be careful of what he said before the child.

'Discarded mistress indeed!' fumed Annie as she set about the morning's chores.

❖ ❖ ❖

Grace stared into the darkness, too weak to move, too miserable to sleep. Tormenting thoughts haunted her. She was now thirty-one years of age, and most of the girls with whom she had grown up had large families of their own and futures mapped out by their children. She had no future, only a past. They would not keep her locked up forever, but when she was released, where would she go? She dare not go back to her own folk. She would not go back to Henry. She wished him well, preferring to believe that in his heart he still had her interests in mind. She did not think she still loved him. She began to wonder if she ever had, or was it the life of everlasting summers and roses and soft beds and full bellies which had beguiled her? Confused recollections of the dazzling splendour of the world which she had lived in, but never belonged to, taunted her. And worst of all was the memory of the face of a child with haunting green eyes. She sat up with a start. If he knew the truth, what would he think of her?

For some time every night, in the relative quiet, she paced up and down, trying to make coherent plans for the future. She wondered what had made her betray her feelings under cross-examination, she who had always been so guarded. In a way Grace felt the better for it. One evening the cell door opened and light from the lamp of the wardress flooded the stone walls as other inmates roused themselves from sleep.

'O'Lochlainn!' A finger prodded her bony shoulder. 'Out you come! You have a visitor.'

Grace had had no visitors, save a well-meaning young pastor who had lent her a bible to read to the others when he discovered she could read. As she had no spectacles, and her fellow inmates were not overly interested in scripture, the opportunity had been wasted.

'Hurry yourself!' the wardress shouted, 'the gentleman is waiting in the governor's room.'

'Gentleman?' Grace's hopes rose. In the dim glow of the lamp she looked into the curious face of the wardress.

'Come on,' the stern woman ordered. 'I'm not standing here all night for the like of you.'

❖ ❖ ❖

Madam Ward had had enough of managing the household, and had decided to go to the Dublin townhouse until everything had returned to normal. She would have felt happier if she had persuaded her brother to join her, but Henry seemed incapable of listening to reason. The only servants in the house were a couple of stupid hussies without a word of English between them, one of whom had been liberally sprinkling herself with the household lavender water, the other the cook, who was feeling precious after her illness. Fanny longed for leisurely strolls through Saint Stephen's Green and visits to her favourite milliner's in Dame Street. She had a lot of tittle-tattle to catch up on, and anticipated comfortable chats with dear Madam Butler. Goodness knows what they would think of the north now. Everything was packed, ready for the coach, but as she came down the stairs in her plum velvet travelling attire Henry emerged from the library, his face drawn and brandy glass in hand.

'Fanny, my dear, I...'

'Really Henry,' she hid her distress beneath a scolding voice, 'you must know how much I was looking forward to getting away. Why, I cannot leave the house without encountering those common billeted soldiers, more often than not with a bunch of chained prisoners. I cannot witness such distressing sights for much longer!'

'I would not wish you to.' He spoke with such despondency that her heart went out to him.

'And how,' she demanded brusquely, 'can I leave you in such a state? That will be all!' she dismissed the maidservant carrying her bags. The girl looked on uncomprehendingly. 'Get out, and leave those bags!' Fanny snapped at her. As the girl left in confusion, Fanny tried to prise the glass from her brother's hand.

'The situation is not of my making,' he sat down heavily on the stairs, burying his head in his hands.

'Please don't fret!' Shocked at his distress, Fanny eased herself down beside him. 'Everything will be all right in a day or so, Captain Walls has assured me. They will catch that scoundrel and that will be that.'

'I doubt it,' he replied, 'I very much doubt it!'

'It was wrong of the Butlers to leave in such indecent haste, but I'm sure they'll be back as soon as Dr Butler comes to his senses!' Fanny prattled on. 'In the meantime, I shall postpone my journey for a few days. It would be wrong of me to desert the fortress at such a time. Grandfather Whitechurch always led from the front!'

'Whitechurch?' cried Henry. 'To hell with his memory! He left naught but a legacy of misery.'

'He did what he had to do! If he was strong, it was because others were weak. If he was good, it was because others were evil,' Fanny stoutly defended the memory of her infamous progenitor.

'My God! You talk as though you believe what you say!' Henry broke away from her comforting arms and strode out of the house. His sister made no attempt to follow.

Henry Valentine felt badly about having lost his temper with Fanny. His sister was kind, and he was grateful that she had decided to stay, for his sake, he knew. He rode to the Barrack, to see if there was any news of the runaway outlaw. He knew from experience that such a man might hold on to his freedom for years in the mountains, and the cost of trying to recapture him was not worth the effort. Both Hall and he agreed that Walls appeared to be pursuing some kind of vendetta, and MacArtain and the old Dissenter were not the real objects of his zeal. As he reached the village he saw groups of soldiers lolling about, and a motley assortment of farming implements – scythes, peat spades, flails and cudgels – had been put on display on the Barrack Green.

'The spoils of war!' He kicked angrily at the presentation, barking at a trooper to get off his backside.

In the Barrack yard Captain Walls was preparing to leave with a horse patrol.

'Ahoy there, Valentine!' he called. 'Come ride with us! We are closing in on our prey!'

'I have just been admiring your magnificent array of captured arms, and was asking myself: "How on earth can a cottier warm his hearth without the help of a turf spade?"' Valentine answered scornfully. 'Or, "How will we cut the corn without the scythe wielders?" In fact, how can any peasant toil without his implements?'

'You ignore the fact that these are potentially lethal weapons,' Walls replied stiffly. 'In the hands of dangerous men, these are more than simple rustic tools.'

'We have very little evidence of anything other than a few isolated incidents. That is no reason to take such drastic measures.'

'Perhaps,' said Walls, 'when we rearrest MacArtain, these lawless men will go to ground once more. At any rate, I shall rest easier.' He spurred on his horse and, after a moment's hesitation, Valentine followed him.

❖ ❖ ❖

As they approached the Priest's Mountain a cry went up. Someone had spotted some figures near the disused altar stone, and troopers had been positioned so that the fugitive could not easily escape. Valentine was uneasy about the mountain and all its bloody associations.

'Be careful!' he called. 'This is known as a place of pilgrimage.'

'These are no pilgrims,' Walls's tone was cold as he raised his pistol. 'And neither are they goatherds.' He watched as the distant figures, realising the presence of the soldiers, huddled together in fear. One began to run towards the officers, waving in agitation.

'Watch him, sir!' a voice called, 'he could be armed.'

'That's a chance I will not take!' replied Walls as he prepared to fire. Without warning Henry Valentine lunged at him, knocking him from his horse.

'You fool,' he cried, 'that's Eamonn! You might have killed him!' Such was the ferocity of Valentine's attack that Walls lay on the ground, temporarily winded, yet he raised his pistol once again. The shot fired uselessly in the air as he was set upon by the furious landlord, his fists landing on Walls's chin and underbelly.

'You bloodthirsty imbecile!' Valentine shouted. 'Would you kill another innocent lad for your pleasure?'

Walls's temper snapped: he would see to this 'toy soldier'. Two of the Newry troopers pulled Valentine off the captain. Walls stood up and carefully brushed the soil from his coat. He regarded Valentine coldly for a moment; then, as the troopers pinned Valentine's arms back, he administered a severe and thorough beating.

Satisfied with his work, Walls remounted and rode off, calling his men to heel. Valentine was left lying amid the bracken and heather.

Eamonn O'Lochlainn rushed to the landlord's side. 'Major Valentine!' he cried, kneeling beside the injured man. 'God save us! What have they done to you?' As Valentine tried to sit up, a rush of blood poured from his mouth.

'Stay there!' said Eamonn. He looked around him helplessly. The group of scholars who had accompanied him to the Mass Rock had dispersed, and only the curious Owen MacOwen remained. 'Keep an eye on the gentleman!' he bade Owen. 'I'll go for help!'

Valentine choked and stuttered alarmingly, holding his hand out to Eamonn.

'Don't leave me with this brigand,' his voice was weak, but insistent.

'Brigand? Owen MacOwen?' asked a bemused Eamonn. Owen looked away.

"Tis the knock on his head that's talking,' he suggested, as the injured man eyed him warily.

'Help me to my feet,' Valentine said. 'I'd rather take my chances than put myself at the mercy of this young reprobate.'

'What did you do to him?' hissed Eamonn as he eased an arm around his wounded benefactor.

'He did nothing!' Valentine cut in. 'What he might have done is another matter.'

Eamonn seemed relieved. 'There is no harm in Owen, but he can be a bit foolish and hotheaded at times, and he's a reluctant scholar. Are you all right?' he asked again, as Valentine winced.

'Help me mount. I've had worse beatings at school.' Eamonn eyed him doubtfully. He had seen what had happened. 'Major Valentine,' he said, 'I am once again in your debt. You may have saved my life.'

'No. He would not have killed you. I over-reacted and deserved what I got.'

'You're a guardian angel!' exclaimed the young man. 'God sent you to good purpose.'

'God will have a lot to answer for when I meet him face to face,' replied Valentine dourly.

Eamonn led Major Valentine's horse down the valley, talking of his plans for the future and the Bishop's faith in him as if the present crisis affected him not at all. When Valentine asked him about Thady's injuries, the young man displayed complete confidence in the Widow Fearon's healing methods.

'She seems to be a remarkable woman, this widow.'

'She is. I would have died in childhood were it not for her ministrations.'

'Yes. You were fortunate. I hope she will do as much for your... father.' Henry Valentine uttered the word with some difficulty, but Eamonn appeared not to have noticed. They conversed easily, as though no chasm of class or creed separated them, and when Henry arrived back at the house, his face swollen and bruised, he felt able to smile at his sister's shocked face. He was developing a fondness for the boy, and already regretted having promised to send him away. Nevertheless he suggested to Eamonn that he might like to avail himself of any books in his library while he prepared for his departure. The young man expressed his delight, promising to make no further intrusion on his patron's generosity. Grace's name was not mentioned. Eamonn wondered if the Major had already forgotten about her.

❖ ❖ ❖

Walls was fuming. He had not intended to let his dislike of Henry Valentine become so obvious, but he felt justified in 'teaching him a lesson'. He wondered what it was about Eamonn O'Lochlainn that had made Valentine react so. Squire Hall, a bumptious fool who insisted on the letter of the law being observed to ridiculous lengths, would never have risked his own safety for any peasant, and would certainly not approve of his landlord friend having 'broken ranks' in front of the common soldiery.

He sent for Coyle first of all, an obnoxious man devoid of grace or manners, with the appearance of one who would betray his brother for a handful of coins. Yet despite Walls's skillful flattery, cajolery and thinly-veiled threats, Coyle remained steadfastly loyal to his master.

It was Fanny Ward who proved to be the best source of information. He sought her out while she was weeding in her garden. Her kilted skirt was studded with burrs and a grubby apron girded her waist.

'Forgive me, Captain Walls. I had completely forgotten the time, so upset am I by this dreadful business.' She prattled on about her garden and the unreliability of servants, removing her apron and tossing it on the path where she stood. Walls listened patiently as she talked. He had found that such a policy paid dividends. She pushed a few unruly curls behind her ears while asking him to admire her yellow May rose.

'You know, 'tis the earliest rose in the county!' she declared proudly, sniffing a bloom. 'Oh, do sit down. I am sure you have more important things with which to concern yourself than my garden. Then we'll have tea!'

'Your brother has recovered from his ordeal?' he enquired cautiously.

'Poor Henry! He would not tell me what happened. Just pooh-poohed the whole thing. Something to do with that O'Lochlainn boy. After Henry promising to send him to that French seminary.'

'To the Roman priesthood?' Walls caught his breath.

'No, no! 'Tis nothing like as bad as it seems, and anyway, Henry would not like it to be generally known.'

'I should think not.'

'Personally, I think it a foolish gesture. Apart from obviously encouraging Romish idolatry, it could easily be misinterpreted in the present climate.'

'He has a fondness for the boy, perhaps?' Walls enquired discreetly.

'Stuff and nonsense!' replied Fanny tersely. 'He has no more time for that sort of thing than you do.' She bent to tackle an offending dandelion.

'Oh, you might as well have it all!' She declared recklessly. 'Henry had, in his youth, an unfortunate liaison with a peasant girl. Of course this sort of thing happens all the time. Grandfather Whitechurch in his day...'

'But this was different.' Walls nipped in the bud what could have been a lengthy historical diversion.

'Yes, it was. He became very attached to Grace O'Lochlainn. She would almost have passed for a lady. Actually, she was employed as housekeeper here, and managed extremely well in spite of everything.'

'But she is no longer here.'

'Heavens no! Henry was getting married and, well, off she went. I was thankful at first, but now I wonder if the pain of their parting has been worth it. He is so miserable.'

'But, as you say, he was getting married. Miss Butler might not have taken kindly to sharing him with the housekeeper.'

'Oh, it wasn't Letitia! It was her! She would not share him with his wife! The strange thing is it was she who suggested going. And she would not take one penny from him! Yes, she was different.'

'And she sent her brother here?'

'Yes! I was setting my borders outside the window when he came. I was, frankly, quite amazed.' She drew herself up. 'He talked about France, and the priesthood, and such things.'

'France? Think hard! What did he have to say about France?' Walls's urgency betrayed him for Fanny's eyes adopted a wary expression.

'I cannot say. He talked a lot of superstitious nonsense. Something about a bell...'

That evening, Walls sent for Pollard. The search for MacArtain had borne no fruit, and he was beginning to accept that the outlaw might have made good his escape. There were reports of sightings of strange men all over Iveagh, and there was no shortage of men seeking to claim a reward for his recapture. However, he knew that MacArtain was in no way strange. He was an ordinary young man who would probably pass for any mountain peasant, and, short of rounding them all up, there was nothing more to be done. In a way, he felt, his quest had now changed to a highly personal curiosity as to the relationship between Valentine and young O'Lochlainn. And if he could publicly discredit the landlord, he would do so.

'Why was Eamonn O'Lochlainn not arrested with the others?' he asked Sergeant Pollard.

'He's a bit of a fool. A guileless fool. "Eamonn a Chloig", they call him in Gaelic, Eamonn of the Bell. So harmless that we let him be!'

'And where would you expect to find him, this harmless fool?' asked Walls evenly.

'He runs a bog-school. For the poor lads. He teaches letters and the like. Even some Greek and Latin, I believe.'

'Quite an academy, this bog-school; we came upon it earlier. The dead boy, Fegan. Was he a pupil?'

'I believe so,' replied the Sergeant. 'And a bright young scholar he was too, they say.'

'What use would brains be to him? The poor lad's better off where he is now.' Walls decided that the activities of Eamonn O'Lochlainn would be worthy of further investigation.

❖ ❖ ❖

Eily applied a soothing green balm to Thady's wounds, one which had been supplied by the Widow Fearon, along with an effective curse which guaranteed to wither the arm that wielded the fearful 'cat'. The curses, maintained the Widow, were good for the nerves, for how else would you ever get back at 'them at the Barrack'. Thady moaned. His had not been the only back to suffer, but it had been the first, and so the worst, an example to loosen the tongues of those who followed him.

'Easy now, *a stór!*'* Eily soothed, as the green emolient caressed his wounds. 'The scabs are knitting on your back and the fine new skin won't take long in growing. You'll be dancing on your feet in no time.'

'At least,' he winced, 'it will put the complaining out of me. The rheumatism was nothing to what I feel now.' He watched while she went about her work. He had often wondered what Eily did during the day while he was out on the mountain. Now he had some idea. His neighbour, the Buller, had dutifully kept an eye on things while the O'Lochlainn men were locked up. That did not mean, Eily remarked tersely, that he had helped her with the work, rather that he appeared in the doorway every time she lifted a crock of praties off the fire. Thady told her not to begrudge him a bite to eat, for he liked to think that there was a man with a head on him about the place. The implication that neither Eamonn, Sosaí nor herself could manage alone, irked her. She also harboured deep concerns for the two youngest members of the household.

Eily began to boil up the strips of linen she had used for dressing Thady's back. Grey steam filled the cabin and Thady complained that she was choking him.

'This will clean out your lungs for you,' she replied confidently, pouring a noxious brown concoction onto the bubbles. The Widow swore by steeping the liquid contents of the piss-pot with yellow whin-heads to kill the infection, and Eily had to admit that the odour was far from pleasant. 'A bad smell never killed anybody,' she announced, but when Thady started retching she decided to lift the crock outdoors. She almost collided with Seán on the threshold.

'Musha! You might have scalded the both of us.'

'Here! Give me a hold of that damned crock,' her burly son insisted.

'Mind your tongue, Seán,' growled his father from the corner. 'I

*A *stór*: my love.

273

suppose you picked up that from the troopers.'

'I could have taught them worse, the same boys,' replied Seán with a grin. He lifted the steaming pot and both mother and son disappeared outside. Their voices were no longer chiding, but hushed and concerned. Thady strained his ears to listen.

'What are the two of you whispering about?' he shouted. He hated being kept out of things. He suspected that young Sosaí was off on her rambles again – he knew she had not been ready for marriage. Eily reappeared, a troubled look on her face. Thady was about to quiz his wife when he saw that she was putting on her cap. She only did that when the priest or William Dwyer came calling, or when she had something of import to discuss.

'What ails you, girl?' he asked anxiously. 'Were you talking about Sosanna? Has she gone off again?'

'No, not Sosanna. 'Tis Grace.' Eily sat and folded her hands, another portent of bad news.

'Grace!' Thady grimaced as he tried to sit up. 'What's happened to her?'

'Don't twist yourself like that,' scolded his wife, 'or you'll start the bleeding again.' She helped him ease himself down. 'No, Grace is all right. I mean, she's safe for the present.'

'She never brought us anything but shame and trouble. I don't think this time is going to be any different.'

'You'll have to go easy on her! She needs you now.'

'It was always going to come to that,' Thady muttered. 'I don't want to see her again about the place! And that's my final word.' To his distress, Eily began to weep.

'As if I don't have enough to worry me without thinking about her lying in gaol.' There was a moment's silence.

'Gaol? You didn't tell me she was in gaol,' he said in a hoarse voice.

'Aye, there's plenty I didn't tell you. You know she'd left him and moved into the Healing House at Levallyclanowen. She was afraid to come home. Afraid of not being welcome.'

'That was her choice.'

'And it was ours. The poor girl had nobody to stand up for her

274

when they attacked.'

'The troopers attacked her?' Thady asked angrily.

'No. A crowd of our own. Children and young lads, I hear. They burned her out of the house, and would have killed her only for Master Dunn, God bless him. Then the troopers took her away, for her own safekeeping, Eamonn said. Then they took her to Newry. That was a few weeks ago.'

'Ask Dunn to find out why they're holding her,' urged an agitated Thady. 'He'll oblige me, I'm sure.' Guilty feelings welled within him as he realised that his daughter was alone and undefended.

Seán appeared in the doorway. 'They wouldn't let him see her,' he said, 'so he went to see Squire Hall.'

'Much good will he do her.' Thady had a low opinion of the planters of Narrow Water.

'He's a fair man, to give him his due,' insisted Seán, 'for he lost no time about riding to Newry with Dunn, and securing her release on his own surety. 'Twas late at night too, by all accounts.'

'I'll pay him back!' Thady remarked dourly. 'When I can raise a shilling or two.'

'You'll do no such thing!' cried a horrified Eily. 'Us that can hardly meet the rent.'

'And where is Grace now?' asked Thady anxiously.

'She was to be brought home today. Only she has no roof of her own now.'

'The bastards. If they as much as laid a finger on her...'

'If they did,' replied Seán realistically, 'there's damn all you or I can do about it, and remember, 'twas our own folk she was rescued from.'

❖   ❖   ❖

Late that evening, Grace was ushered unceremoniously out of a military provisions cart which she had shared with two muzzled hounds.

'This is as far as you go!' called the driver before steering his horses through the gates of the Barrack. She was tired and weak after her ordeal, but savoured the fresh air as she filled her lungs with the breath of freedom. The houses of the village seemed watchful and secretive, and Grace was aware of peeping eyes at the windows. She smiled, realising that there was little harm they could do to her compared to what she had already been through.

Ricketty Dick came out of the inn with a barrel of refuse, and she wondered if the billetees were still ensconced there. A shaggy donkey with a mountain cart attached to it rested by the horse trough, but there was no sign of any fashionable carriages or the smartly groomed ponies of visiting gentlefolk. It seemed that they would most likely leave Rostrevor from their itinerary until things had settled down and order was restored. As usual, the ancient sages sat under their favourite tree, taking advantage of the late evening sun. Grace disliked these old men. She had often felt their disapproval and scorn in former days, and was loathe to pass them once again. Gathering her pride, she prepared to walk as far as Dunn's, knowing that Annie would let her sleep alongside Betsy's cot until some other arrangements could be made. As she passed the old men, an unexpected movement caused her to turn to look at them. To her surprise, first one, and then the others raised gnarled hands in salutation. She inclined her head in return before continuing onwards, wondering if she had misinterpreted this sign of goodwill.

'Grace!' A voice rang out across the square. She stood still as a man walked towards her, someone she had not seen for a long, long time.

'Come on, girl,' said Seán. 'We're going home.'

Chapter Eighteen

IT MEANT LITTLE to Murtagh Fegan that he had his daughters to comfort him. That Briony was only one of a large family simply meant that more people were affected by the loss, and so there were more left to grieve. Two nuns came to pray with the Fegans, so celebrated had the tragedy become, and they were startled to find Murtagh working at his forge as if nothing had ever happened. The little girls clung to Brigid, their mother, but no one dared go near Murtagh. The brazier burned with a new intensity as the silent blacksmith thrust irons deep into its centre, as if trying to purge his heart of the hatred he felt. He had had few customers in the weeks following the death, as folk felt that they were looking at a man without a soul, and uneasily withdrew with their broken implements, telling Brigid they would return when Murtagh was more like himself.

Brigid had burned the straw from the lad's cot. She would have burned the cot too, had her practical mind not persuaded her that they would be able to put it to use, not in the near future but perhaps when the baby had grown a bit. She worried about the way grief had taken its toll on Murtagh, and wished he would come with her to the grave and cry like any other bereaved father might. It hurt her to think that he nursed a torment she could not reach, and bore a burden which he would not allow her to share. When she had suggested that they might ask for permission to erect a little cross in Briony's memory, he had said, 'You do what you must do. I will do what I must do.'

Murtagh had taken to standing in the shadows of the Barrack wall, clutching Briony's 'sword'. He would follow the comings and goings from the Barrack, his face like a mask, his eyes unfathomable. It was agreed that he had the makings of a madman, and that he was trying to find the marksman who had killed his son.

❖ ❖ ❖

Sosanna came looking for Thomas Dunn; any nervousness she had previously felt in the presence of the great man was swept aside by the urgency of her errand. Clutching her shawl tightly about her she stole into the yard at Dunn's Hill, where the master was grooming his mare.

'Master Dunn!' she called breathlessly. 'I need to talk to you!'

'Why, Mistress Sosanna!' he bowed gallantly. He was very taken with the girl and stood back to admire her. She had certainly grown in beauty, but where Grace was serene and reserved, Sosanna was full of vibrant youthful energy. He laid down his brushes and took her hand in his.

'Your father sent you?' he decided. 'You know he is constantly in our thoughts...'

'No. I did not come about him. 'Tis Donal MacArtain!'

'I trust that by now the young rebel has gone far away,' Dunn remarked warily, suddenly foreseeing a dangerous development.

'I love him, Master Dunn!' she protested. 'I would have run away with him only...'

'Only?'

'Only he didn't want to go.'

'MacArtain?' cried Dunn, 'is he still around here? By God he'll bring more trouble on us all if he's caught. You must make him go, Sosanna.'

The girl sighed. 'You see, he knows that Makepeace Agnew is still alive. Ever since that, he has refused to go, even though I offered to accompany him.'

Dunn brushed aside this added complication. 'Did you tell him the trouble his escapade has cost us, the arrests, the floggings...'

'He knows about the arrests, but,' Sosanna maintained loyally, 'it was not he who fired the barns, or raided the pound. And,' she added dismally, 'it must have been one of our own who informed. That was not his fault.'

'No. But if he is recaptured, how many more will suffer? He will most likely contradict Agnew's story, and could implicate us all.'

278

'I did not distress him by mentioning the floggings, for he is tormented with guilt and determined to rescue Master Agnew. He is a very loyal foster son.'

'And very foolish, if that is what he is planning. Not even a French invasion could save a self-confessed traitor now. Sosanna,' Dunn looked intently at the girl, 'he must go. Tell him to make for Ballynahinch, and the cooper will advise him from there. Don't be tempted to go yourself. You will only draw attention to him.'

'I would not willingly bring him any harm,' she whispered tearfully, 'but I don't want to leave him.'

'No. But 'twill be for the best if you do. Think of the old Dissenter. He has confessed to everything. A man who would not lightly tell a lie has taken all the blame on his own brave shoulders. For the sake of Donal, and the rest of us. He faces a fearsome death at Downpatrick, for they disembowel traitors...'

Sosanna's face blanched and she turned away. 'It will be the same for your young man if he's caught.'

'I know!' she whispered sadly. 'He must go.'

❖   ❖   ❖

From his headquarters in the Barrack Captain Walls surveyed the scene on Rostrevor square where his men were drilling. His attention was drawn to the presence of Murtagh Fegan, the village blacksmith, standing beneath the flogging tree, still stained with the recent bloodletting. As the drilling men marched back through the gates, he called for Pollard.

'That blacksmith is still loitering out there. He appears to keep a constant vigil on this place. What does he want? Or whom?'

Pollard too was uneasy about the presence of Murtagh Fegan. It was unsettling for the soldiers and annoying for him. There was also little to be done about it, for Fegan was no more breaking the law than the old men gossiping beneath the oak trees.

''Tis grief,' Pollard ventured. 'He has not yet recovered from the loss of his son.'

'Has the man no backbone?' Walls was not sympathetic. 'I

could tell you stories, Pollard, of unfortunate men who have lost a lot more than a child!'

Pollard turned a deaf ear to the Dublin man. If Fegan was over-reacting to the tragedy, he was not going to stand in judgement on the matter. Children were vulnerable in this cruel world and no family could hope to escape for long, but this death had been so unnecessary.

'Bring him over to me,' ordered Walls. 'He needs a stern dressing down.' Pollard was privately of the opinion that the last thing the poor man needed was a reprimand.

Within minutes, Murtagh was standing before the Captain. His hat had been wrenched from his head and thrust into limp hands. He looked pathetic for all his size, staring blindly ahead. As Pollard left the room he felt thankful that young Davies had been shifted to Newry, and the two were not likely to meet each other.

'Now then, Fegan!' Walls spoke in a crisp, forthright manner. 'What is this all about? Grieving for your son? Only natural. It's a pity these things happen, but there you are.'

Murtagh stirred. How often before had he heard that phrase, 'These things happen?' Was it an explanation or an excuse? 'These things happen...'

'Diseases happen. Bad harvests happen. Storms happen,' he whispered. 'But this did not *happen*. Someone *made* it happen.'

'Well, don't go blaming a common soldier for it!' Walls pontificated. 'If you are going to blame anyone, blame yourself for allowing the child to become involved in the incident.'

'I do blame myself. To my death I'll blame myself. But I also blame the hand that set the trap, the trap that ensnared Briony,' cried Murtagh.

Walls listened. The blacksmith talked not of the hand that held the gun but rather the 'hand that set the trap'. All the blacksmith's wrath was directed towards the one among his own who had broken faith.

Looking closely at Murtagh, Walls decided to throw out a bait.

'Tell me, Fegan, what do you know of this Eamonn "a Chloig", as I believe he's called?'

'Eamonn O'Lochlainn?' Murtag[h] [...]
know?'

'He taught your son. I believe h[e] [...]
priesthood.'

'May God take care of him.'

'He seems to be an ambitious youn[g] [...]
Raised in poverty, determined to study [...]

It was of no importance to Murtagh w[here...]
to go. He shook his head. ''Twas Paris b[...]

'Before?'

'When I was a lad, they sent Matthe[w Ga]non to Paris. He
worked hard to raise the fare, but everybody that could, and many
that couldn't, did their bit. It was a great blessing to make a priest
of a man. There were powerful indulgences going, if you could
afford it.'

'Isn't it fortunate for young O'Lochlainn that he won't have to
pay his own way?' Captain Walls raised the idea softly. 'Don't you
know that he's Major Valentine's protégé? A very privileged young
man indeed.' The captain sat down and contemplated Murtagh's
vacant face. The stupid man did not understand. Walls spelled the
message out for him.

'Major Valentine has given Eamonn a fortune! We know he is
an ambitious fellow, but why would he be sponsored for the
Roman priesthood by a Protestant landlord?'

He watched with satisfaction as understanding dawned on the
face of the blacksmith.

'You are telling me... it was him?' he whispered.

❖   ❖   ❖

William Dwyer saddled his horse and locked up his store for the
last time. It was a quiet enough fair day, for there were few folk at
Hill Town square who did not have good reason to be there.
Scattered around was an unusually large proportion of redcoats,
and it would follow that trade in certain commodities would be restrained. There were none of the usual shifty faces from Attical
and Kilcoo, and the innkeeper, fighting his nerves since the arrest

...aken to his bed, claiming an attack of palsy. ...love Bushel the preacher remained at his post, ...npalatable fate for those within hearing distance, al-...e were few at the fair to hear his words. Even the cry of ...ntainy sheep in the pens seemed plaintive and distressed, ...aps reflecting the feelings of their handlers and, more likely, those of William Dwyer himself.

He led his horse past the inn. At the corner where the village street met the meagre road from Rathfriland the untidy briars reminded William of the elderly dandies who had created such a commotion some weeks earlier. He supposed that they were now safely back in Dublin, brimming with tales of the barbarous north with its cut-throats and unpruned roses.

His mother's parting words were still ringing in his ears as he left Hill Town. She had asked him many searching questions, none of which he answered truthfully.

'Yes, 'tis only to deal in brown linen while the market's high. Oh, I'll be back in a week's time! No, I'm not in any sort of trouble.'

But as the hard old face peered from over the half-door, there was sadness and loss in her eyes, for they both knew that they would never meet again. He thought he could hear her keening and lamenting in the distance, as though he'd been lost at sea and waked without a body.

The horse turned towards the well-worn road past the Bolie, the way to the O'Lochlainn close, and William had to redirect her towards the Poorlands and down through Knockbarragh. In the past, he had always kept a sharp eye out for Sosanna, following the herds to their pasture. He had been ecstatic with happiness when she had agreed to be his wife, but black jealousy had got the better of him and his hopes for the future now lay in ruins. He was used to travelling alone but his present anguish made the loneliness almost unbearable. He was bound for the Bridge of Mayo but, on impulse, turned towards the priest's house in Knockbarragh.

The man William saw fetching his water from the well was

indeed the Parish Priest, although he could have passed for any elderly peasant in his homespun breeches and shirt.

'God save you, Master Dwyer,' he called, 'and are they saying their prayers in Clonduff?' He plunged his head into a pail of water; emerging seconds later, he explained: 'I was up half the night. This is the best way to wash out the sleep.' William watched doubtfully as the priest shook his head and combed his white hair backwards. 'You look as though you are in want of sleep yourself,' observed Father Mackey. It looked as though the postponement of his wedding had upset the merchant considerably. He filled the horse trough for the two animals before speaking again.

'You had better step inside,' he said, lifting the latch. 'I suppose you'll be wanting to talk about the marriage.'

'No, your Reverence,' replied William, 'I would have you hear my confession.'

❖ ❖ ❖

Father Mackey said his night prayers, but his mind kept straying to what William Dwyer had told him. It was strange, he thought, how a righteous man could be destroyed by the love of a woman. It was stranger still that a shrewd Clonduff dealing man would be so gullible as to believe that the troopers would stick to their promise and arrest only the pair of outlaws. Dwyer had always lived by selling. Intelligence was just one of the many commodities in which he dealt, although he usually confined himself to informing on violent law-breakers and criminals who were a scourge to rich and poor alike. Sheer jealousy of a younger, lustier man had provoked him into betraying his own friends, and the poor man was now filled with remorse.

The priest had lived through changed times, and knew how brittle and transient any period of peace could be. Things would settle down he was certain, as most of the troops were being moved to quell a riot in County Armagh. His most compelling worry now was the case of Eamonn O'Lochlainn. He had seen how Eamonn had reacted during the recent emergency. The lad appeared to remain aloof from the suffering of his family and friends, and had foolishly visited the home of his wealthy patron as though there were no grievances against the landlord. Father Mackey was uneasy about Major Valentine's offer, instinctively feeling that money so easily gained must carry some kind of forfeit. Most of all he knew that the Major's benevolence was directly due to the influence of Grace O'Lochlainn, a wanton woman who had flouted her sin in defiance of all things decent and the Church's teaching. Not only had she sinned openly, but she had cut herself off from his congregation and no longer received the sacraments.

'This is what comes of allowing a woman to learn to read and write!' he said as he shuffled into bed. Our Blessed Mother, he always maintained, had no need of learning, and neither had her Irish daughters. During the night he tossed and turned and dreamed of galloping black horses. He woke up in a sweat.

'No good can come of bad!' he cried aloud. He had to talk to Eamonn.

Early next morning he rode off to celebrate Mass in Killowen townland on the outer borders of his parish. The clannish Killowen men were building their own Mass house on the land of an elderly Protestant lady, and had laid out a fine altar for him when he arrived. All during the Mass his concentration wandered, and he shocked the pious Killowen men when he almost dropped the Communion wafer.

He rode back through the village, calling at the forge to ask after Murtagh Fegan. He found Brigid stoking the fires herself and lamenting the uselessness of her husband. While privately acknowledging that Mistress Fegan had reason to complain, Father Mackey felt obliged to remind the woman of her conjugal duties and the onus on her to produce another son as quickly as possible.

'You must know that 'tis the only thing which will ease his conscience,' he told her sternly as she struggled with rusted scythes and holed crocks. He did not like to see a woman toiling like a man when her duties lay elsewhere.

His mood worsened as he arrived at the hedge-school. There

were only three pupils in attendance, a further sign, if he needed any, that there was disquiet over Eamonn's role in the recent purge. The young man was reading aloud from Thomas a Kempis' *Imitation of Christ*, and the boys looked extremely bored.

'Ah,' said Father Mackey, 'a gift from the Bishop I take it?'

'No, sir,' replied Eamonn. 'It came from the library of my patron.' Father Mackey noticed from the surreptitious glances of the scholars that they guessed of whom he was speaking.

'He must be quite a theologian then!' he remarked testily.

'Perhaps not,' responded Eamonn, 'but he is a good Christian.'

'Dismiss your scholars!' Father Mackey told him sharply. Eamonn complied, reminding the boys that he would continue their class the following evening. The priest added his own instructions about hurrying home without loitering, and reminded them as to what the Devil did to boys who played pitch and toss.

'I think, Eamonn O'Lochlainn,' he said carefully, 'that you should shelve your plans to travel. Until the French War ends, at least.'

'But Major Valentine has assured me...'

'Enough of Valentine!' the priest interrupted. 'Use your brain O'Lochlainn. Why is this man so ready to see you on the road to France? Why should he give you anything, let alone a small fortune?'

'Because God has spoken.'

'Yes, yes, we know all that. Let me tell you, O'Lochlainn, the Lord does not work through the sins of fornicators and wretched women like Grace O'Lochlainn!' Father Mackey did not like to be so blunt about one of Eamonn's own family, but the lad did not appear to understand anything other than straightforward words. 'You cannot accept so tainted a gift.'

Eamonn was unabashed. His faith in Grace was almost as great as his belief in his future. 'Perhaps,' he suggested, 'it is her way of asking forgiveness for her sins?'

'The Sacrament of Penance is a lot less expensive.'

'I meant,' said Eamonn slowly, 'forgiveness from her family.'

'Your father is too righteous a man to condone what that girl has done. And have you thought for one moment how others will see this – this outburst of generosity from one who is content to see widows and children evicted from their homes?'

'They will not know. I have told none but you, and by rights I should not even have spoken with you.'

Father Mackey was affronted at the suggestion that he should be kept in the dark over so serious a matter.

'You have a lot to learn about obedience, boy,' he muttered darkly. 'Now, for your own sake, I am ordering you to cease all intercourse with this man. If his intentions are holy, he will approach His Lordship the Bishop, or myself,' Father Mackey drew himself up, 'and in the meantime you will submit yourself to self-mortification and prayer.'

'But the books...'

'You will not need them. You are to hold no more classes here.'

Eamonn stayed alone at prayer for some time after the Parish Priest had left. He had difficulty concentrating as his fingers traced the familiar heraldic emblem on the book's leather binding. His thoughts went to Makepeace as he examined the carefully stretched and polished skin. It was only a matter of weeks since they had first met, here amidst the ruins, and yet the cantankerous old Dissenter had gained a place in his troubled heart. It was that meeting with Briony that had eventually lead to his following the outlaws across the mountain to the spot where the little boy met his death. His eyes were drawn towards the oak tree – Briony's tree. The little boy had aspired to climb that tree. Now he never would; one of the many children, like his own dead brothers, who never grew up. Eamonn wondered if his dreams would be so withered.

'If only...' he began. Then, realising the futility of such speculation, he turned once more to his prayers.

❖ ❖ ❖

It was late in the evening, and the sky was dark and brooding. Eamonn was oblivious of the omens around him, and while another man might have started for home before the storm broke,

Eamonn remained engrossed in prayer. When he lifted his head it was not because he heard a sound or because a light rain had started to fall, but rather because he felt a presence close by.

'Briony?' he said, looking around as if expecting to see his young scholar lounging against the slabs in his usual impudent manner. There was no one to be seen. Eamonn picked his steps through the long grasses towards the spot where the little boy was buried, near the ancient cross of Bronach. There was no slab to mark his grave, and already a haze of growth had begun to appear on the disturbed earth. In a while it would be like all the other peasant graves, poor simple mounds, known only to those who cared enough to remember. Unless Murtagh had a stone erected. He had always expressed admiration for the planters' memorials to their dead. Eamonn intoned the words of the *Agnus Dei* to himself as the rain began to fall more heavily on his bare head and neck as he bowed in prayer. Looking up, he was startled to see a still figure watching him from the south portal of the ruins. It was the blacksmith.

'Murtagh!' he called softly. They had exchanged few words since Briony's death, the blacksmith's mood too fey and dark, Eamonn's plans too urgent.

'Murtagh, my friend,' he stepped towards the smith, 'your sorrow is my sorrow. I was thinking of Briony as I taught today. He was always so bright, so full of hopes and wild imaginings.'

'And your own dreams, your own ambitions O'Lochlainn? How do they proceed?' whispered Murtagh.

Eamonn felt a chill at the blacksmith's tone. Murtagh had never spoken to him in such a manner before. He looked away into the gathering storm.

'You are leaving these shores, I hear,' continued the blacksmith. 'A fortunate chance!'

The smith's huge hand gripped Eamonn's thin shoulder in an almost friendly gesture.

'Do you remember this, O'Lochlainn?' he said.

'The Dissenter's knife,' replied Eamonn. 'Briony made a hero of the old vagabond!'

'Knife? How little you know of Briony. Look you on the Sword of Achilles! The sword of vengeance!'

He plunged the knife hilt-deep into Eamonn's chest. 'You bought your own dreams with the life of my boy!'

'Murtagh!' Eamonn gasped only once, sliding silently to the ground to lie on Briony's grave. The smith withdrew the blade and held it high as the rain lashed and the wind howled.

'Briony!' he cried, his grief released at last. 'Briony!'

And as the storm raged around him, and the branches whipped and groaned, amid the rack and ruin of all their lives, from close by came the sound of a ghostly bell.

Chapter Nineteen

CAPTAIN WALLS WAS leaving Rostrevor. He had, it appeared, other more important duties to attend to elsewhere. The news of the departure of the Fencibles was generally greeted with relief, although there were the inevitable complaints about lack of security and the need for special protection for the law-abiding community after the recent disturbances.

The Valentines had already left for Dublin. Some said that the Major had been very shaken by the death of young O'Lochlainn, others that Madam Ward could not stand the stench of rotting flax in the hot weather. They were going to stay with friends at Powerscourt, south of the city, and would not be back for some time. There was some gossip from Mistress McIntyre about Major Valentine's melancholic fits since his parting from Grace O' Lochlainn, but most village folk preferred to believe that he was happy with his new love, a lady fit to be his bride, and had probably gone to be near her. The O'Lochlainn woman had returned from whence she had come.

Sergeant Pollard saluted crisply as Captain Walls and his escort party rode through the Barrack gates for the last time. He watched them cross the Square at a brisk trot before turning towards Drumreagh. He heaved a sigh of relief.

'Maybe now we can get back to where we left off,' he said as the sound of hooves faded. He wondered if there were any who regretted their departure. There would always be a few pining girls and one or two susceptible boys who would see themselves in uniform, but he did not think that there would be many others.

He took a stroll around the village, stepping past Napper Donnan, who was lying drunk at the pump.

'Some things never change,' he thought, 'especially the simple ones.'

In a while, one of the women along the lane would give the drunk a good dousing and send him home to his wife. Napper's old companion, Mick the Fox, had seemingly disappeared off the face of the earth. He had not been seen since the night before the ambush, and there were those who would maintain that Mick had fled to Newry and jumped on a boat bound for the South Seas. His mother, Minnie the Fox, had kept a stony silence when interrogated, but informed Pollard that if she knew the whereabouts of her good-for-nothing son, she would personally hand him over and pick up the reward money. Pollard had replied that since the Treasury had considered Mick's head as worthless as the rest of him, she need not build her hopes on any reward.

Armed with a sermon on drunkenness, Spendlove Bushel the preacher from Hill Town had just arrived on the square and was setting up his pitch close to the elderly sages under the tree. Pollard wondered why Bushel bothered coming so far; Rostrevor was traditionally stony ground for preachers, and the drunken men never listened to him anyway. The innkeeper's wife, who was supervising the delousing of her mattresses following the departure of the billetees, ignored the rantings of Spendlove Bushel who instead turned towards his ancient listeners under the oaks. Pollard was amused by their indifference, and almost collided with Mistress McIntyre, who was on her way to visit an ailing friend with a can of hot broth.

'Your pardon, ma'am!' he apologised to the petulant woman who had splashed some of the contents of her can over his boots. She muttered something about his being better suited to locking up Napper Donnan than annoying decent women going about their lawful business. Things had surely not changed much around Rostrevor, he thought, cleaning his boots on the sward.

Some things had changed. There was the disappearance of William Dwyer. No one knew where he had gone, but his round had been taken over by an enterprising individual from Hill Town known as the Darner. Unlike the quiet William, the Darner was known to have a woman at every stopping point along his route, including a certain house at the head of the lane where his cart was presently stationed. Pollard was walking past the cabin when the Darner emerged amidst a furious barrage of screams and flying piss-pots. He fumbled with the drawstrings of his breeches as he leapt onto the cart and whipped his somnolent nag back to life. The commotion had distracted the attention of Master Bushel's half-hearted congregation, prompting him to alter the subject of his sermon to the sin of lust. Sergeant Pollard was aware of the prying eyes from the window of the Agent Coyle. In that respect also, he thought, things were returning to normal.

❖ ❖ ❖

Coyle's conscience had been numbed by years of obedience to his master and the law. He did not consider himself in any way responsible for the death of Eamonn O'Lochlainn. It had never occurred to him that some secrets had best remained hidden, and that if he had not drawn the Major's attention to the existence of Grace's child the tragedy would not have unfolded as it did. The Widow Fearon felt differently. She was tormented by guilt, and could confide in no one. She could not even bring her troubles to the confessional, suspecting all priests of feeding on titbits of scandal.

Outside her mountain hovel, she laid out a few scraps she had gathered for the dog.

'Eat up, lad,' she instructed, unnecessarily so for the dog had wolfed down his food before the words were out of her mouth. 'You're an ill-mannered cur!' she said fondly, ruffling his ears. 'But you're welcome company!' Owen MacOwen had left her, to take up residence in the ruins of the Healing House. He was a wild boy, and it would do him no harm to live out his hurt there during the summer months. She would keep a sharp eye on him. In the meantime Thady O'Lochlainn's soothing balm was bubbling in the crock, and the steam was stinging her eyes. She dabbed at them with her grubby skirt, wishing that she could produce an ointment to mend poor Thady's broken heart, and her own troubled mind.

It was some weeks now since her encounter with the Major. On

291

that occasion he had asked her about a baby, a child which Grace O'Lochlainn had borne at the age of fourteen years. The Widow had always been afraid of the Valentines. Even her most powerful incantations had no effect on them; indeed, the more she cursed them, the more they prospered.

Henry Valentine's powerful figure had towered over her, and the expression in his green eyes was alarming.

'You're a fine build of a man,' she declared spontaneously, 'and no wonder the young girl was taken in by you!' At first she told him that there was no such baby, and that even if there had been she would not remember after such a passage of time.

'There are so many childer born,' she muttered, 'and precious few of them live past their first year. My own went that way. But weren't they the fortunate creatures?'

'I am sure you will remember if you try,' he said quietly, but there was a hint of menace in his tone. 'It was during the year 1763.'

'Years mean little to me. I couldn't tell you my own age.'

'The boy would be seventeen years now. Come, surely you know them all hereabouts?' He had alternatively coaxed and threatened her, while she tried to evade his questions. She desperately feared eviction at her age, for even the workhouse would spit on her.

'Did she give him up for fosterage?'

'A baby born out of wedlock was a shameful thing for a young cailín, although it happens anyway. It happened to myself, though 'tis better not spoken about. Rape, it was, a dirty beggarman with stinking breath.'

'This child,' Valentine interrupted softly, 'was born of love, not rape.'

''Tis better, I suppose, for the child to know that.'

'Then tell me who it is!' He looked keenly at the Widow. 'Did Grace's parents take the boy?'

After he had left, she convinced herself that she had done nothing. Valentine was not a bad man. At least, he was not as bad as Whitechurch. And Eamonn, the most vulnerable of men, might do well with the landlord's protection.

Now, as she poured Thady's balm into a small pot, she told herself that she would never be redeemed for causing the death of a poor young scholar.

'Come on, boy,' she told the dog. 'You may accompany me up to the close.' Try as she might, she could not lighten her spirits.

❖ ❖ ❖

Father Mackey was not surprised by Eamonn's death. The galloping black horses of his dreams were not just pagan portents of sudden death, he thought, but real and justified fears for the young man's safety. Even now he shuddered at the memory of their advancing hooves and the terrible breath from their nostrils. He had been one of the first people to come on the scene, early on the morning of the storm, when he had been called out at the request of the Poundwarden. The man had been on his way to Hill Town when he noticed a movement from within the ruined burial ground, and, expecting to find a wayward animal, he investigated further. At first he had been afraid to approach Murtagh, crouching by the muddy grave where the body of a young man lay. The blacksmith was grasping a knife and crooning to himself. He had behaved as a simple child, handing over the knife before wandering off.

The priest had had to break the news to the O'Lochlainn family, and worse, to poor Brigid Fegan. Murtagh would never again practice his craft in the forge, for if he escaped the gallows or the convict ship he would undoubtedly spend the rest of his life in an asylum, an incurable lunatic. In this instance, most of the priest's sympathies lay with poor Brigid Fegan and her girls.

The people of Kilbroney reacted quietly to the killing. Most were shocked by the spilling of blood on consecrated ground, but there was also confusion because of the absence of a common enemy, the killer having stepped from among themselves. There was much soul-searching, some attributing the murder to army deserters who had taken advantage of Murtagh's mindless state to plant the murder weapon in his hands. Others, more honestly, accepted the guilt of their own community.

Seán, the Buller, Paddy O'Linden and Tom Dunn carried Eamonn's body to its resting place. Behind them walked the women of the house, Eily and her two daughters. It had been the first time Father Mackey had come face to face with Grace in many years, and he was unsure as to how to react. He wanted to spare Thady's family any further anxiety, but still he could not bring himself to acknowledge her presence. He was determined that Grace should be seen to come to him, not the other way around. It would not do for sins of such great magnitude to be treated lightly.

'Aye, 'tis a pity,' he sighed to himself as he watched Grace supporting her lamenting mother, 'that some are ever born...'

Sosanna wept until the tears would come no more. Eamonn and herself had grown up together. They had been friends and allies through childhood and adolescence, and although he had been the learned scholar, it was she who had been the stronger and more forceful of the two. She had always known that life would one day part them, but so abruptly, and in such a cruel way... She began to weep again. 'Sosaí!' she heard her father's feeble voice call from below. 'What ails you, a chroí?' Concern for him roused her.

'Is your back paining you?' she asked, 'Will I help you shift a little?'

'No, no,' he reassured her, 'I'm well used to that by now. I was wondering what was bothering you?'

'Eamonn.'

'Ach, don't mind Eamonn!' he answered quietly. 'The wonder of Eamonn is that he lived as long as he did. We'd given him up for dead more often than enough. The poor lad. He's as well off where he is now, an innocent boy that meant no harm, but caused it all the same. We'll miss him, for certain, but then we would have lost him either way. And look at it this way,' he stroked her hair, 'Grace came back to us, and we had thought to lose you, but you're still with us. Now don't be starting again!'

'I would have been away,' she wept, but told no more.

'Hush, a chroí, I know. You wouldn't leave us.'

Sosanna was on Donal's mind as he neared the end of his journey. She had wanted to accompany him, and their parting was harder to bear than the evening they had first taken leave of each other, before the ill-fated ambush. Now he felt helpless and lonely as he trudged over mountain wastes and bogland, heading north from whence he had come. The fine June weather with a dry southerly wind made the going easy, and there was no old man to hinder his progress. Yet it was on account of Master Agnew that he was making this journey, a pilgrimage of sorts, to the place of public execution in Downpatrick where the brave old Dissenter would be hanged.

Leaving the Mournes behind him, he traversed the flax country, where the stench of rotting fibres hung heavy in the warm air. There was plenty of work for poor migrant labourers, but it was backbreaking toil. At least, he realised, another stranger on the byways would attract little attention. If his mind was on Makepeace as he walked, at night he thought of Sosanna. She had told him about the impending execution, and had tried her best to dissuade him from going to Downpatrick, but without success.

'What if they catch you?' she had cried.

'If they do, I will say nothing to incriminate any of you,' he had insisted stubbornly. Now as he made his way through the narrow old lanes towards the Gaol, he wished that she were with him.

Donal had abandoned any boyish hope of rescuing Makepeace, and the last thing he could do for his old mentor, he realised, was to be near him at the moment of death. His beard had grown in the past few weeks, and he hoped he could pass himself off as a simple mountain man. Not that any he had encountered were that simple, but many of them owed their survival to the naive belief of their conquerors that men of inferior intellect could pose no threat. Donal felt confident enough to mingle among the crowds which had gathered to witness a popular public spectacle, the death of a traitor.

Few seemed to be aware of the identity of the diminutive old man in preacher's garb, bereft of his spectacles, who hobbled along to the gallows with his fellow condemned criminals. Donal looked anxiously, but lost sight of Makepeace as the crowd gathered and thickened. There was some jostling for the best viewpoint as a murmur went out that 'the French agent' was on his way. The onlookers were, for the most part, respectable citizens of Downpatrick, who had strolled up the winding cobbled streets of the ancient town for a glimpse of the dangerous traitor who had held an entire family at knifepoint and betrayed his King. Not all were so bloodthirsty, for a few mothers and young girls stood amidst the throng, tearfully waiting for a last glimpse of sons and sweethearts. They were very much outnumbered by the many who had climbed Gallows Hill to savour the excitement of the occasion.

Donal, avoiding the redcoats who mingled with the crowd, willed Makepeace to look in his direction. The old man would not be able to see him, but so close had they been in life that Donal felt certain that Makepeace would know of his presence in the hour of his death.

A cheer went up, and Donal overheard some of the onlookers identify a swaggering highwayman from Newry who had eluded the law for many years, but had been finally brought to justice. The white-throated rogue gave little bows and nods to the spectators, insolent and defiant to the last, before he was led towards the scaffold. Donal pushed his way through the crowd to observe the bedraggled little parade in chains. Makepeace could not walk to the rhythm of the drumbeat, but he stuck his chin proudly in the air and gamely tried his best. Donal bit his lip as the white head suddenly turned. Makepeace was frowning.

'He knows I'm here,' thought Donal, 'and he's worried I'll be caught.' The foolishness of his own situation struck him for the first time as he realised that the only comfort Makepeace had left was the knowledge that he, Donal, was safe. Yet he wondered; he had a strange feeling that Makepeace was actually enjoying being the central figure of such a public spectacle. It would be a dramatic end to an otherwise dull and ordinary life, and the Dissenter, of all of them, had his God-given assurance of a better future.

The prisoners stopped by the scaffold. Alongside Makepeace and the highwayman were a couple of sheep-stealers from Kilcoo, a coachman who had pocketed all his fares, and a wild-tempered maid who had pushed her mistress down the stairs.

'Where is he?'

'Where's this traitor they're talking about?'

Donal could hear the buzz of interest pass through the assembled spectators. He began to move away, trying to call to mind a prayer of which the old Dissenter would approve. He could think of none. On the outskirts of the gathering children were playing hide and seek, laughing and squealing, oblivious of the morbid proceedings which had caught their parents interest. Then he heard a distant voice call 'Makepeace Theophilus Agnew, book-binder and traitor.' He forced himself to look at the blindfolded figure with the rope around his neck, still standing stiff and proud. In accordance with the punishment allotted to traitors, Makepeace was to be hanged, drawn and quartered.

Donal recalled the rosary entwined in his mother's hands and the rough feel of Makepeace's coat, that moment so long ago when he had lost one parent and found another.

'Goodbye, old friend,' he whispered as the drums rolled. There was a sharp crack, a gasp, and a groan of disappointment from the crowd. Instead of dangling and choking as was expected of most hanged men, Makepeace's neck had been broken. He died instantly.

An hour later, Donal was on his way to the town of Ballynahinch, in search of the cooper. He did not stay to witness the aftermath of the execution, when the dead man's head was severed and exhibited on a spike for all to see, with the accompanying legend:

MAKEPEACE THEOPHILUS AGNEW
A traitor to his King

❖   ❖   ❖

297

Donal arrived at the home of the cooper early the following morning, footsore and weary, having taken advantage of what little cover the short summer night could provide. Somehow his heart had been lightened by his friend's death, for instead of worrying about Makepeace manacled in prison or enduring a whipping, he knew the Dissenter was now free from all pain and hardship. There were times on the course of his journey when he felt as though old Makepeace was still with him, hobbling along behind, advising about bogholes, badger traps and any other hazards a nocturnal wanderer might encounter. He felt comforted by the thought and it made his solitude easier to bear. The ache of sorrow and remorse which had tormented him since the night of the ambush was beginning to fade for the first time.

He was given a short welcome by the taciturn cooper, who seemed to have been expecting him. Picking his way over half-seasoned barrel staves, the cooper remarked on the difference in the pathetic appearance of the bedraggled soul who had just arrived and that of the lighthearted young coxcomb he had entertained some months previously. A soft-hearted man underneath his surly veneer, the cooper called his wife who was only too willing to mother the poor lad. She half filled a barrel with steaming water and ordered him to shed his clothes. Donal had grown unused to such luxury, and strangely shy about undressing in front of a clucking woman, but felt his tired muscles ease within the warmth and friendliness of the cooper's kitchen. She scrubbed his back and scolded him about his tatty hair, and for the first time he began to weep. The woman bathed his head with distilled gorse water which, she claimed, would soothe his sorrow away and help him sleep. She sat by his side as if he were a child, until he was oblivious to the world.

Next morning, the cooper visited him in the barn where he had spent the night.

'Walls is gone,' he said.

Donal, correctly interpreting this brief report to mean that the search had been called off and that Captain Walls had withdrawn his men, jumped up in excitement. 'So he is no longer hunting me. He is returning to Dublin!'

'Nay! Tanderagee!'

It took Donal some time to discover that the troopers had moved to quell sectarian rioting between Protestant Steelboys and Catholic Defenders in County Armagh. For a while, at least, the French threat had receded as the internal security of the country took precedence. It took the cooper's more loquacious wife to persuade him that his instinct to double back to Kilbroney was unwise in the extreme.

'Have a titter of wit!' she said scornfully. 'What manner of man are you to go stirring up trouble with folks that have suffered enough on your account.'

'But I promised Sosanna.'

'Promises made by a man on the run for his life mean nothing. If the girl has any sense, she'll be wed to her fat old merchant by now,' the cooper's wife continued bluntly, 'and as for yourself, we'll wait to see what Master Russell advises. He'll soon sort you out.' Then, in a more kindly tone she added, 'You look like a few hot meals in your belly wouldn't harm you.'

Donal was more than grateful for her solicitude, but stung by her warnings about the consequences of returning to Kilbroney. He decided that he would bide his time. Should it be weeks, months or years, some day he would go back for Sosanna.

Some days later, a young man arrived at the cornmill of Mistress Matty MacGinn on the Upper Bann looking for work. He bore the alias of McAteer, but Donal MacArtain found that the whispered name of Tom Dunn had more the desired effect on the stalwart woman of the mill.

Chapter Twenty

THE SUMMER PASSED without incident, and the grass and ferns grew thickly around the deserted forge. Weeds and straggling brambles contended for space on the floor of the sad little building which had once resounded to laughter and chatter. The brazier was cold, lying on its side amidst some pots and spades which had never been collected, as their owners were afraid to go near the forge, claiming that it was haunted. There was talk of a new smith, Turlough MacCormac, coming to take up the tenancy, and the Agent Coyle was certainly anxious to let it out before the building fell into total disrepair. Brigid Fegan, with her daughters, had gone to live with her own people in Lisnacree, vowing never to return to Rostrevor. The little girls were blessed with kind grandparents who would help them recover from their ordeal, but most people were sorry to see them go, in spite of what had happened.

The big house was still empty, and Mistress McIntyre lost no time in telling everyone that the Major had gone to visit his mother in England.

'She must be of a ripe age by now!' commented McIntyre. 'I mind how she used to cut a fine figure on horseback. There's many's the man would have jumped up behind her.'

'And many's the man that did,' commented his wife tartly.

Major Valentine had always spent a lot of time away from home, whether through attending Parliament or travelling abroad, so it made no difference to his tenants and staff that he was not in residence.

The flax harvesting had been disrupted by the events of the previous spring, and several skilled workers had left their village homes and gone to offer their services elsewhere. With them went young men and boys from the Poorlands, wary of the return of

Captain Walls. Anxious to make up the shortfall in estate income, the Agent Coyle was forced to consider increasing the rents. He was aware of Major Valentine's concern after the fate of Dervla MacOwen, but felt that there was no other way to ensure compliance with the law than the tried and tested threat of eviction. In the meanwhile, he made sure that every tenant and subtenant fulfilled his duty and provided their labour for the harvest, and by mid-August all the flax had been pulled and the land was ready for winter ploughing. The family might not be in residence, but the wily Agent still kept an eye on the plum trees. He would be retiring at the end of the year, but, until then, he would be as vigilant as ever on his master's behalf.

The quarry had been closed down. There were no further plans for extending the building programme, and the labourers were either redeployed in the flax fields or dismissed. Seán O'Lochlainn found himself toiling amidst the stench of wretting flax fibres. He hated the tedious, back-breaking work, although he was told that he was fortunate to be able to earn a wage. He said little, and few knew what was going through his mind as he waded through the stinking millponds. His old eye injury was irritated by summer pollen, and he was forced to wear a patch for protection. Towards the end of the summer Tom Dunn had prevailed on him to take on another task in the late evenings, the tuition of Eamonn's young pupils. He was a good teacher, confident and thorough. Better than Eamonn had ever been, the lads told their parents. Seán was not the raw dog he pretended to be, they said. Some Protestant children from the village joined his class, such was his reputation, and soon he had assembled a group considerably bigger than Eamonn's.

'He is saving up to marry the Widow Murphy next door,' it was whispered. Grace did not think so. One Sunday evening, returning from a visit to the graves, she asked him why he was working so hard.

'You need not!' she said gently. 'I can meet the rent with what I earn from Master Dunn.'

'Meet the rent? Is that all you aspire to now, sister?' Seán asked.

'No. And neither do you. You are not so different from the rest of us, are you Seán? You dream of far horizons too,' she said, softly but challengingly, and waited for a response.

'Isn't it strange,' he sighed, 'that all my father ever wanted was a stone chimney.'

'That was the most he could hope for then. I will try to persuade him to build a stone house,' replied Grace.

'At his time of life? You'd bother him to his grave. He worries enough about the rent as it is.'

'I know that, so I intend,' said Grace, 'to have a word with Coyle on the matter. 'Tis time all these rotting sod cabins were replaced.'

'And would he listen to you?'

'He daren't ignore me. Oh no,' she hastily raised her hand to his protests, 'I will not invoke the name of Major Valentine. But I do know the law. I have not been idling during the past eight years. And I hope I will be able to persuade him that sturdier, healthier homes are in everyone's interests.'

Some of the old distrust had reappeared in Seán's eyes. 'I would rather you left well alone,' he muttered.

'When all is well,' she countered.

'Still, I'm glad you came back,' he said. 'It makes what I have to do easier.'

'You are going away, Seán?' Grace had half expected to hear as much.

'The Bell has been tormenting me.' He turned to look back at the little churchyard nestling in the evening sun. 'Eamonn's Bell. I hear it in sleep and on waking.'

'Eamonn was sure that what he heard was a real bell,' suggested Grace.

'Maybe he did. I wish I was so convinced. This sound haunts me to distraction, and I cannot ignore it.'

Grace looked fondly at his dark face with the fearsome eye-patch. He was in many ways Eamonn's opposite, but yet she could see that he was driven by the same yearning. She knew that, whatever his present plans, he would not return to Ireland as a submissive curate, but rather end up as a zealous missionary in some distant land.

'Yes,' Seán spoke softly. 'I, too, must pay heed to the Bell.'

❖ ❖ ❖

The young girl of the house was causing concern. Sosanna felt that life had passed her by. William Dwyer had gone, no one knew where, and had not even returned for his mother's funeral in August. Donal MacArtain had not been heard of since the day before Eamonn's death, when he had left for Downpatrick. Sosanna wondered if he had forgotten about her, and her promise never to marry another. Her frustration and resentment grew daily. Grace worried about her and there were several quarrels, most of which ended in Sosanna rushing out of the cabin and threatening never to return.

'Pass no remark!' Thady would say with confidence. 'In a year or two she'll learn sense.' Grace was wary of such complacency. What her father meant was that eventually Sosaí's spirit would be subdued; she would marry one of the Murphys and end up a worn-out drudge in some damp cabin.

It was one day in early September that the Darner called with his wares. He usually got short shift from Thady, who had been told of his reputation with women, but Grace was amused by the rough-featured little man with the smooth tongue. The cart pulled up at the head of the track and Grace left her chores to exchange a few words with the merchant, and to purchase some China tea-leaves for which she had developed a taste during her life in the big house.

'Mistress O'Lochlainn!' the Darner said unexpectedly. 'Would you recognise this?' He furtively produced a shabby scrap of linen, pressing it into her hand.

'The lad that gave it to me told me you'd know what it meant. A handsome young buck, there's no doubt, and an older woman like yourself that's held on to her looks might be just what he needs.'

Grace hid her ignorance. 'Did he say anything more?'

'Aye!' The Darner looked around him in a clandestine manner, before bringing his black teeth uncomfortably close to the woman's ear.

'He told me not to let your father know. He's coming for you one of these days, just as soon as he puts a few shillings together.'

'Oh, is he indeed?' replied Grace tersely. 'And where is he now, this young man of mine?' The Darner was pleased to be able to give Grace some details of the whereabouts of the lad. He urged her not to worry about her secret.

'You learn to keep your trap shut in my business,' he assured her. 'Your ears would burn up if you knew the half of what was going on along between Rostrevor and Hill Town.' Obviously disappointed that Grace was not prepared to tap this inexhaustible well of information, he bade her good day and goaded his cob onwards.

Grace looked at the scrap of ribbon. Next morning she announced her intention of going away for a day or so, on business of Master Dunn's. Some time later, she again passed the close, astride Dunn's mare, travelling in the direction of Hill Town.

On the following night, while the Buller was visiting Thady and Eily, Sosanna sat out by the well, watching the trail of the harvest moon in the lough below. She had a longing to leave home, to go in search of Donal, yet other considerations, not least her feelings of guilt at the prospect of deserting her parents, held sway. The others, Grace and Seán, would all leave her to be the dogsbody, for she had no learning like the rest of them and no hope of escape. She felt aggrieved that Donal had not sent for her, and angry with Tom Dunn for persuading her to stay in the first instance.

Grace appeared by her side, rebuking her for being out in the cold without her shawl.

'You could get a cold to last the winter!' she scolded. In truth, the young girl was hardier than any of them and had never coughed in her life, but Grace felt it was time she showed some signs of responsibility towards herself. Sosanna was not sure how to react to this recently returned sister.

'Much care you about whether I'm cold or not!' she replied in a sulky manner. Her chin dropped to her knees.

'And where are your shoes, and the hose I gave you?'

'The shoes nip my toes.'

'The Cobbler McChesney told me they were his best. I'll take them back.'

'Oh no,' said Sosanna quickly, stretching out her legs to wriggle her feet, 'I'll put them on tomorrow.'

'You will not be able to go anywhere until you are used to wearing them,' said Grace, sitting beside her.

'And where would I be going?' The tears loomed in the younger girl's eyes as she contemplated her future.

'I thought you might have wanted to go with Donal MacArtain,' suggested Grace. Sosanna started.

'And what do you know of him?' she cried.

Grace produced the ribbon.

'My ribbon! He had it! Where did you get hold of this?' she whispered in excitement, peeping over her shoulder towards the open door of the cabin.

'He wants to take you away. What do you have to say to that?'

'I would have gone with him before, only Master Dunn persuaded me to stay my ground. I have regretted it since.'

'I've seen him and told him to take himself off, and not to entertain coming back for you.'

'Grace, no!' Sosanna's voice was beseeching. 'I will go with him this moment. You went with your love, and cared not what hurt the rest had to suffer!'

'Sosai, I want you to think carefully before you decide to go. You will have a long lonely road by the side of an outlaw, a life of hardship and pain. And for him there will be no return.'

'I care not. I want to be with him.'

Grace looked at the wide eyes of the young girl, sparkling in the moonlight with her newly awakened hopes. She wanted to shake her, to tell her to be sensible, but something held her back. She knew that however hard Sosai's life would be on the road with the outlaw, it would be just as intolerable at home with a buried mound of unfulfilled wishes. Grace's heart went out to the young girl as she watched her rise to her feet and stand gazing out to sea.

'I always wanted to find out,' murmured the girl, 'what was beyond those mountains. My father told me there were just mountains, and more mountains, but I didn't care. I didn't even care if there were monsters and dragons. I just wanted to find out for myself. I've never had the choice of anything...'

Grace was resigned. She threw her great-shawl around Sosanna's trembling shoulders.

'I will have to see that you marry before you go. 'Tis ill enough having one bad woman in the house.'

A few days later, on the eve of the last big fair of the year, Grace left her work at Dunn's Hill early and came home. Eily wondered what was ailing her, as she planned to take the egg basket to Hill Town on the morrow. When Grace told her she was going to pay someone a visit in Knockbarragh, Eily hid her delight. A visit to Knockbarragh could mean only one thing. Their recalcitrant daughter was going to make her peace with Father Mackey and be received back into the fold of the Church. Her prayers, she told a sceptical Thady, had been answered.

'Now don't you think of coming back in the twilight without company. Bed down with Minnie the Fox, and walk back at first light,' Eily insisted as Grace prepared for her departure. Minnie, Grace's friend when she first went into service, was a distant connection of Eily's who always had a warm welcome for her kin from the other side of the mountain. She also had a strapping son, well into middle age, and Grace suspected that her mother was embarking on one last desperate matchmaking bid.

'Will I tell Mick the Fox you were enquiring after him?' she called back.

'If there was an ounce of wit left in your head, you'd get him to walk you back home!' Eliza fired one parting shot. She watched for a while as her daughter followed the little goat track towards Levallyclanowen before veering off towards Knockbarragh. She had been reared on tales of the ghosts and pookas and other such fairy creatures that roamed the dark, wild corners of the earth, and, in truth, it was hard to imagine a darker, lonelier wilderness than the Poorlands of Knockbarragh at night, when gaping chasms and bottomless pits were likely to swallow up lonely wanderers. Thady ridiculed such travellers' tales, and bade his wife sit down by the fire and show some sense.

Grace, as she scrambled over a mountain ditch decided that she would would rather cope with any number of ghosts than the amorous advances of Mick the Fox. She knew him of old; in the company of his diminutive mother he was weak and submissive as a newborn kid, but was somehow transformed by the sight of an unescorted woman. The thought of having to endure the Fox's company on the homeward journey jolted Grace into a faster gait, and a tighter grip on her blackthorn stick and the oatencake which her mother had given her for Minnie's pleasure. As she reached the Gap from whence the winding track led downhill, the wind whipped her skirt about her legs and a dark cloud shrouded the valley below. Alongside each other lay the townlands of Drumreagh and Knockbarragh, the gentler hollows giving shelter to several doughty cabins and poor hovels. Higher up, protected by a copse of hazel and ash, was the priest's house. A bubbling stream separated it from the little peat cabin of Minnie the Fox and her son.

Father Mackey was returning home from a sick call near the village, but his mind was not occupied by his elderly patient, rather by the gift of fine mushrooms he had just received from John Rooney. If the superstitious beliefs of his parishioners prevented them from enjoying these tasty morsels, Father Mackey was not inhibited by any such qualms. An education in France had considerably widened his gastronomic horizons, and he kept a sharp eye open for the herbs, berries and fungi which would add interest to the staple diet of potatoes, porridge and buttermilk.

His heart sank when he saw a black-shawled figure waiting by the ditch to the side of the cabin. In expectation of another sick call the weary man consigned the mushrooms to the back of his mind.

'Yes? What is it?' he asked. To his astonishment, Grace O'

Lochlainn turned towards him. The simple dark tweed framed a face of chiselled, timeless beauty, with fine grey eyes as unfathomable as ever. Father Mackey felt qualified to appraise and appreciate womanly beauty with the eye of the celibate non-combatant, and, to give Grace O'Lochlainn her due, he had never seen as fine a specimen, even after this passage of time and trouble.

The priest felt let down by Grace. Old Priest Pullein had defended her from scorn and criticism when she had borne a babe outside the sanctity of wedlock. He had silenced any wagging tongues with the direct threat of divine retribution. He had, above all, protected the baby from being lifted and taken away to be reared under the shadow of a misguided heretical church. And then, in spite of these efforts on her behalf, she had publicly rejected all the values of modesty and decency, and had gone to live with the spawn of a priest-hunter. Years of living in shame, he noticed, had not weakened her neck sinews, for she held her head as proudly as ever. But, for all his misgivings, he was pleased to see her.

Grace walked towards him. He would have expected a humbler, more subservient demeanour from a penitent with sins of the unsurpassed magnitude of Grace O'Lochlainn, but yet – the parable of the Good Shepherd sprang to mind. After all, a sinner had returned to the fold.

❖   ❖   ❖

'Come out of that, you great lump of lard.'

'Has she gone yet?'

'She's waiting outside the priest's house this half-hour.' Minnie the Fox hobbled back to her vantage point on a mound to the south of the cabin, where an upturned pail amidst the straggly bushes allowed her a decent view of the priest's house.

'Well?' called a muffled voice from within.

'Oh holy God, 'tis himself. He'll curse the same one to hell and back, and she knows it's coming to her. Jesus, he took of his hat to her.'

'What?'

'He's going mad in his old age. He never the once did that to me, and myself with a path beaten to confession.'

'I doubt you may go again after calling the priest mad,' the voice advised.

'They're away inside the oratory. I can see no more.' The commentary slowed as Minnie eased herself off her perch, cursing a protruding bramble which caught her skirt. She hurried back into the cabin.

Mick the Fox poked a scraggy grey head from the churn in the corner, a relic of Minnie's service in the big house. Strangers to Kilbroney Parish would have expected to find the Fox McCanns, as they were collectively known, to have red hair, cunning minds, or some other vulpine attribute, but in truth they were so called in order to distinguish them from the Badger McCanns, skilful bakers who lived by the sea, but who had their origins in Badger Mountain.

'Ma! Did you see what she was after?' Mick hissed. 'Spying on me!'

'Spying my arse,' snapped his mother, 'the poor woman was only paying a neighbourly call. If you were any good at all, you'd have got out of that churn and courted her.'

'You wouldn't see your only son wed to a fallen woman?' pleaded Mick.

'You could bloody well practice on her, if nothing else.'

Weeks of hiding in the cabin had caused Mick to put on weight, and he heaved and grunted his way out of the churn with great difficulty.

'Save me a bit of that oatcake, ma,' he implored, puffing.

'Bedad, you're a bit late to be talking of saving anything,' replied Minnie, casually finishing off the last delicious crumbs. 'And you think about your oatcake the next time you go setting alight to other folk's barns.'

❖ ❖ ❖

'Good day, your Reverence,' said Grace with a demure curtsy which she hoped would please the priest.

'You were not waiting too long, I hope, child.'

'Indeed, no. I paid a call with Mistress McCann. I was distressed to learn that her son has left the country.' Her mouth twitched.

'Mick the Fox? A lazier cur never walked on two legs. He wouldn't make it as far as the port should there be one alehouse on his route.' This comment was delivered with some force and was probably, Grace deduced, intended for the ears of the occupants of the neighbouring cabin. Father Mackey held the sin of drunkenness in almost the same distaste as fornication.

'You have come, Grace O'Lochlainn, to make your penance!' he declared with confidence. 'Just wait until I dispose of these mushrooms.' He entered his little living-room and lifted the fungi, one by one, into a crock.

'You should try them fried in garlic,' suggested Grace. 'They are tasty cooked that way.'

'Garlic!' exploded Father Mackey. 'If you had to hear a man's confession,' he divulged in a more restrained tone, 'and the same man telling you about selling a sick pig at the fair, while he had garlic on his breath – not,' he pulled himself up, 'that such ever occurred here in this parish...'

'Of course not.' Grace watched while he completed his task. He turned back towards the oratory, considering the prospect of a confession which would shame the usual market-day frauds and missed evening prayers.

Father Mackey indicated for Grace to kneel, while he adjusted his cushion, and made himself comfortable for a long sitting.

'To make a good confession, child, and to receive God's absolution, you must be truly meek and humble of heart, and vow that you will never sin again.' Grace, while obligingly complying with all his requests, raised her eyes to meet his.

'I could not do that,' she said.

'What?'

'Vow never to sin again. I know I would.'

'Hear me, child.' Father Mackey, infinitely patient, took a deep breath. 'Every one on this earth was born to sin, and is capable of sinning, even the most innocent infant. To think that you can't sin is a sin. I sin, for the Devil tempts priests more than other men. Yes, do not be surprised, for I, too, am a sinner! Although not,' he added cautiously, 'that any of my sins were quite in your league.'

Grace felt her skin burn. This man could only see her love as sordid and evil. 'Holy Father,' she stumbled over the words, 'I could not make such a vow, because I do not believe I have sinned in the first place.'

'Mother of Mercy!' The priest kissed his worn crucifix. 'I do not believe you to be a suitable candidate for the sacrament at all. You are not suitably contrite.' He rose to his feet. 'You must,' he demanded sternly, 'submit yourself to a suitable period of instruction...'

'Father Mackey,' she interrupted him. 'I did not come about my confession. I would have Sosanna wed.'

Chapter Twenty-One

AJOR VALENTINE AND his sister were on their way home to Kilbroney. The wedding had not taken place and there were even rumours that Miss Letitia Butler had found a new beau. Only Coyle and a few privileged or observant retainers were aware that the Major was suffering from a severe depression, and that Madam Ward had persuaded him to go away 'for the sake of his health'. The dust sheets were lifted and preparations began for a return to the regime of a family in residence. McIntyre was content that there was plenty of game and fishing for the amusement of the Major and his friends, and there had been fewer poachers in operation this year than ever before.

Fanny Ward had resolved to help her brother through his melancholy, and that included keeping him in plenty of gay and lively company. His distant, aloof manner, forlorn eyes and reputation as a wealthy man ensured that a regular bevy of the season's beauties were constantly on his trail, and Fanny felt sure that in only a matter of time he would be his old self again. Then she began to wonder to herself what his 'old self' really was. As a child he had been shy and withdrawn, neglected by his mother, scorned by his father. When she came to rejoin him after leaving Armagh she had found a happy, confident, good-humoured man. But Grace O'Lochlainn had been around then.

A summons from their mother in Gloucestershire interrupted her plans for the summer, but Fanny thought it would be a welcome respite and a chance to bury some unhappy ghosts from the past. The woman was approaching her seventies, and the prospect of a lonely old age and the intimation of her own mortality prompted her to call Henry and Fanny to her side.

After a pleasant sailing to Bristol, there was a fatiguing road journey, broken by inns vastly superior to anything in Ireland but nonetheless tedious given Henry's inclination to drown his sorrows. At the end of the road lay a formal, and not particularly warm welcome from Lady Calmont, as Daphne Valentine had become. Selfish as ever, she neglected to notice her son's problems, but rather added to them by criticising his failure to marry, and finding fault in the way she had done through his childhood. Fanny waited in vain for some sign of affection or change of heart, but none came.

The Valentines remained with their mother only as long as was decently necessary, until Fanny decided that it was time to depart. Assuming the role of her brother's keeper, she arranged for them to spend some time in London, but finding the city too hot and stifling for her liking, returned to Dublin. After a few more miserable weeks, Fanny was at her wits end wondering what to do with him. Then, out of the blue, he took his fate in his own hands. On a morning after a night's heavy drinking, he took his sister aside. His face was pale and his eyes darkly shadowed, but he was calm and seemed to have arrived at a decision.

'I am going home!' he announced, quietly but firmly.

❖   ❖   ❖

Sergeant Pollard had received his orders. Within a week he would be back in Newry, before returning home to Wales. He had had little chance, of late, to reflect on the vagaries of his military career. Memories of battles, clashing steel and roaring cannon, were dim and distant. He could hardly remember the names of fallen comrades, nor friends buried in far-off places with no one to mourn them or keep watch by their graves. His present situation was different, but then, Ireland was always different. The Irish in his experience were treacherous, vengeful, misguided, and yet there lingered a strange reluctance to leave, a feeling of unfinished business.

Being honest with himself, the Sergeant had to admit that his reluctance was due to Grace O'Lochlainn. He had a limited experience of women; dirty camp-followers, the haughty wives of officers, poor women of the roads - they all seemed sordid and unreal.

Grace O'Lochlainn was like no one he had ever known. She was warm, she was sympathetic and gentle, belying any opinion he had ever held regarding peasant women. It was hard to think of her as such, yet that was what she was. He admired her most of all because she had spoken her mind. She had chosen poverty rather than to be pampered in captivity. Yes, he would miss Grace, and he would never forget her.

❖   ❖   ❖

Grace stood by Eamonn's grave. The scutch grass had thrived, and pale seed-heads hung suspended on delicate stems. The hedge-school had deserted the burial ground after the violent act of the previous spring, as Seán had no more heart for the place. Occasionally one of the Kielty brothers would come and scythe a path through for mourners, but Grace liked the small signs of new life, of rebirth and resurrection amidst the tombs of the past. Grace had little time for graves and she visited only rarely. It was Eily who faithfully kept a weekly vigil by the graves of her children, and those of her parents before her. Grace had often wondered how anyone could have endured so much hardship as her mother, taking one blow after another without complaining, and still go on hoping and wishing for better times to come. Grace was the one who had travelled, who had seen life as it could be lived, and yet she envied her mother her understanding of life. She looked sadly around the little mound where ended all Eamonn's wishes and aspirations, and kneeling, she combed the grass with her fingers and removed the offending weeds. None of his dreams had come to fruition, and although she had tried to help him it was her interference which had led to his death. It had been her intention to retrieve some good from the impossible situation in which she had found herself with Henry Valentine, but God had thrown it all back in her face with a vengeance. Thady had tried to persuade her that she could not hold herself responsible for Fegan's actions.

'He was mad, *a chroí*,' Thady had said, over and over again. 'Fegan would have killed the Pope of Rome, had he had the notion.'

As she stared at the grave the doubts crept back. She should have left well alone.

'Grace?'

Startled by the sound of her own name she spun round, catching her breath. Her eyes alighted on what looked like a ghost, framed by the portal of the ruined church. For some moments she gazed on the dark face of the man she had loved for so long. Henry Valentine's hair was dishevelled, his shirt crumpled and unbuttoned. His green eyes were hooded.

'Come back to me, Grace. Come home.' His voice was no more than a whisper. She rose to her feet, appalled by his appearance. He reached towards her, and she instinctively recoiled backwards, aware of the spasm of pain which crossed his face as she did so. She looked away, as if hoping that the vision would melt.

'I could not marry,' continued the voice, a little stronger now. 'I could not marry, for I love you, only and always.'

He reached for her hands. Grace felt her wounded heart in a turmoil and did not trust herself to speak.

'Come with me. I will leave my home,' he whispered. 'We will go away. We will marry and to hell with them all!'

At one time she had longed to hear him speak so. Now her feelings were confused as she felt him at least in part responsible for the tragedy which had shaken their lives. There was bitterness now, a feeling of contempt. This man had power, real power, over her, over his land, but he did not know how to wield it. The grave between them served to remind her that he was the son of her conquerors, she the daughter of a vanquished race. Part of her protested that she loved him, but yet... A new grief surged through her.

'Poor Eamonn!' she cried. 'He was very dear to me. I built up false hopes with him. He trusted me, he believed in me. I loved him, and now I have lost him. I cannot love anymore. I cannot endure losing what I loved.'

'Hush, *a chroí*,' he used her Irish endearment. Then he was beside her, holding her trembling body as she sobbed against his chest. Thus they remained for some time before he wiped away her tears and spoke again.

'Why did you never tell me,' he asked gently, 'that Eamonn was our son?'

Grace stared uncomprehendingly at him. 'Eamonn?' she whispered. 'Henry, Eamonn is my brother. We have no son!'

'But Grace, I...' He looked at her intently, examining every feature of her face. Her teeth bit her lip tightly, but her eyes, as ever, were clear and open. He knew that she was not lying to him. Drawing away from her he stared down at the grave, trying to come to terms with the new truth. He felt all at once numbed and bereaved, unable to explain or even understand the emptiness and pain in his heart.

'They told me so, and I believed them. I asked, I threatened. God knows, *a chroí*, this is no more than what I deserve.'

Grace stared at him. She had never before seen him so helpless and forlorn.

'I thought,' he continued, 'that losing a son was painful enough. Now I know, 'tis worse never to have a son at all. Forgive me, Grace, I am a fool.' He could not look at her, and bowed his head in misery, the tears coursing down his haggard face. Grace felt unable to offer any comfort, for the chasm between them was wide, and fearful memories came flooding back to her.

1763

GRACE HAD TAKEN a long time to recover from the beating she had received on the orders of Madam Valentine. In spite of the intense pain of the wounds the young girl had carefully kept herself covered for fear that her father would see the marks. Annie Dunn had warned her that Thady was likely to act on impulse and might end up losing his home, his freedom, even perhaps his life. Annie had deliberated before announcing to Grace that she was going to call on the good offices of the Widow Fearon. Grace, a little timid in the presence of the indomitable Widow, meekly revealed her wounds. The Widow clucked and scolded, and agonised her patient by rubbing rancid butter into the stripes. She followed the initial treatment with a carefully selected array of balms and ointments, but in spite of all her ministrations, ugly marks still remained a few months after the event. The Widow was determined to get rid of the scars, finding any disfigurement of skin so perfect an affront to her senses and pride in her office as a healer.

'The pain has gone,' Grace tried to persuade her, 'and no one will notice the scars.'

'No matter. They are there all the same!' At the first light of dawn the following morning, the Widow set out to walk the twenty miles or so over the mountains to the village of Annalong on the Irish Sea, where resided a master healer. This dirty old fellow lived in a sizeable stone cabin by the shore and was patronised by folk from far and wide, including several gentlepeople. A seventh son, he had miraculous healing hands, although he also pulled teeth painlessly and carried out quick and clean amputations. He had no sons of his own, but hired out his several daughters as wet-nurses. The Widow held his skills in high esteem and, fortified by Mistress Dunn's ample purse, she approached him and duly received a small pot of mackerel oil and an accompanying charm with special incantations which he required to be repeated at regular intervals.

Back at Levallyclanowen the Widow meticulously carried out the instructions which she had been murmuring to herself all the way from Annalong. As she had expected the scars soon began to fade, but something else caught her attention.

'Stand up girl, 'til I see the shape of you,' she instructed. Grace obeyed. 'Have you started your monthly curse yet?' she enquired, almost in a whisper. The young girl lowered her eyes in embarrassment.

'Yes,' she said, 'a year ago, but you need not worry on that account.'

'And why would I worry?'

'Because it has cleared up. Since September.'

Eily, of course, would have to be told right away; Thady in due course, when the time was right. The Widow was the last woman in Ireland to stand in moral judgement on anyone, least of all Grace O'Lochlainn. Her quiet courage through her recent ordeal had been admired by many, and the Widow knew that she would need it all in the future. She could have produced an abortive potion, but it was as likely to kill Grace as it would anything growing in her belly. Anyway, it was too late to think of that course of action, and old Priest Pullein had warned her of dire consequences in the past. Now her only concern was for Grace and her baby. Such occurrances were common with young girls hired into service, and many a sobbing child was cast onto the road when a pregnancy was discovered. Her chances of being employed in the future were remote, as upright gentlewomen and their housekeepers only employed staff of high moral fibre.

The poorest people, those who most often had to deal with such situations, were usually the least censorious, taking a philosophical view of the problem. Where possible, the children were adopted by the grandparents and enfolded by the wider family.

Grace gave birth on a May Eve, bearing her pain with hardly a whimper. The baby was small and sickly, but in case it might live old Priest Pullein imposed silence on all who knew of the birth. The planters, he said, always came looking for their own bastards, to raise them in the perfidiousness of heresy, away from the influence of the true church. Eily feared for the baby with whom she had quickly formed a strong bond. A future mistress of the big house might not take kindly to the existence of an illegitimate child in the parish. They might all be dispossessed. She had to make Grace understand the seriousness of her situation.

'What would we do,' she asked her daughter, 'if the Valentines found out, and had the wee lamb carried off to England?' Eily believed every tale she had ever heard about how the English treated Irish children.

'You know what they do with Irish babies – meat on a rich man's table...'

Grace complied.

The birth would be kept secret.

So many years had passed since then, and once again she stood with Henry Valentine, no longer proud and handsome, but sad and distressed. He had done his best for Eamonn because he had believed that he was his son. Now respect for Eamonn's memory demanded that the truth be spoken at last.

'Henry,' she said, ''tis you who must forgive me.' She cupped his face in her hands and looked into his eyes.

'It is true that Eamonn is not our son, but Sosanna is our daughter.'

Chapter Twenty-Two

THE CORNMILLS ALONG the streams from the Mourne foothills had never been busier. Ricketty wooden carts drawn by asses and heavy plough-horses arrived hourly from the surrounding fields and the outlying townlands, laden with newly-harvested grain. Cartmen and mill-hands whetted their thirst with buttermilk and home-brewed porter at a few enterprising cabins in the vicinity of the mill, where the potency of the ale and the good-natured bonhomie provoked lively conversation between friends who had not had a chance to meet since the previous year. Topics ranged from a cure for piles to the war, from sheep-rot to the Rathfriland Volunteers.

The young hired man at McGinn's mill said nothing, but listened much. He worked hard, it was noticed, but no drink ever passed his lips, yet he would sit as though enjoying a good draught. He passed the time of day with the Darner, who peddled his wares anywhere that folk gathered in numbers, but otherwise kept himself to himself.

Mistress Matty McGinn, a stout, dark-haired woman with a heart of gold, was determined to keep an eye on her young employee, having reason to be grateful to Tom Dunn for past favours. She trusted the Darner and assured Donal that since the softest part of the merchant was his teeth, he could be relied upon to deliver a message to Kilbroney. The young man had grown in wisdom since the death of Makepeace, and was now more cautious than before. He had endured the most tedious and back-bending labour without complaint, and proved to be well worth his board and wages.

Donal had been a pitiful specimen when first he arrived at the mill, nursing a private grief which he eventually revealed to the sympathetic Matty. His sunken face and skinny arms were hardly fit for mill work, and, in his bedraggled garments she might have set the dogs on him had he not invoked the name of Tom Dunn, the man who had once saved her husband from the gallows.

Now, after three months in Matty's care, his shoulders had filled out and bronzed under the summer sun, and he was attracting the attention of the young maids from far and wide. Such was the degree of curiosity that Mistress McGinn was compelled to pass him off as her sister's son, apprenticed to the mill. Many an evening she had to shoo away a bevy of giggling girls, as though they were wayfaring chickens. Donal, she suspected, was encouraging their attention out of boredom and frustration, and she took him to task for his display of profligacy.

'You'll be giving a decent mill a bad name,' she declared loudly, but without real anger, for she too had a weakness for his charm.

There had been the customary calls from red-coated military men, and one from a colleague in plain clothes, but fortunately Mistress McGinn could spot a soldier in a silk petticoat. During such visits Donal always managed to make himself invisible, although she was not aware of any particular urgency on the part of her inquisitors. In truth, she advised Donal, it did not seem as if they were on his trail at all.

As the summer wore on Donal grew restless and began to ask Mistress McGinn about her seafaring husband.

'Surely to God you're not thinking of running away to sea yourself, are you? You're not so soft that you'd fall for their tall stories of mermaids and easy wenches?' She looked at him suspiciously as she folded away the ironing. The kitchen was warm and cosy with a Swiss clock ticking away in the corner. She had grown used to Donal's company and would miss him when he went. She had not set eyes on McGinn for nigh on four years, and for all she knew he was feeding the fishes at the bottom of some distant ocean. Yet the clock was there to remind her that he could walk through the door at any moment with a sackful of souvenirs. He would kiss her and tell her how much he had missed her, and vow never to leave home again, and he would mean it until the wanderlust struck him once more, and off he would go with a pack of laundered clothing.

A singeing smell brought her back to earth as Donal leapt forward to lift the iron off one of her white kerchiefs. 'Mistress Matty,' he chided. 'You're away in a world of your own. You haven't been listening to a word I've been saying.'

'Go on with you,' she chuckled as she tried to repair the damage. 'You put other things into my head. What was it you wanted to tell me, lad?'

'I will be off at the end of the week,' he said firmly, as if he had considered the difficulties and carefully reached a decision. Matty hid her anxiety as she tackled her linen sheets.

'And where were you thinking of going?' she asked casually.

'To the Port of Derry, if there's a chance of a ship.' He rose to his feet with a grin. 'But first, I am returning to Kilbroney for Sosanna.'

◇ ◇ ◇

'Do you know anything at all about him? Who are his people? Has he papers?' Father Mackey could think of several more reasons why he should not permit Sosanna O'Lochlainn to marry, her recent engagement to William Dwyer not the least of them. The frail and careworn face of Eily persuaded him to hold his fire. She looked bewildered and turned to her son Seán for support.

The priest added one more point for consideration. 'He may already be married.'

'He has no wife,' Seán interrupted. 'He has been in the care of Master Agnew all his life.'

'A Dissenter,' the priest muttered darkly.

'A good man! He had the boy raised in the faith of his mother.' Seán, remembering the old man's sacrifice, was not going to be deterred by what he saw as irrelevancies. Father Mackey flicked through his breviary as if it were a rule book containing some obscure exclusion clause. He was uneasy about secret marriages.

'I don't know. I supposed if he was baptised...' He began to worry about what the Bishop would say, but Seán was growing impatient.

'With Sosanna gone from our midst,' he tempted the priest, 'there would be one less reminder of the past. She may go with or without the sacrament. Would you condemn her to a life of sin?' As Eily began to weep Father Mackey took time to admire Seán's ability to produce such a reaction from women. He undoubtedly had the makings of a good priest.

'I suppose,' he conceded reluctantly, 'that there are extenuating circumstances which must be taken into consideration.'

❖   ❖   ❖

Henry Valentine rode into Newry. His main bankers were in Dublin, but old Mr Fisher handled estate finances. Mr Fisher made no comment when the Major announced that he was cashing in several bonds, but wondered if his reserves would meet the request. He left his desk, to the surprise of his clerks, to watch Major Valentine's departure from the window.

The Valentines' solicitor in High Street was equally surprised to receive a personal visit from his most important client, but more surprised still by the instructions he received. He took some time trying to dissuade the Major from his chosen course of action. As Major Valentine set forth to return to Rostrevor, he left behind him a general consensus: the landlord of Kilbroney had lost all reason.

❖   ❖   ❖

Mistress McGinn dabbed her eyes and sniffed. Donal, she believed for certain, was one of the best workers she had ever entertained around the mill, and she would miss him sorely. She had a maternal fondness for the boy, for good and generous as McGinn had been to her, he had never given her a son of her own. She scolded the young man about looking after himself and keeping a flannel close on his chest. He gave her a hearty kiss, lifted his pack and departed with three months good wages in his pocket and a real French jabot glistening on his throat, another of Sailor McGinn's souvenirs. She could see a new spring in his step as he crossed the field and mounted the stile, marvelling in, and taking some personal credit for the transformation of the past few months. She had fattened him up, assuaged his anger and his grief, and had put him back on his feet. Now she knew that she would never see him again. She watched until he was a small speck on the distant hills before returning to the mill and another day's work.

❖ ❖ ❖

As the sun rose on Kilbroney House there was an unusual amount of bustle. The maids had been up, as usual, kindling fires, preparing breakfast trays and baths, and the aroma of fresh bread from the ovens wafted through the house. The choice Jersey cows had arrived for milking and there was a general air of activity about house and yard, more agitated than usual for the family had risen early.

Fanny Ward was red-eyed and sniffing as Henry descended the stairs in his travelling cloak. He seemed unnaturally buoyant, as if a great weight had been lifted from his shoulders. She was forced to admit to herself that he looked carefree, excited, and more like the handsome young brother she had known in the past. Yet it was beyond her comprehension that he should feel happy, considering what he had just done.

'You cannot have thought this through,' she berated him as he went to stand on the terrace which looked across the meadows to the woods.

'I have never been more certain of anything in my life! My dear Fanny,' he turned towards her, 'you of all people must understand.'

'No! I do not understand! Whatever about your private wishes, have you no sense of responsibility towards your family? To your retainers?'

'That is why I am leaving everything to you,' he replied, not surprised at her belligerence. 'You are my family. This house, this land, I am giving to you! God knows, you care more for it than I ever did.'

'If Grandfather Whitechurch heard you say...'

'Grandfather Whitechurch is in his grave, and there I am l. to leave him. I am sorry to see you distressed, but my mind is made up. I will take Grace and our daughter away from here. We will be happy again.'

❖ ❖ ❖

Sosanna gathered together her little bundle, a few precious items to accompany her into exile. Grace did not need to persuade her this time to wear her thick shoes, with well-darned hose and a heavy shawl. Eily had succumbed to a fit of depression, throwing a blanket of melancholy over the whole family. Only Sosanna seemed unaffected, humming a spirited tune as she hopped down the ladder from her loft.

'What will become of her?' Eily sobbed, 'away in some distant land with nothing but strangers to abuse her!'

Surprisingly, Thady took the opposite view. The new skin was beginning to form on his back and the itchy scabs had left him snappy and cantankerous of late. Now he told his wife to sit down and dry her eyes.

'She's well out of here, *a stór*, and perchance the strangers will treat her better when they don't know her lineage and who she's related to. Certainly I'll miss her, but I'll sleep all the better for knowing she has a strong lad to mind her. A strong lad and a smart lad.'

Thady had spoken to no one of his heartbreak over the dishonour of his daughter Grace. It had been a slur on his idea of fatherhood that he had not been able to protect her, let alone seek retribution. When she had given birth to Sosanna, his first reactions had been of rage and humiliation. It was bad enough that his daughter, who was little more than a child herself, should have been so treated while in his care, but that the child should be a Whitechurch offended him to the core.

In the winter of the year 1763, the worst potato harvest of the decade had forced him to go cap in hand to the Agent Coyle, and to take his place in the queue alongside pathetic old men and poor widows, all pleading hopelessly against eviction orders. In the end

a year's grace, not for any charitable reasons but
new that Thady O'Lochlainn would work himself to
raise the rent. After all, the Agent knew that he had
two girls and an ailing mother to feed. But then, Coyle
there was to know about everybody.

Thady had hung his head in shame every time he passed
Kilbroney House while he thought of the young scoundrel who
had dishonoured his daughter and then cleared off out of the
country. He never attached any blame to Grace. She was his only
daughter and he loved her. Yet ten years later Grace left home,
went freely and brazenly back to her molester, the man who had
blighted the O'Lochlainns' life. From then on, Thady had vowed
that Sosanna would never suffer the same ignominious fate,
should he have to put a langle on her legs. In time, he grew to
love the little girl just as much as he had loved Grace.

'Father!' Sosanna's voice brought Thady back with a start. 'This
is my wedding day! Are you not going to wish me well and give
me your blessing?'

Thady regretted not being able to go to the priest's house to see
Sosanna safely wed. Eily also had decided not to go. The parting
would be too much for her.

'I'll stay here to keep an eye on your father,' said Eily, 'in case
he does something foolish! Besides, we don't want to draw
people's attention to the house. They're a nosey crowd in Knockbarragh.'

'You don't call Minnie the Fox a crowd now, do you?' Thady
replied, then whispered to Sosanna, 'And anyway, I thought that I
was keeping an eye on her!'

Sosanna, sensing that Eily was going to break down once more,
tried to reassure her.

'Don't be worrying about me, mother. You were always worrying. We'll see each other again in happier times. I'm sure we
will!' The young girl's optimism lightened Eily's heart, but Thady
made no comment. The child had no understanding of what lay
ahead for her. He painfully held out his arms to her and she em-
braced him slowly, carefully, mindful of his healing injuries. Then

with a final bittersweet kiss, she was gone.

The three O'Lochlainns, Seán, Grace and Sosanna set out ov
the mountain towards Knockbarragh. A horseman appeared on
the horizon at Levallyclanowen, causing the walkers to stop in
their tracks.

'Say nothing if it's the troopers,' advised Seán nervously.

'Why, 'tis Master Dunn!' called Sosanna happily. 'Have you
come to bid me goodbye?'

Seán and Grace looked sadly at each other. She was still not
much more than a child, and this was all one great adventure for
her. Tom Dunn gallantly raised his hat.

'Your father has honoured me,' he explained, 'by asking me to
witness the marriage for him. Your brother and I will be your
escort.'

'And you, Grace,' added Sosanna fondly.

'Sosaí,' Grace sounded hesitant.

'You will, won't you?'

'I will be your maid as far as the oratory!'

Seán's tone was humorous. 'Your big sister saw fit to engage the
priest in an argument. They don't like being put down by a
woman.'

'Did you argue over me?' asked a perplexed Sosanna.

'Of course not,' Grace reassured her. ''Twas a discussion on a
point of interpretation.'

'Oh!' Sosanna was in awe of anyone who would question the
authority of Father Mackey.

'I will wait for you at the Fox's house! I will have to spin Minnie
some convincing yarn!'

As they descended towards the Knockbarragh stream, Grace
pulled a cluster of heather. 'Now,' she said, thrusting the flowers
into Sosanna's hands, 'you look more like a bride.'

❖ ❖ ❖

It never occurred to Henry Valentine that Grace and her daughter
might not want to leave. He had held Grace in his arms again and
she had not shrunk away. She still loved him, and she had wanted

327

their child. He wondered who Sosanna might re-
...d to conjure up a picture of her in his mind's eye.
...as he rode up the valley towards the O'Lochlainn
...e now had the chance to put things right.

...l lamenting Sosanna's departure, became hysterical at
the ...t of the rider, like a luckless ghost from the past, approaching the close as he had done before. Thady forced himself
to rise and hobbled to the door wielding his stick. If Thady was
surprised to see the landlord in his yard, Valentine seemed equally
puzzled to find only this wizened old man glaring malevolently at
him. The woman, Grace's mother, began wailing in terror, and
turned to run down towards the river.

'I mean no harm,' called Valentine after her.

'Save your breath!' the old man hissed, 'she hasn't a word of
English.'

'I wish to speak with Grace. Where can I find her?'

'Away home with you! You'll not get her back again, should you
burn the roof over our heads!' Thady lifted his stick menacingly,
as Valentine dismounted.

'You are her father,' the younger man realised, 'I can see that
now.'

'And what damn business is it of yours who I am?' Thady enquired fiercely.

'I would not take Grace against her will. Neither her nor our
daughter.'

Thady's eyes narrowed. 'So you want her, too? Well you've
come too late; she's safe from you now!'

Valentine was uneasy. There was no sign of anyone about the
place, save for these old people.

'Where have they gone?' he asked, his stallion skittish and impatient. The old man stood defiantly on his threshold, grasping his
stick.

'Are they in the cabin?' Valentine demanded, pushing Thady
aside. It was not the Major's intention to hurt the old peasant,
and he was surprised by the cry of anguish as Thady's injured
back scraped against the doorpost. He stammered an apology as

the old man felt his way back to the litter and eased himself down on his stomach. The woman of the house appeared in answer to her husband's cry; as she ministered to him, the Major looked round the cabin, then left in haste. He knew that Thady had been whipped during Walls's visit, and did not wonder at this hostile reaction to him.

He mounted his horse and considered. He thought that the old man had glanced towards the mountain path to the west, so he started to ride in that direction, depending more on his instinct than anything else.

❖ ❖ ❖

Sergeant Pollard was puzzled. With William Dwyer gone, a valuable source of information had been lost to him. Dwyer's successor, the Darner, far from filling the vacancy was himself an object of suspicion. He traded in contraband; but then, they all did that in Hill Town, and few remarks were passed. It had been suggested in the past, by a reliable source from Kilkeel, that he had been actually trafficking arms, probably destined for the warring factions of South Armagh. No weapons had ever been uncovered in his innocent-looking cart – the most that had been found was a stout cudgel, one of the type that any travelling merchant would find essential.

The Sergeant had been on a routine visit to Knockbarragh, where the men of the valley were burning the whins and stubble prior to the autumn ploughing. He was accompanied by a veteran trooper from Cork who seemed to know what the Knockbarragh men were about. Pollard's main concern was that they kept to the laws concerning stubble burning and did not ignite the whole countryside. Most of Knockbarragh was part of the Batt plantation, belonging to the profligate Narcissus Batt, although some parts remained in the Valentine estate. The Batts had an agent who was as lackadaisical as Coyle was industrious, and did not keep as careful an eye on his tenants. As a result Pollard felt obliged to oversee the burning.

The appearance on the scene of the Darner and his cart caught his attention. The man, he knew, was a creature of habit, and although he sometimes visited Rostrevor on a Tuesday he nearly always came from Hill Town via the Kilbroney valley, returning home by Knockbarragh and over the Poorlands. He halted the cart, and although the man answered the Sergeant's questions without the usual excuses about not understanding the King's English, he seemed a little edgy. A close inspection of the cart revealed nothing but the customary bales of cloth, meal, sugar and a small sheath of tobacco leaf, and that in itself was unusual, too. He would have expected the odd few bottles of smuggled brandy or poteen from some remote mountain distillery, for there were always private customers from among the gentry and clergy along the route. It was almost as though the Darner was taking no chances on this expedition. The cart, usually overladen with goods, did not seem as full as it could be, considering that there were precious few dwellers on the Poorlands to relieve him of his wares.

'Did you have a passenger, by any chance?' enquired Pollard.

'Aye. A lame beggarman. An old soldier like yourself.'

'You picked him up in Hill Town? And where did you put him down.'

'Around Rooslieve. He wanted to walk to the Bridge of Mayo.'

'A lame beggarman? Why the hell did he set out for Rostrevor in the first place?'

'He thought there'd be rich pickings. I made him the wiser, and told him they're as mean as sick weasels.'

'But open-handed at the Bridge of Mayo?'

'Aye.'

'On your way, man.'

The Darner's shifty backward glance confirmed Pollard's suspicion. He pounced, landing a fist on the merchant's chin.

'Beggarman my backside,' the Sergeant shouted. 'What rogue did you have in your cart, and where the hell is he now?' The Darner, reeling from the blow, seemed taken aback as he rubbed his jaw.

'Take it easy, Sergeant,' He winced as Pollard pulled him to his feet. 'I'm telling you the truth! There was no rogue,' he said earnestly.

'You had better do just that, unless you fancy peddling your wares on a prison ship.'

'I don't like divulging secrets,' the Darner recovered his hat and pulled himself up. 'Especially when I've made a promise to the party involved.' He brushed his hat as if trying to salvage his affronted pride.

'You'll have to overcome your scruples,' replied Pollard dryly.

'A young man is getting wed. I think there is some family disapproval somewhere along the line. But he's no outlaw! A mill labourer who works to earn an honest wage.'

'And the bride?'

'That name I can tell you, for I've spoken with her myself. She's Sosanna, the daughter of Thady O'Lochlainn of upper Kilbroney.'

'Sosanna O'Lochlainn.' Pollard pondered on the name. He recalled his last meeting with William Dwyer. Dwyer was betrothed to the fair Sosanna, and yet he was prepared to implicate the O'Lochlainns in the French conspiracy. All to get rid of a rival, Donal MacArtain.

❖   ❖   ❖

'You may as well partake of a bowl of porridge, lad. We've already broken our fast.'

'Thank you, Father,' replied Donal meekly, 'but there is no great hunger on me.' He had had to endure the Darner's unoriginal opinions on the state of matrimony, and what with that and the jolting passage of the cart over the Poorlands he was in no mood to face the cleric's oaten brew.

Father Mackey, who treated every meal with the reverence of the Last Supper, had no patience with poor appetites. They indicated a weakness of the brain. 'You have a long and hazardous journey ahead of you! Eat up!' he commanded, pushing a steaming bowl towards the bridegroom.

'Now, while you're enjoying your gruel, you may recite to me, if you please, the Seven Deadly Sins.' Father Mackey had to reassure himself of the young man's fitness to receive the sacrament.

It was somewhere between 'drunkenness' and 'sloth' that the bridal party arrived, and Donal, sweating at the brow, heaved a long sigh of relief. Father Mackey felt reassured at the sight of Tom Dunn, for although the man lacked piety he had a Jesuit priest somewhere in the wider family. He ushered the bride into the oratory.

'Step in here, Sosanna. I want a word with you.' He was always concerned that a young girl might be forced into marriage against her will, the fate of many poor lassies. He was the curse of the local matchmakers, many of whom had lost hard-earned commission when brides had a last-minute change of heart. Other priests, he knew, performed the Holy Rites on young maids dragged kicking and screaming to the altar, without a thought for their feelings. He had no doubts about Sosanna's intentions, as her eyes, already turning in search of MacArtain, glowed fiercely with an expression which he could easily interpret.

'Why, 'tis high time this one was married,' he muttered to himself. 'Come in here, lad!'

❖   ❖   ❖

Valentine rode like a man possessed, urging his horse up the steep mountainside. He wondered what the old man had meant when he said, 'she is safe from you'. He reached the mountain of Leckan and the spot where he had nearly lost his life. Below the precipice, a sparse winding trail led down through the townland of Levallyclanowen towards Dunn's Hill. In the other direction a mountain gap led to the neighbouring valley of Knockbarragh. He closed his eyes to pray for guidance, then turned back to take a steeper, faster route into Knockbarragh.

In the lower part of the glen the air was thick with the dense billowing smoke of burning whins. His own land in the upper regions lay peaceful and virtually deserted. There were two cabins by the stream below, the larger stone house, he knew, was that of the Parish Priest. Outside the house, two horses were tethered. He dismounted and walked down the valley, passing through the copse of ash and hazel, despairing of ever finding Grace. He had all but decided to return to Kilbroney House when he noticed from out of the smoke and the mist the approach of two red-coated figures.

'Pollard!' he hailed him. 'I have been looking for Mistress O'Lochlainn! Could you have seen her?'

'No, sir,' replied Pollard grimly, 'but I think I know where she might be found.' He relayed some of his suspicions to Valentine. The Corkman was despatched to the Barrack to bring back an armed party.

'A clandestine marriage, sir.' Pollard was wary about the landlord's association with Grace, but knew that he would not allow any personal feelings get in the way of his duty. 'And the bride is Thady O'Lochlainn's young daughter.'

'No, Pollard. She is my daughter, mine and Grace's.'

❖   ❖   ❖

Donning vestments paper-thin with age, Father Mackey thumbed through his breviary. There would, of course, be no Mass, just a short ceremony bestowing the Church's official approval of the union. Tom Dunn felt a sense of disquiet and followed Donal outside to advise him to make all haste to leave the valley as soon as the vows had been exchanged. The young man was leaning on the ditch humming a love-song when Father Mackey ordered him to attend within.

'I hope you can sing your responses as well!' The rebuke was wasted on Donal.

'Et cum spiritu tuo!' he intoned, lowering his eyes with a grin. Tom Dunn quickly urged him into the oratory. The irreverence in his heart evaporated when he saw Sosanna awaiting him: there was room only for love. She was as radiant a bride as any grand lady, in spite of her coarse homespun garments. Her eyes sparkled with joy, her cheeks were flushed, and her fair hair curled into little tendrils on her forehead.

Seán observed the meeting of the lovers with a wry smile. He fingered his rosary beads as the prayers commenced, thinking of the attempts they all had made to keep the pair apart. Beside him

Tom Dunn seemed only half aware of the priest's words. His eyes kept straying towards the door from where a shaft of white morning sunlight fell across the rush-strewn floor. A sudden shadow crossed the floor. Father Mackey looked up and faltered on the liturgical words: there at the end of the church stood the Sergeant.

'Donal MacArtain,' Pollard cried, 'you are under arrest! You are all under arrest!'

The wedding party made to scramble from their seats, but froze as the Sergeant's gun was trained on them. Donal looked towards his young wife, hopelessness in his eyes. He had gambled too much in coming back and now the others, including his bride, would help him pay the price. Sosanna was stunned, her head slumped in dejection. In one awful moment all her dreams had been dashed.

A second shadow blocked out the sun as Henry Valentine entered.

Valentine looked at the prisoners. Father Mackey, still garbed in ancient vestments, faced him with the demeanor of an early Christian on his way to the lions. The other men avoided his gaze; beside them was a young girl, not much more than a child, head bowed and body trembling. He wanted to say her name, but the word caught in his throat. He wanted to tell her that he would take her with him, this daughter he had never seen before. He would give her everything that had been denied her...

Sosanna suddenly tossed her head and faced him squarely.

'How dare you!' she cried with passion. 'How dare you arrest my husband!'

Valentine stared into eyes as green as his own, ablaze with a fiery anger.

'Where is your army?' she hissed. 'Is this the best you can muster?'

'Sosanna,' Dunn warned, ''tis Major Valentine...'

'And should I run for my life then? From a drunken landlord and an old man in a red coat? You know you'll be needing twenty armed dragoons to take Donal. And another ten to take me!'

'In the name of Jesus, Sosai,' Seán intervened, 'will you hold your tongue or you'll get us all hung!'

But Valentine was enthralled. What courage! He looked at Sosanna proudly.

'Mistress Sosanna,' he began.

'Mistress MacArtain!' she interrupted proudly. Then, looking around at the bowed heads, her shoulders drooped and her face fell, the fighting talk no more than foolish bravado. She knew that they were helpless against even one armed man, and the twenty dragoons she had so injudiciously mentioned were, no doubt, making their way up the valley at this very minute.

'All right,' Pollard instructed, 'you may start walking. And if any of you step out of line, you'll get shot for your trouble.'

'Pollard,' the Major interrupted. 'I wish to interview this young man. Take the others outside.'

Pollard felt uneasy, but he obeyed orders. He would do what he could to spare the O'Lochlainns, for Grace's sake, but as for MacArtain – there was a score to be settled with him.

❖ ❖ ❖

Grace accepted the clay pipe and took a long, slow draw. The fumes filled her lungs and she felt the better for it. The beady eyes of Minnie the Fox peered through the haze.

'That will do you the world of good, girl! 'Tis a powerful balm for the nerves.' Minnie leaned forward to prod Grace on the shoulders. 'And you're getting too thin, like a plucked hen past laying, you that used to be a fine big build.'

If Minnie had hoped to bring a smile to Grace's lips she was to be disappointed, for she was scarcely listening. Minnie's prattle wafted over her head as she stared into the embers. At the back of her mind was a deep-rooted fear at having divulged Sosanna's identity. It had seemed the right thing to do at the time; he was so lonely, so grief-stricken. Yet she would be glad when the young girl was safely out of the country.

Minnie poked at the fire and lifted the pot on to boil. Grace rose to her feet, disturbed.

'Settle yourself! Sit down, *a stór!*' chided Minnie, "tis not often I have company, and sure the wee girl will come over once the deed's done, for 'tis the lucky house is first-footed by a bride. I can tell you,' her brow furrowed darkly, 'she will be the only bride this house is ever likely to see.' She stopped, seeing Grace's face white with shock.

Below Minnie's cabin, a small hazel copse straddled the stream. The sun was clouding over as a light mist crept down the mountains on either side of the valley. To the south the smoke billowing from burning whins was pushed up the valley by a mild southwest wind. As Grace shifted her gaze from the fire to the cabin window, she saw Sergeant Pollard emerge from the oratory. He ushered out the priest, then Dunn and finally Seán, his arm around a weeping Sosanna, all at the point of a gun. Of Donal there was no sign.

Grace shot to her feet and rushed to the door. She lifted up her skirts and hurried towards the copse, wading through the tumbling waters of the stream and pulling herself up on the opposite bank. She lay there for some moments, her heart pounding wildly, before scrambling up the nettled embankment towards Father Mackey's cabin. She pressed her body against the gable wall, unheeding of the nettle stings on her hands and legs. She had somehow to save Sosanna.

❖ ❖ ❖

'I wish you to leave Ireland as soon as possible. I do not care where you go, provided I never hear from you again.' Major Valentine stated his case to an astounded Donal.

'How? On a convict ship? I'd rather hang.'

'And so you will if you do not accept my offer.'

'What offer?' asked Donal suspiciously.

'I will do what I can to secure your safe passage out of Ireland,' replied Valentine. 'I will see that arrangements are made.'

'You would see us out of harm's way?' Donal sounded incredulous. 'Why? Are you afraid of me still?'

Valentine resisted the urge to lift his whip to the insubordinate youth, attired in his polished boots, sturdy hose and breeches, and a heavy great-cloak which had, undoubtedly, seen better days. A jaunty lace jabot adorned his neck, and his wavy brown hair was brushed neatly back from his brow and caught with a black ribbon. He looked every inch the legendary rapparee, although, for all his insolence, there was a touch of anxiety in his voice.

'You are quite the gentlemen tory. Even down to the white throat,' Valentine smiled. 'You seem dressed for travelling.'

The anxiety in Donal's voice became more marked.

'I had hoped to take Sosanna away – far away. I thought you might have forgotten about me by now.'

'We hanged your companion, Makepeace Agnew.'

'I know. I was there. In Downpatrick.'

'I see. You take too many risks. You are not afraid of hanging?'

'Not now that you have offered to let me go.'

'I did not say that,' the Major spoke sharply. 'I will not have the security of my country put at risk again. You must have no more contact with the French.'

'I can give you that assurance.'

'And you must travel alone. Without Sosanna.' He watched while Donal considered his offer. 'I am offering you freedom. Do you have to think twice about it?'

'Why do you do this?'

'Because Sosanna O'Lochlainn is my daughter. I do not wish to see her married to a traitor. I do not like to be insulting, but I would wish for better things for her.'

'I too wish for better things for my wife. And I am not insulted to be called a traitor. But Sosanna, your daughter?'

'Her true mother is Grace O'Lochlainn. She is a child born of a great love, and she is not a simple peasant. She is a Valentine.'

The young man spun round.

'She was born an O'Lochlainn. Whatever blood flows in her veins, she knows herself as Thady's daughter. Now she is my wife, and you have no claim on her,' he said bitterly.

'Do you hate me so much as to deny me my child?'

'No. You misunderstand. I have never hated. I was reared by a

337

man who taught me that hatred is a poison. You see, Major Valentine, I am a MacArtain, and it is my mother's name I bear. And if I ever found the man who sired me, I would still be a MacArtain.'

'I will arrange things with the Sergeant if you go now,' the Major responded sharply. They had digressed from the matter in hand. 'But you must promise to have no further contact with Sosanna.'

'I would walk to the scaffold twenty times rather than be separated from her.'

'With me,' insisted Valentine, 'she would have everything you cannot give her, and more besides.'

'I can, and will give her her heart's desire, should I have to break my back to get it. I promise you that. Besides, if you are her father, think how she would feel towards you if you were to separate us now.'

Valentine looked sadly at the young man, so full of vigour and hope despite the desperation of his position.

'So,' he said slowly, 'you wish to take her with you.'

'I will not leave without her.'

'And she loves you enough to chose a life as an outcast, hunted and harried, forever in danger?'

'She has already chosen such a future.'

The Major sat in silence for some moments. Eventually he shifted in his seat. 'I hope that you value my daughter's trust in you. It was the only thing missing between her mother and I,' he continued heavily, 'yet she is the only woman on earth I could ever love. Let it be like that for you.'

Donal could hardly believe his good fortune. He understood the landlord's great distress, but his own anxiety was paramount. Valentine produced a purse from his pocket, but Donal stubbornly refused.

'I have three months' wages here!' he declared proudly, patting his chest pocket. The Major smiled. It seemed that the rapparee had not been idle, and perhaps his daughter had made as good a choice as had been available to her.

'What about the Sergeant?' the younger man began.

'Sergeant Pollard has only seen you once. In poor light. He dare not question my judgement that you are not, after all, the man he is seeking.'

❖ ❖ ❖

Grace surveyed the scene. In her fear she saw in the rowan berries and haws a myriad of redcoats, and as the brown smoke billowed closer she imagined the relentless pulse of beating drums and marching feet. She must act, and quickly. A turf spade rested by the ditch.

Sergeant Pollard glanced over his shoulder, trying to hide his anxiety from his prisoners. He wished for the backing of a few more troopers, for there were so many of them he could easily be overpowered. If it were not for Major Valentine's damnfool idea about interviewing MacArtain he would have marched them all towards the village. The Major had lost his sanity. His daughter, indeed! Pollard looked closely at the weeping girl. He could see no resemblance. And yet, there had been rumours of a child...

A movement drew his attention to the priest, a black crow with the shrivelled face of a witch. He distrusted Father Mackey more than any of them, for he had heard his mother talk about the 'evil eye'. It was, of course, superstitious nonsense, but all the same he avoided looking directly at the man. Tom Dunn slouched casually, as if he were in a queue at the village pump, while O'Lochlainn comforted the fretting girl. Pollard had been surprised but relieved to find that Grace was not there. It made his unpleasant duty easier.

As he waited, Seán O'Lochlainn muttered something to Tom Dunn.

'Speak English, or hold your tongues!' Pollard snapped. He had a working knowledge of Irish, but there were so many local expressions that sometimes it was impossible to understand what was being said.

'We were just wondering if the Drumreagh lads would clear

the stubble before the rain starts.' Dunn scanned the darkening sky above and Pollard's eyes followed. The last he saw was a swelling cloud before he blacked out and crumpled on the ground in a heap, his pistol by his side. His assailant, still tightly grasping the shaft of the turf spade, looked helplessly at the captives.

'Grace!' Dunn relieved her of the weapon, 'MacArtain is inside, with Major Valentine.'

Breaking free from Seán's protective arm Sosanna rushed towards the unconscious Sergeant and lifted the pistol from his side. Before anyone could stop her she had reached the door of the oratory where the two men were concluding their business.

'Come now, Donal!' she cried wildly. 'We have but one chance!'

'Sosanna! You will hurt yourself!'

'Sosanna!' Major Valentine rose to his feet. He was too tall for the little church as he walked towards her, hands outstretched.

'No!' Donal cried a warning, but the terrified girl was already aiming the gun. Shivering with fear she pulled the trigger. Major Henry Valentine stared wildly at his daughter before falling to the ground at her feet.

Chapter Twenty-Three

'TAKE MY HORSE!' shouted Dunn. 'The two of you go, this minute!'

'Master Dunn,' Donal was pleading. 'I must tell you the truth. He would have saved me. He wanted to save us both!'

'In God's name! Will you take yourselves to hell out of here before the troopers arrive!' Dunn yelled savagely. 'We may all hang for this foolish act.' He cursed himself for being involved in the wedding at all. He had no right to risk leaving his Annie a widow.

'Take care of her, MacArtain!' Seán kissed Sosanna, still trembling as he lifted her onto the horse. 'And may God speed you, *a stór.*'

Donal quickly mounted, holding his wife firmly around the waist. Unexpectedly, he produced a sealed billet, crumpled and stained. He handed it to Dunn.

'What?' Dunn looked perplexedly at the paper.

'You may burn it,' he said. 'I'll never deliver it now.' With that he spurred Dunn's horse and they galloped off into the mountain mists.

❖ ❖ ❖

Sergeant Pollard awoke to find the priest ministering to his injuries.

'Get that into you, lad,' urged the priest, holding a cup to his lips. It will clear your brain.'

The injured soldier spluttered. 'What poison are you giving me?' he cried, grasping out wildly.

'Poison? 'Tis nothing of the sort!' reassured Father Mackey. 'Strong whiskey. I keep it for medicinal purposes only.'

'Give me it then.' Pollard swallowed a large gulp, feeling the better for it. He got to his feet, shrugging off the priest's offer of assistance. Feeling his aching head, he staggered towards the oratory. Seán O'Lochlainn met him in the doorway.

'It should not have happened. No one wished for it,' he said hoarsely. 'It was a terrible accident.'

Pollard pushed past him. On the floor of the church Grace knelt, cradling the Major's body. His arms hung limply and his eyes stared blindly upwards. Grace crooned and hummed to herself, as if she were trying to send a child to sleep. She was soaked in blood, the blood of Henry Valentine.

❖ ❖ ❖

The horse galloped onwards, eating up the miles. They crossed the Poorlands and headed north, knowing that their only chance was to reach Derry with all possible haste. Once the crime was discovered there would be no mercy for them.

'I did not want to kill him. I only wanted to save you!'

'It could not be helped. We're both free: I intend to see that we stay free. Now put your fears away and think only of the future.'

'What about the others?'

Donal did not know what would happen, or if he would ever find out. In the meantime he intended to honour his promise to Henry Valentine and get his bride to safety. After that he would tell her some, but not all of the truth. She would never know that the man she had killed was her own father.

❖ ❖ ❖

Pollard stared wretchedly at the pitiful sight of Grace O'Lochlainn stroking the lifeless face of her old lover. He felt sick with apprehension, unable to understand what had happened. Valentine had been determined to save his daughter, to stop her from running away with the young outlaw...

'The outlaw shot him,' Pollard began, but Seán interrupted.

'I see redcoats in the distance. They're on their way.'

'Twenty armed troopers,' the Sergeant whispered to himself. He looked around him for an explanation. 'You let MacArtain kill this man? But he meant you no harm. He wanted only to save young Sosanna.'

'You know what happened, brave Aeneas Pollard.' Grace spoke softly, with the familiarity of an old friend. 'You saw me, did you not? It was I who hit you.' Her eyes turned to Seán's in mute appeal. 'And then,' she continued, 'I killed Henry Valentine.'

❖ ❖ ❖

Tom Dunn, having seen his horse depart, knew that escape was not an option. Annie, young Betsy and the boys might be left to ruination and poverty even though he had been no more than a witness, and even he could not say, for certain, how Valentine had met his death. Father Mackey, who also remained to face the consequences, was engrossed in prayer when Dunn touched his shoulder. The priest struggled to his feet, brushing down his vestments.

'What will we do now?' he said. 'I knew that no good would come of this marriage.'

'Why could Pollard not have let well alone?' Dunn mused sadly. 'Was the old Dissenter not enough?' As he spoke he looked at the crumpled billet, reading the name written thereon. His eyebrows lifted.

'This must be burned at once!'

'What is it,' asked the priest, 'a confession?'

'No. But it seems he has aborted his mission.' He showed the parchment to the priest.

'Well, now!' replied Father Mackey. 'So much for the mercenary soldier of France. MacArtain must have been an American agent!' The ink had watered and run, but the name on the billet was still visible.

'Dr Benjamin Franklin,' read Dunn, 'American Ambassador to Paris.'

❖ ❖ ❖

Shouts and warnings and the jangle of horses sounded round the clearing, but Grace O'Lochlainn was aware of none of it. She saw

343

the shadowy figure of a seventeen-year-old boy in the autumn flax meadow, struggling to control his prancing pony. She saw the young man, his black hair rippling in the wind on the sunny heights of Slieve Bawn. And she saw her lover on a moonlit balcony so far away. Had she agreed then to be his wife, had she known how sincere was his proposal. His green eyes, once warm and vibrant, stared past her into the void, lifeless and loveless, yet she was loathe to close them forever. She loved him now, just as she had loved him then, as a boy, and as a man. As his life's blood seeped into her clothes, she vowed she would never leave him again.

'I love you, dear, dear Henry Valentine,' she whispered and kissed his cold lips. 'I love you.'

And so she held him, until the blood grew cold and congealed, and firm hands prised her away.

❖ ❖ ❖

Squire Hall watched as the troopers bearing the pall began their journey down to the village. In order to avoid the raging whin fires, now burning without control, they turned to the gap by Leckan, taking the route down through Levallyclanowen, past the shell of the Healing House, over Dunn's Hill and into the village. It was fitting, the Squire decided, that the procession should move slowly, out of respect for the lord on his own land.

The Squire, accompanied by a distressed Sergeant Pollard, rode on ahead. The master of Narrow Water saw it as his duty to break the news to Fanny himself, and wanted to arrive there before the pallbearers. Poor girl, he thought, she has no one now. He wondered if the estate was entailed. If so, some distant English cousin would in all probability squeeze the life out of the place in order to keep up some London townhouse. That was what usually happened. He did not expect Fanny would want to stay. This was no place for a woman on her own.

'The girl, Grace O'Lochlainn,' enquired Pollard. 'Do you wish to speak with her? I shall have to make out a report.'

The Squire recalled the frail figure, a pale waif who looked as though her soul had left her body, leaving behind a brittle waxen case. She was the woman who had loved and had been loved by Henry Valentine. Now their relationship would be exposed in the courts, and the Valentine name held up to ridicule. He was silent for a while. He could not allow this to happen.

'What happened, Pollard? You were there.' He looked towards the Sergeant. 'If anything, we must avoid a scandal.'

'Yes, sir,' the Sergeant replied. 'I was made aware that a clandestine marriage was taking place, and I suspected that it might have involved the outlaw, Donal MacArtain.'

'And can you say it was him, without question?'

'No, I cannot.' Pollard was leaving for Wales within a week, but he would do what he could to save Grace O'Lochlainn.

'The young man, sir, was a mill labourer. He was not the outlaw we sought. The bride was Sosanna O'Lochlainn, the daughter of Grace O'Lochlainn and Major Valentine, born out of wedlock and in secrecy, but their daughter nevertheless.'

'Valentine's daughter?' The Squire was astounded. 'He certainly did not acknowledge her.'

'I speak the truth, sir. As told to me by the Major.' He related the sequence of the arrest, how the priest had revived him, and the finding of the body. 'I do not believe,' he ventured, 'that Grace O'Lochlainn killed the Major, as she claims. I think she wants to shield the truth.'

'I always admired my neighbour. A fine landlord. A member of the Grand Committee, a magistrate and soldier. Pity. He'd been so melancholic of late. Couldn't marry the girl, you know. Wouldn't betray his class.'

'He was in a very despondent mood when I spoke to him, sir.'

'I think we owe it to him, and to his daughter,' said Squire Hall with gravity, 'to avoid further disgrace on the name of Valentine.'

Pollard was quick to seize the opportunity.

'I am loathe to suggest this, sir,' he deliberated, 'but it seems to me that, given his state of mind...'

'He took his own life? No. Can't have that. It would kill Madam Ward. I'll settle for death by misadventure. Shooting accident.

That should hold.'

'Yes, sir. Death by misadventure it is.'

❖   ❖   ❖

Seán walked home that evening with Grace. No charges were being brought against her and she was free to go. The sticky, blood-soaked clothes clung to her thin frame, and she was shivering. He lifted her in his arms and began to carry her. A soft rain was falling.

'Why, Grace,' he jested, 'I've carried new-born lambs twice your weight.' He would have taken her to Dunn's Hill, but all she wanted was to get home for the night. His heart went out to the sorrowing girl. She had said little, nor had she shed a tear since he had prised her hands from the body. When the grief had tempered, he would be there to help and offer what comfort he could. Grace was strong, and she would recover. She would have to: she was needed.

As the O'Lochlainn close came into view Seán called to Eily:

'Mother,' he cried. 'Rake up the fire for us!'

Eily emerged from the cabin, arms extended as her son quickly assured her that it was not O'Lochlainn blood that stained their clothes. He related the sequence of the day's events to his parents as Grace was tightly cocooned in blankets and fleeces before the hearth.

'She's frozen, the poor child,' Eily choked. 'Such a terrible thing to happen.'

Thady shuffled around on his stick as he questioned Seán closely. He knew that the official version of Valentine's death was the one he must accept, for Sosanna's sake. Confused, he returned to sit by his daughter's side, smoke his pipe and think.

'Try to sleep, Grace,' Eily soothed, 'a sleep will do you good.'

'Seán,' she tentatively asked her son, 'when you've eaten your supper...'

He placed a hand on her shoulder and smiled.

'I'll away for the Widow Fearon,' he replied.

Thady sat by Grace and thought for a long time about the

Major, and his confrontation with him earlier that day. Had things been different he might not have hated the man. It was unfortunate that he was who he was. He stroked his sleeping daughter's hair and thanked God that she had been spared, and returned to him. Then he said a prayer for the soul of Henry Valentine.

❖ ❖ ❖

Henry Valentine was buried in the family crypt after a modest service in Saint Paul's Parish Church in the village. There was no pomp or ceremony as Madam Ward, the Halls and a few family friends and retainers followed the coffin to its resting place. Some curious faces framed by black shawls watched from a distance but did not approach the cortège. Word had got round that Madam Ward was the new landowner, and some of her late husband's relatives from Armagh had found it prudent to call to pay their respects to the dead.

The crumbling walls of Rory's Castle, the MacAongus castle, cast long shadows when Fanny visited the crypt later that evening. It had been a tiring day, what with the funeral and entertaining sympathisers at the house. Here, in the quiet of the churchyard, she sat listening to the waves of the incoming tide on the shore below. She had refused to display any unseemly grief at the funeral, but now allowed herself to shed a few tears in memory of her brother.

On one thing she was intent: before leaving to winter in Dublin she would call upon Grace O'Lochlainn.

❖ ❖ ❖

The snow was melting and only the higher peaks of the Mournes remained white. They had got over the worst of the winter, and Thady looked forward to the lengthening days. The winter had not been without its casualties. They buried Adam Coyle on Saint Stephen's Day and one of the little Fegan girls, the youngest, had died out in Lisnacree. Her father was still in gaol. They said he'd never hang, for he was mad, but he'd never be free again. Thady

347

thought it would have been kinder to hang him.

Another casualty, not of the winter but of South Armagh highwaymen, was William Dwyer. His body was found stripped of all valuables, including his hat and boots. Even the bone buttons of his waistcoat, his only vanity, had gone. His body was found along the wayside near the 'Gap o' the North', where only the foolhardy ventured without armed escort. William Dwyer had never been foolhardy, but he was friendless.

Dunn visited the close regularly, bringing with him talk of reform in Dublin. Tidings of fresh laws to ease the lot of the common man. Thady wished he had a fill of tobacco for every time he had heard such news. In the meantime, Grace was resolutely determined to provide him with a stone house before the following winter. He was proud of his lovely strong-willed daughter, who was in constant dispute with the new agent over the living conditions of folk on the Poorlands. She was on familiar terms with the late Major's sister, who had decided to revert to her maiden name of Valentine and snub her deceased husband's family. Seán grumbled at the extra workload Grace's building plans had left him with, but as he intended to leave Ireland soon, he was content to know that at least his parents would have a sturdy home and a well-thatched roof.

Grace had received word via the Darner from Mattie McGinn of the Bann cornmills. Her seafaring husband had arrived home with the news that Donal MacArtain and his wife had safely arrived in Boston. Grace was relieved to know that Sosanna was safe and well in her new home. She kept Fanny Valentine informed of events. Fanny wavered over whether or not to make a settlement on the girl, her natural niece, but Grace dissuaded her in the belief that the young pair would do better without any temptation to return home.

Although Fanny often talked fondly of her brother, Grace never mentioned her lost love. She sometimes visited the places where they had been happy together, like Slieve Bawn and the oak woods, but that was only once in a while, and she did not linger.

In June 1781, the Widow Fearon asked Eily to accompany her

on a pilgrimage to the sacred hill of Saul in northern Down, where the boy Saint Patrick had once slaved as a swineherd. Eily was reluctant to go with so much work to be done around the close, but with some coaxing from Thady she agreed to join her friend. She had, it was clear, a lot to be thankful for.

The two women set out barefoot, Eily leading the Buller's donkey which he had graciously offered for their journey. When nearing the town of Downpatrick, the Widow revealed that she had another purpose in making the journey. At the gates of the Gaol she retrieved the skeletal head of Makepeace Agnew, which, having been exposed for a year, could now be taken away for burial, and as he had no living relatives the authorities agreed that the Widow, a friend of the traitor, could be accorded the dubious honour. All the way back from Saul she spoke to the skull, which she carried in a linen bag, causing Eily to feel most uneasy. She buried the last remains of Makepeace Theophilous Agnew in Saint Bronach's churchyard, and said over him a few prayers of her own.

Thady, his wounds long healed, and his other pains eased after his enforced winter's rest by the fireside, was glad that the old Dissenter had returned to Kilbroney.

'Damn it, for all his heretical ways, he wasn't a bad fellow,' he would say to people, before lifting the shafts of his turf cart and heading back up the mountain.

Historical Background

THIS STORY IS based on actual events and people of late nineteenth-century County Down. Thomas Dunn became the leader of the United Irishmen in the Kilbroney area, and his barn, where pikes were manufactured for the 1798 rebellion, still stands on Dunn's Hill. His headstone can be found in the old graveyard beside the ruined church, and reads:

> IHS
> HERE LIETH THE REMAINS
> OF THOMAS DUNN
> WHO DEPARTED THIS
> LIFE AUGUST 22ND
> 1798 AGED 62 YEARS
> MAY HE REST IN PEACE

Owen MacOwen, an associate of Thomas Dunn, met his death during the disarmament of 1797. The MacOwens were hereditary Keepers of the Staff of Bronach. The Bell of Bronach is a ninth-century bell which was uncovered circa 1785 when a violent storm felled the oak tree in which it had been hidden since Cromwellian times. The Bell was taken to the National Museum in Dublin, where it remained until claimed on behalf of the people of Kilbroney by the parish priest in 1885. Since then it has been kept in the Church of Saint Mary, Star of the Sea, Rostrevor.

Matthew Lennon, Bishop of Dromore; Priest Pullein; Father Mackey; Squire Hall; Denis Hempson and Thurot O'Farrell are also based on historically authentic figures.

An annual pilgrimage still takes place to the Mass Rock of Alt na Sagairt – the Priest's Mountain – where a massacre occurred during the Penal Years. The savagery of the conflict of those and later years was matched by the wildness and poverty of the area. In a letter written while on circuit in Ireland circa 1759, Edward

Willes, Chief Baron of the Irish Exchequer, described the territory as he saw it:

'... it is a hard day's journey, being over the Alps and Appenines of Ireland: they are called the Mountains of Mourne and the Mountains of Newry. Within these twenty-three years, it was an absolute uncivilized country, and anyone who ventured to go among them did it at his peril, it being the almost inaccessible retreat of tories and rapparees and outlaws.. the wildest and most mountainous country I have seen.... The cabins one sees on the sides of the hills are the most miserable huts I ever saw, built with sods and turf, no chimney, the door made of an hurdle, the smoke goes all out of the door, the cocks and hens, pigs, goats, and if perchance they have a cow inhabit the same dwelling.

'They seem much upon a rank with the American savages excepting that they have some notion of making the Sign of the Cross, and stand much in awe of their priests.

'And yet there must be times when the master and mistress of the family are merry and jolly, for one sees the cabin doors crowded with little naked boys and girls. In one part of these mountains is a place of resort for people of fashion who come to drink goat's whey which in Ireland is esteemed preferable to asses' milk, and a great purifier of the blood, and the herbs that grow on these mountains are thought to be the most medicinal of any.'